The Art of Lainey

The Art of Lainey

by paula stokes

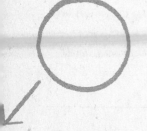

HARPER TEEN
An Imprint of HarperCollins*Publishers*

HarperTeen is an imprint of HarperCollins Publishers.

The Art of Lainey
Copyright © 2014 by Paula Stokes

Library of Congress Cataloging-in-Publication Data
Stokes, Paula.
  The art of Lainey / by Paula Stokes. — First edition.
    pages cm
  Summary: "When Lainey gets dumped, she employs an ancient Chinese warlord's
tactics to get her ex-boyfriend back"— Provided by publisher.
  ISBN 978-0-06-223842-9 (pbk.)
  [1. Dating (Social customs)—Fiction. 2. Interpersonal relations—Fiction.] I. Title.
PZ7.S8752Art 2014   2013037299
[Fic]—dc23   CIP
                                                                           AC

Typography by Ellice M. Lee
14 15 16 17 18 LP/RRDH 10 9 8 7 6 5 4 3 2 1
❖
First Edition

for the city that raised me,
the music that saved me,
and the ones who got away

Chapter 1

Maybe if I'd paid more attention to my mom and her tea leaves, I would have seen it coming. Instead, all I see coming is Jason, my boyfriend of two and a half years. His dark uniform shirt clings to his muscular back and shoulders as he turns to shut the passenger door of the ambulance. He's been doing ride-alongs with local medics this summer because he's thinking about becoming an EMT after we graduate.

I stop right in the middle of taking an order to watch as he saunters across the street. Pulling a chunk of strawberry blonde hair down over my forehead, I try to hide where an ill-advised visit to the tanning salon resulted in a big glom of overlapping freckles shaped like New Jersey. Next time I will be strong when one of my friends tells me my fair, freckly skin will turn all bronze and glowy if I "take it slow." Lies. All lies. Some people are simply destined for spray tanning.

The door to my parents' coffee shop plays a weird wooden tune as Jason opens it, courtesy of the coconut wind chimes Mom got on one of her hippie sabbaticals. Tahiti? Tuvalu? Who can keep track?

"I said I'd like a skinny iced chai and a Death-by-Chocolate-Moose Brownie. Did you get that?" The girl on the other side of the register waves a hand in front of my face. She's one of our regulars but I can never remember her name. She's majoring in something artsy and likes to dress monochromatically. Today she's wearing a long, sky-blue skirt with a navy tunic and head wrap.

"Got it," I tell her, sliding a brownie onto one of our colored ceramic plates and plunking it down in front of her. I fill a cup halfway with ice, slosh some chai concentrate and milk over the top, and finish by giving the drink a half-hearted stir. "Here you go." I quickly run her credit card through the machine and then slip out from behind the counter.

"Hey, is this skim milk?" she asks.

"Yeah," I say, and then mumble, "I think so." I head across the shop to the long, wooden bar where Jason is now sitting with his back to me, tapping one of his black leather shoes to the music blaring from the speaker above his head. Weird—he never sits at the bar.

"So, what can I get for you, hotness?" I lean in close to stroke one of the blond curls sticking out from the bottom of his cap.

He looks up at me and flashes his trademark dimpled smile, only today I don't see any dimples. A little voice inside my head whispers a warning: *something's not right.*

I tell it to shush. Everything is better than right. I finished my junior year with decent grades so my parents are only making me work a couple of days a week at Denali, our family coffee shop. My older brother, Steve, is doing a summer study-abroad program in Ireland and left me the keys to his small but reliable Honda Civic. And my boyfriend—the smoking hot slice of savory goodness in front of me—just scored his own place. Well, technically his dad owns the condo, but he travels a lot for work so it might as well belong to Jason.

"I'll just have water," Jason says.

I frown. "You sure? Yesterday we got in this awesome Madagascar spice—"

"Just water, Lainey," he says. "Alex is waiting out in the ambo for me."

I glance through the big glass window in front of us, but the ambulance is parked across the street and I can't really see him. "Well, you didn't have to leave him outside like a dog. Did you at least crack the window?" I smile at my own joke.

But Jason doesn't smile. Crap. Something *is* wrong. Or I'm being paranoid. I go get a glass of water and a mug of Madagascar tea for me and then rest my elbows on the bar next to him. Behind me, I hear my best friend Bianca picking up my slack at the counter. I shouldn't have left her up there by herself, but I need to make sure everything is fine—a few minutes with Jason to make that little voice in my head be quiet. It's not like anyone will die if they have to wait for their ultra-mocha-blended frappé with extra whipped cream.

"What's going on, Jay? You all right?" I rub one of my hands across his shoulders, being careful not to snag my freshly manicured nails on his nubby polo shirt. Jason thought his ride-alongs would be all glamour, nonstop excitement. Maybe the reality that EMTs spend a lot of time waiting around for work has started to set in. Then again, a job doing nothing doesn't sound like something Jason would mind.

He turns away from the window to look at me. No dimples. No smile. "I need a break," he says.

"Are they working you too hard?" Maybe I was way off about what EMTs do.

"No." He laces his fingers together in front of his body. "It's just—I don't think we should see each other anymore."

Tea sloshes over the edge of my mug as I start to shake. "I'm sorry . . . what?" My brain barely registers Bianca's voice telling the customers to hang on a second. She hurries over with a rag and swipes at the floor while I continue to stare at my Jason. "Are you breaking up with me?"

I'm not slow. I'm just stunned. Jason and I have been together since the middle of freshman year. Less than a week ago we christened every room in his dad's new condo, if you know what I mean. He talked about all the ways we were going to kick it this summer. Pool parties. House parties. We're even supposed to be playing on a coed soccer team with some of our friends from varsity. It sure didn't seem like he was unhappy with me.

"Sorry, dude." Jason stands up, leaving his untouched glass of water on the bar.

Dude? Years of being practically inseparable and I am now reduced to the status of "dude"? Like we weren't ever anything but drinking buddies? Bullshit. I put my hand on his arm to stop him. "You can't just show up at my job and break up with me. Who does that?"

What I mean is, things like this are not supposed to happen when everything else is perfect. In April, I got picked out of over a hundred girls to star in a commercial for Hazelton Forest University. In May, I scored the winning goal at the state soccer championships. And the summer was shaping up to be truly epic.

What the hell happened?

Jason looks everywhere but at me. "Please don't make this any harder."

I told you I told you I told you, the little voice says. I want to strangle it. This can't be real. The coffee shop blurs in front of my eyes and I wobble slightly in my platform sandals. I tighten my grasp on Jason's arm to keep from falling over, but he pulls free so we're no longer touching. For a second, I think about my mom's face as she studied the bottom of her teacup yesterday. *"Separation,"* she warned. *"Sadness."*

Crap. This *is* real. All I can do is clutch the edge of the nearest stool and stare at the metal sign on the wall above Jason's head: *Dogsled parking only. Violators will be peed on.* "I—I don't understand," I say.

He gives me a pitiful look. "I just need to be on my own for a while. Sorry, Lainey." He heads for the door.

The dining area of Denali is dead quiet, except for the music, which has faded away to a dull hum. It's so quiet I'd be able to hear myself breathing if I wasn't holding my breath. I can't help but stare at Jason's muscular back as he disappears out into the heat.

The wind chimes clunk together like thunder as the door swings closed. I turn around slowly, praying no one in the shop heard our conversation. Bianca is holding a rag saturated with Madagascar spice tea. Her eyes are dark and her face is heavy. She looks like she's the one who got dumped. Behind her, two tables of college kids and Micah, the prep cook, are staring at me.

"Enjoy the show?" I ask, plastering a tight-lipped smile on my face. "I was getting tired of him anyway." A couple of the college kids clap. Monochrome Girl looks at me with the same sad eyes as Bianca. Micah fiddles with the hem of his black T-shirt as he helps himself to a cup of Colombian drip.

"I'm going to take a short break, Ebony." I turn toward the back without waiting for my manager's response.

Ebony is sitting in a corner booth working on next month's schedule. She looks up with a bored expression. "Have you actually done anything today?"

Bianca jumps in. "I can cover the front."

"Thanks, Bee," I say, my voice starting to waver.

I keep the fake smile cemented on my face as I make my way around the counter, but it breaks apart right as I hit the door to the kitchen. I need to hide, and quick, but the only bathrooms are out front, which means there's no place I can safely be alone.

Unless . . .

I turn and find the door to the manager's office cracked open. Ebony doesn't like us loitering back there, but she won't know. Besides, my parents own the place. What is she going to do? Fire me? Dare to dream.

I barely make it through the door before the tears come, hot and fast. I collapse into the rolling chair in front of Dad's dinosaur of a computer. Sobs force their way out of my throat. I feel like I'm trapped in a disaster movie where everything is shriveling into darkness and ash. Sunflowers are being uprooted. Puppies are being trampled. Whole cities are crumbling to dust.

Pushing the keyboard to the side, I rest my head on the desktop, wishing I could turn off all the lights and sounds, and maybe the air too. I can still see the customers staring at me, snickering behind their eco-mugs. And Monochrome Girl with her sad eyes.

I haven't felt like this since I got cut from my middle school select soccer team. I warmed the bench as a seventh grader and hoped to get moved up to the starting line in eighth grade. Instead, I had the worst tryouts ever and was the only player not invited back. I felt like such a loser walking away from the list of who had made it, my former teammates either avoiding me completely or patting me awkwardly on the back. I swore I would do whatever it takes to never feel like that again.

Someone knocks softly on the door.

"Go away," I say, hoping whoever it is will take the hint and come back later.

No such luck. I look up as the door squeaks open. Micah is peeking through a one-inch crack, looking like he'd rather be in a dentist's office awaiting several root canals than anywhere near me.

"What do you want?" I mumble through my tears.

He slides into the little room and shuts the door behind him. "Sorry. Just need to get the recipe for Caribou Cookies." He reaches above me to the binder where Dad keeps the dessert recipes. The scent of smoke lingers on his clothes, like maybe he just came back from a cigarette break. Flipping through the binder, he pulls out one of the laminated pages.

But then he doesn't leave.

"Are you some kind of weirdo who gets off on girls crying?" I wipe my eyes on the collar of my shirt. The teal fabric comes away dark with eye makeup.

Micah laughs softly to himself as he slides the binder back onto the shelf. "I hope you don't really think of me like that."

Something in his expression stings like lemon juice

poured directly on my broken heart. Pity. I *hate* pity.

"I don't think of you at all," I say.

Micah nods. "That figures."

I know I'm being a bitch, but I can't help it. Jay didn't hang out long enough for me to tell him exactly what I thought of his breakup strategy, so the rage is seeping out of me bits at a time, targeting anyone unlucky enough to be nearby. Better Micah than Bianca. He can take it. He's got a tattoos and a mohawk. Clearly he doesn't care what anyone thinks.

"Hey," I mutter, the closest I can manage to an apology. "Be cool and don't tell my dad about this, okay?"

Micah runs a hand through his spiky hair. Dark brown roots are showing beneath the black dye. "Your dad doesn't really talk to the kitchen people," he says. He lowers his voice to a whisper. "I think he's afraid of us."

I pinch my lips together. It's a little funny because it's totally true. Dad thinks the cooks snort coke in the walk-in coolers and worship Satan in the parking lot. Sometimes I make up stories just to freak him out. That's what he gets for letting a bald chick in a band do the majority of the hiring. Talk about unfair. I had to beg and plead to get Bianca hired on as a barista for the summer, but Ebony gets to staff the whole kitchen with dregs she fishes out of the gutter in front of The Devil's Doorstep, Hazelton's premier (and only) live music venue.

"I could have him killed if you want," Micah says with exaggerated seriousness. "Jason, not your dad. I bet C-4 knows people who would make it look like an accident."

C-4, also known as Cal. Another member of Denali's crack-team kitchen staff. He's always going on about his collection of homemade weapons and telling everyone his locker is booby-trapped with explosives. Now there's a guy who makes Micah seem almost normal.

"I'll pass," I say, wondering why he's being so nice to me. Eager to change the subject, I zero in on his hands as he brushes some loose flour from the bottom of his T-shirt. "Why don't you wear an apron?"

"Because aprons are for losers?" Micah swipes at his shirt again. He's got what looks like a coil of barbed wire wound around his left wrist. It's also caked with flour.

"Apparently gloves are too."

"Nobody wears gloves unless the customers can see them," he says, heading toward the door. He pauses, looks back at me for a second. "My girlfriend and I broke up a few weeks ago. I know how bad it sucks."

I bristle again. More pity. "Why are you trying to make me feel better? You haven't said, like, five words to me since grade school."

He shrugs. "Bee asked me to check on you. Also, Ebony said I have to work the counter if you can't go back up there." Micah inches toward the door. "You know how we kitchen people tend to scare away the customers."

My breathing has finally returned to normal. I dry my eyes again and try to pretend nothing happened, that Jason didn't just dump me like I was a total loser. I hate that a coworker saw me break down, but it could be worse. Micah and I knew each other when we were kids but we've never rolled in the same circles. He hangs out mostly with other guys at work and I'm not overly concerned about what the Denali kitchen weirdos think of me. "I don't see why Bald Beauty couldn't man the counter," I grumble. "That schedule isn't going anywhere."

"Why are you such a bitch to her?" Micah asks.

"Because she's lazy? And bald?"

Not to mention, she's been a bitch to *me* since the day we met. Pretty sure she sees me as a threat to her management position, like I'm going to graduate high school and immediately use my family connections to steal her Denali power.

Micah rolls his eyes. "It's just a style, Lainey."

"It's a lack of style." I run the tips of my pinkie fingers along my lower lash lines in an attempt to remove some of my smudged mascara. "You'd think she could help out for five minutes. It's not like my whole world ends every day."

Micah glances back at me as he slides out of the office. His face twists into a mixture of sympathy and disgust. "That douchebag was your whole world? I feel sorry for you."

"I don't need you to feel sorry for me," I snap a little too loudly. But I mean it. I'm Lainey Mitchell, varsity soccer star. I have my own freaking commercial. I'm not a loser. I rock—I know it. And underneath whatever is going on with Jason, I'm sure he knows it too. All I have to do is figure out a way to make him remember.

Chapter 2

PONDER AND DELIBERATE, BEFORE YOU
MAKE A MOVE.

—SUN TZU, *The Art of War*

Bianca and I head to my house immediately after
work. We both flop down on my zebra-print comforter and I lean my head against her shoulder.
"Mom knew this was going to happen," I wail. "She said the
leaves showed big changes, separation. I thought she meant
Kendall!" Jason's twin sister, my other best friend, just left
town for the summer.

Bianca puts an arm around me and squeezes. "But you've
never believed in your mom's tea-reading stuff. Why start
now?"

I've actually always kind of believed in my mom's readings. I only pretend not to because—and this might be an
understatement—tea leaves are not cool. But according to
Mom, when she got pregnant, her doctor told her I was going
to be a boy and she kept disagreeing because she dreamed
I was a girl. Then her doula, aka the world's biggest hippie, saw something feminine when she was reading Mom's

leaves and that clinched it—Mom asked for all pink baby clothes. Of course Dad and her friends thought she was having a breakdown so they bought lots of green and yellow stuff to be safe. And then I popped out looking all girly and perfect and Mom got to go around shrieking "in your face" at everyone. Well, maybe it didn't go down exactly like that, but she's been reading tea leaves herself ever since. And *sometimes* I listen.

But it's not an exact science. She can look at a cupful of glop and pretty much see what she wants to see. And since she and the rest of the world knew Kendall had recently jetted off to New York after being selected for the special teen edition of *So You Think You Can Model*, I wasn't too worried about the separation reading.

"I don't know. But apparently this time Mom nailed it. What are we going to do?" Okay, so it's technically my problem, not Bianca's, but any crisis of mine is a crisis of hers, and vice versa. That's just how we roll.

She pulls a pair of wooden chopsticks out of her bun and shakes out her thick Latina hair. "Maybe you should try to call Kendall and see if she's got any inside information."

"Ooh, good idea." Not only is Kendall closer to Jay than anyone else, she also knows how to "handle situations," as she likes to say.

I send her a quick 911 text, but she doesn't respond right away like usual. I tell myself it's no biggie, that she's probably off somewhere posing in body paint or getting an überchic pixie haircut. Still, nothing stings quite like an unanswered text message.

I wait five whole minutes and check my phone again. "I think she's forgotten about me," I say, only half kidding.

"She's probably not allowed to use her cell phone," Bianca says. "Didn't you say they wouldn't even let her email anyone during filming?"

"Yeah, I guess." It's nice of Bee to make excuses for Kendall, since they don't like each other very much, which sucks because the three of us all play varsity soccer now and I wish we could hang out together. Bianca's been my best friend forever, but being around Kendall is like getting swept away by a tornado, in a good way. She and Jason lived in Los Angeles until eighth grade when their mom got transferred here for work, and there's just something glamorous and unpredictable about everything she does. When we go out, I never know where we'll end up.

Kendall makes me better too. If it weren't for her excellent assist, I wouldn't have scored the winning goal at the championships. I probably wouldn't have gotten together with Jason either. She pushes me to do things I'd be too scared to try on my own. Bianca finds her "a bit overbearing."

"You're probably right," I tell Bee. "Maybe she's getting ready for a shoot, being draped in some glamorous dress while a team of designers revolve around her, brows furrowed, mouths full of pins." Kendall's mom is the district manager of a chain of fashion boutiques and she's always making her daughter try on outfits before she lets the buyers order them. Kendall bitches about being a human Barbie Doll, but she gets to keep all the samples. Talk about having the best wardrobe in school.

As for me, my mom's an anthropology professor, which means all I have is the best collection of creepy tribal masks. They used to hang on the wall of my room, but last year I finally said enough and put them up in the coffee shop. You have no idea what it's like to be fooling around with your boyfriend and look up to see a bunch of painted-up African warriors glaring at you. Major mood killer.

Now my walls are full of pictures and posters. My lower lip gets quivery as my eyes land on a framed photo of Jason and me from last year's junior prom. Him in his tux, and me in a long pale blue gown. Both of us tall, tan, blinding smiles. We look like the little people on top of a wedding cake.

"I can't figure out what happened." My voice wavers. "Everything was fine last week."

"No warning at all?" Bee asks.

I shake my head violently, and my brain is assaulted by thoughts of Jason from all sides, from the pictures on the wall, to the DVDs he loaned me scattered across my desk, to the three bottles of perfume—one for each Valentine's Day—arranged in a line on my dresser. An old soccer jersey of his that I sometimes sleep in lies crumpled on the floor. As I pick it up and toss it toward the hamper, I catch sight of my jewelry box on the highest shelf of my dresser. There are only a couple of necklaces inside it—one of which is the golden soccer-ball pendant Jay gave me when I turned sixteen.

He and Kendall threw me a pool party that night. It was epic—I bet at least a hundred people came. Then, after everyone left, Kendall distracted their mom while Jay snuck me into his room. I lost my virginity that night, and while it was everything people said that it would be—awkward and nerve-wracking and a little painful—Jason was so amazingly sweet that I wasn't afraid. I just . . . trusted him. I knew he wouldn't hurt me. I never thought he would hurt me.

Until now.

I bite back tears. That was also the night he told me he loved me for the first time. It took him almost a year to say it, but I didn't mind because to me that showed he really meant it, you know?

Sniffling, I turn to Bianca. "I mean, did I do something wrong?"

She hands me a tissue. "This isn't about you."

I want to believe her, but it's hard. I guess it sounds stupid, but a little part of me thought Jason might be "the one." My parents met when Mom was twenty and Dad was twenty-two, which isn't much different from meeting in high school. Even though I'm hoping to go to college on a soccer scholarship, I never planned on going far enough away to risk my relationship with Jay.

"He's just confused," Bee continues as I wipe my eyes. "Maybe it has to do with meeting his father for the first time."

"I guess that's possible." But he didn't seem too traumatized when his dad showed up in town last month. Especially when the first thing he did was toss Jay the keys to a sweet condo. But his parents have been estranged since before he and Kendall were born, and Kendall still refuses to speak to her dad. When all you know about your father is that he's a professional photographer who lives out of a suitcase and never wanted kids, having him suddenly arrive and buy a place in town is probably a big deal. I don't know. Maybe it messed with Jason's head more than he let on. "You know what? I'm going to text him." Before Bianca can stop me, I've got my phone out and I'm rattling off an "Is this about your dad?" text.

Bee chews on her naturally plump lower lip. "I'm not sure if—"

I wave her quiet with the back of my hand. Thirty seconds. Forty-five seconds. A minute. There is no way Jason is not going to answer me. He *always* answers me.

Another minute passes. Bianca sees me teetering on the edge of pathetic and tries to pull me back. "We need a plan," she announces, grabbing my laptop from my desk. I've got about eight windows open—most of them to soccer or gossip websites, one of them to CalebWaters.com. "Oooh, Caleb," she says, immediately distracted. She enlarges a picture of him at a red-carpet premiere and turns the laptop toward me. "This will cheer you up."

I give her a halfhearted smile. Caleb Waters is a former pro soccer player and the star of *Victory Dance* and *Only One*

Shot. He's currently shooting a movie called *Flyboys* in cities all across the Midwest. I've been checking his page a lot for updates in case they shoot some scenes in nearby St. Louis. Meeting Caleb Waters is one of my major life goals.

"Do you think *Flyboys* will be as good as the other movies?" Bee asks. "You know, since he doesn't get to play soccer in it?"

"I'm sure it'll be awesome." I blot my eyes with the tissue again. "Maybe he's reinventing himself as a serious actor."

"Hopefully not." She peers at the screen. "What good is a Caleb Waters movie if he doesn't get sweaty and take his shirt off?"

As wrecked as I am right now, I have to giggle a little at that. Bianca may act all prim and proper most of the time, but when it comes to Caleb Waters she's every bit as obsessed as me. I force my face back into a serious expression. "Enough celebrity stalking. We have a different soccer star to focus on, remember? I thought you were coming up with a plan to fix my life."

"Right. Sorry. A life-fixing plan." Bee opens another window to a search engine. "I don't think I've fixed your life since that time in seventh grade when you tried to give yourself highlights and ended up looking like a crooked skunk."

I shudder. "Thank God that color fixer stuff worked." I lean over Bianca's shoulder while she types in various permutations of "how to win back your ex-boyfriend." Hundreds of thousands of hits come up. "Wow. A lot of people get dumped." I feel a tiny twinge of relief. Somehow, it's better knowing I'm not the only one.

"Yeah, but I'm not sure if we'll find anything useful." Bee scrolls through a bunch of websites that are trying to sell thirty-dollar e-books with "secret psychological techniques." Some are written by people whose grasp of the English language is debatable.

Undaunted, Bee keeps clicking. A pink-and-gray page pops up. "This one looks good." She nibbles at a pinkie nail. "Tips from Maverick the Master Dater, MD, in Loveology."

"Clever. Probably some thirty-year-old virgin living in his mommy's basement, but what do I have to lose?" I read over her shoulder. Maverick has a basic list of Dos and Don'ts.

- Do keep on living. Even though you're sad, you need to keep going to school or work.

- Don't wallow. It's pathetic, and you don't want him to realize how much the breakup has affected you.

"I can do those," I say. "I'm pretty sure my parents wouldn't even give me the option of bailing on my shifts at Denali, and I definitely don't want to seem pathetic."

Next:

- Don't contact him. At all. No emails, text messages, phone calls, letters, unannounced drive-bys, etc., for at least three weeks. Men inherently crave what isn't readily available. If you stay away, he'll wonder why. And he'll come sniffing around to find out.

A strangled sound works its way out of my throat. "Three weeks without any contact from Jason would seem like several lifetimes. No way," I tell Bianca. "Find something else."

A rattling sound from the floor makes me flinch. Bee's backpack is vibrating. While she digs around for her phone, I click desperately through links from so-called relationship experts, but they all seem to say the same thing: the best way to win back a guy is to avoid him . . . for weeks!

"There *has* to be a better way," I say.

Bianca peeks quickly at the text message and puts her phone away without replying. She holds up a tattered red-and-black paperback.

"Maybe there is."

Chapter 3

"*The Art of War*?" I raise an eyebrow. It sounds vaguely familiar, like I heard it referenced in a movie or something. It also sounds as old as dirt. "Why do you have that?"

"Seriously? It's on our summer reading list. Don't you ever do your schoolwork?" Bee slaps me on the leg with the book. "It's by a Chinese military strategist named Sun Tzu. It's mostly about war, but people have applied it to all kinds of scenarios—business, law, college, sports, relationships."

I squint at the cover. It figures brilliant Bianca would turn to some dusty schoolbook for advice. "You think a dead Chinese guy can help me get Jason back?"

"A dead Chinese *warlord*," Bianca corrects.

My eyebrow creeps up even farther. "My world is ending and you're channeling your inner warlord?"

Bee smiles. "Hear me out." She flips the book over and starts reading the back cover. "'*Master Sun Tzu's military treatise is required reading on battlefields and in boardrooms.*

Countless people of all ages have benefited from his wisdom.'" She tosses the book to me.

I snatch it out of the air. "This is never going to help." The cover is decorated with a bunch of symbols that look like tic-tac-toe boards on crack. I flip past the introduction and start skimming from the top of a page. *"'The art of war, then, is governed by five constant factors, to be taken into account in one's deliberations, when seeking to determine the conditions obtaining in the field.'"* I roll my eyes. "Whatever that means."

"Read them," Bianca says. "The five factors."

"'Moral law, heaven, earth, the commander, method and discipline.'" I clear my throat. "Which is six things, not five. I'm supposed to take advice from some dead guy who can't count?"

Bee ignores me. "So you can think of those as loyalty, timing, natural resources, leadership, and organization. These are the things you need going your way to be successful."

"Super. All I have to do to win Jason back is become my mother."

"No, really, Lainey. Give it a chance. Millions of readers can't be wrong."

"That's like saying millions of boy-band fans can't be wrong," I mutter, but I flip through a few more pages. They're full of words I've never heard of, like *ramparts* and *bulwark*. Even the words I do understand don't make much sense. My eyes start to glaze over. "Is there a translation?"

"This *is* a translation."

"Is there maybe a translation to the translation? *The Art of War* for Dummies?"

"You can do this." Bee reads over my shoulder. *"All warfare is based on deception."* She points at the next page. *"Hold out baits to entice the enemy. . . . Attack him where he is unprepared, appear where you are not expected."*

I stare down at the text. "So how do I use that to win back Jason? Sneak up on him when he's at the gym and offer him a protein smoothie?"

"You have to read the book first," she says. "Then we'll make a plan."

"You're giving me a homework assignment?" I ask. "Because honestly, I don't feel like reading a book right now. I feel like hunting Jason down and forcing him to tell me what I did." I sigh dramatically. "Which was *nothing*. So if I can make him see that, show him we're fine and he's just being mental, then he has to take me back, doesn't he?"

"Yes," Bee says. "About the assignment. Sorry, no about everything else. And you need to stay away from him at least for a few days, give him space, don't be clingy."

"I am *not* clingy," I snap. At least I don't think I am. Crap, now I'm having doubts about everything. "Fine. You're right. I'll stay away." I pause. "But maybe I should call him just to see if he still wants me to play on his coed summer team. He was talking about it last time we hung out and sign-ups are really soon."

She shakes her head. "How would that conversation go? 'Hey, I know you just crushed me publicly, but I'm wondering if we're still going to play soccer together?' Sun Tzu would not approve."

"Okay. Stupid idea," I admit. "But I have his varsity jacket, and his jersey, and some DVDs. I shouldn't keep that stuff . . ." I trail off hopefully.

Bianca's too nice to laugh at me but the look on her face says exactly what she's thinking—that I am the lamest person alive. "Keep it temporarily. Like Sun Tzu says, attack when the enemy isn't expecting it. Right now Jason is probably expecting you to be all over him."

"Fine." I wrinkle my nose at the paperback. "And I'll read this book, if you really think it'll help." My reading generally consists of soccer and gossip magazines, so struggling through *The Art of War* is going to feel like self-mandated summer school. But hey, at least it's short. And if it works for armies and athletes, maybe it can work for me. I'm a girl who believes in fighting for what she wants.

Kendall calls me the next day. "Laineykins!" She half screams into the phone when I answer. "I miss you so much."

"I miss you too." There's a lot of chatter in the background. I hold the earpiece slightly away from my head. "How is everything going?"

"I swear." She huffs. "I have to share a room with *three* other girls and they are all treating me like I'm a *farmer* because I live in the Midwest."

"That sucks." Kendall is supersensitive to being treated like a hick since she and Jason grew up in LA.

"You have no idea," she continues. "And the people running this place have so many rules. Eleven p.m. curfew. Seven a.m. group breakfast. It's like military school."

"That sucks too," I say. "Why don't you just quit?"

"Because quitting means I lose, and losing is for . . . losers," she says. "If I win this thing I get a hundred grand. If I leave, my mom will be all pissed and I'll also get to deal with that waste of space who likes to call himself my dad."

I suspected that Kendall mostly tried out for *So You Think You Can Model* to get away from her parents for the summer, but this is the first time she's basically confirmed it. Don't get me wrong, she loves the idea of being on TV, but I know she has no desire to actually work in the fashion industry. Her mom was a high-fashion model before she got pregnant and she seems determined to make Kendall to take over where she left off. She's forced her to do lots of catalog stuff for the boutique, and Kendall says it all sucks. Apparently the designers and photographers poke and prod at her like she's an alien and act like it's her fault if she gets a freckle or—God forbid—a zit.

I'm pretty sure the only reason she even made it on the show is because her mom called in some favors from people she used to work with. Then again, Kendall is gorgeous and she does have the perfect confrontational attitude for reality TV.

"Um, hello? Lainey? Are you still there?"

"Yeah, I was just think—"

"Oh, great. One of my *roomies* is talking about me."

Kendall swears under her breath. "She's tattling about something to one of the production assistants."

"So . . . ," I start. "Not sure if you've heard about this or not . . ."

"Hang on." I hear muffled voices, a stern-sounding man, and then Kendall sounding extra-indignant. "Apparently I have to go in two minutes," she says. "Heard about what?"

My eyes flick to the picture of Jay and me at prom again. "It's not important. I'll talk to you soon, okay?"

"For sure. Give my brother a hug for me."

The phone clicks softly as she hangs up. I'm not sure why I didn't tell her. It doesn't take two minutes to say "Jason broke up with me." Maybe it's because there wouldn't have been time left for her to give me advice. Maybe I didn't want to dump my problems on her when she already sounded so stressed.

Or maybe I just didn't want to start crying again.

Chapter 4

THOUGH WE HAVE HEARD OF STUPID HASTE IN
WAR, CLEVERNESS HAS NEVER BEEN ASSOCIATED
WITH LONG DELAYS.

—SUN TZU, *The Art of War*

A few days later, I have a dream about Jason lying in
a ditch, calling out to me for help. It's four o'clock
in the morning when I sit up suddenly in my bed,
positive he's in some kind of trouble. I should call him.
What if he's really hurt somewhere?

I debate it for about five minutes but then decide to call
Bianca instead. She went through a phase in fifth grade
where she had night terrors and she used to call me at crazy
hours when she woke up and couldn't fall back to sleep. We
would end up talking about movies and the cute boys in our
class until Bee felt better and then we'd both doze off in
class the next day. She hasn't made a late night call in years,
but she won't mind if I wake her up just this once.

She picks up on the third ring. "Are you okay?" she asks.

"Sort of." I explain the situation.

"Don't do it, Lainey." Bee yawns. "Nothing says pathetic

like a middle-of-the-night text message."

"But what if he was in a terrible accident?" I ask. "What if he really *is* lying in a ditch somewhere and I'm, like, psychically connected to him?"

Bianca mutters something in Spanish under her breath, but she stays on the phone with me while I do an internet search for recent crimes and car accidents. The Hazelton police department has logged exactly two incidents in the past twelve hours: a car break-in and a vandalized doghouse.

"Who would vandalize a doghouse?" I ask.

"Cats?" Bee suggests. She yawns again. I laugh. I love her. She lets me keep her on the phone for another half hour, talking about soccer strategies and *Undead Academy*, our favorite TV show. We trade opinions on which of this season's zombies have the best hair, and then discuss which of the JV girls might make varsity soccer in the fall. It feels almost like fifth grade all over again. For a minute, I miss how simple things used to be.

Finally Bianca says, "You should get some sleep, Lainey."

I sigh. "There's no chance I'll be able to fall back asleep. But I shouldn't keep you awake just because I'm all freaked out."

"There's nothing to freak out about," Bee says. "Did you read *The Art of War* yet?"

"I skimmed it a little," I say. "I mean, I did look at it a couple of times." In between reading and rereading every single email Jason ever sent me and moping around the house.

"Why don't you go read it for real," Bee suggests. "Think of me and you as one army, Jason as the opposing army, and your relationship as the country being fought over. I'll come by around eight and we can go for a run and start strategizing."

"Okay. Thanks, Bee."

"See you soon," she says.

I hang up and dig *The Art of War* out from beneath a stack of magazines on my dresser. Using the light on my phone, I open the book and start to read. The first part makes sense—the five factors, planning, all warfare being based on deception. But then Part II starts talking about chariots and how much it costs to raise an army. How the hell can that be relevant? I skim forward until I find something that makes sense to me: *In war, then, let your great object be victory, not lengthy campaigns.*

I keep reading. Part III is about when to attack and when to retreat. *If you know the enemy and know yourself, you need not fear the result of a hundred battles.* That's sounds promising. Obviously I know myself, and after almost three years, I know Jason pretty well too. I'm starting to feel like Bee's idea isn't so crazy. I flip forward a few pages. Part V talks about combining direct and indirect strategies. *The quality of decision is like the well-timed swoop of a falcon.* I hold out my hand and imagined my manicured fingernails as talons. I see myself swooping in and snatching back Jason's love. *Therefore the good fighter will be terrible in his onset and prompt in his decision.* I flip to the next part. *March swiftly to places where you are not expected.* That sounds like I'm supposed to attack quickly, an idea I like a whole lot better than sitting around doing nothing.

I'm only about halfway through the book, but I'm already feeling more hopeful. Later today, I'll talk things over with Bee. Then, I'll officially start my battle.

Bianca arrives promptly at eight while I'm in the process of putting my hair in a ponytail. She follows me from the front door back to my room.

"Did you stay strong?" she asks. "Resist the urge to text?"

"Yeah," I say. "And I even read part of *The Art of War.*"

She flops down on my bed. "Won't your English teacher be pleasantly surprised."

I start pinning back my flyaways. "Don't talk about school." For a second, I imagine going back as someone other than Jason Chase's girlfriend. My heart starts to race. Who would that girl even be?

I don't want to find out.

Bianca spends a few minutes admiring the newest poster of Caleb Waters tacked to the wall behind my bed. "Come on," she says finally.

"Almost done." I peer at my freckle tumor. "You don't get it. You're one of those people who can just roll out of bed and look good."

She snorts. "No I'm not."

"I've only been to about fifty sleepovers with you. I know what I'm talking about." I turn around and give Bee's thick braid a squeeze. "I, unfortunately, require a little more polish than you."

"How much polish do you need to run?" She gestures at my posters. "Are you expecting to bump into Caleb?"

"Dude. I hope so. That'd be enough to make me forget about Jason for at least a day." I drop the remaining bobby pins back onto my dresser. "Fine, I'm ready."

"So how much did you read?" Bee asks as we head outside and start our usual three-mile loop through the main streets of Hazelton.

"I only got about halfway through," I admit. "I feel like it kept saying to strike fast and be decisive. I think it's time for me to do something."

"All right. But remember it also says something about stupid haste being a bad idea." Bianca turns the corner, her feet pounding the pavement in an even stride. "As long as you're not just acting out of emotion."

"Who? Me?" I'm pretty much always acting out of emotion, so I see what she means. "I'm not going to break down crying and beg Jason to take me back. Maybe that first text I sent was too quick, but now I'm ready."

I pull even with her as we pass The Devil's Doorstep. It's a bar during the week and a live music venue on weekends—mostly for local punk and hard rock bands. The main windows are papered over with flyers announcing an upcoming concert for an all-girl group called Hannah in Handcuffs. I've never heard of them. The girls on the poster look like a cross between circus clowns and dominatrices.

Two guys sit cross-legged in front of the covered window, smoking cigarettes and flipping through the latest issue of the *Riverfront Times*, St. Louis's alternative newspaper. They either didn't make it home last night or have showed up extra early hoping to meet whoever is playing tonight when they roll in for sound check. Between the two of them, they have an eyebrow ring, two lip rings, and at least eight visible tattoos.

"They'll probably end up as our coworkers someday," I say, nodding toward the guys. "If Ebony wasn't gay I'd totally think she was hiring herself a harem of rocker boys to seduce."

Bee laughs. I lengthen my stride and concentrate on the way it feels when each shoe hits the pavement, on the way the wind flares my ponytail out behind me like a flag. I don't usually get up before nine, and running feels different this early in the morning. Quieter. Less humid. Kind of nice.

Halfway through our usual loop, Bee veers off into an alley.

"Where we heading?" I ask.

She flashes me a mysterious grin over one shoulder. "It's a surprise."

"You hate surprises," I say, but I let her lead.

The alley runs behind a strip of small businesses and ends at an abandoned lot overgrown with weeds. Bianca jogs from the pavement up onto the uneven ground, tromping down the high grass as she disappears back into a thick grove of trees. I should have known. Bee is such a nature bunny. She's always going camping and hiking and stuff with her family.

I skid to a stop. I'm not a big fan of the woods or the bugs living there. "Bianca, where are we going?"

She ignores me and I have no choice but to follow her into the trees. We twist our way through the branches until we come out on a path that seems to spiral around the large hill that forms the northern boundary of Hazelton. I watch Bee's thick braid flap like a horse's tail. Somewhere in the trees, a bird trills. A butterfly flits past me, its pale wings beating furiously. Suddenly I hear the whoosh of cars. Bee slows to a stop at the edge of a sheer cliff cut into the side of the hill.

I catch up to her, my blood accelerating in my veins as I look down. We're higher up than I thought we were. Below us, an eighteen-wheeler whizzes by on the highway, the driver oblivious to the fact he's being watched. "This must be where the thugs come to drop rocks on windshields," I say.

Bee exhales hard, winded from the steep climb. "You always focus on the negative. I think it's great. It's like looking down on the whole world."

"I guess, if your whole world consists of an interstate, a strip mall, and a graffiti-covered airport terminal," I mumble. A patch of forest stands beyond the airport's high fence. The view sums up how I feel about Hazelton. A little bit of nature. A little bit of business. Not enough of anything.

"Hazelton isn't that bad," Bee says.

"Then why are you leaving?"

"Mizzou has the most affordable med school in the state," she reminds me. "And they'll accept all of my college and AP credits. I can have my MD in seven years, maybe six and a half if I go to summer school. Besides, Columbia is only two hours away."

She's told me this before, but it's still weird to think of her not being around all the time. "Maybe I should apply there too. Mizzou's got a great Division I schedule." My ultimate dream would be to play soccer for Northwestern like Caleb Waters did. Both their men's and women's soccer teams are national contenders most years. Plus, Chicago! I could live in a big city and still be just a weekend train ride away from Jason. But I have about as much chance of getting into Northwestern as I would have getting into Harvard—about zero.

"Definitely," Bianca says. "Mizzou might offer you a scholarship."

"I don't know. I didn't really get scouted by anyone last season. And Mizzou only gives out a couple of soccer scholarships to entering freshmen each year."

"So then you can get loans if you need to," she says.

"It seems stupid to go into debt when I can take classes where my mom teaches for free." I stare off into the distance. "I'm not sure I'm good enough to play for a Division I school."

"You're totally good enough." Bee sits at the edge of the cliff, dangling her legs over the side. And for some people that would just be them telling me what I want to hear, but I know Bianca means it. My eyes start to water.

"Thanks." I turn and wipe away a stray tear before she sees it. "How'd you even find this place?" I ask, changing the subject.

She pats the ground next to her. Reluctantly I take a seat. I'm a little afraid of heights. "The new guy at work said he likes to jog this route," she says.

"What new guy?"

"Leo. You've seen him. He goes to school with us. Kind of preppy?"

"Oh, right." I do remember my dad giving the standard Denali tour to some kid dressed like a golfer. "Did Ebony hire him? He seems too normal to have attracted her attention." I raise an eyebrow suggestively. "Maybe his tattoos and piercings are in more discreet places."

"You're bad." Bee giggles. "I think Micah recommended him."

I snicker. "He seems too normal to have attracted *Micah's* attention."

"They live in the same apartment building. Your dad had me training him on the register yesterday and we got to talking." Bianca, pauses, looking down at the cars. "I'm glad you're making jokes, Lainey. I was starting to worry about you."

I wrap an arm around her shoulders. "Sorry about getting all dramatic and keeping you on the phone. That was pretty lame."

"You're not lame," Bee says. "With or without Jason, your life is still amazing, you know?"

"I guess." But ever since the day Jason dumped me, I've felt less and less sure about that. Almost anyone can be successful at sports if they work hard. Even popularity is more about who you know than who you are. Being Jason's girl-friend was different. A guy who could date almost anyone picked *me*. With him, I felt part of something bigger. Just like Kendall, he made me feel invincible, like things would work out for me no matter what. Once you've experienced that, it's kind of hard to give it up.

Bianca and I finish our run at the park across the street from my house. We guzzle water from a fountain shaped like a lion's head, and then Bee jogs over to the curb and pulls a soccer ball out of her trunk. I groan.

"What? Are you tired?" she asks. "You were the one ready to *beg* to play on Jason's coed team. How about you practice with me?"

"I don't know. I'm kind of exhausted just from the drama of the past few days."

"I get it," Bee says. "But I know how much you want a scholarship. This thing with Jason is out of your control at the moment. But soccer—no one can take that from you unless you let them."

"How'd you get so smart?" I snatch the ball out of her hands and twirl it between my fingers.

"I watch people. I see things."

And that's Bee. A watcher. A "think first and leap later" girl.

"I just figure instead of obsessing about what is out of your hands, why not control the things you can?" she adds.

"Okay." I toss her the ball and mop the sweat from my forehead. "But prepare to be dominated."

For the next thirty minutes, we play one-on-one, chasing each other up and down the full-length field. I score the first goal and impulsively turn cartwheels all the way back to midfield.

"That's the Lainey I know," Bee says as I collapse in a heap of giggles.

She fights back and ties the score, pulling a couple of nice moves to pass me on her way to the goal.

"Somebody's been practicing without me." I chase her down the field.

"Two brothers," she hollers back.

"No fair. My brother never played soccer." I put my game face back on and manage to score twice more. When we finally decide we've had enough, I'm still ahead, three goals to one, but both Bianca and I are smiling. I realize our "game" is the first time in days that I've thought about something other than Jason.

After a break, Bee practices throw-ins and then plays goalie so I can take a few penalty shots.

I'm feeling giddy, so good I could probably practice all day, when I notice my arms are looking a little pink. The sun seems to be centered exactly over the field where we're practicing and I only put sunscreen on my face.

"I'm turning into a lobster," I say, passing the ball to Bianca and heading for the nearest shade. We both collapse onto the ground beneath an ancient oak tree. I feel my stomach rise and fall with each breath.

"So." Bee blots her forehead on the sleeve of her T-shirt. "You're sure you're ready to see him?"

"Ready," I confirm. "And thanks for the workout. It felt good."

"Maybe we can still get on a rec team somewhere." She tosses the ball up into the sky and then catches it on her fingertips.

Bianca wanted to sign us up to play soccer for her church on Saturday nights. I told her no because I figured I'd be playing on Jason's team and hanging out with him on the weekends.

"It's okay," I tell her. "Like you said, we can work out together. Besides, August practices for the Archers will be here before I know it." The St. Louis Archers is the select team I play for during the off-season. "You should try out too."

"Nah. I get enough soccer in the spring," Bee says. "My fall schedule is full of AP classes. I'm going to need my free time for studying."

"Sounds boring." I nudge her in the ribs. "Think about it. I bet you would totally make it."

"All right. I'll think about it." She hops to her feet and lifts one of her legs behind her, pressing the heel of her shoe against her butt. She does the same thing with the other side, and then pulls the foot almost all the way up to her head. I watch with envy. I'm not even close to that flexible. "So what's the plan for Jason?" she asks.

"I'm thinking maybe I should wait until Monday," I say. "That'll be a whole week since we've talked, and I know he has a ride-along shift so I can catch him if I go by his dad's place in the morning."

Bee leans against a tree and starts stretching her hamstrings. "You don't think that's a little stalkerish?"

"I think he shouldn't have given me his schedule for all of June if he was going to break up with me at the beginning of the month," I say. "Besides, if I call him, he'll just ignore me. I need to swoop in like a falcon or something, right? Be unexpected. Be bold. Whatever."

"Good point. You want me to spend the night Sunday so I can help you get ready?"

"That would be all kinds of epic." I look up at her. "You can keep me from chickening out."

"I've known you for what, ten years? I've never seen you chicken out," Bee says. "If anyone can make this work, it's you." She reaches down and pulls me to my feet.

"With your help," I remind her.

"With my help." She smiles. "All right. I need to take off. My mom wants me to watch my brothers so she can sleep." Bee's mom is a nurse who works night shifts, and her dad travels a lot for work. Her little brothers, Elias and Miguelito, are cute, but rowdy.

"Doesn't your grandma ever watch them?"

"Ha," Bee says. "I think someone needs to watch her too. I caught her making flan at three o'clock in the morning once. When I asked her what she was doing, she said she was hungry."

I smile. "Go give your mom a much-deserved break." Working out calmed my mind, and thinking strategically makes me feel like I've regained some control over my life. Maybe Bianca's right. Maybe *The Art of War* can fix things.

It's time to put my plan into action.

Chapter 5

Monday takes forever to get here. I set the alarm for five o'clock so I have plenty of time to get ready. Jason has to be at work by seven, so he should be up by six.

In the morning, I can't eat anything. My hands are shaking, but I'm pretty sure it's not from lack of food. "This is a bad idea," I say. "Maybe I should at least text him and let him know I'm coming."

"That would *not* be unexpected," Bee says. "Don't give him a chance to weasel out of seeing you."

She's repeating back what I said last night, when an unannounced visit seemed like the best plan. I mean, it's word for word from *The Art of War*: *The spot where we intend to fight must not be made known.* But now that little voice in my head is back and it's whispering things like *danger* and *bad idea.* I rub at a bump on my left cheekbone that wasn't there last night. Crap. Am I getting a zit?

"I feel like I'm going to puke."

"You can't. You haven't eaten anything," Bianca says. "You need to relax. And you look amazing, by the way."

She's right. About the relaxing. Well, also about the amazing part, I hope. I put a lot of thought into my outfit, a pair of cutoff jean shorts and a teal-blue tank top that accentuates my spray-on tan and bright green eyes. Of course he won't be looking much at my eyes because thanks to the miracle of engineering known as the "Stick-'em-up Stunner Bra," my B-cup breasts appear to be defying the law of gravity. I give myself a once-over in the mirror. I'm all arms, legs, and cleavage. "Too much skin," I say. "I look like Hooker Barbie."

Bee hands me a lacy black cardigan from my closet. "Try this."

I slip it around my shoulders. "Better. Thanks." My strawberry blonde hair is straight and shining thanks to a half hour of flat ironing and I've done my makeup as daytime flirty—light lips, brown eyeliner, a touch of mascara. Most of my freckles are hidden under a thin layer of foundation. I rub at the bump on my cheek again.

"Don't mess with it," Bee says. "You'll make it worse."

"Easy for you to say. You're one of those people with invisible pores. I'm pretty sure it's medically impossible for you to break out." I dot some concealer over the bump and turn to let Bianca look me over. "What do you think?"

"Perfect," she says without a touch of envy. "Irresistible."

I nod and take a deep breath. Together we tiptoe down

the hallway and into the kitchen. I poke through the refrigerator but it's full of hummus and organic produce—nothing Jason would eat.

"Let's stop by Denali," I say. "If I bring breakfast, he'll have to invite me in. I mean, it would just be rude not to, right?"

Bianca nods. "Good call. You can get some of Micah's famous chocolate chip muffins. It'll be baiting the enemy, just like Sun Tzu said to do."

We hop into the Civic and arrive at Denali a few minutes later. Humming along to the weird indie rock music Ebony likes to put on before my dad gets there, I grab a couple of muffins out of the front case. Then I pluck a honey oolong tea bag from a box next to the register and fill my travel cup with hot water.

Ebony looks up from her usual booth. "Were you planning to pay for that stuff?"

"Take it out of my check." I stroll back toward where Bee is still lingering just inside the door. A pair of elderly men look up from their chessboard to stare at my outfit for an inappropriately long amount of time.

I spend a moment reviewing my game plan. I decided to hang on to Jay's jersey and letter jacket for now, but I've brought all of the DVDs he left at my house. That's my "legitimate" reason for stopping by. The muffins are just extra, to remind him of how sweet I can be and to score a few extra minutes with him, to *show* him just how sweet I can be. I can't help but feel like Dead Chinese

Warlord would be proud.

Now all I have to do is not chicken out at the last second. There is no backing down once you have committed to a course of action. You have to rush forth like floodwater or strike like lightning or something. Besides, getting busted doing a stalker drive-by would be an epic-fail move. I'd have to transfer to a new school.

"Do you want me to go with you?" Bianca asks.

"Nah. What if he's outside and sees you?" I say. "Or what if things go so well he skips his ride-along shift so we can have delicious makeup sex? I don't want you to have to wait for me. That'd be awkward." Really I'm thinking more like what if he laughs in my face or walks right past me like I'm invisible, but I can't say that or I might start crying. And I've done more than enough crying at Denali already.

Bee pets both sides of my silky flat-ironed hair. "I'll be here all morning, maybe behind the counter if it gets busy. Come by afterward and share the good news, okay?" She walks me up to the front door.

"I will. Thanks." I throw my arms around her neck, give her a squeeze, and then turn to leave. I open the door halfway, but then hesitate. The coconut wind chimes dance above my head. "What if this doesn't work?" I ask, my voice so quiet only Bee can hear me.

"It will," she says. "And if for some reason it doesn't, well, I always thought you could do better than Jason anyway."

Better? Jason might be going through a thing right now, but he loves me—I know it. And he makes me stronger. Not to mention he's hot, popular, and superathletic. We're practically two halves of the same person. There is no one better, not for me. Bee's just being a good friend, building me up.

It gives me the confidence to keep going.

On the drive over to Jay's condo, the bad feeling returns. I try to shake it off as the blocks fly by. Maybe it's just because Bianca's not here to be my cheerleader. I envision her sitting next to me in a pep squad outfit, chanting, *L-A-I-N-E-Y. Time-to-go-get-your-guy.* It's ridiculous, really. She would probably rather get nipple piercings and a sleeve of tattoos than be a cheerleader. She doesn't like when people stare at her. Even in soccer, she's the girl who passes instead of taking the shot.

I used to be that girl too, before I started hanging around with Kendall.

My stomach feels like it's full of angry hummingbirds. I try to think of what Kendall would say if she were with me. Probably something about how Jason is just a guy, and I should grab him, flash my girly parts, and then lead him to the bedroom. The problem there is that I've been doing that since I turned sixteen, so if it quit working for some reason, why would it work today?

And why did it quit working in the first place?

The traffic signal in front of me turns red. I sit at the intersection for what feels like a million years. I cycle through my brother's radio presets. Red. I check my reflection in the rearview mirror. Still red. Pretty sure the stoplight has broken. It's like the universe is conspiring to keep me and Jason apart. Suddenly I need more than a pep talk. I need divine intervention. If only my mom were here to do one of her readings.

I glance at my black plastic travel mug. It's worth a try, I guess. Grabbing the mug from the cup holder in the center console, I roll down the window and pour out most of my tea as the light finally turns green.

I pull over around the corner from Jason's condo, where I can see the front of his building but hopefully he can't see me. The soggy tea bag is stuck to the bottom of my travel mug. I rip the tea bag open and squeeze the wet pulpy leaves into the mug. I swish them around with the half ounce of liquid still hanging out in the cup. Then I invert the whole mess onto the lid, splattering my bare legs with droplets of tea in the process.

I swear under my breath. If form counts for anything, my cup is going to be full of skulls and tombstones. Laying the lid gingerly on the passenger seat so as not to make more of a mess, I pray for a symbol of happiness or good luck. A bell. A dove. Maybe a kite that means my wishes will be granted. As I look down at the tea leaves that stayed stuck in the cup, I see . . . wet leaves. I rotate the cup slowly, looking for anything familiar. Nada. Crap. The story of every teenage girl's life—I should have paid more attention to my mother.

I hear a door open and I look up, forgetting all about my leaves as Jason appears from the entrance to his building. My chest feels like it's being crushed in one of those blood pressure thingies the old people are always using at the Supermart. As he heads across the grass, my breath catches in the back of my throat. I pause just long enough to consider the likelihood that I may, in fact, be having a heart attack at age seventeen. Not. Likely.

Inhaling deeply, I grab the bag of muffins from the passenger seat and start to slide out of the car. And then the condo door opens again and an arm wearing navy blue appears. Jason isn't alone. He must be with the EMT who is training him. Alex. Yeah, that was the name. It conjures up images of a short, slightly pudgy, thirty-year-old guy. But when Alex comes into view, he's anything but a boring old dude.

For starters, he's a she.

Chapter 6

ALL ARMIES PREFER HIGH GROUND TO LOW.
—SUN TZU, *The Art of War*

The bag of muffins slips from my fingers and hits the street with a deafening crunch. Or maybe that was my heart breaking? I snap out of my shock and realize Jason and Alex haven't noticed me. Slipping back inside the car, I pull the door closed slowly, praying neither of them will look in my direction. I slouch down in my seat, my eyes peeking out the bottom of the side window.

Alex is a few inches shorter than me, with hair so long and shiny that mine probably looks like yarn in comparison. Hers is movie-star red, definitely from a box, but still gorgeous. Even through her EMT cargo pants and high-necked uniform shirt, I can tell she's built like a lingerie model. Suddenly my stunner bra doesn't seem very stunning.

I realize I'm gripping the steering wheel so tightly that my knuckles have blanched white. My whole body is shaking and my inner warlord is screaming things like *attack* and *kill*. I need to calm down before I punch a window and they see me. I try to channel my inner Bianca instead.

Maybe they're carpooling. She probably has a boyfriend. How could a girl that pretty ever be single?

I loosen my grip from the wheel and shake out my fingers. Everything is going to be okay. My inner Bianca has to be right. He's only been doing ride-alongs for a couple weeks. There's no way he dumped me for a girl he just met.

I almost have myself convinced. Until Jason and Alex make it across the lawn to his convertible Mustang, and he presses her up against the side of the car playfully. And she laughs. And then he kisses her.

I squeeze my eyes shut. "Image deleted," I whisper. But it doesn't go anywhere. It's like a movie playing on the back of my eyelids. Jason and Alex kissing. Jason and Alex kissing. I squeeze tighter, scrunching up my whole face until I hear a car engine purr to life. It's probably the Mustang but I'm taking no chances. I cannot handle one more second of them together. I stay slouched down in the driver's seat for a count of one hundred. When I open my eyes, Jason and Alex are gone.

Bianca sits in our usual spot at Denali, the big, round table by the bookshelf. She's sipping from one of Dad's ceramic painted eco-mugs. It's probably a skinny chai. Bianca loves chai.

As I approach, she looks up, a concerned frown forming on her face. "Do you want to go back to your house?" she asks immediately.

I can tell by the hippietastic music that my dad is here somewhere. He's really big into tribal drums and monks chanting and stuff like that. Apparently it adds to the ambience.

"Nah, let's stay here. My mom is at home, writing. Even if my dad comes around, you know him. He likes to steer clear of the girly drama."

"Okay," Bianca starts as I slide into a chair. "So was Jason mad you came over?" She toys with the end of her braid.

"I don't know. I didn't even talk to him."

"Why not?"

I lower my voice. "He was leaving when I got there." I sigh dramatically. "And he wasn't alone."

"What?" Bianca sucks a straw full of chai straight into her lungs. Her tan face turns bright red and she coughs for about three straight minutes.

"His ambulance partner," I say. "Alex? Well, Alex is a girl. And they were leaving his place together at six thirty in the morning, so . . ."

"Are you sure he wasn't just giving her a ride to work?" Bee takes another sip of her drink.

I wait until she swallows. "He kissed her."

She gasps. "No way."

"Yeah way." Reality starts to set in for me. My life. My epic summer. It's gone. It's like I'm back in eighth grade, not making the soccer team. And this time it's even worse because I didn't mess anything up. I didn't fall on my face at tryouts. I just . . . lost. I'm a loser.

I bite back tears. I will not freak out in the coffee shop again.

My dad strolls out from the back. "What's this? Meeting of the minds?"

"Just girl talk." I keep my voice light.

"Ah," he says. "Covert ops. Carry on, ladies." He makes a loop around the dining area, stopping to wipe down a few tables and ask a pair of college kids how their drinks taste. Then, satisfied that everyone seems content, he turns back toward the office.

Bee waits till my dad is out of sight. "You know what this means, right?"

That I'm a total loser? "That Jason is an asshole?"

"Well, maybe. More like if you want him back you have to step up your game." She pauses. "*Do* you want him back?"

I lower my voice. "I do. Is that terrible? We've spent the last two and a half years together, Bianca. I don't even know who I would be without him."

"You would be my amazing friend, Lainey," Bee says vehemently. "The same person you've been since second grade. Seriously. You don't need Jason to define you."

"You don't think? Remember how the soccer team joked that instead of 'Mitchell,' my jersey should say 'Chase's girlfriend,' because that's how everyone knows me." I lean forward in my chair. "It's more than that, though. I can't imagine my life without him. It's like I try, but nothing makes sense. Everything was perfect, and now everything is crap. I need him back. I need everything to go back to the way it was."

Bee purses her lips together. I can tell she still doesn't agree with me, but she's not going to argue. "Okay," she says. "Then we need a better plan." She drums her fingernails on the table and stares off in the direction of the tribal masks.

They stare back. Grinning. Laughing at me.

Her eyes light up. "I've got it. Where's your book?"

"*The Art of War*? I didn't exactly think I would need that at Jason's." I wasn't even planning on needing the muffins. I seriously thought after almost a whole week apart that Jay would miss me. Dude, who is this Alex girl and what does she have that I don't?

"I knew you were going to say that. Which is why I downloaded a copy onto my phone." Bianca pulls out her cell and starts swiping the screen.

"I'm not sure I'm up for ancient Chinese literature right now." I sink even farther down in my chair.

"Come on, Lainey. I know you. Strategizing will make you feel better."

"Maybe." I'm not convinced, but if I go home I'll end up facedown on my bed crying, which definitely won't make me feel better. "Okay, but I'm going to need ice cream for this." Pushing back my chair, I head through the back dining area and around to the front. I slide behind the counter and help myself to a big scoop of Caramel Meltaway, loading it down with whipped cream and chocolate-covered espresso beans. I grab a spoon and head back to the table.

Bianca frowns at my monster-sized dessert. "Are you expecting company?"

I down a big spoonful of nothing but whipped cream. The airy consistency makes me cough. "Obviously not," I say. "I'll probably be alone forever."

Instead of responding, Bee opens *The Art of War*, scrolls to Part IX, and sets her phone down in front of me.

"'*The Army on the March*'?" I scoff. I skim a few passages. "So I'm not supposed to attack Jason in a river or a salt marsh?"

"Keep going."

"Or from the bottom of a mountain?" I take a bite of ice cream.

"Exactly," she says.

"Exactly what?"

"This whole section is basically saying you have to be on even ground to fight. Or better yet, you want to be the girl on the mountaintop. Think of it like in soccer. If the field isn't level, it's easier to score when moving downhill."

"Oh, I get it. Jason is dating someone new so he has the upper hand, the better position."

"All we have to do is find you a guy to date and you'll be back on level ground." She smiles. "Then Jason will see you, get jealous, and *voilá*—you'll be the one on top."

"A guy to date," I repeat slowly. I feel like eating my way to the bottom of this bowl of ice cream and then getting a refill. I feel like crawling into bed, pulling my covers up over my head, and crying myself to sleep. What I *don't feel like* is finding a guy to date.

"Yes." Bianca peers around Denali as if one of the college kids bent over their laptops is just going to volunteer.

"Wait," I say. "What if the guy falls for me and gets all stalkerish, like when the Swedish exchange student got a crush on Kendall sophomore year?" I'm actually thinking more along the lines of what if I flirt with a guy and he blows me off and I get to experience that crushing rejection feeling all over again. I take another bite of Caramel Meltaway.

Bee slides the ice cream toward her, out of my reach.

"Get your own," I whine, grabbing for the bowl.

"No. You are not doing this," she informs me, her hand wrapped firmly around the base of the dish. "I'm not going to let you drown yourself in ice cream. Gaining ten pounds will not make you feel better."

"Neither will dating some other guy," I say. "Let me finish reading the book. Maybe it'll give me a better idea."

"All right," Bee says. "You work tomorrow, right? We can talk more then." She tucks her phone back into her purse and then gives me another quick hug. "Let's get out of here before your dad puts us to work."

As we head out the front door, Micah and the new guy, Leo, are strolling over from the parking lot. They look weird walking together: Micah and his mohawk, Leo and his baseball cap and polo shirt. Micah raises one hand in a half wave, and Leo mutters something that sounds like "Hiya." They're both smiling at Bee. Neither one of them even glances in my direction. Normally it would not faze me that I'm being ignored by kitchen weirdos.

Today it does.

"Nice to know my Invisible Woman costume still works," I mumble. I can't remember the last time I felt this alone.

Chapter 7

THE DIFFICULTY OF TACTICAL MANEUVERING
CONSISTS IN TURNING THE DEVIOUS INTO THE
DIRECT, AND MISFORTUNE INTO GAIN.

—SUN TZU, *The Art of War*

The next day, Bianca and I grab the table by the bookshelf again after we finish our shift.

"I ordered us a barbecued chicken pizza," she says as I settle into the chair across from her. "I figured we could go through *The Art of War* together, break it down, make a list." She's already got the book open on her phone.

I slide up a third chair and prop my feet on it. "Show me the way, Warlord Woman." I pull *The Art of War* out of my purse. "I read the second half last night. The part about exploiting enemy weaknesses made sense, but then there was some stuff about spies and alliances that doesn't seem as helpful."

"All right. Let's brainstorm strategies," she says.

I flip through several dog-eared pages, reading certain passages as Bianca makes notes.

I'm on Part VII, Maneuvering, when Ebony strolls out of

the back with our barbecued chicken pizza. She's wearing camo pants, a black sleeveless tee, and a studded leather necklace that looks like a dog collar. I resist the urge to tell her that her head is looking particularly shiny today. She frowns at my feet as she sets the pizza and two plates in the middle of the table. "Try not to make a mess, okay?" Without waiting for a response she disappears into the back.

Snatching a chunk of chicken from the slice of pizza nearest to me, I flip to Part VIII, Variation in Tactics. *"There are five dangerous faults which may affect a general,"* I say. *"Recklessness, cowardice, a hasty temper."* I pause. *"A delicacy of honor? Over-solicitude'?"*

"Pride and excessive worry," Bianca translates, helping herself to a slice of pizza. "Maybe not *exactly* what Sun Tzu was thinking, but close enough for our purposes. So we need to make sure you avoid all of those feelings while you're utilizing the rest of these strategies."

I nibble on another piece of chicken. "Those feelings probably make up 85 percent of any given day for me, especially lately."

Bee blots her lips on her napkin. "No one ever said war was easy."

We finish going through the last few parts and then I slide around to Bianca's side of the table so I can see the list she's compiled:

1. Plan your attack
2. Know your enemy

3. Be flexible, unpredictable, deceptive,
    decisive
4. Seize opportunities as they present
    themselves
5. Attack from a position of power
6. Attack directly and indirectly
7. Don't be too aggressive
8. Exploit enemy weaknesses
9. Divide and conquer
10. Utilize spies and allies

"It's like a top ten list," she says proudly. "Top ten ways to win back your ex-boyfriend."

I read through the list again. "So what does all this mean for me and Jason?"

Bee takes a bite of pizza before answering. "We're obviously planning your attack right now. Number two: Know your enemy. You know enough about Jason, but we need to learn more about this EMT girl."

"EMT Girl. It's like she's a superhero. How am I supposed to compete with that?"

"What's her name again?" Bee asks.

"According to Jay, his ride-along partners were a paramedic named Lance and an EMT named Alex. So unless he's been lying to me for weeks, her name is Alex."

"Do you know anything else about her?"

I see her walking out of Jay's condo, her plain navy uniform hugging her curves, the sun shining brilliantly off her scarlet ponytail. "Hair is fake. Boobs are probably fake."

"Helpful," Bianca says drily. "So she either works for the Hazelton fire department or Gateway Transport?"

"She works for Hazelton. I remember the ambulance from the day Jason broke up with me, and every other excruciating detail. I could tell you what color socks he had on."

"So then we need to do a little research on the Hazelton FD."

I dig into a slice of pizza while Bee goes a-googling on the local fire department website. Denali's barbecue sauce is actually a mix of barbecue, powdered onions, and hot wing sauce. It's delicious but after a few bites I'm fanning my mouth. "Find anything on her?" I ask. "X-rated blog? Slutty EMT calendar?"

Bee wrinkles her forehead in concentration. "There aren't any first names on here. There's a A. Malincheck. It says EMT-B, certification through Hazelton Community College."

Jason told me it only takes one year to get EMT certified at the community college and two years to become a paramedic. That would mean Alex could be as young as nineteen. A nineteen-year-old girl and a seventeen-year-old guy? It's weird, but within the realm of possibility. "Okay, so let's say it's her. Alex Malincheck. So what? What happens next?"

Bianca shakes her head. "I still can't believe someone older is interested in Jason. He's so immature."

"You think? I always saw Jay as way more mature than

most of his friends."

"Yeah, but that's not saying much. Didn't some of his friends get suspended for peeing in a girl's Coke when they were selling refreshments at Homecoming?" Without waiting for a response, Bee goes back to her googling. "I can't find her on any of the social networking sites," she mutters. "I can't even find a home address."

"Gee, imagine how hard it must have been to find addresses back in the time of Dead Chinese Warlord," I say. "How did he learn to know *his* enemy?"

"Sun Tzu," Bianca corrects. "He probably enlisted the help of spies."

Spies. Right. Strategy number ten.

"I bet we could get her fired." I slide a second piece of pizza onto my plate. "She shouldn't be hitting on the high school boys she's supposed to be mentoring. Not to mention, if she's nineteen, isn't that technically illegal?"

Bianca's dark eyes widen. "I don't know, but it doesn't matter because that would be really mean."

"Meaner than stealing my boyfriend?"

"It would also be counterproductive," Bee says. "Remember: we're supposed to divide and conquer. If you get her fired, you'll only unite them against you."

I fan my mouth again. "Then what good does knowing anything about her do?"

"That depends on what we find out. I'll handle the spying." She smiles mischievously, clearly psyched at the idea.

"You?" I'm surprised. "I figured you'd find anything like

that to be inappropriate and criminal."

Bee winks. "For you, Lainey Mitchell, I will sink deep into a life of crime."

"Have I told you lately how amazing you are?" I ask. "Are you going to stalk her?"

"Yes, you have," Bee says. "And *stalk* is a strong word." She's still grinning. "But you shouldn't get involved. Jason might see you. It could blow your whole plan."

I envision myself tailing Alex from the fire station back to her house, hiding out in the bushes to see if Jay comes over. I can totally see myself sneezing or getting a phone call at the worst possible moment, being dragged out of the shrubbery by Jason himself. If dying of embarrassment is more than a figure of speech, getting caught stalking him and his new girlfriend would do it.

"Okay," I say. "You're in charge of spying. As far as some of the other stuff, I can work on being unpredictable and flexible and deceptive and decisive, but how am I supposed to get close enough to Jay to display these fabulous traits?"

"You'll have to figure out how to run into him, prefer-ably in places where Alex isn't with him."

There are a handful of places Jason frequents regularly that I might be able to "accidentally" cross paths with him. I nod. "Got it." I consult the list again. "I'm all about seizing opportunities. And I won't be too aggressive." I skip over the positioning strategy because I don't want to listen to Bianca tell me I need to date someone else again.

"Exploit enemy weaknesses," I say. "I wonder what kind

of weaknesses Alex has. Younger men, apparently."

"What would you say are Jason's weaknesses?"

"Sex?" I offer.

"What else?" She's not going to say what we're both thinking—that sex probably isn't a weakness if he's getting it from another girl.

I tick a few more off on my fingers. "Alcohol. Food. World Cup soccer."

"Does he get jealous?"

"Uh . . . I don't think so." I slump down in my chair a little.

"What about that time sophomore year?" she asks. "You and Matt Clifton after the Aquinas game?"

"Oh, right." We lost when I missed a penalty shot wide, and I refused to go home until I put twenty shots in each upper corner of the net. The boys' varsity goalie saw me practicing as he was walking to his car and offered to stay and play keeper for me. "It wasn't even like Matt was hitting on me. He probably just felt bad that I had to chase down the ball each time I kicked it. But you're right. Jason made snide comments about how he was a no-talent hack for at least a month afterward."

"So then if you were to date someone else, that might do more than level the field. It might put you in a position of power . . ." Bianca's voice trails off meaningfully.

Dude, she is fixated on this idea. "Forget it, Bee. It's not like it would be fair to date some other guy when all I'm doing is thinking about Jason."

"So find a guy to pretend to date," she says. "Adding a little deception to the mix."

"Where am I supposed to find a guy like that? Fakedates dot com?"

"Not online." Bianca shakes her head violently. "I said a guy, not an ax murderer trolling for victims. Let me think on it."

The wind chimes do their weird clunking thing, and Micah and Leo saunter into the shop. I glance up at the clock. It's almost four. Time to set up for the evening. The guys cruise past our table without even so much as a grunt in acknowledgment. As I watch Micah swipe at the screen of his phone, I get the beginnings of a great idea. "Micah," I say, my voice slick like honey.

"No." He doesn't even look back.

"Come on," I wheedle. "Come talk to us."

He pauses just outside the doorway leading into the kitchen. "I have to help Leo prep the line, Lainey."

"Oh, sorry. I just had a quick question about your girlfriend." I clear my throat. "I mean, your *ex*-girlfriend."

Bee inhales sharply. She looks from me to Micah back to me again. She's onto my plan. "Now *that* would be unpredictable," she says.

And deceptive.

And flexible.

Micah mutters something to Leo, who nods in reply and disappears into the back. Then he turns toward Bianca and me. He's sporting a new eyebrow piercing, a shiny silver barbell above his right eye. It's probably a starter piercing that he'll replace with something black and spiky, but right now it looks strangely delicate amongst his masculine features.

"So what?" he says. "What's your point?"

"She broke up with *you*, right? How'd you like to get her back?" I give him my most charming smile as I smooth the wrinkles from my Denali T-shirt.

His face tightens up. Something—pain or doubt—flashes in his hazel eyes.

I've got him. I reel him in. "I have a foolproof plan."

He rests his hands on the back of an empty chair. "What? Did you find some Wiccan love spell on the internet? All I need is a lock of hair and three tears?"

"This is the real deal," I say. "We can make her think you're over her. She'll get jealous and then wonder if she made a mistake."

"Oh yeah?" Micah's voice is full of skepticism but I can almost see him turning the idea over in his mind. "And how are we going to do that?"

"We can pretend you and I are dating." I've been feeling more and more undesirable since I saw Jason and Alex together, but for some reason even just the thought of a fake date replenishes some of my confidence.

"A pseudo-date," Bee interjects. "It can help *both* of you win back your exes."

Micah spins the chair around and straddles it backward. "I don't know," he says with exaggerated seriousness, looking back and forth from Bianca to me. "I miss Amber and all, but dating Lainey? Even for pretend? Not sure if it's worth it."

"Oh, ha-ha," I say. "You don't really think I'm that bad."

Micah smirks. "I don't think of you at all."

Zing. Ouch. I remember flinging those exact words at him the day Jason and I broke up. I had no idea they could draw blood.

"It wouldn't work anyway," Micah continues. "Amber would never believe we were dating."

I gather my hair into a ponytail and drape it over my left shoulder. "Why? Because you like your girls a little less smoking hot? A little freakier?"

Micah's eyes flick down to my hair for a second. Then he smirks again. "More like a little smaller."

I gasp. "You asshole. I am all muscle." He ducks out of the way as I make a move to slug him in the arm. "Take it back," I demand. "Take it back or else I might get, like, an eating disorder."

Micah snorts. "Pretty sure an eating disorder won't make you any shorter, dummy."

Oh. That. I never really thought about it. I guess at five eight I am almost as tall as he is.

"Wow," Bianca says. "It's like you guys are already dating."

We both give her a dark look, but she's got a point. Micah and I sat next to each other in fourth and fifth grade, back before I got popular and he went all freaktastic rocker boy.

Maybe that's why I still feel like I know him, even though we haven't really said much more than "Excuse me" and "Do you have any more of those Caribou Cookies?" in years. My heart starts skipping in my chest. This plan could actually work.

I give him my most pleading look. "I'll wear flats. Come on. Do it for Amber."

Micah gets up and heads to the kitchen. He looks back at me over his shoulder right before disappearing into the back. "I'll think about it."

Chapter 8

After torturing me for a couple of days, Micah finally calls. "So how would this work anyway?" he asks.

I flop down on my bed. "We pretend like we're dating and take each other to places where we know our exes will see us." I cross my fingers as I glance around my room full of Jason mementos. Micah has to agree—he has to. I can't ask just *any* guy to fake-date me. He needs this too. It's like fate delivered him into my lap.

"And you think it's that simple?"

"I think it's a start." Without mentioning *The Art of War*, I explain about leveling the playing field.

"So how long would we keep up this charade?"

"Good question. What about five dates each?" I suggest.

He whistles long and low. "That's a lot of quality time together."

"Well, what about either side can terminate the agreement early if it's not working out," I say. "I wouldn't want us to spend our whole summer being miserable or anything."

"What about rules?" he asks. "Things we can and can't do?"

"Rules, yes. Good call. I think we both should be able to make any rules we want, but I haven't thought that far in advance. Does that mean you're in?"

He doesn't say anything for a minute and I feel like he just needs one more nudge. "I'll even let you have the first date," I offer. "That way if it's a disaster, we can call it quits and you haven't wasted any time at all."

"You are one determined chick." He laughs under his breath. "Sure your ex-boyfriend is worth all this trouble?"

Two and a half years of kisses and late night texting and an almost perfect life as Jason's girlfriend flashes in my head. And then the thought of my senior year ruined while I watch from the sidelines as he hangs out with all of our mutual friends.

"Positive," I say.

"All right. Let's give it a shot."

I meet Micah at his apartment at the end of the week for our first official "date." His room looks about like I expected: band posters, mounds of dirty laundry, black sheets taped over the windows.

"You know, they have these things called curtains." I stand with my back against the wall. There's no way I'm sitting down in here.

Micah is sprawled across his unmade bed. He looks up from the TV long enough to roll his eyes. "So, the rules.

What are they? You strike me as the kind of girl who probably came up with a thousand of them."

"Actually I only have a few." I clear my throat. "Number one: no telling anyone else about the plan."

Micah nods. "Okay." His eyes flick back to the TV. He's watching the Cartoon Mayhem channel—an episode of *Happy Cheetah*.

"Two: no touching. Three: absolutely no kissing."

"As much as I have no desire to turn myself orange by brushing up against you and your spray-paint tan, I think we might have to touch occasionally to look like we're dating," Micah says.

"Fine. Minimal touching." I hold out my arm and admire my silky bronzeness. "And by the way, this isn't orange. It's Desert Glow."

"More like glow in the dark." He yawns. "Is that all you got?"

I nod. "Go ahead. What are your rules?"

"I'm kind of a no-rules guy." He turns to me, a slow smile spreading across his face. "I'm curious, though. What are you going to tell your friends? And your parents? That getting dumped by Jason drove you to the dark side?"

"Well, Bianca knows and Kendall is out of town. They're the main ones I talk to outside of soccer. And my parents are pretty laid-back as long as I'm home for curfews, so I don't have to tell them anything specific. I mean, for all they know we're just work friends hanging out."

Micah snorts, as if the idea of us hanging out as work

friends is all kinds of hilarious. "So no other rules?" he asks. "At *all*?"

The way he's looking at me makes me feel like there should be tons more, but I can only think of one. "No making up X-rated stories about me."

He runs a hand through his mohawk. "What about R-rated?"

"I'll give you PG-13."

"Middle school kids can get pretty rowdy these days." Micah licks his lips suggestively.

"That's your sister you're talking about, right?" I say sweetly.

"Not cool." He throws a pillow at me. "Ugh, she's actually going to be a freshman."

As if she can sense us talking about her, Micah's sister pokes her head into the room without even knocking. "Oh, hey," she says. "I'm Trinity. I just wanted to say hi."

"Hi. I'm Lainey." I give her a smile and a beauty pageant wave. I've seen Trinity hanging out at Denali, but today is the first time we've officially met. She has dark brown hair like Micah, with little streaks of blue and green protruding from behind her left ear. She's wearing a flowered dress, a trucker hat, and these weird black shoes shaped like cats. It's a mix of masculine, feminine, and just plain weird that I don't think I could pull off, but it totally works for her.

"I know who you are." She giggles. Micah punches the volume on the TV up a couple of notches. "Cool, *Happy Cheetah*," she says. "Is this the episode where Cheetah and

Bipolar Bunny go to the zoo to torment Anxiety Zebra?"
Trinity looks back and forth from Micah to me.

"I have no idea," I say.

"Lainey's not into *Happy Cheetah*." Micah changes the
channel to an episode of *Celebrity Sightings*. "This is more
her speed."

He's right. I listen as celebrity reporter Ashton Leigh
reports the latest updates on Caleb Waters and *Flyboys*.

"*Flyboys* is the story of two Air Force pilots who get
kicked out of the military for reckless behavior and have to
try to make a living as commercial pilots," Ashton chirps.
She flicks her stick-straight blonde hair back over her shoulder. "Currently the crew is filming scenes in Chicago." The
camera cuts to some grainy footage of Caleb Waters in what
looks like a hotel.

"Ohmygod," I say as Micah flips back to *Happy Cheetah*.
"Chicago! That's pretty close. What if Caleb Waters comes
here?"

"Ohmygod," Micah mimics. "I'm getting all horny just
thinking about it."

I wrinkle up my nose. "Ew, don't talk like that in front of
your little sister."

"Don't talk like that in front of your date," Trinity
chimes in.

It is superweird to hear myself referred to as Micah's
"date."

Trinity clasps her hands together and I notice her fingernails are painted blue and green to match the streaks

in her hair. "So, Lainey," she says like she's known me for years. "I've been wanting to tell you how much I love your commercial."

Micah makes a gagging sound without looking away from the TV. "I can't wait to go to Hazelton Forest University," he says in a high-pitched voice. "I'm doing a double major in soccer and celebrity stalking and a minor in tanning. It's going to be totally to die for!"

Trinity laughs. A big laugh that shows a lot of gums and teeth. I used to laugh like that, before Kendall informed me belly laughing was uncool, especially with big horsey teeth like mine.

"Those would be the best majors ever," I admit. I smile at Trinity. She's so enthusiastic about everything. It's pretty cute. "I like your streaks," I tell her, mostly because I know how much being complimented by a popular senior will mean to her.

Trinity's eyes go so wide that she looks like one of those anime girls my brother used to be obsessed with. "Really? I could give you one."

"I, uh—" Crap. This is what I get for trying to be nice.

"I'll use a clip instead of glue so you can take it out right away if you don't like it." She looks so hopeful that I can't bear to tell her no.

Micah, apparently, isn't as reluctant. "Let her be, Trin. Lainey would look weird with one of your extensions."

"I would not." Turning to Trinity I say, "Hook me up. I think I would look cool."

She smiles her huge smile again. "Awesome sauce! Be right back."

She returns carrying a camouflage tackle box and when she pops open the lid, I can see it's full of jewelry, makeup, and hair extensions.

"Pick a color." She's got little swatches of hair in every color of the rainbow.

I reach for a teal one. "It'll match my work shirt."

Trinity cocks her head to the side and toys with one of her streaks as she looks me over. She fingers the top of my hair and then the area behind my left ear, her pale forehead crinkling up in concentration. I feel a little self-conscious, which is ridiculous. I mean, she's a kid. Still, I wonder what she thinks of my outfit. Micah wouldn't tell me where he was taking me, so I tried to dress as rocker as possible, which isn't too easy when your wardrobe consists mostly of secondhand designer dresses and pastel tank tops. I opted for a black T-shirt dress and the biggest, most metallic jewelry I own. I flattened my hair extra straight. It's so shiny it's almost reflective.

"I think you look great," she says. "But a streak will make you look even cooler. You'll look right at home where my brother is taking you."

I focus my attention back on Micah. "Where are you taking me?"

"You'll see." He hums a little tune under his breath. "It's going to be torture."

Trinity steers me over in front of a full-length mirror

hanging on the closet door. She uses the pointy end of a comb to create a part down the left side of my scalp. I barely feel it as she threads a tiny silver clip around a lock of my hair. My mind tries to imagine all sorts of horrific places Micah might take me, but it comes up empty. Hazelton is the smallest suburb of St. Louis. I've been pretty much everywhere there is. Even if we go into the city, the number of places that would qualify as torture are pretty limited.

I think.

"You guys are still going to Ms. Creant's, right?" Trinity leans away from me and admires her work. She finger-combs the left side of my hair.

"Yup," Micah says, smiling at his sister or my discomfort. Maybe both.

"You'll like it then," Trinity says, heading for the bedroom door. "Be right back."

"Maybe we need to make some rules about where we can and can't go," I say, once she's out of earshot.

Micah drops the remote control on the floor and turns to see the look on my face. "Oh, come on. I have to get some enjoyment out of this."

"I don't have any immediate plans to torture *you*," I say, sounding just the slightest bit whiny.

"That you know of," he says. "Maybe just being around you will be agony."

"Ha-ha. So what's Ms. Creant's?" The name reminds me of a voodoo bookshop in New Orleans that my brother and I snuck into on a family vacation a few years back.

"It's a restaurant in the city." Micah hops up and crosses the room toward me. Without warning, he reaches out for my hair.

Instinctively I slide away from his outstretched hand, bumping my back against his closet doorknob.

"Chill, Lainey." He raises his hands in mock surrender. "I was just checking out my sister's mad skills."

I got so distracted thinking about where Micah might take me I completely didn't realize Trinity had finished threading the streak into my hair. I twist around to check myself out in the smudgy mirror. A teal-blue stripe runs behind my left ear. I have to admit I kind of like how it looks.

Trinity returns with a pair of needle-nose pliers. She pinches the clip tight where she attached the colored extension. "Now it won't fall out," she explains. "Not for a while."

"Are you done making her hot, Trin?" Micah asks. "I'm starving, and you know there's always a wait."

"Unless Lainey wants to borrow my shoes." Trinity kicks one of her clunky cat shoes up in the air. They actually have little braided tails coming off the heels. "We look about the same size."

"I'm good," I say. And then I start wondering if Micah just implied that I was hot? Or did he mean to say I *wasn't* hot without his little sister's help?

Dude, this breakup is seriously messing with my head.

Trinity nods. She packs up her tackle box of beauty products and slides out of the bedroom. "Have fun, you guys," she calls over her shoulder.

Micah turns off the TV. He grabs a tube of something from a drawer and squirts it into his hand. With the tips of his fingers, he combs his hair toward the ceiling until it stands about three inches tall. It looks cool. Creepy, but cool.

The door to his room bursts open again. A woman with bleach-blonde hair and a whole sleeve of tattoos pokes her upper body into the room. "What's going on, Micah?" she asks.

"Hey, Mom. Nothing." He fidgets with his barbed-wire bracelet. "What are you doing here?"

"I live here," his mom says. "My last appointment can-celed. What are *you doing* with a girl in your room?"

"Oh, I'm not—" I start to explain to Mrs. Foster that Micah and I are just friends.

He cuts me off. "It's Elaine from elementary school," he says. "She barely even counts as a girl."

"Micah! Don't be rude." Mrs. Foster flashes me an apolo-getic look.

"Trust me. I'm used to it," I tell her. "And I go by Lainey now."

She gives me a quick once-over but doesn't seem to rec-ognize me without the crooked teeth and straggly hair I sported back when I was eight. "Well, aren't you pretty," she says after a few seconds.

"Don't encourage her," Micah says. "Seriously."

Mrs. Foster blinks rapidly. "Is that your father's?" She gestures at Micah's shirt.

He's wearing a black T-shirt as usual. This one has four gray bars on it, with the words BLACK FLAG printed below them. It must be a band or something.

"So what if it is?" he asks. "I have lots of his shirts."

"It's fine. I just didn't realize you wore them." His mom sniffs the air. She narrows her eyes, causing a fine network of wrinkles to form at her temples. "Have you been smoking in here?"

"No, Mom." He sighs. "Jeez. Quit embarrassing me."

Mrs. Foster turns back to me. "Has he?" she asks. "Has he *ever* smoked around you?"

Only, like, every single day at work. "No, ma'am," I say quickly.

Her eyes return to normal but she doesn't look completely convinced. "Where are you two headed?"

"We're just going out to eat." He grabs his wallet out from under a pile of dirty clothes and clips the chain to one of the loops on his jeans.

She nods. "Don't be too late, okay? I've got to work until midnight at the diner. I expect to see you home when I get here."

"Right." Micah grabs my arm and tugs me past his mother and down the hallway. "Let's get out of here."

I smile a good-bye to Micah's mom over my shoulder as he practically drags me out of the apartment. I stare at his mohawk as we head down the steps and out of his building. Individual tufts of hair lean to the left in the warm breeze. I can't help wondering what his hair feels like. Is it soft? Is it prickly? I could touch it if I wanted to. I mean, he was going to touch *my* hair before I pulled away. I think about it for a moment, but then decide not to. I wouldn't want to give him the wrong idea.

Chapter 9

THE QUALITY OF DECISION IS LIKE THE WELL-
TIMED SWOOP OF A FALCON.

—SUN TZU, *The Art of War*

"This is what you drive?" We're standing in front of a car-shaped heap of lime-green metal parked across the street. "How have I never noticed this monstrosity in the Denali parking lot? Does it even run?" I zero in on a big arc of rust above one of the tires. I'm not trying to be a bitch, but the car seriously doesn't look like it would make it around the block, let alone fifteen miles into the city.

"It runs like a dream," Micah says, frowning at me. "It's a Mustang."

I laugh. "What year? Like 1950?"

His eyes narrow. "1965. It's a classic."

"Sorry. It's just that Jason drives a Mustang, and his car looks nothing like this."

"Yeah, I didn't pay extra for the douchebag package." Micah opens the door for me. "Get in."

Reality crashes down as I slide into the passenger seat.

I've never ridden in another guy's car before. I start to sweat before Micah even makes it around to the driver's side. What the hell are we going to talk about on the way to the restaurant? The new beans we got in at Denali? The latest heavy metal bands coming to The Devil's Doorstep?

I flail for a distraction. As soon as he slips the key in the ignition, I punch the radio on and tune it to K-HOT, the hip-hop station Jason likes to play in the car.

"No chance." Micah hits the first preset and something that sounds more like screaming than singing erupts from the speakers. "I'm driving. I pick the music."

I plug my ears with my fingertips. "I'd rather listen to static."

"Fine. How about a compromise?" He connects his phone to the stereo and fidgets with the screen. A happy punk song starts playing.

"What is it?" I ask, nervousness making my voice come out high and snippy.

"It's a playlist of different stuff." He shifts the car into drive. "Nothing too hard-core. Give it a chance, okay?"

"Okay." I'm not really sure what else to say, so I pull my phone out of my purse and check my email. There's a message from my brother with pictures of his dorm room in Ireland, and also an update from CalebWaters.com with a few stills from *Flyboys*—mostly photos of Caleb in a pilot's uniform posing in a cockpit. I forward it to Bianca. I wonder if Caleb likes acting better than playing soccer. He used to be a striker forward like me, but he had to retire after he ruptured his Achilles tendon in a play-off match a couple of years ago.

I think acting would be awesome, but I can't imagine giving up soccer. It's not like it's the only thing I'm good at—I get decent grades and stuff—but racing up and down the field gives me that rush of power. Kind of the same way I feel hanging out with Kendall.

And Jason.

I pull *The Art of War* out of my purse. Desperately, I flip through my dog-eared pages looking for something to latch on to, something that will reinforce the idea that this whole plan isn't insane. *"The quality of decision is like the well-timed swoop of a falcon,"* I mutter under my breath.

"What?" Micah gives me a sideways glance. "Are you . . . reading?"

"Believe it or not," I say without looking up, "it's part of my impressive skill set."

"Should I be offended you brought a book on our fake date?" He sounds amused.

For some reason, I don't want to tell him the truth. Probably because I don't feel like being made fun of at the moment. "I'm just getting a head start on our summer reading list."

The music switches to something dark and slow that matches my mood. The song is an instrumental, with piano and violin layered on top of the rock guitars and bass. Something about it makes my heart beat funny. Tears form out of nowhere, hot behind my eyes. I glance down at my lap, swallowing hard to dissolve the lump in my throat.

Micah switches lanes and brakes gently as he prepares to exit onto a different highway. "Is it a sad book?"

He looks over at me again. There's something different about his voice. It's so gentle, so smooth, like rain falling against stained-glass windows. The image freaks me out. This music is apparently making me crazy.

"I'm just thinking about something," I reply.

Now he's got both eyes back on the road. "I thought maybe you were going to start crying on me."

"Don't worry." I try to infuse my voice with sarcasm. "The last thing I plan to do is break down on our fake date. I am all business." The dreamy instrumental song ends and something more upbeat comes on. It's got a catchy hook but the guitars are a little shrieky for my taste. "This music is giving me a headache," I mutter.

"You're giving me a headache," Micah says, but he turns the volume down a notch.

The afternoon sun blasts me head on. I don't usually wear sunglasses because they make those ugly red marks on my nose, but today I wish I had some. I turn my face back to the side to protect my eyes. Strip malls slide past me, one after the next. Gaudy billboards line the highway. UP TO 50% OFF. ONE DAY ONLY. THE BIGGEST DEALS ARE HERE. Lies. All lies.

"I remember when this whole area was fields," I say, immediately regretting it. I sound like my grandpa.

But for once Micah doesn't jump on an opportunity to

make fun of me. "Me too," he says. "My dad used to take us camping out here."

"Oh," I reply, startled by the mention of his dad. Micah's father, a guitarist for a local rock band, was killed in a convenience store robbery back when Micah and I were in fifth grade.

It was big news in Hazelton. Everywhere you went in school, people were clustered together talking about it, how terrible it must have been for Micah, who was waiting out in the car when the robbery occurred. Micah, who wandered into the store right in time to see his dad bleed to death. Those were the rumors anyway. No one ever dared to ask if they were true.

What do you say to someone whose dad has just been shot and killed? If you're a member of Mrs. Simonson's fifth-grade class, not much. You tiptoe around the person, trying not to make physical contact in case "dead dad" is contagious. You offer timid smiles and awkward greetings until eventually the person snaps, knocks over a couple of desks during class, gets in a fight with the security guard, and then disappears until the beginning of the next school year.

We didn't talk much in middle school. Micah didn't talk much to anyone. I feel the urge to apologize for the shitty way I treated him back then, but I can't quite make the words come out.

"I've never gone camping," I say finally. I lick my lips and peek over at Micah.

He catches me looking and misinterprets my distress as being about our fake date. "You're not going to freak out if this plan doesn't work, are you?" he asks. "Because I'll be fine either way."

And just like that, the moment passes. It's probably for the best. I bet he doesn't even remember the way everybody acted back in elementary school. Or if he does, he wouldn't want me to bring it up. I stare through the smudgy glass. A megamall. An electronic sign. More empty promises. I tuck the book back in my purse.

"I'll be okay," I say without turning to face him. It's the least convincing answer ever, but Micah doesn't question it and I'm glad. How am I supposed to explain to him I *won't* be okay if our plan doesn't work? That without Jason I'm not even sure who I'd be anymore.

Kendall is the one who is going to really freak out when she finally hears about the breakup. Jason must not have told her or else I'm sure she would have called me. The three of us spent a lot of time together last year because her boyfriend, Nicholas, went off to college in California at the start of our junior year. When they broke up officially a couple months later, Kendall decided high school guys were lame and college guys were only out to score. I hated seeing her alone, so whenever Jason and I went out—to the movies, to the soccer park, to someone's party—I always invited her along. Jay never seemed to mind and Kendall loved it. Maybe if she stays in New York for most of the summer, I can win him back before she even hears about the breakup.

I don't want her to feel like she has to pick between us, because I know I'll lose.

Micah's voice cuts into my thoughts. "Hey. Thanks for telling my mom I don't smoke."

"You thought I would narc you out on our first fake date?" I force a smile. "Don't you think she knows, though?"

"Probably. But I try to hide it. My grandma died of lung cancer and if Mom even smells smoke on me, she gets pissed. I plan to quit . . . eventually. It's just been hard."

Micah pulls off the highway. The outer part of St. Louis is all industrial buildings and vacant lots. As we head toward the river, we pass Union Station and the hockey arena. On the left is a green space dotted with random modern art and panhandlers. The courthouse looms in front of us.

"We're almost there," Micah says.

I focus on my lap, wishing I could rewind to before Bianca and I came up with this silly plan. This can't be what Dead Chinese Warlord had in mind by deception and leveling the battlefield. This is like me putting down my weapon and going to grab a bite to eat with a random nomad who accidentally wandered into the war, isn't it?

I need to get it together. *Don't be a coward. Don't worry too much.* I remind myself of the five deadly faults I'm supposed to be avoiding. I'm just nervous because I've never gone out with another guy before.

Micah turns left onto a one-way street. He switches lanes to avoid a parked delivery truck and then dodges a giant pothole. He's a really good driver, but the stop-and-go traffic is making me queasy. I watch out the side window as the city flies by. Through gaps in the skyline, I see the sun reflecting off the top of the Arch. Jason and I went there together last year for a history class field trip. There's a museum at the base of it and a tiny elevator goes up to a viewing area where you can see the whole city. We went up to the top with most of our classmates and kissed every time our teacher wasn't looking.

Micah cuts through a decidedly seedy area of North St. Louis where the redbrick houses sit so close together you could probably reach out your window and into your neighbor's house—if it weren't for the bars on the windows. A man sits on one of the porches, drinking straight from a whiskey bottle. A pit bull paces back and forth in front of him. I slouch down in the car. A train whistle blows from somewhere nearby and I flinch.

As Micah slows the car to a stop, I peek out the window and see a two-story house that is straight out of a horror movie. The bricks have been covered in white paint that has worn away in uneven scabby patches. My heart thuds against my rib cage as I check out the boarded-up windows and the field of three-foot-tall weeds in the front yard.

"Are we lost?" I ask hopefully, double-checking to make sure my door is locked. "Or have you brought me here to kill me?"

Micah grins as he shakes his head and points toward a wooden sign half buried in the high grass. I can barely make out what it says: MIZZ CREANT'S HOUSE OF TORTURE.

Chapter 10

IN ALL FIGHTING, THE DIRECT METHOD MAY
BE USED FOR JOINING BATTLE, BUT INDIRECT
METHODS WILL BE NEEDED IN ORDER TO SECURE
VICTORY.

—SUN TZU, *The Art of War*

"House of Torture?" I ask through clenched teeth.

Micah laughs, a big belly laugh like Trinity. "Read the fine print," he says.

I squint. Underneath the big, bloody word *torture*, someone has stenciled something in black ink. " 'And pancakes'?" I turn to him. "Seriously?"

"Trust me, we're only indulging in the food today," Micah says. "Unless you're into—"

I lash out with my fist and it connects with a pyramid tattoo on his right bicep.

He doubles over in pain. "Ow. That tattoo is brand-new."

"No it's not." My eyes turn to slits. "You've had that for, like, a year."

He gasps in mock surprise. "Why, Lainey. And here I didn't think you paid me any attention."

My face flushes. "I don't," I insist, but it just sounds defensive. "How many tattoos do you have anyway?" I ask. "Your mom doesn't care?"

"I have three. When I turned sixteen, she told me I could get whatever I want, as long as she gets to do them."

Besides the pyramid, he's got a tattoo of three overlapping circles on his neck. For a second, I wonder where the third tattoo is, but that's probably one of those "Don't ask if you don't want to know" questions. "Wow. Your mom must be really cool."

Micah fiddles with his barbed-wire bracelet. "I think she sees it as safe self-destructiveness, you know? Better for me to get a tattoo or pierce an eyebrow than to go buy drugs if I'm feeling like shit."

I wonder what else besides Micah's dad dying made him feel bad enough to turn to "safe self-destructiveness." His eyebrow ring is new. Did he do it when he was hurting about Amber? Before I can even decide if I want to ask him, he opens his door and slides out of the car. "Come on. Quit stalling," he says.

We follow the stepping-stones made of shards of broken mirror through the high grass and up to the porch. Someone has spray-painted a red line on one of the boarded-up windows. Scribbled in Magic Marker below it are the words: *You must be this tall to enter the House of Torture (and pancakes).* I try to peer through a spidery crack in the warped plywood but all I can see is darkness. Micah could be taking me to a crack den for all I know.

He practically has to yank me up the stairs. Half-rotted steps groan under my feet. A wind chime made of fake (I hope) bones and pieces of broken chain clanks in the soft summer breeze.

"I bet someone got murdered in this place," I mutter.

"I'm about ready to murder me some pancakes," Micah says. The door creaks impressively as he pushes on it. He holds it open for me.

The inside of the restaurant is crowded with clusters of teens and college kids who look like they could be extras on *Undead Academy*.

"Popular," I say. As my eyes adjust to the gloom, I see that we're standing in a dim room underneath a tarnished candelabra filled with misshapen red candles. The black-and-white-tiled floor is smeared with drips of crimson wax—it totally looks like a crime scene. I half expect some supermodel-hot CSI tech wearing a body-hugging gray jumpsuit to greet us. Instead, a hostess wearing fishnet stockings, a patent-leather strapless dress, and a bored expression doesn't even bother to say hi. She stands behind a guillotine-shaped podium, clicking her sparkly, black fingernails against the wooden surface to the beat of a song she's humming to herself.

"Hey, Lyla." Micah strides up to her like they're old friends. "Is Phoenix working?"

The hostess licks her lips, as if Micah has asked something extra perverted. "Are you looking for more than a server?"

"Oh no. Food only." Micah shudders.

"Wait time is about fifteen minutes." Lyla jots down Micah's name on a notepad full of unintelligible scribble. "I'll see if Phoenix is available." She slides out from behind the podium and heads toward the kitchen.

"Who's Phoenix?" I ask.

"Amber's sister." Micah rests one shoulder against the wall. The burgundy wallpaper is peeling in places, revealing plain concrete beneath.

"Oh. So Amber won't actually be here?"

"She doesn't work a regular job so she's harder to accidentally run into." He picks at a loose spot of wallpaper. "I figured the indirect route might be less obvious anyway."

The indirect route—vintage Dead Chinese Warlord. "Wow, you're good. It's like you've done this before." I watch the tiny scab-like flecks of maroon flutter to the floor.

Micah stops picking. "No, but I know Phoenix will report back to Amber in excruciating detail." He winks. "Feel free to hang all over me."

"Ha-ha," I say. "Minimal touching, remember?" I peer past the guillotine and into the main dining room. Replicas of old-fashioned torture devices—a rack, a hangman's platform, a dunking booth—are stationed throughout the dining area like some sort of depraved physical fitness circuit. "Where the hell have you taken me?"

"Check this out." Micah heads toward a pair of doors marked SADISTS and MASOCHISTS. I think they're the bathrooms, but I'm not sure. I make a mental note not to drink too much so I don't have to find out. He points at a silver rectangle that looks like an old-fashioned pay phone. As I squint to try to read the instructions mounted above the box, Micah slides a quarter into the machine.

"Hold these," he says, giving me a pair of brass handles attached to metal cables.

"What are—" Before I can get my question out, a wave of electric current races through my body. *Ouch!* I drop the handles. "What the hell?"

Micah laughs. "It's a shock generator. I hit you with the voltage of an electric eel."

"Dude! Why would you do that?"

He laughs again and then grabs my wrists as I lunge for him. "You're kind of a brute, you know?"

My face crumples. Jason used to call me butch sometimes. It made me so mad. I could do fifteen really girly things an hour but the one time I punched him or belched or scored a kick-ass goal off him, he always made me feel like the least sexy person in the world.

Micah drops my hands. "What? I was only kidding, Lainey." He backs slowly away from me like I'm a bomb in danger of detonating.

"I'll show you brute," I say, faking a smile. I pass the brass handles to him. "My turn."

"Okay," Micah says, "but be gentle. Don't hit me with taser or I might piss myself."

"Ew." I bend in to look at the five choices: 1. NERVE CON-DUCTION TEST. 2. BABY ELECTRIC EEL. 3. CANINE SHOCK COLLAR.

4. CATTLE PROD. 5. TASER. "There's no way this is *really* taser strength, is it? People would be collapsing on the floor."

"Not sure. I've never been brave enough to try it."

I don't know if it's because I'm feeling nice or because I'm skeeved out at the thought of Micah peeing his pants, but I give him a blast of baby electric eel.

He yelps. Then he grins. "You went soft on me, didn't you?"

Before I can answer, Lyla coughs meaningfully and gestures to us with one of her glittery black talons. "Your table's ready."

We follow her to a booth near the back of the dining area. There's a potted plant on the table—a Venus flytrap.

"That's one way to take care of bugs, I guess." I stare at the tiny teeth adorning each pair of leaves, wondering if they're as prickly as they look.

"Check that out." Micah nods toward something behind me.

I turn. On the far wall, there's an old-time film projector screen. A hazy black-and-white movie from before I was born is playing. Some guy's getting electroshock treatment. His body spasms and convulses as the current moves through him. I get a little jittery just watching.

"Is there an age requirement for this place?" I ask.

"There's the height requirement outside, but I don't think it's enforced," Micah says. "But you have to be eighteen to tour the interactive torture museum in the basement." He makes air quotes when he says the word *interactive*.

"What does that involve?" I try to fight back the blush creeping up in my cheeks.

"I've never been down there so I can't say. Probably nothing *too* deviant." He gives me a suggestive look. "You want to check it out? I bet Phoenix wouldn't card us."

"No," I say quickly. A trio of girls with Kool-Aid dye jobs and big sunglasses turn to look at me from the next table over. One of them snickers. I grab the menu and hide behind it.

The food choices at Mizz Creant's include not just pancakes, but also waffles, omelets, and other assorted breakfast items. The laminated menu is shaped like a skull and crossbones. I skim the choices under the heading PANCAKES: SAW-BERRY SURPRISE. CHOKE-A-LOT CHIP. SIN-A-MON SPICE.

A girl with short, white-blonde hair, wearing a black rubber skirt and a tank top made of what looks like overlapping safety pins, sidles up to the table. She's got a spiked collar around her neck and rings of black eye makeup around her eyes. "Look who's come out of hiding. What's up, kid?"

"Hey, Phoenix." Micah nods toward me. "This is—"

"No one cares." The girl makes a throat-slitting gesture. "I assume you're not here because you want me to make you my bitch, so what are you eating?"

"I like a girl who gets right to the point," Micah says. "I'll have the Destructor omelet. With bacon spears and hash-browns."

Phoenix is carrying a little notebook with the metal spiral partially unbent and formed into a shank. She nods at

Micah but makes no move to write anything down. "Would you like your hashbrowns asphyxiated?"

"Oh yeah. Smother away," he says.

She pops her gum. "And what does your rebound chick want?"

I make a noise somewhere between a gasp and a yelp. Phoenix doesn't even glance in my direction.

"She can order for herself," Micah says.

"Aww. Wait till I tell Amber you've gone all submissive." Phoenix turns her black-ringed eyes toward me and gives me her best bored expression.

I start to order but no sound comes out. I clear my throat. "I'll have the Saw-berry pancakes. With bacon spears."

"Fabulous." She spins around and heads toward the kitchen. Between the straps of her tank top, I can see part of a giant pair of wings tattooed on her back.

"She seems nice," I say.

Micah stares at me for a second, then bursts out laughing. I laugh too. He reaches toward my face and runs his finger down the teal streak in my hair. "That was cool of you to let Trinity put this in. I can take it out later if you want." He folds my hair up and away from my face so he can get a look at the tiny clip.

"I kind of like it." I smile. "It makes me feel alternative."

He snickers. "You're about as alternative as skim milk, Lainey." He drops my hair and runs his finger along the prickly edge of one of the Venus flytrap's lower leaves.

"Gee, thanks," I say, but I didn't mean alternative like

Micah. Or Phoenix, God forbid. I meant more like getting to be someone else for a change. No one knows me here. I can do or say whatever I want without having to worry about what anyone thinks.

"Hey. Speaking of Trin. I thought of a rule I want to make." Micah looks up from the plant.

"Let's hear it."

"She may have said something about how being the sister to the guy dating soccer star Lainey Mitchell was going to make school suck less in the fall. I didn't know what to tell her. But if she says hi to you in the halls, promise me you won't ignore her, okay? No being mean to my sister."

Being friends with a varsity soccer player is actually a big deal at Hazelton, especially when you're a freshman. It never occurred to me that this little charade had the potential to hurt anyone besides me or Micah. "Rule accepted. I would never ignore her."

"Cool," he says. "I just don't want her to have a hard time. You're more than welcome to ignore *me*. I got my own reputation to look out for too, and it does not involve palling around with a soccer chick."

"Right. You wouldn't want our classmates to confuse you with someone normal," I tease.

"Normal is overrated." He points at my teal streak. "You practically said so yourself." He gestures with his head at the table next to us—the girls with the Kool-Aid hair. "Obviously not trying to be normal. So who do you think they are?"

"Um, weirdos?" I offer.

"More specific." He lowers his voice. "I think they're members of an all-girl rock band who just hit the big time, hence the glasses."

"Oh, I get it." I sneak another peek at the girls. One of them has a *Happy Cheetah* Band-Aid on her thumb. "I think they're hookers who all just got beat up by their pimp, *hence the glasses*," I whisper.

"Not bad." Micah nods slowly at me and I can't help but smile. I wasn't expecting hanging out with him to be fun.

The two of us scope out the other customers while we wait for our food, trying to guess their identities. We've identified potential school bus drivers, Satanists, illicit lovers, professional ballerinas, and a coroner by the time Phoenix returns with our food. She clunks down our plates in front of us without so much as a word.

My pancakes are heart-shaped and tinted pink, with spatters of strawberry puree drizzled across the top to resemble blood. A serrated knife protrudes from the stack. I pull the knife out hesitantly and saw off a square from the tip of the heart.

The pancake is delicious, soft and sweet like it was soaked in butter before the strawberry sauce was added. The whole forkful practically melts in my mouth.

"Ohmygod," I say. "These are totally to die for."

"I know, right?" Micah closes his eyes momentarily. "Now you see why even normal people are willing to come here and be treated like shit."

I take another bite. Another explosion of sweetness and tanginess. "There aren't any illegal substances in these, are there?" I ask. "I'm feeling sort of . . . euphoric."

Micah swallows a big bite of cheesy-bacon hashbrowns before answering. "Nope. Just good food." He laughs under his breath. "But I have that effect on girls a lot."

"Oh, I'm sure." I ball up my straw wrapper and flick it at him. My aim is about two feet wide and I nearly hit Phoenix as she strolls by on the way to take another table's order.

I study her out of the corner of my eye. Her skin is impossibly pale except for the tattoos on her back. She's so waifish that the bones of her spine stick out, and the snake armband she's wearing slips down around her elbow as she walks.

"So are Amber and her sister a lot alike?" I ask. Micah's girlfriend goes to a different school and I've never seen her up at Denali. "All tattoos and bad attitude?"

"No," Micah says. "Despite my choice of eatery, I'm not into being abused." His voice softens and he looks down at his omelet as he talks. "Amber is really awesome. She's funny and cool and amazingly talented. I felt lucky to be with her, you know?" He glances up. "Like she was probably too good for me."

I nod. "Yeah, I felt the same way about Jason. For the first six months we dated, I kept expecting him to break up with me. And then, I don't know, the more time we spent together, the better we seemed to match up."

"Really? He always seemed like kind of a tool to me."

"Yeah, but all you see is the person he is in school. He's different with me."

"If you say so." Micah shrugs. "But blowing you off like that, in front of everyone? I would never do that to a girl."

"I'm sure he had a reason," I say sharply, even though I can't imagine what it was. I look down at my plate and concentrate on cutting my remaining pancake into small squares.

"Forget I mentioned it." Micah runs one finger along the edge of the Venus flytrap's leaves again. "I didn't mean to upset you."

I nibble at another bite of pancake and swallow hard. "It's no big deal." I feign interest in the black-and-white movie until the awkward moment passes.

When our plates are empty, Phoenix slinks up to our table and rests one of her hands on the back of Micah's neck. He makes a face at me as she runs her fingernails through his hair. "Sure you two don't want to take our interactive tour?" She smirks as she drops the check in the middle of our table. "I'm cool with a group thing."

Micah gives her the finger as he grabs the check.

"I can—" I start to say, but he kicks me under the table.

"I got this," he says.

"Thanks, *hon*." I give him an exaggerated smile as I reach down to rub the sore spot on my shin. Phoenix makes a gagging sound.

Micah slides a couple of bills into the black studded-leather check holder. "Keep the change."

Apparently satisfied with her tip, she plants an air kiss next to Micah's face. "Come back and see me sometime," she coos as we stand up to leave. I'm pretty sure she's not talking to me.

We head back through the restaurant and outside to Micah's car, which surprisingly has not been vandalized in any way. He turns to me as he fires up the engine. "So what'd you think?" he asks. "Not too much torture, right?"

I'm not sure if he's talking about the restaurant, Phoenix, or just hanging out with him. "It was pretty fun," I admit. "Except for the shock therapy."

"Sorry. I couldn't resist." He pulls away from the curb and turns south to cut back across the city. "So what now, O Great Planner?"

"I guess now you wait for Phoenix to tell Amber you're hanging out with some other girl. And see what happens."

He nods. "Sure, but what do I have to do for you?"

"Oh, right." Funny. I had almost forgotten about that part of the deal. "Give me a couple days. I'll get back to you."

Micah nods. His phone rings and he looks away from the road just long enough to answer. From my side of the conversation it sounds like he's telling someone he's going to be a little late to work. I fiddle with the stuff in the center console: an insurance card, a lighter, a pack of gum, and a small, black-and-gray rectangle that looks like a knife handle. I press the tiny silver latch embedded in the metal and a blade shoots out.

Micah swerves halfway onto the shoulder. "I have to

go," he says quickly into the phone. He lets it fall to his lap and turns to me. "What are you doing? Don't mess with my stuff."

"Why do you have a switchblade?" I ask.

"Because I'm not old enough to own a gun." With one hand on the steering wheel, he grabs the knife from my hand and retracts the blade. "You need to be careful."

"But what would you even do with it?"

His hazel eyes go dark. "Nothing, hopefully," he says. "But you never know." I can tell he's thinking about his dad again. Maybe the whole world becomes dangerous if you lose a parent the way Micah did.

"You work tonight?" I ask, eager to change the subject.

"Not at Denali. I volunteer at the Humane Society once a week."

"You work with the puppies and kitties?" I raise an eyebrow. "I figured you'd be more interested in biting their heads off."

"They let me do that sometimes after we close," he jokes.

"No, seriously," I say. "I never saw you as the volunteering type. That's kind of sweet."

"You are so dense." Micah keeps both eyes on the road but shakes his head. "It's not sweet. It's court-ordered community service. Better playing with puppies than picking up beer cans and dirty diapers along the side of the highway, you know?"

"Oh," I reply, adjusting the hem of my T-shirt dress. "So you really went to jail last year?"

"Juvie."

"For what?" The question leaves my mouth before I even have time to think. I've heard all the usual rumors that you hear about someone working the loner-rocker-boy image like Micah. He smokes weed. He deals drugs. He beats up preppy kids behind The Devil's Doorstep. I always figured the stories were bullshit.

"Why do you care?" He glances over. "You afraid of me now?"

"No," I say quickly. And it's true. Even if he carries a switchblade and pretends to be a badass, he doesn't seem much different from the kid I knew in fifth grade. "I'm just trying to . . . get to know you again."

"That's kind of sweet," he says, throwing my words back at me in a high-pitched girly voice. His lips curve upward, just barely. "Maybe I'll tell you. Someday."

Chapter 11

WEAK POINTS . . .

YOU MAY ADVANCE AND BE ABSOLUTELY
IRRESISTIBLE, IF YOU MAKE FOR THE ENEMY'S
WEAK POINTS . . .

—SUN TZU, *The Art of War*

Later that night, I'm crashed out on the sofa watching a rerun of a World Cup game when Bianca calls.

"Hey." I watch as Caleb Waters puts a free kick in the upper-left corner of the goal. The crowd goes wild.

"Hey, yourself. Weren't you going to call me the instant you got home from your pseudo-date?" she asks. "I want to hear all about it."

"Oh, right." I mute the TV. "So Micah took me to this completely freaktastic place where his ex-girlfriend's sister works." I give her a quick rundown on Mizz Creant's.

"That sounds . . . strange. Did you guys get along okay?"

"Other than the fact that he blasted me with some weird shock device." I start to smile thinking about it, even though it was totally not funny at the time. "It was awkward at first. He mentioned his dad in the car and I didn't know what to say. But there were plenty of conversation starters at the restaurant."

"Well, I'm glad it wasn't terrible," Bee says. "Where are you going to take him?"

"Not sure yet. Got any great ideas?"

"Hmm." She yawns. "I'll have to sleep on it."

"Sounds good. Talk to you soon."

Right as I hang up, a commercial for a home game against the Chicago Cubs comes on. That would be perfect. Jason has baseball season tickets. He would never miss a chance to see the Cardinals waste the Cubs. I've been to a handful of games with him so I know exactly where he sits. Micah and I can get tickets for the same section.

But how to make sure Jay sees us at a crowded baseball game? I head into my room and paw through the old birthday cards, notes, and ticket stubs in my bottom dresser drawer until I find a Cardinals ticket from last summer. Right-field bleachers. Fifth row. Seat 14. I'll just have to look for open seats as close to there as possible.

After texting Micah to make sure he's available on Sunday afternoon, I get online and check out the available tickets. Most of the first ten rows are already purchased, but there is a pair of seats way at the outside edge of the fourth row. If Micah and I entered from the wrong side we'd have to squeeze past the entire section. I'd pass right in front of Jay—there'd be no way for him to miss us. I start imagining the look on his face when I stroll by with my new "boyfriend" in tow.

Hello, mountaintop.

* * *

"I can't believe you're taking me to a Cards–Cubs game," Micah says. "This might actually be kind of fun."

"It's the perfect place to run into Jason," I say. "He's got season tickets."

We're meeting up at Micah's house again because his mom has to go straight from her job at the tattoo parlor to her job at the diner tonight, so no one will bother us.

During the school year, I also get a lot of parent-free time, but Mom spends her summers camped out in the study writing anthropology books and journal articles. Even though she's been known to get so into her notes that she forgets to eat, I'm pretty sure me dragging a guy with tats and a mohawk into my bedroom would not escape her attention.

"Please tell me you're not really going to wear that," Micah says.

"What?" I'm wearing jean shorts and one of the only red things I own—an official Caleb Waters replica jersey.

"You can't wear a soccer jersey to a Cardinals game. It's sacrilegious." Micah shakes his head in disbelief. "Let me see if Trin has something you can borrow." He leaves the room and returns a few minutes later with a tiny red-and-white scrap of cloth that looks like a dinner napkin. He tosses it to me.

I unfold it and hold it against myself. It's a baby-doll T-shirt, not even enough fabric to cover half of my chest. "No way," I say. "This'll never fit."

"It looks like it would fit great to me," Micah says

innocently. And then, when I frown: "Fine. You can wear one of my shirts." He ducks his head in his closet and comes back with two Cardinals tees on hangers.

"Why do you have all these baseball shirts?" I ask, trying to decide between the red shirt with a cartoon bird on it and the black one with the more traditional STL logo. "I wouldn't have thought you were into sports at all."

"Everyone in St. Louis is into the Cardinals, aren't they?" he asks. "My dad used to take Trin and me to games when we were little."

"My dad and my brother go a lot. Steve loves baseball." I pull the red shirt from the hanger. "I'll wear this one." I start to remove my soccer jersey and then realize Micah is staring at me. "Turn around," I order him.

"But you've got another shirt on under there," he says.

"Yeah, but it's a tank top. Just turn around."

He mutters something under his breath about me strutting around Denali in less—not true!—but gives up and turns to face his closet. I back away to the other side of his bed and tug the replica jersey over my head. Micah whistles and I almost drop it on the floor. He's totally checking me out in the mirror.

"Micah!" I hurriedly pull the Cardinals T-shirt over my head. "What is wrong with you?"

"What? You said turn around. You didn't say close your eyes."

"Perv." I give him a dirty look.

His lips twitch, like he's trying not to laugh. "Man. I had

you figured for a lot of things, but uptight wasn't one of them."

"I am *not* uptight," I say in what is probably the most uptight voice ever. "Now be quiet and find a hat or something to cover that freaktastic hair of yours."

"You like this hair," Micah says. But he digs a red Cardinals cap out of his closet. He flips the hat around in his hands and then puts it on backward. It's amazing how normal he looks already. Well, except for . . .

I point at his eyebrow ring. I cough meaningfully.

"Not happening. It'll close up if I take it out."

"But—"

"No. It stays," Micah says. "It'll be like you replaced him with a bad boy. He'll wonder if you've got some deviant fantasies he totally missed out on."

The way he says it is almost flirty and I feel my cheeks growing warm. I ignore the comment and check my phone, even though I know exactly what time it is. "We should get going soon."

When Micah stands up, other than the pierced eyebrow and tattoo on his neck, he looks like any other high school guy. But what will Jason think? Will seeing me with any other high school guy be enough to make him jealous?

"Want to drive my car?" Micah asks with a gleam in his eye.

"No freaking way. That thing doesn't even qualify as a car." I jingle my brother's keys in front of his face. "I thought we'd take the train so we don't have to worry about traffic." Traffic would mean long periods of time trapped in the car together with nothing to say. Not to mention I've never driven downtown by myself and would probably end up going the wrong way down a one-way street or parking in a tow-away zone. Best to play it safe.

"Whatever you want," Micah says. "I'm just a fake date along for the ride."

We leave my brother's car at the nearest MetroLink station and hop into the first car of a Red Line train that's heading east toward St. Louis.

The car is half full of people in Cardinals apparel. Micah and I find forward-facing seats together. We're ten stops from the stadium and I talk nonstop through the first eight. As the train gets progressively more crowded, I talk about the weather, Jason, soccer, Denali, Bianca, etc. The funny thing is, my brain is so busy playing out worst-case scenarios where Jason doesn't even notice me or my "date," that I have almost no idea what I'm saying and even less of an idea of how Micah is responding.

Or even if he's responding.

I stop talking for a second. Crap. He's *not* responding.

"Sorry," I say. "I ramble when I get nervous."

He punches me lightly in the side of the arm. "You ramble all the time. No wonder you got dumped."

I frown. The words sting even though I know he's kidding. What if that's part of why Jason left me? If he decided I was annoying, he'll probably be *glad* to see me with some other guy. Suddenly the whole plan seems like a terrible idea again, more art of insanity than art of war.

Micah hands me an earbud that's connected to his phone. "Here. This will relax you." A pulsing rhythm blares out of the tiny speaker. It reminds me of one of the songs we listened to on the way to Mizz Creant's. Not the instrumental one. One of the faster songs. It's got a catchy little chorus.

"Who is this?" I ask, momentarily setting aside my doubt.

"It's Hannah in Handcuffs. I saw them in concert not too long ago. The song is called 'Terrible Beauty.' You like it?"

"It sounds like a bunch of cats being crushed by a steam-roller," I say, even though I don't totally hate it.

Micah smiles. He's not fooled.

The train slows to a stop and the stadium rises up in front of us, all red brick and black metal. I take a deep breath. Too late to turn back now. We exit with everyone else decked out in Cardinals gear, funneling out the MetroLink doors and across the platform in a stream of red. The gray pavement reflects the sun back at us. It's shaping up to be a scorcher.

We pass the statue of Stan Musial, who according to my dad was one of the greatest athletes of all time. I'm thinking he couldn't have been as good as Caleb Waters, but St. Louis never manages to keep a professional soccer team for very long, and the Cardinals have won, like, eleventy million championships, so baseball is much more popular here.

Micah and I enter the stadium where I am glad to be out of the sun for a few minutes. Vendors carrying coolers of beer and soda gracefully navigate the throngs of people. Pockets of blue—Cubs fans—snake their way through the red-and-white masses.

"Do you want food or anything?" Micah asks.

It's a nice gesture considering that food here would probably cost more than I paid for our tickets. "No, that's cool. I'll eat later."

We find the right-field bleachers and it only takes a few seconds to pick out Jason in the fifth row. I'd recognize his broad shoulders anywhere. A shock of blond hair juts out from his fitted Cardinals cap. I'm torn between wanting to run toward him and wanting to hide.

He's sitting next to Dan Spencer, a guy who just graduated, who Kendall dated briefly when she went through what she called a "slumming phase." I barely hear Micah saying something as I stare at Jason's back, at the way his muscles pull the fabric of his replica jersey taut. A family of four squeezes past us carrying nachos, hot dogs, and a tray full of sodas.

Micah nudges me. "Are we going to sit or what?"

"Yeah. He's in the fifth row." I nod my head toward Jason and then slowly make my way down the concrete steps, keeping my eyes locked on him the whole time. Jay's row and the row right in front of him are mostly full already. I pause halfway down the stairs, praying he doesn't turn around. I'm not ready for him to see me yet.

Which is stupid. The whole point is for him to see me with another guy. *Don't be a coward,* I tell myself. Boldly I move down to the fourth row. Micah and I start squeezing our way toward the center.

"Do you know the guy he's with?" Micah asks.

"Yeah. Kendall went out with him a few times." I do a quick check of the surrounding seats but don't see Alex, the world's sexiest EMT. Score one for divide and conquer. Well, divide anyway.

When we pass Jason and Dan, I look up and pretend to be surprised. "Oh, hey," I say.

Jason's got sunglasses on so I can't see his expression. "How's it going, Lainey?" His head angles slightly toward Micah, but he doesn't say anything. Dan gives me a nod and a slow smile, but there's no time to say more since people behind us are pushing forward to find their seats.

"Enjoy the game," I say brightly, resting my hand on Micah's lower back as he makes his way to the end of the row. As I settle next to him, I casually sling my arm around the back of his chair, lean over, and murmur in his ear. "That was perfect." Hopefully from Jason's vantage point it looks like I'm giving Micah a kiss on the cheek.

He turns and brushes my hair back from my face and I catch of whiff of his cologne. "I think you just violated our minimal touching rule." His breath is hot against my cheekbone. "I feel like a whore." He traces one finger across the bare skin of my leg and I stiffen. "Chill, Lainey. Pretend you're an actress. Shouldn't be too much of a stretch, a big commercial star like yourself."

I make like I'm going to hold his hand, but instead I give

him a hard pinch above the knee. He smells really good. In fact, he smells like Jason. "Is that Red Lynx you're wearing?" I ask, smiling as he winces in pain.

"Yeah. Why?" He tries to pinch me back, but I slap his hand away. This is perfect. To anyone who doesn't know what's going on, we totally look like a couple play-fighting. "Oh, don't tell me what's-his-face uses that too. I'm going to go buy something else as soon as we're done here."

"Why are you wearing cologne for a fake date anyway?"

Micah widens his eyes into a pretend-innocent look. "It's aftershave. I splash some on when I'm too lazy to shower."

I laugh. "You're gross, you know that?"

"Yup," Micah says, smiling. "And proud of it."

The section fills up quickly and we're surrounded by chatter from Cubs and Cards fans alike. As Micah gets engrossed in the pregame warm-up, I risk a couple of glances back at Jason, but I can't tell if he's paying me any attention. The electronic scoreboard informs the crowd that the air temperature is 94 degrees, and the temperature down on the field is a tropical 102. I pull a floppy hat out of my purse and adjust the brim down to protect my face from the sun. At this rate, the SPF 50 I slathered on my face will sweat off before the third inning.

The Cards take an early 2–0 lead on a Cubs error and the whole section goes crazy. I jump up and cheer along with everyone else in red, trying to stay out of the path of the guy next to me whose beer threatens to slosh all over my sandals each time he moves.

The game continues to be almost all Cardinals and by the end of the fourth inning, we're leading 5–1.

"Man, that was one of the most beautiful bunts I've ever seen," Micah says.

"I know, right?" I say, even though no one ever makes it on base when they bunt so I couldn't tell a good one from a bad one.

I spend the next two innings laughing loudly at everything Micah says, even though I'm not really paying attention. I just want Jason to feel like I'm having more fun with Micah than I ever had with him. He's competitive, so that sort of thing will get to him even if he's not feeling jealous. Look at me—exploiting a weakness I didn't even think about with Bianca.

Blotting the sweat from my face, I turn my attention back to the field. The Cardinals are up to bat again and the first batter hits a home run. The whole crowd is cheering in time with the organ player. Micah exchanges high fives with the people sitting around us. I smile and do the same with Sloshy Beer Guy.

The Cardinals score twice more and now we've got an 8–1 lead. It's shaping up to be a long game for the Chicago fans. When the Cubs finally come up to bat again, I pull my phone out of my purse and check my messages. There's an email from my brother that says he's finally settled in and starting to explore Ireland, and he hopes I'm taking good care of his car. The way he babies the Civic, you'd think it was Lamborghini. I email him back and tell him I'm at the game. I glance up at the field—one out, a man on first—and then scan the pro soccer scores and CalebWaters.com. Nothing new has been posted about *Flyboys*.

The crowd roars and I reluctantly get to my feet again, clapping one hand against my phone, even though I'm not sure what happened.

"What is more important than a perfectly executed double play?" Micah peers down at my phone.

I shrug. "I was checking my messages." I fan myself with one hand.

He scoffs. "Expecting your ex to text you from the next row?"

"I was emailing my brother." When Micah looks confused, I lower my voice and add, "Sorry. I'm not really into baseball."

"Don't you think this is going to look a little obvious then? You showing up here with me?"

"I don't know." I pick at a fraying thread on my jean shorts. "This is one of the only places I knew for sure we'd run into Jay, and *you* seem to like baseball well enough." A gnat buzzes in my ear. I claw violently at the air around my head. "Maybe if it wasn't ten million degrees. Aren't you dying in those jeans?"

"A little," he admits. "You want to go hang out in the shade for a bit?" He winks. "Maybe Jason will think I'm dragging you off to some deserted corner so I can do bad things to you."

My eyes narrow. "You wish."

"You wish I wished," Micah says. "Come on. If you're nice, I'll buy you a water."

"Woo, big spender," I say.

We wait for a break in the action and then I make a production out of standing up and gathering my purse. Micah takes my hand as we tromp down the long row of bleachers and back onto the steps.

Dan leans over and whispers something into Jason's ear as we pass and both guys burst out laughing. My stomach twists itself into knots. What if my plan is totally transparent? Or what if Jason thinks I was so devastated by our breakup that I just went out and grabbed the first guy I could find? No. Must. Not. Panic. I smile brightly and act like everything is fine.

I stare at my tan fingers curled inside Micah's pale ones as we head back into the stadium tunnels. I'm a little sweaty, and so is he, but it doesn't feel nearly as weird as I thought it would to hold hands with another guy. Jason used to squeeze too hard sometimes and practically crush my fingers, but Micah's grip is firm and relaxed. Kind of nice. It feels almost normal, really. Like, in another world, the two of us could actually be on a date.

Chapter 12

MILITARY TACTICS ARE LIKE UNTO WATER; FOR
WATER IN ITS NATURAL COURSE RUNS AWAY FROM
HIGH PLACES AND HASTENS DOWNWARDS.

— SUN TZU, *The Art of War*

I drop Micah's hand the second we're back inside and then excuse myself to slip into a restroom and freshen up. Pulling off my floppy hat, I cringe. I look like I've played about three overtimes. My hair is frizzy on top and the ends are curling in all directions due to the humidity. Sweat has made my skin all shiny and wreaked havoc on my eyeliner. My left eye is doing the raccoon thing; my right eye looks basically naked. Maybe Jason and Dan weren't laughing about Micah. Maybe they were laughing about how hideous I look.

Pulling a paper towel from the dispenser, I blot my whole face and apply powder until I'm not causing a physical glare in the mirror. I redo my eyeliner and then put my hat back on.

By the time I'm done making myself look human, Micah is leaning against the wall outside the bathroom holding two sodas. "I hope you're not one of those skinny girls who drinks diet," he says. "I got you a Coke."

"No way. Diet soda tastes like poison." I gratefully take the cup he offers and swill down a long drink.

"Feel better?" he asks.

"Yeah. I wish we could see the game from here." I gesture around at all the shade. "It's about twenty degrees cooler."

Micah's face is a little flushed. I'm not sure if it's from the heat or if he's getting a sunburn. "The Cards scored another run while you were in the bathroom," he says. "I'd say this one is in the bag. There's no reason to stay if you don't want."

I take another sip of my drink and let out a happy sigh. Soda has never tasted so good. "Are you trying to get rid of me?"

"Nope." He takes a drink of his soda and mimics my ecstasy. "But there's no point in wasting your time if you're bored. We've accomplished what we came here to do, and like I said, if we don't come back, your ex will wonder what we're doing."

"Good point." I run my fingers across Micah's forearm. "You're looking a little pink. Let's get out of here before we both end up with third-degree sunburns."

Back on the MetroLink, I soak up as much air-conditioning as possible. As we near our stop, thick storm clouds begin to blot out most of the blue sky.

"I still can't believe you don't like baseball," Micah says.

I shrug. "Jay and I usually go to a couple of games a year. I don't hate it or anything. I just like soccer better."

"Maybe next time you should take me somewhere you and Jason went together that you actually like."

A smile plays at my lips as I think of the perfect place, a place I'm sure Micah would hate. But it would be fun to see him totally out of his element. "Good idea," I say. "So next time we'll go to Beat."

"The dance club?" He makes a face like he swallowed a wasp. "Amber tried to drag me there for one of their full-moon parties. How about we forget I said anything?"

"Too late." I elbow him in the ribs. "You offered. And speaking of Amber, did she call you yet?"

Thunder rumbles in the distance. Even as the sun cuts its way through the clouds, raindrops begin to plink against the train window.

Micah shakes his head. "Not yet."

"Have faith," I say. "It might take a couple more dates."

As the words tumble out of my mouth, I hope I'm right. The only thing that's kept me sane without Jason the past couple of weeks is all the plotting and scheming in the name of getting him back. I try to imagine what my life would be like if it doesn't happen. Days spent watching him from afar in the hallways, agonizing about whether to run toward him or away from him. Nights at home alone, wondering who he's with. No. That's not how I'm going to spend my senior year. I refuse to even entertain the possibility.

The MetroLink purrs to a stop and Micah and I jump

off. The rain is coming down in soft sheets now, drowning out what's left of the sun. The air temperature has dropped a few degrees.

I pause at the edge of the platform and watch the silvery droplets add to puddles of pooling water at the edge of the parking lot. "I think I'm going to go by work and grab a pizza," I say. "You want to come?"

"Nope. You can drop me off on the way." Micah heads for the stairs leading down from the platform. "I get enough of that place as it is."

"Okay. Hang on a sec." Shielding my phone with one hand, I send Bianca a quick text.

I'm hungry. You want to meet up at Denali? I can tell you about fake date #2.

She replies right away:

I wish I could, but I'm taking my brothers to their soccer game tonight. You'll have to fill me in tomorrow.

"Everything cool?" Micah asks.

"Yeah. It's all good." I slip my phone back in my purse, a little disappointed that Bianca is busy.

"You want me to get the car so you don't get wet?"

"Nah. I like rain," I say. "It beats sweating my ass off."

Micah and I race across the parking lot to the Civic. We slip inside the car and I use my hat to blot a few stray droplets from my face. Flipping on the radio, I tell him to pick a station. He finds something playing music I've never heard before. Once again, I kind of like it. When I slow the car to a stop in front of his apartment building a few minutes later, I turn sideways to look at him. "Let me know if you hear from Amber."

"Yeah. You too." He watches me warily, like he's expecting me to give him a hug or something.

I fiddle with the radio preset buttons. Commercial. Commercial. Annoying boy-band song. I end up going back to the station Micah was listening to. The Civic idles loudly. "Otherwise I guess we'll talk at work. . . ." I trail off.

"Yup." Micah slides out of the car with a wave.

"Hey," I call after him. "I'll wash your shirt and get it back to you soon, okay?"

"No hurry. It looks better on you anyway." He grins. "See you around."

As he crosses the lawn in a few long strides and disappears into the building, I feel a little lost.

I'm not used to being all by myself.

Chapter 13

MOVE NOT UNLESS YOU SEE AN ADVANTAGE; USE
NOT YOUR TROOPS UNLESS THERE IS SOMETHING
TO BE GAINED.

—SUN TZU, *The Art of War*

When I wake up the next morning, there's a note on the table that says Ebony called in sick so my dad will be at Denali all day. He'd love it if I came in and helped out, but it's okay if I already have plans or don't want to work.

I don't want to, but going to work is about the only thing that will keep me from staring at my phone all day waiting for Jason to call. Plus Bianca is working this afternoon, so I can fill her in on the baseball game later.

When I get to the shop, the line of customers is out the front door. I catch a glimpse of my dad through the front windows, and he's actually taking orders at the counter. Dad's the kind of guy who still does his taxes on paper. He's terrified of the computerized cash register, so they must be slammed for him to be working the front.

I quickly park between an old station wagon decorated

with dancing bear decals and Micah's lime-green rust bucket. I thought he was off today. My dad probably figured there was a .0001 percent chance of me coming in on my day off so he dialed up the more reliable members of the staff too.

I struggle to make my way into the shop. "Excuse me," I say, elbowing my way past a bunch of kids dressed in hoop skirts and fake armor. Now I see why it's so busy. A Renaissance festival must be going on somewhere nearby.

The line is starting to turn into a mob, and people are actually beginning to block part of the street. No wonder Dad was trying to recruit extra help. "Coming through." I slide between a pair of pale, gangly boys sparring with wooden swords, narrowly avoiding a thwap in the ribs. "Watch what you're doing." I give the offender my patented "back the hell up" look. The boy mumbles an apology and sheathes his sword. His friend calls me a "saucy wench."

Inside, the wind chimes and music are drowned out by the bean grinder, overlapping animated conversations, and the occasional clank of armor against armor. I fight my way through the crowd to the counter. My dad's glasses are starting to fog up. He mops sweat from his brow with one of the gray rags we use to wipe down the tables. He doesn't see me until I'm practically on top of him.

"Lainey!" He says my name like I'm some sort of superhero who has come to save the day.

I grin. It feels good to be needed. "Just let me clock in."

He grabs me by the wrist. Dude, he is really sweating.

"I'll clock you in later," he says. "Take over for Micah so he can help out in the back."

I nod and toss my purse in the drawer beneath the register. Then I slide over to the back counter where all the stainless steel coffee machines are lined up. "Messing up everyone's orders?" I joke.

"Hey," Micah says breezily as he looks up from the bean grinder. "What are you doing here? Don't you need your beauty sleep?"

"Obviously not." I turn a small pirouette for effect. "I didn't even know you knew how to make drinks."

Micah whistles innocently. "I don't." He gestures to the mob at the counter. "But they don't know that."

I bite my lip to keep from laughing. "Go help out whoever is cooking before he quits. Maybe if we feed the masses they'll stop making so much noise."

It takes us about two hours, but eventually the crowd thins out and Bianca comes in to work the front. My dad immediately heads for the safety of the back. Bee clocks in and then takes her place in front of the register.

"Did you dye your hair?" She strokes my teal streak.

I can't believe I haven't seen her since the day I went to Mizz Creant's. I completely forgot to tell her about my streak. "It's a clip-in. Micah's sister did it for me."

"Cute," she says.

Smiling, I make myself a skinny iced chai and survey the dining room. Most of the tables are taken. No one looks like they need anything. "I'm going to take a break," I tell Bee.

She nods. "Go ahead. I'll yell if I need you."

Micah is in the back making pizza dough while Cal—aka C-4, though all the girls refuse to call him that—is keeping up on the orders for salads and sandwiches.

"What's up, freaks?" I ask.

Micah spreads a glob of dough onto a silver pizza pan. "Well, if it isn't our TV star and future alumna of Hazelton Forest University. Anyone ask for your autograph today?"

"Ha-ha." I lean against one of the prep tables as I sip my chai.

Cal plates up two Alpine Slammer sandwiches and a salmon salad. His beard is so long it's practically dragging on the dishes. He looks in my direction. "Food runner?" he asks.

I cross my arms. "I'm on break."

"Whatever." Cal balances the plates on his arm and heads toward the dining area. My dad will kill me if he sees I let Cal run food. Between his monster beard and the shocks of bushy hair protruding from both sides of his ponytail, he looks more like a Sasquatch than a human. I cross my fingers that Dad stays back in the office for at least a couple more minutes. Then I turn back to Micah.

"Why do you give me so much crap about that commercial? There's nothing wrong with Hazelton Forest." I pluck a black olive from the salad station. "Half the kids we go to school with will end up there."

The smile fades from Micah's face. "I wish my mom worked at a college so I could go for free."

"Sometimes I wish mine didn't so I could go someplace else," I reply. "Hazelton Forest's soccer team is only Division III. They don't play anyone good. I want to go to a Division I college but I'd need to land an athletic scholarship to pay for it."

Micah sighs. "I'll be lucky to afford community college. I could save all of my pay for ten years and not even come close to paying for where I really want to go."

I imagine Micah and his mohawk strolling down the ivy-lined paths of Princeton or Harvard, a sorority girl on each arm. I hold back a snide comment. "Where's that?" I toss the olive up in the air and catch it in my mouth.

"The CIA."

"With tattoos and a mohawk? Aren't spies supposed to blend in?"

"Not that CIA, dummy," Micah says. "The Culinary Institute of America. Their pastry chef program is one of the best in the country."

I raise an eyebrow. "You want to make pies for a living? Seriously?"

Micah grabs a walnut from the salad station. He flicks it in my direction. Direct hit. It pings right off the blotchy tan spot on my forehead. "Pastry chefs make all kinds of stuff. Sorry, not everybody wants to be a big, badass EMT like your loser ex-boyfriend."

I pull my bangs down and glance around, considering my options for ammunition. "He is *not* a loser."

Micah grins. "Keep telling yourself that."

My hand reaches out for the nearest thing I can grab and flings it in his direction. It's a half full measuring cup of flour and it ends up everywhere—the counter, the floor, all up and down Micah's T-shirt and baggy chef pants.

A white cloud hangs in the air. Micah coughs from the dust. "You little . . . ," he starts. But he can't even finish his sentence because he's laughing too hard.

I'm laughing too. "Dude, you're such a cokehead. I'm totally going to tell my dad."

Micah tosses a raw egg in my direction. I reach out and catch it without it cracking. "Ha. Is that all you got?"

"Actually, no." He lobs another egg at me. And then another. And then one bounces off me and cracks onto the kitchen floor. Micah advances on me, pantomiming like he's going to slam an egg onto the top of my head, but I wrap my hand around his wrist and use all my strength to push his arm away from me.

He tries to wriggle free of my grasp but can't. "Mr. Mitchell," he hollers at no one in particular. "Tell your daughter to stop groping me."

"You wish."

"No I don't." Micah points to my arm up against his. "I'm not into girls who are orange."

I push him back away from me. "Shut up. At least I'm not whiter than this flour."

"At least I don't look like I was made in a lab," he says. "Good thing I'm not allergic to yellow number 5."

"Good thing you're not allergic to eggs." I smash one

against his pyramid tattoo.

"Oh, you are a dead woman." Micah grabs me around the neck and bends me into a headlock.

"Stop," I beg as he starts to drag me across the prep kitchen to where an entire carton of eggs is waiting. My foot lands in a smear of broken egg goo and we both nearly end up on the floor as my leg slides out from under me.

Cal reappears from the dining room. "What the hell are you two doing?" he barks.

His voice draws my dad out of the manager's office. Micah releases his hold on me. Dad's jaw drops a little when he sees the mess. Micah and I exchange a look.

And then a curl of smoke wafts from the oven.

My dad sniffs. "Is something burning?"

"Shit." Micah yanks open the oven and pulls out a pan of three quiche. They're black. Not brown. Not just burnt. Black. He reaches out to touch the edge of the nearest one and the delicate fluted crust crumbles into ash.

"Ohmygod." I have to bite back a giggle. I've never seen anything so charred in my entire life.

My dad looks from me to Micah. "Please tell me that's some kind of experiment and those are chocolate."

Micah deflates a little as he shakes his head and I immediately feel guilty. It's a well-known fact I can be a slacker, but Micah actually has a reputation around Denali as a hard worker. He might need a recommendation from my dad someday and here I am messing things up for him.

"It's my fault," I say. "I've been bothering him."

Both Micah and my dad turn to look at me with surprise.

"I'll get this place cleaned up and then head back out front." I walk to the end of the prep line and grab a broom.

Micah brushes the loose flour from his clothes. Then he pulls a rag from his back pocket, wets it in the sink, and then bends down to mop up the broken egg. "Sorry, Mr. Mitchell," he says. "It won't happen again."

"Good." My dad polishes his glasses on his shirt. "I'll grab more quiche shells from the freezer."

"Sorry," I mumble as soon as my dad disappears into the walk-in cooler.

"Not your fault," Micah says. "I should have been paying attention."

I put the broom back in the corner and head back to the counter as Micah and my dad start re-prepping the quiche.

I make drinks and serve pastries for the next few hours. For once, work doesn't seem so bad. It's actually kind of fun trying to keep up on all the orders while Bianca works the register and buses tables. A couple times I catch myself smiling for no reason. I guess there's nothing like an impromptu food fight to take the edge off a busy day.

My dad pokes his head out of the back a couple times, probably to make sure I'm not destroying the dining room too.

"Don't worry, Dad." I set a pair of mango-blueberry smoothies on the far end of the counter where people pick up their drinks. "We got this."

When things slow down a little bit, I fill Bianca in on the

baseball date. She's still working on her end of things with the spying and doesn't have anything to report yet.

"So you're feeling better?" she asks, her eyes dark with concern. "And hanging out with Micah is still going okay?"

"He's actually kind of fun," I admit. "And yeah, I'm feeling better. But even though our plan has been distracting in a good way, I'm still not any closer to winning back Jason. He hasn't even called." I wipe at a smudgy spot on the counter. "Maybe Micah was right. Maybe bringing a date to the baseball game was all kinds of obvious."

Maybe Jason is laughing at me right now.

"Nah. Jason is pretty dense," Bianca says. "Just give it time. Wars aren't fought in a day."

I don't run into Micah again until a few minutes after six p.m. when we're clocking out. "Sorry again about the quiche," I say, waiting behind him as he punches his ID number into the red-and-silver time clock.

"Don't flatter yourself." The machine beeps and he scoots out of the way for me. "You're not *that* distracting. I just forgot them is all."

"I don't think my dad was too mad." I key in my numbers and the machine logs me out. Micah and I head toward the exit.

"He actually got me thinking." Micah pushes open the glass door, holding it behind him for me. "Chocolate quiche might not be a bad idea."

"Sounds kind of gross." The summer heats wraps around

me like a soggy blanket as I step outside. How can it be so hot this late in the day? A trickle of sweat forms at my hairline and threatens to run down my forehead. I look over at Micah as we head across the parking lot. He's managed to get his black-on-black wardrobe covered with flour again, all the way down to his studded bracelet. "You're like this punk-rock baker," I say, shaking my head.

"What's wrong with that?"

"A bit of a contradiction, don't you think?" I wipe the sweat from my forehead, running my hand over my hair to tame the flyaways. I can feel it starting to frizz.

Micah looks hard at me for a moment as we reach our cars. The sun catches his hazel eyes, reflecting ribbons of green and gold through the warm summer air. "Most people are."

Chapter 14

THERE IS NO INSTANCE OF A COUNTRY HAVING
BENEFITED FROM PROLONGED WARFARE.
— SUN TZU, *The Art of War*

I can't shake Micah's words on the drive home. I'm active
and sporty. I hang out with active and sporty people. I
like active and sporty things. I'm not a contradiction. I
run through everyone close to me: my family, Bianca, Kendall, Jason. They all make sense too. What you see is what
you get. Most people are *not* contradictions.

My purse vibrates against my hip as I park the car and
head into my house. Just the act of having to fish my phone
out from beneath a pack of tissues and a cracked compact
feels weird. I used to carry it around everywhere in my hand.
That was back when I was always expecting a text from Jay.

It's Kendall. She hangs up before I can answer. I call her
back right away before she can compose a scathing message
accusing me of ignoring her. Kendall does not like to be
ignored.

"Elaine Mitchell," she hisses as soon as the phone connects. "What the hell is going on with you?"

I feign innocence. "What do you mean?"

"Were you ever going to tell me that you and my brother broke up? What happened?"

This is pretty much the freak-out moment I was expecting. Kendall also does not like change.

"I don't know, K. One day we were fine. The next day he was telling me he needed to be on his own or some crap." I twist a strand of my hair around one of my fingers. "I texted you the day it happened," I finish, a hint of accusation creeping into my voice. "But you didn't respond."

Kendall ignores my tone. "I'm only allowed to use the phone here twice a week. Besides, we've had a conversation since then and you didn't even bring it up."

Her idea of having a conversation is her talking while I listen, but she's right this time. I could have mentioned the breakup if I had really wanted to. "What did he tell you?" I ask. "What's the story with the EMT girl?"

"What EMT girl?" Kendall asks. "He didn't even mention another girl. Just that you guys broke up."

"He's hanging around with this redheaded chick named Alex. She's one of the medics who have been taking him on ride-alongs. You think you can try to find out more?" When it comes to spies and alliances, no one is more powerful to have on your side than Kendall.

She sighs. "Not sure what I can do from here, but I'll try to sneak an email to him if I run out of phone time. I swear, our dad comes to town and a month later Jay is acting like a deadbeat. Coincidence? I think not."

"Are you ever going to talk to him?" I ask. "Your dad?" It feels good to focus on someone else's problems for a second.

"I don't know. I probably can't avoid him forever, but he doesn't get to breeze into my life after seventeen years like nothing happened. Maybe if he'd been around at all, my mom would be less of a psychotic bitch to everyone." Kendall huffs. "Now that I'm still doing okay on the show she's saying she won't pay for me to go to college until I'm twenty-one and have given modeling a 'fair try,' whatever the hell that means. Why can't she accept the fact I'm not her?"

The whole situation sucks. It's wrong of Kendall's mom to force her to be a model. I get that she gave up her dream of modeling to be a single mom, but that doesn't mean Kendall owes her.

"What about applying for student loans?" I ask.

"My mom would have to sign off on them, I think. And she won't. Besides, why should I go into massive debt just because I refuse to be her little puppet?"

"You could probably get a soccer scholarship somewhere. Didn't you get scouted last year?"

She sighs again. "Not by anyone good. And I'm not even sure I want to play soccer at college."

"What? Why?" Kendall is one of those girls who are naturally good at sports. She hasn't practiced all summer, but when she comes home she'll still dribble rings around me. I can't believe she's thinking of giving it up.

"I don't know. I feel like soccer is a high school thing. I want college to be a whole new life, you know? But I want to go someplace cool, like NYU," she says. "We did a shoot with some of their photography students yesterday. It was amazing."

"Well, I'm glad you're having some fun at least."

"What? Hang on." Kendall says something harsh to someone in the background. She's probably giving the finger to one of her housemates or some poor production assistant. "*Apparently* my time is almost up," she says. "But, hey. My mom's doing the annual trip to Costa Rica again this August. Ask your parents if you can come. You could crash in my room . . . or my brother's. The time-share is paid for so all you'd need to do is save enough for the airfare. Maybe the right atmosphere would heat things up again between you and Jay."

I imagine a full week partying on the beach with Kendall and Jason while their mom downs glasses of expensive champagne on the veranda. Me in my tiniest bikini. Jason just buzzed enough to find me irresistible. Sun. Surf. Sand. Sex. Talk about exploiting my enemy's weaknesses. Not to mention dividing and conquering. It would work, but there's no way I can afford it.

"I don't know," I say. "I can't come up with that kind of money. But that doesn't mean I'm giving up. Bianca and I are kind of working on a plan." I'm glad Kendall is out of phone time. I don't feel like listening to her make fun our Dead Chinese Warlord strategies. Better to wait until they work and then tell her the good news.

"Bianca? What does *she* know about dating?"

"She's really smart, Kendall. She knows a lot about everything. We've been practicing soccer together while we strategize, and her footwork has really improved too. I'm trying to get her to try out for the Archers with us this year."

Kendall makes a snorting sound. "Smart doesn't make you good at dating, Lainey. Or soccer. Bianca seems nice and all, but she's only been on varsity for a year—not exactly select team material."

I start to protest, but Kendall swears under her breath. "I have to go," she repeats. "They're threatening to take my phone or kick me off or some shit. Stupid rules. I swear! Anyway, do what you have to do, but do it quick, because the longer you and Jason stay apart, the harder it's going to be to get back together."

She's right. I know it.

I have to step up my game or I could lose Jason forever.

Chapter 15

WE CANNOT ENTER INTO ALLIANCES UNTIL WE
ARE ACQUAINTED WITH THE DESIGNS OF OUR
NEIGHBORS.

—SUN TZU, *The Art of War*

Two days pass and Jason still doesn't call. I spend my downtime at work rereading highlighted passages from *The Art of War*. I remind myself not to be reckless or afraid or prideful or obsessively worried.

"Get this." Micah slides a tray of Death-by-Chocolate-Moose Brownies in the pastry case. They smell like my grandma's house, warm and sweet. My mouth starts to water.

"Yeah?" I shake the contents of the blender into a tall eco-friendly cup and top it with an uneven spiral of whipped cream.

"Leo and I both worked last night, and I might have told him about our plan." Micah shuts the case with a click.

The can of whipped cream slides out of my fingers and rolls across the counter, leaving a trail of white foam behind. The girl waiting for her blended ice coffee taps her dark purple fingernails on the counter and stares at me.

"Micah!" I hiss. "Wasn't that rule number one? This was supposed to be our secret." I put a lid on the drink and hand it to the girl.

"Straw?" she asks, as if I'm the world's biggest idiot.

"Over by the napkins," I snap back, like she's not very smart herself.

Micah pulls a towel out of his back pocket and swipes at the trail of whipped cream. "What's the big deal? You told Bianca."

"Bianca basically came up with the plan. The big deal is that if word gets out this isn't real, it'll get back to our exes and we'll look like idiots."

"I'm sorry, but he knows we've been hanging out," Micah says. "Would you rather I told him some of those PG-13 stories?"

My face gets hot. I glance quickly around the front of the coffee shop. Ebony at her usual table, sipping a latte and reading the *Riverfront Times*. Monochrome Girl rocking a mix of plum and indigo hunched over her computer. Five tribal masks grinning demonically. No one is paying us any attention.

"Okay. So you told him. So what?" I start mentally calculating how many people Leo could tell, and how many they could tell, and how many degrees of separation there are between practically invisible Leo and soccer superstar Jason Chase.

Micah picks up on the look on my face. "No, it's cool. He

was actually wondering if you might be willing to fake-date him too."

"What?" I screech. "Why? I'm pretty sure Leo hasn't spoken one word to me since he started working here."

"Chill," Micah says, lowering his voice. "It's kind of a hard thing to ask a girl to do, but since you're already doing it . . . He figured you'd say no, but he's willing to pay you and everything."

"Pay me?" The image of me and Jason on a beach in Costa Rica, half naked, both of us with drinks in our hands, flashes before my eyes. "Does he think I'm a hooker?"

Micah's eyes flick momentarily to the hem of my mini-skirt. He coughs into his hand. "Why would he think that?" He ducks out of the way as I go to slug him and then continues, "Forget it. I'll tell him you're not down with the idea." He swings his towel in a circle as he heads back to the kitchen.

"Hang on," I say. "Tell him I'll think about it." After all, I am supposed to be seizing opportunities that arise. "What about us? It's your turn. Dare I ask where you'll be taking me next?"

"Don't worry." Micah snaps his towel at me and I jump back. "I'm working on something for us," he says. "I'll be in touch."

It's a couple of days later when Leo and I both work an opening shift.

"So," I say, hopping up onto the prep table, my hip just

inches from the edge of the cutting board. I can't help but grin. There's something empowering about knowing a guy wants to date you, even if it's only for pretend.

The knife blade wobbles in Leo's hand, but he keeps dicing. "So," he says back. His pile of tiny ham cubes grows in size.

I look him over. He's about six feet tall with brown hair and gray eyes. Not thin, not fat. Jeans. Polo shirt. Nice tan. There's nothing wrong with him. There's just nothing that really stands out about him either.

"Micah says you have a proposition for me." I pluck a piece of ham from the top of the mountain and pop it in my mouth. The saltiness makes me wince.

Leo nods. He adjusts the brim of his cap. "Two hundred up front," he blurts out. "Another two hundred if it actually works."

The ham tries to lodge itself in my windpipe. I cough hard. "You're willing to pay me four hundred dollars to hang out with you a few times?" That's more than half the airfare to Costa Rica. "You do realize this is all pretend, right?"

"Yep." He slices the ends off a white onion and peels back the skin. "Getting Riley back would be worth every penny, and then some."

My eyes immediately start to water. "You saved all that money working here?" I feel a little guilty about potentially fleecing him. I know nothing about his ex-girlfriend or why they broke up. What if she dumped him because he was a terrible kisser or because she realized she liked girls?

"I work a second job in the summer. Landscaping. It pays pretty good."

"Why'd you guys break up?" It suddenly occurs to me I was so focused on my own problem of getting Jason back that I never bothered to ask Micah why he and Amber broke up. I should probably do that.

"She's a year older than me and started taking college classes at the beginning of summer. She said it just felt like we were growing apart."

"Well, there's no guarantee I can help you. I mean, it's not like I've helped Micah much yet."

Leo shrugs. "I'm a pretty patient guy. And Micah said he found you . . . entertaining."

"He did, huh?" I hop down from the prep table and flip the brim of Leo's baseball hat to the back. Peeling the label off a can of chickpeas, I write my phone number on the back. "Let me know what you have in mind and I'll see what I can do."

Chapter 16

ACCORDING AS CIRCUMSTANCES ARE FAVORABLE,
ONE SHOULD MODIFY ONE'S PLANS.
— SUN TZU, *The Art of War*

I decide two hundred bucks up front is too good to pass up, so when Leo texts me Thursday night asking if I want to go to a play at Hazelton Forest University, I don my most studious outfit and call him back to confirm.

"What are we going to see?" I ask, straightening the pleats of my plaid miniskirt.

"*The Tragedy of Faust*," he says. "Part One."

I wrinkle up my nose. "Sounds tragic."

"You don't know the story?" Leo's voice raises at the end, as if he can't believe I'm not an expert on classic literature.

"I'm more into current theater, like movies."

"I think you might like it," he says. "I'll pick you up in thirty minutes."

I give Leo directions to my house and then peek my head into the study. My mom is sitting at her computer, half buried behind a stack of textbooks. Handwritten notes on yellow lined paper are splayed out around her. A collection of painted coffee mugs lines the left side of the desk, the nearest one venting wisps of steam into the air. She frowns at her computer screen.

"Hey, Mom. I'm going to Hazelton Forest to see a play." I fiddle with the collar of my button-up shirt.

She looks up, her lips pursed as if maybe she's heard me wrong. "With Jason?"

"No, with a friend of mine from Denali."

She spins her chair around so she's facing me and reaches out for the steaming mug. "I haven't seen Jason in a while."

"Yeah. We sort of broke up."

"And you're all right with that?" She sips from the mug.

Leaning against the door frame, I cross my arms. "No, but I don't really want to talk about it."

"Well, Jason is charming, but you're both young . . ."

Oh, brother, here we go. "I should let you get back to work," I say brightly, edging my way back out into the hallway.

"Just remember, I'm here if you ever do want to talk," she calls after me. "With your brother gone, I feel almost like I've been slacking in the parental department."

I peek my head around the corner again. "No chance. You're the least slackingest person I know."

"Says the daughter with the blue hair. Your father and I were hoping that was a clip-on or a barrette, but it never seems to go away. Are there any other bodily alterations I should know about?" Her voice is light but I can hear concern in her words.

"It's a clip-in extension I can take out whenever. And no other alterations, I promise." I flash her a quick smile. "You don't need to worry. I'm totally fine." I dart back to the living room before she can ask any follow-up questions.

I wish I were as fine as I'm pretending to be, but hearing my mom tell that classic mom parable about other fish in the sea is not going to help right now. Collapsing onto the sofa, I try to relax to the beat of her fingers tapping out her latest masterpiece.

Grabbing my phone, I text Bianca. She knows about my plans tonight.

Me: This Leo date. I feel weird about it.

It takes her a few minutes to respond. She's probably working the register.

Her: Is it the money?

Is it? I suppose it could be.

Me: Maybe.
Her: So then don't take it.

That's what Bee would do, help Leo out of the goodness of her heart. But Costa Rica . . . so much time alone with Jason . . .

Before I can respond, another text comes through:

Her: I gotta run. What looks like an entire softball
team just got in line. But just try and enjoy the night.
Leo seems pretty cool. You might have fun.

I pluck the remote from the coffee table and skim
through the channels. I pause on *Celebrity Sightings*, hoping
for a mention of *Flyboys* or Caleb Waters, but it looks like
he's not in the news this week.

Two channels up, I catch the end of my commercial. I
watch myself stroll across the quad with a backpack slung
over one shoulder. A camera zooms in. "I can't wait to go to
Hazelton Forest University. Affordable education and professors who care," TV-me says. "What more could you want?"

"Maybe a Division I soccer team?" I mumble under
my breath. I keep flipping until I find an episode of the
Los Angeles season of *So You Think You Can Model*. The
remaining six girls are doing a black-and-white photo shoot
wearing lingerie and old-time movie star makeup. I wonder
what Kendall is doing right now. I wonder what she'd think
of me hanging out with Leo. She might actually approve if I
told her it was going to provide the money I needed to go to
Costa Rica. Kendall is very goal oriented.

The doorbell chimes and I unstick my legs from the sofa.
"Later, Mom," I holler toward the open door of the study.

The tapping stops. My mom peeks her head out of the
study. "Remember, curfew is midnight," she says.

"Got it." It's only six thirty. I can't imagine Leo and I
being out past ten, let alone midnight.

I open the door and slip out onto the porch. Leo is wearing black pants and a pale blue dress shirt with the top button undone. His hair is slicked back on the sides and slightly spiked up on top.

"Hey, Lainey." He laces his fingers together in front of his body and shifts his weight from one foot to the other.

He's nervous—how cute. I smile. "Hey. I like your hair that way." I tug on the hem of my miniskirt as I make my way down the driveway toward Leo's sky-blue Ford Taurus. Maybe I should've worn something a little longer.

"Thanks," he says, unlocking the door for me. The first thing he does when I get in is toss me a wad of twenties. I debate counting it, but then decide that would make an awkward moment even weirder, so I quickly slip the money in my purse. If he's willing to pay for this, then I shouldn't feel bad about it.

We head toward Hazelton Forest. Suburbia flies by. Pizza places, dry cleaners, Bianca's church where I learned to play soccer, even though I'm not and never have been Catholic. I pick at the vinyl trim on the edge of my seat. Leo drums his fingertips on the steering wheel. Neither of us says anything. One of us needs to. We might as well be driving out to the desert to bury a body together.

"So how'd you meet Riley?" I ask finally.

"We were both in Karlsson's Intro to Acting class together," he says.

"Cool. I wanted to take it last year but Kendall talked me out of it. I probably shouldn't have listened to her."

Leo smiles big enough to show teeth. "It was the best. Almost like not even going to class. I probably never would have talked to Riley if we hadn't been paired up for a skit. She is so funny. And gorgeous." The smile fades from his lips. His body sinks back into the car seat. "Probably out of my league."

"You can't think like that," I say. "Or else you'll make it true."

"What do you know about people being out of your league?"

"More than you think." I toy with the strap of my purse. "You didn't know me in middle school. I used to be an awkward mess. Everyone was out of my league."

"Oh yeah?"

"I remember when I first started liking Jason, at the beginning of freshman year. Kendall forced me to talk to him when she caught me staring out her bedroom window, watching him swim laps in the pool. 'At least say something to him,' she insisted. 'Or I'm going to tell him I caught you drooling over his half-naked body.' Rather than endure life-threatening humiliation, I managed to squeak out a few words when he came back inside." I shake my head. "I can't believe I'm telling you this story."

"Go on." Leo has both eyes on the road but a smile plays at his lips.

"Over the next few weeks, Jay and I became friends. I was shocked when he asked me to Homecoming. All I saw was this guy who could have his pick of girls, but for some reason he wanted me," I say. "For the first few months we dated, I was always waiting for him to break up with me."

"What did you do?" Leo asks. "How did you get over it?"

"I think a lot of it was Kendall. If it weren't for her constantly reminding me of my fabulousness, Jay and I probably wouldn't have lasted as long as we did." I stare straight ahead through the windshield, watching the reflective road markers zoom by. "But enough of that. Tell me more about this play." I don't like thinking of the Lainey I used to be. What if it was dating Jason that changed me? Does that mean if I don't win him back I'll go back to being awkward and insecure?

Leo brakes slowly and smoothly as we hit a pocket of traffic. "It's the story of a guy who sells his soul to the devil."

I snort. "Why would he do something so dumb?"

"It's complicated," Leo says. "He's disillusioned with his life. But basically he does it for a girl." Cars on either side of us fly past as he accelerates in the same controlled manner. He pulls off the highway and turns into the Hazelton Forest campus. We drive past the student union and the social sciences building where my mom has her tiny windowless office.

"Well, just so you know, I'm not the devil," I give him what I hope is a devilish grin.

"Pretty sure your friend Kendall has dibs on that title," he says.

Kendall and I have managed to share almost every class since sophomore year, and I don't remember Leo being in any of them. "You don't even know her," I protest. "She's not that bad."

"A failing grade is not that bad. Mono is not that bad," Leo says. "Kendall Chase is evil. Everyone knows that. You practically said so yourself."

"She was just trying to help me with Jason," I say. "And *everyone* must not know that, or else she wouldn't be the captain of the soccer team. And the front-runner for student government president."

"Those are just positions of power handed down from one despot to the next." He pulls the car into a parking space outside the student amphitheater.

"What's a despot?"

His lips curl upward, ever so slightly. "A dictator. Like Hitler."

The messed-up thing is I'm thinking Kendall might not be offended by the comparison. Her need to dominate everyone and everything at school probably comes from the fact she has no control at home. I'd probably be exactly like her if I had grown up with her mom. I have no idea how Jason ended up so laid-back.

"Kendall has it tough at home." I unclick my seat belt and slide out of the car. "And really, her bark is worse than her bite."

"If you say so." Leo doesn't sound convinced.

We cut across the parking lot where families, other couples, and clusters of college kids are making their way toward the auditorium. Even though the sun is starting to set, the air hangs heavy and humid around us.

Inside the building, I let Leo lead me down the plush-carpeted aisle to a seat in the second row. The walls of the amphitheater are covered with gold-embossed dark purple wallpaper. Above our heads, glass-blown chandeliers tinkle from the breeze each time one of the theater doors opens.

Leo pulls his phone out and holds it in front of us. "To commemorate the night." He leans over close to me and takes a picture.

I peek over his shoulder as the saved image pops up on his phone. Our faces come out extra pale against the dark backdrop of the room, but it's a cute photo. "We look like a real couple," I say.

Leo smiles. "Do you care if I post it online? No caption or anything. I'll just let people wonder."

"I don't mind," I say, settling back in my seat. If it leaks out, it'll be just one more thing to make Jason jealous.

Leo slips his phone into his back pocket.

"So, what part does Riley play?" I ask quietly. Other people are talking, but there's something about the fancy décor that makes me feel like I should whisper.

"She's Gretchen."

"And who's that?" I smooth invisible wrinkles out of my miniskirt, adjusting the hem to cover more of my legs.

"The girl Faust is in love with."

"Do they end up together?"

"If they did," Leo murmurs, "it probably wouldn't be called a tragedy."

The lights dim and the thick curtain in front of us parts soundlessly to reveal a blue backdrop and fluffy, white clouds. The chattering of the audience fades away as two boys come to the center of the stage and begin speaking.

The language is kind of old-English sounding, but I can tell the boys are supposed to be God and the devil. I miss a few things, but Leo is watching raptly and I don't want to disturb him.

"That's her," Leo whispers, when Riley first comes on the stage. Those are the only two words he says to me during the whole first act. It's hard to tell what she looks like beneath her wig and heavy stage makeup. It surprises me how seriously the students are taking everything. The stage sets look like someone spent weeks designing and constructing them, and as far as I can tell no one flubs a line during the whole first section of the production. At one point, they close the curtain for a few seconds only to reopen on a completely new set.

What surprises me the most, though, is how much I like the show. There's something otherworldly about the whole deal. I can almost see myself up there, in a fun costume with cool makeup. Preferably a play I actually understand, but still, I never imagined I would enjoy theater so much. Even my desire to enroll in Karlsson's class was mostly because one of the projects everyone does is film a fake *Celebrity Sightings* segment and put it on the internet.

The curtain closes again and Leo turns to face me. "Intermission," he says. "Fifteen minutes. Do you want to get up and walk around? Get something to drink?"

"I'm okay." I'm still kind of dazzled by the ornate theater, by the glistening chandeliers and the golden threads embedded in the wallpaper.

"I'm going to use the restroom. I'll be right back." Leo squeezes past me and I pull out my phone and check my messages. No texts, but there is an email from Steve:

> Hey L—
>
> So far Ireland is really wet, but I don't even need my fake ID to drink here, so it's got that going for it, which is nice. How is everyone? How's your summer going? I hope Dad's not making you work too much since I'm not there to play barista.
>
> Since when do you like baseball? I know you're crazy about Jason, but don't forget to do some things for yourself this summer too. The fall will be here before we know it.
>
> More soon,
>
> S

I type him back a quick reply:

> Hey S—
>
> Actually, Jay and I broke up and I was at the game with someone else. We might get back together though. I think he's having some family issues or something.

Mom and Dad are the same as always (so, you
know, kind of lame but points for effort, ha-ha) but
they're not overworking me. I gotta run because I'm
actually at a play. I know, right? Since when do I like
plays? Let's just say I'm broadening my horizons this
summer.

Stay dry,

L

Leo returns to his seat just as I am slipping my phone
back into my purse. "Sorry if you're bored to death," he
says. "I don't even know if Riley saw us. She used to tell me
it can be hard to see anything out in the audience because
of the lights, that even the first rows are mostly just silhou-
ettes of people."

"What about at the end?" I ask. "Do the actors stand at
the door or anything?"

"They come out for curtain call, but everyone will be
clapping and she still might not notice." He pauses. "There's
this after-party," he says hesitantly. "I figured it might be a
lot to ask."

"We can go if you want."

"Really?" Leo sounds hopeful. "The guy who's throwing
it lives a few miles away."

I pull my phone out of my purse to check the time. It's
only eight thirty p.m. "No problem." I twist my legs sideways as an older couple squeezes past us back to their seats.
"I just need to be home by midnight."

The house lights dim again and this time I find myself getting almost as engrossed in the play as Leo. I watch how the characters move around the stage, listening to the way they make their voices louder without shouting. Afterward I stand with Leo and clap as Riley and the actor who played the devil come out for their curtain calls. Leo puts his fingers in his mouth and whistles. Riley looks over at him. A little smile appears on her face, like she's surprised to see him there.

"Nice one," I whisper in Leo's ear. "She's definitely looking at you."

The after-party is being held at the devil's house. "This is awesome," I say as Leo leads me up the steps toward the porch. "My first college party."

Leo smiles. "Glad the night isn't a total loss for you."

I grab a couple plastic cups and head over toward one of the beer kegs. "Nothing is a total loss if beer is involved," I say. It's actually one of Jason's favorite lines. I don't even drink beer that much, but I'm not going to pass up an opportunity to drink at my first college party. "And I liked the play, even if I'm not exactly sure what happened."

Leo takes the cup I hand him without even looking at me. He's too busy staring across the room at a petite blonde girl with a pixie haircut. The girl is standing in a group with the devil and two taller girls.

"Is that her?" I whisper. The girl he's staring at looks nothing like the girl onstage, but there's something familiar about the way she gestures with her hands as she talks.

Leo nods. The beer cup teeters in his fingers and a bit of frothy head sloshes over the top, barely missing my strappy sandals.

I nudge him in the ribs. "Hey. Get it together. I'm your date, remember?" I put my hand on his arm and laugh. "Dude. You are so funny," I say brightly.

I'm not sure Riley can hear me over the pulsing dance music but out of the corner of my eye I see her look over. Her smile flattens momentarily. I put my lips next to Leo's earlobe like I'm telling him a secret. "She totally just saw us together," I whisper. "Grab my hand and lead me somewhere."

Leo's beer cup wobbles again and I imagine the explaining I'll have to do if I return home reeking of Bud Light. "What? Like upstairs?" he asks.

"No, silly." I resist the urge to bop him on the forehead. "She's not going to want to take back a guy who's into drunken hookups. She'll think I'm just a rebound chick you snagged to make yourself feel better." I laugh loudly again, as if Leo is telling me one funny joke after the next. "Take me outside in the back to look at stars or something."

"Pretty sure all guys are into drunken hookups," Leo mutters. But he wraps his hand around mine and leads me through the sea of bodies, past the kitchen, and out the back door onto a large wooden deck. There's a patio table with four metal chairs, but three of them are taken up by a group of boys playing cards. We walk to the far end of the deck and lean against the railing. Leo drops my hand.

I crane my neck upward. The night is clear, and even with all the lights around us, the black sky is awash with silvery specks. "I love the stars," I say.

"Which one is your favorite?" he asks.

It's a weird question. I have trouble picking a favorite flavor of soda, or even a favorite color. Who would think I actually have a favorite star? But I do. "My brother and I used to wish on stars when we were little. Not about anything important. Mostly for stuff like snow days and extra Christmas presents." I point to a shining dot of light, lower on the horizon. "That one. It's always so strong, so full."

"That's because it's not a star," Leo says.

"What do you mean?"

"It's Venus."

"Seriously? How can you tell?" I squint at the point of light until spots swim in front of my face.

"Well, for one, it's not winking," Leo says. "Stars, their light pulses."

"Wow, you're smart."

Leo looks down at the ground. "Yet another trait that makes me irresistible to the ladies."

"Girls like smart guys." I think about it for a few seconds. Jason probably isn't particularly smart, but it wouldn't bother me if he was. "Well, we don't *dislike* them," I clarify.

My phone suddenly buzzes. It's too early for my mom to be checking up on me. I fish it out of my purse and swipe at the screen. It's a text. From Micah.

Chapter 17

IF YOU KNOW THE ENEMY AND KNOW YOURSELF,
YOUR VICTORY WILL NOT STAND IN DOUBT.

—SUN TZU, *The Art of War*

"Everything all right?" Leo asks. His eyes keep flicking toward the door leading back into the house. He's probably hoping Riley will come outside. Or maybe hoping she won't. I remember the way I felt at the baseball game, like I was both dying and terrified for Jason to see me with another guy.

"Funny, that's the same thing he asked." I hold up my phone. "Micah."

I tap out a quick response telling Micah that everything is going fine. I wait for my phone to light up again, but the screen stays dark.

"Aww, he's checking up on you," Leo says. "Almost like a real boyfriend."

"Shut up." I slide the phone into my pocket where I'll feel it vibrate if I get another text. "Me and Micah—that's just business."

Leo cranes his neck to look through the small kitchen

window. I follow his gaze. I think I see Riley's pixie haircut float by, but I'm not sure. "I don't know," he says. "I see you guys at work and you're always laughing and having fun."

My lips quirk upward as I remember our impromptu food fight. "Sometimes, when he's not being mean, but it's the same way I have fun with Bianca."

"If you say so." Leo shrugs. "Just keep it real with him."

I roll my eyes. "Why are you acting like Micah is some delicate flower? The dude carries a switchblade. I don't think I'm a big threat."

"He's a good guy. That's all I'm saying."

"I know he's a good guy, which is why I'm helping him get back together with Amber." Now I'm the one with the shaky beer glass. I feel like Leo's accusing me of something, of taking advantage of his friend. Am I using Micah? Yeah, I guess I am, but he's using me too. And it's fine—no one is getting hurt because of our agreement. I chug the rest of my beer and slam the empty cup down on the wooden railing. Then I make a big show of digging my phone back out of my pocket and checking the time. It's still early. "I should prob-ably be getting home," I say.

"Okay," Leo says. We cut through the house and walk out to the car in silence. If Riley is around, I don't see her.

I flip on the radio as soon as Leo fires up the engine. I hit the tuning arrow up until it lands on the station Micah put on for the ride home from the baseball game.

Leo looks over at me. "I didn't know you liked this kind of music."

Me neither, but I do. Kind of, anyway. "I've been branching out. Anything gets old if you listen to it 24/7, you know?"

"I hear you. I like new stuff too."

I don't answer. If you asked me whether I was the type of person who liked trying new things or preferred sticking with what was familiar, I would have told you I was the second girl. The if-it-ain't-broke-don't-fix-it girl. I also would have told you plays were lame. It suddenly occurs to me that I don't seem to know very much about . . . me. It's a weird feeling, like maybe a stranger is inhabiting my body. Or maybe a stranger was, and I kicked her out.

The beginning of *The Art of War* said something about knowing yourself and your enemy, that without that basic knowledge you can't hope to be successful in battle. Is that my problem? Do I know Jason better than I know myself?

I sneak my compact out of my purse and pretend to check my eye makeup. Bronze shadow. Bright green eyes. I think I even see freckles on my left eyelid. Normally that would be frustrating, but tonight the smattering of rogue spots is a comfort. I might *feel* different all of a sudden, but I'm still me.

Leo navigates the car onto the highway. "It seemed like you were getting into the show."

The interstate is mostly empty, even though it's not that late. Brake lights dance in the distance, red blurs in an otherwise black night. "Yeah, I can't believe it was based on classic literature. Who knew old German guys had such a flair for the dramatic," I say. "Lying, betrayal. Unplanned pregnancy. It was like a cliff-hanger episode of *Undead Academy*. All it was missing was zombies."

The dark highway gives way to the soft glow of street-lights as Leo pulls onto the exit ramp. I lean my head back against the seat.

"Have you heard from your ex-boyfriend yet?" Leo asks.

I shake my head. "No, but Bianca's helping me strategize. Don't laugh. She seriously has us pulling ideas from *The Art of War*. Crazy, huh?"

Leo thinks for a few seconds. "That's actually brilliant. War is basically head games and fighting. So are relation-ships."

"What an uplifting thought."

"There's even that quote about how all's fair in love and war," he continues.

"Also said by someone who's been dead for, like, a zillion years, right?"

"Most people attribute it to Shakespeare, but it's actually from John Lyly, who's even older," Leo says. "But it's not like relationships have changed much." He taps his fingers on the steering wheel. "You might also want to check out *The Prince* by Machiavelli. You can probably find the text online."

"Whoa." I hold up a hand. "One dead guy at a time, okay?"

"Okay. But let me know if there's anything I can do to help you and Bee."

"Sure." Dead Chinese Warlord said something about

utilizing all available resources, but it seems weird that Leo wants to volunteer to be part of my "army" since he's paying me and all. A tiny flicker of guilt moves through me. I shouldn't take his money, but without it there's no possibility of Costa Rica. Maybe I can pay him back after everything works out.

"Listen." Leo glances at me. "What I said about Micah— I hope I didn't upset you. It's none of my business what you guys do."

"It's fine," I say. "But we're not *doing* anything." Leo and I are almost to my house. I lean forward and crank the radio up a couple of notches, singing along to the song. I'm hoping he'll take the hint. The idea of me hurting Micah is ridiculous. He's practically bulletproof.

When Leo pulls up at the curb in front of my house, I lean over toward the center console and give him a quick half hug. "I hope Riley calls you."

"Yeah, me too. Thanks again for going with me tonight."

"Sure. I had fun," I tell him. And I mean it.

The next day, I wake up to streaks of sun burning through my eyelids. I open one eye and swear under my breath when I realize my blinds are open.

"You awake?" It's my mom's voice. I roll over. She's puttering around near my dresser.

"I am now." Raising one of my arms, I block out the offending sunbeams and watch my mother paw through a stack of magazines. "What are you doing, Mom?"

"I was leaving you a note." My mom drops an issue of *Celebrity Tattler* onto my dresser and tucks her pencil back into her bun. "But now that you're awake I can tell you." She smiles. Her teeth are almost as bright as the sun—unnaturally white for someone who drinks so much tea.

I fall back on my bed and cover my face with my favorite pillow. "Why did you feel the need to open the blinds?"

"Sorry, I didn't want to write on anything crucial," she says. "You should probably clean things up in here someday."

"Someday," I say, my voice muffled by two inches of feathers. "What was so important you couldn't wait till I got up?"

"I'm heading out for the day with some of the other assistant professors. I was curious about how things went on your date last night so I did a reading for you with my breakfast tea. I saw a bird—a swallow." She clears her throat. "Love. New beginnings."

I groan. I swear my mom keeps my picture on her desk for the sole purpose of reading leaves for me against my will. It's her weirdo way of spying or something. "Are you sure it wasn't a raven or a vulture?" I ask. "Maybe a headless chicken foretelling a future full of . . . headless chickens?"

"Joke all you want. I just thought you'd want to know," she says in a singsong voice. "Am I right? How was it? Is new love blooming in my daughter's life?"

I peer out from underneath the pillow. "It wasn't even a date. It was business."

Her brow furrows. "Do I need to worry about what kind of *business* has my daughter donning tiny miniskirts and going out with strange boys?"

"No, Mom. I haven't turned hooker or anything, I promise." I sit up and rub my eyes. "Think of it more like an anthropology project. I'm interacting with different, um, subcultures."

My mom's eyes narrow to little snakelike slits. "You've never had any interest in anthropology before," she says wryly. "Or plays, for that matter. You saw *Faust*, right? What did you think of it?"

I stifle a yawn. "I kind of liked it, the parts I understood anyway."

She tucks a chunk of unruly hair back out of my face. "You know, I was in a couple of productions when I was in college. It's exhilarating being up there on the stage, living someone else's life."

Was *that* what I liked? The idea of being someone else? No, that's crazy. There's nothing wrong with my life. Well, there won't be once I win Jason back. Most girls would trade places with me in an instant.

"Well, keep an eye out," my mom says. "The leaves are never wrong. New love. How exciting." She pulls the blinds closed and practically scampers out of my room. It's disturbing how giddy she can be sometimes.

I squeeze my eyes shut and try to go back to sleep but it's pointless. I grab my phone to check the time and see that I have two text messages from earlier in the morning. The first is from Bee, asking if I want to go running with her. I do, and I should, but maybe later. I tap the screen. The second is another message from Micah.

> Micah: Concert tomorrow night at TDD. You in?
> Me: Will Amber be there?
> Micah: Yup
> Me: Okay. What time?
> Micah: I'll pick you up at 8. Wear something hot.
> Me: Ha-ha. Everything I own is hot.

I call Bianca and give her the lowdown on last night's date with Leo. Then I tell her about my plans with Micah.

"Do you want to come with?" I ask, crossing my fingers that she'll say yes. "I'm sure Micah wouldn't care. Two hot dates are better than one, right?"

Bee pauses on the other end of the line. I can almost hear her brain whirring as she tries to come up with a polite excuse. "The Devil's Doorstep isn't really my scene," she says finally.

"Like it's *my* scene?" My voice gets shrill. "I'm half expecting the bouncers to turn me away for being a fraud and a poser." It's kind of like those super-goth stores at the mall. I like to peek in from the outside and I'm pretty sure there's stuff in there I would want, but the thought of the sales clerk with the tattooed face and triple lip rings treating me like I don't belong makes it not worth the hassle.

Bianca yawns. "You don't need me for this, Lainey.

You've got Micah. He'll protect you. Meanwhile, I'll prob-ably be playing goalie for Elias and Miguelito."

"I can't believe you'd rather spend the night playing soc-cer with your brothers," I whine. "You're going to leave me all alone to be doused in pig's blood by a bunch of guys wearing leather and face paint." I sigh dramatically. "But whatever. I'll survive. Micah and I made a deal and there's no backing out now."

Bianca giggles. "I doubt it will be that bad. And look on the bright side—"

"*What* bright side?"

"You'll finally get to see what Amber is like."

I guess I am a little curious about that.

Chapter 18

THEREFORE, THE CLEVER COMBATANT IMPOSES
HIS WILL ON THE ENEMY, BUT DOES NOT ALLOW
THE ENEMY'S WILL TO BE IMPOSED ON HIM.

—SUN TZU, *The Art of War*

"So hanging out with Leo went okay?" Micah asks.

We're in his car on the way to The Devil's Doorstep. I keep slouching lower and lower in my seat so no one will see me in what I'm now referring to as "the Beast."

"Were you expecting it *not* to go okay?" I peek over at him.

He's wearing the standard rocker-boy uniform: jeans, strategically frayed, with a black concert T-shirt. In addition to his barbed-wire bracelet, he's also wearing a silver anarchy pendant, and his hair has been spiked to maximum height. "Well, I would have felt responsible if you had a miserable time since I hooked it up."

"Stop talking about me like you're my pimp," I say, fiddling with my colored streak. "It was my decision to hang out with Leo."

"Did it go *better* than okay?" Micah asks. I can see his lips curl into a smirk out of the corner of my eye. "You sound a little defensive."

"And you sound a little jealous." I arch an eyebrow.

Micah hums to himself as he pulls into the gravel parking lot behind the club. "Now you sound a little delusional." He shuts off the ignition and checks his reflection in the rearview mirror.

"Whatever." I pull out my compact to give myself a quick once-over. I'm wearing a flowy green-and-black sundress with a lace neckline and hem. Between my outfit and my bronze eye shadow, my eyes are looking super green tonight. "Who's playing again?" I ask. He's told me about six times but I keep forgetting. I reach down to retie the strap of my left platform sandal, frowning when I notice one of the tiny rhinestones has fallen off. My shoes are tall enough that I'll tower over my fake date, but Micah doesn't seem to care. "A bunch of bands that'll make my ears bleed?"

"Arachne's Revenge and Bottlegrate."

"Right." I nod, even though I don't think I've heard anything by either one of them.

"You going to be okay?" Micah's still wearing half a smirk, but his voice is serious. "I can assure you the place isn't as scary as you think."

"I'm fine," I snap. "I'm not scared."

He pulls a couple tall cans of beer out from under the seat. "We won't be able to get served inside. I stole a couple of my mom's just in case you needed something to take the edge off."

I grab a can out of Micah's hand and pop the top. It's a brand I don't recognize and it tastes awful, like someone took the cheapest beer they could find and spiked it with nail polish remover. Still, for some reason I chug almost the whole can before I come up for air.

"Damn, girl." He stares at me in disbelief. "That's kind of hot."

I smile. "Jason would have told me to quit being a dude."

Micah pops open his own beer. "This Jason guy seems to have a lot of issues, almost like a chick."

"Funny." I wipe my mouth with the back of my hand and let out a satisfying belch.

"Okay, that's less hot, but I'll let it slide." Micah slams his beer and makes a point of belching even louder. "Almost like hanging out with C-4," he teases, slipping the empty beer cans back under the seat and then getting out of the car. I hop out on my own side and gingerly close the door behind me. Micah walks around the back of the car so that we're standing next to each other. He's wearing Jason's aftershave again. "If C-4 were an insanely tall soccer diva."

"I'm not that tall," I insist, even though I have to look down at Micah to say it.

"You are tonight," Micah says, nudging my platform sandal with one of his black boots. "Very supermodelesque."

I give him a skeptical look as we walk side by side toward the front door of the club. "I had one beer," I say. "I'm not drunk enough for you to schmooze your way into my pants."

"You're not wearing pants." Micah glances down at my bare legs. "Looks like I'm halfway there." He winks at me and I give him my "back the hell up" look in response.

We get our hands stamped by a bald guy who looks like an ogre, and then pass through a dingy hall into an even dingier main room.

I've never been inside The Devil's Doorstep before, but it looks pretty much like I expected. The floor is made of wood, scraped in some places and warping in others. A narrow bar runs along one side of the room. Three-legged barstools are lined up in front of it, their cushions bleeding stuffing out of various rips and tears. Behind the bar, pictures and posters, most of them autographed, hang at crooked angles. The walls of the place are painted black. A pair of red fiberglass devils flank the stage.

Above our heads, half-rotted wooden ceiling beams dip low. An exposed wire dangles from a hole in the wood. The whole place looks about one equipment malfunction short of burning to the ground.

People stand around in little clusters talking and drinking. I see a girl in a rubber dress and I think of Phoenix, of her slicked-back blonde hair and giant tattoo. I peer around, trying to pick Amber out of the crowd. She'll probably make Micah look normal.

"Where's Amber?" I ask. "Do you see her?"

He glances around the club. "Not yet, but she'll be here."

"Should I look for a girl who's more tattoo than person?"

Micah laughs. "I think you'll be surprised at how normal she is," he says. "She doesn't have any tattoos, in fact."

"Really? And here I would have thought that was one of your requirements."

A bank of round lights above the stage snaps to life with a sharp hum. I watch as someone cycles through the lighting options: bright white, pale blue, green, white spotlight. The stage goes dark again.

"What are your requirements?" Micah asks. "Chiseled abs? Fake tan? A shelf full of sports trophies?"

"Dude, you think I'm such a bad person," I say.

A bald guy in oversized headphones makes his way to the middle of the stage. He taps the microphone twice and says. "Check. Check two."

"Not bad," Micah says. "Maybe a little shallow." He nudges me in the ribs to show me he's kidding, but his words sting.

"Just because I'm popular and in love with a guy who is also popular doesn't make me shallow, does it?"

"I was only—"

"It's not like I can just change who I am or what I like. I can't just turn off feelings and quit giving a crap about stuff that's important to me." I lift my chin. "I think of shallow more like only caring about owning fancy stuff and being beautiful. Most girls want to feel beautiful, but it's not my number one goal in life or anything."

"Hey." Micah gives my shoulder a squeeze. "Chill. I didn't mean to upset you."

I look away, part of me still feeling wounded and the rest of me trying to figure out why I even care what he thinks.

"So what is your number one goal then?" he asks.

"Getting a soccer scholarship, I guess. I know I can't turn that into a paying job, but I'm not like Bianca—I don't have the next twelve years already planned out." I frown. "Still, I want to do something meaningful too. I just haven't figured out what yet."

"You've got plenty of time to decide what you want to do," Micah says. "That's what college is for."

Headphones Guy moves from microphone to microphone checking each one. Then he picks up a guitar and strums it lightly, producing a barrage of chords that sounds more like a car accident than music.

"Please tell me he's not in the band," I say.

"He's not." Micah is looking across the room at a pair of girls sitting behind a card table selling T-shirts and stuff.

A flash of jealousy sparks through me. I can't believe he's checking out other girls while we're supposed to be acting like we're a couple. "So, is Amber prettier than me?" I blurt out, mentally kicking myself as soon as the words leave my mouth. It's one of those things you think, but never actually mean to say, but once it's out there you've got no choice but to own it.

"Relax, Lainey," Micah says. "It's not a competition."

I think of *The Art of War* tucked inside my purse. "It's totally a competition," I mutter under my breath. "It's a battle."

But Amber isn't the enemy.

Right. It doesn't matter if Micah's ex is hotter than I am, so then why do I want him to like me better? I feel a twinge of shame. Maybe I *am* shallow. Kendall is all about collecting "fan club members" as she calls them, but I've never been one to lead on boys I wasn't interested in. Again, I wonder if being without Jason is wrecking my self-esteem.

The lights in the club dim and the stage lights flare to life again. "Come on." Micah urges me forward and I stomp on the toes of the guy in front of me.

"Sorry," I mutter. People from the back of the club and the bar area are flocking to the small rectangle of space in front of the stage, jostling me from all sides. I'm not sure where Micah wants me to go. I try to turn around and ask, but then I feel his hands on me. Fingertips, really. Barely grazing my sides, right below where my rib cage ends. I let him guide me through the people. When we stop moving, my arms are actually resting on top of the stage. Micah is directly to my right. To the right of him, stacks of black amplifiers hum with energy.

The crowd starts clapping and whistling as the opening band, Arachne's Revenge, walks out onto the stage. The drummer is an overweight guy wearing a backward baseball cap and a T-shirt with the sleeves cut off. The guitarist and bassist (I can never tell which is which) are both lanky and tall. One has dark skin and dreadlocks. The other is pale with unruly, curly blond hair. The lead singer is a Kendall-pretty girl who looks a few years older than me. She's wearing a black-and-red kimono with a layer of black mesh peeking out from beneath the hem. Her heavy combat boots are half unlaced, but she glides across the stage like she's part swan and part panther.

"Wow," I say. I'm impressed and she hasn't even started to sing.

"I know, right?" Micah's eyes follow the girl as she walks from one side of the stage to the other, stopping to ruffle her bassist's (I think) dreadlocks. He tugs on one of her pale fish-bone braids and winks, as if they're sharing a secret joke.

The girl heads back to center stage and sidles up to the microphone. "What's up, Hazelton?" she asks. The crowd roars in response. The guy standing next to me, whose toes I smashed, reaches out to touch the singer's boot. She smiles down at him but steps back out of his reach.

The first two songs aren't bad. The lead singer has a decent voice but it's being swallowed up by the screaming guitars. Still, it's way better than one of those shows where the band dresses up like grim reapers and throws buckets of pig guts at the audience.

Then the drummer leaves the stage and returns with a dual keyboard setup. A guy wearing a staff T-shirt brings the lead singer a violin.

"This is called 'Wake Up Dreaming,'" the lead singer says. Her voice is a mix of throaty and little girlish. "Someday we hope to perform it with a full symphony." Around me, people are pulling out their cell phones, lighting up the screens and holding them above their heads. The girl counts out a beat and the whole band begins to play at once. It's one of the songs Micah played on the way to Mizz Creant's. The song that almost made me cry.

The bright lights blink off and suddenly the stage is awash in rotating blue circles. I can feel vibrations from the amps, from the floor. I swear I can even feel the individual notes moving through the air. My blood hums in my veins. I look over at Micah. He's got his eyes closed.

The music pitches and swells, violin and guitars, drum-beats and thudding bass. As I sway back and forth in front of the stage, it's like being in the eye of a tornado, where it's calm, but everything is going crazy, whirling around me. I can't stop looking at Micah, at the way the lights reflect off his mohawk, at the way he's completely lost in the storm of overlapping chords.

I see every part of him, tiny pieces I never knew existed. The slight bend in his nose, the wedge-shaped scar on his right temple, the outline of his bicep hiding beneath the pyramid tattoo. His lips part, just barely, when he exhales. As I imagine the invisible mist of his breath hanging in the air, I inch closer to him. Here, in the strange blue light, while the bass pulses and pounds, all I can think about is touching him. Our fingertips brush. A shock wave courses through me. I want to grab him and pull him into my calm spot, closing my eyes and kissing him while the world spins topsy-turvy around us.

My thoughts feel hot inside my head, like they should

be radiating a laser beam across the club, but Micah's eyes are still closed, his body loose. He's oblivious to the fact I'm thinking about kissing him. He has no idea my eyes are skimming their way down the lines of his body. His cheekbones. His beard stubble. The ridge of muscle connecting his jaw to the center of his chest. The faintest trace of sweat glistens where his neck meets his right shoulder. I want to touch my lips to it.

This is crazy. It's Micah. I don't like Micah. He doesn't like me. We have about as much in common as, well, nothing. I sneak another glimpse at him. He's still completely entranced by the song. He's still completely kissable. It has to be the beer, or the music, the violins and guitars and electronic pulsing, the whole otherworldly quality to this song. Or maybe it's just because I'm not myself here, and I don't have to obey the rules of Lainey.

Micah's eyes snap open and he looks over at me, as if he can finally sense the strange intensity of my thoughts. My heart does a somersault in my chest. I mutter something about needing air even though I know he can't hear me.

Turning, I thread my way through the crowd. The music is crescendoing now. Louder and louder. I feel it pounding in my skin, my blood, my ears, my head. Every beat is punctuated with the split-second image of Micah and me kissing. His lips, white-hot on mine. I plunge forward, swimming through swaying arms and sweaty torsos.

I swear he says my name, but I don't turn around. I'm imagining it. I have to be. There's no way I'd be able to hear him over the music. Besides, I don't dare look back. If I do, he'll know. He'll see everything reflected in my eyes.

I escape out into the night, embracing the breeze that cools my skin and dries the damp tendrils of hair at the nape of my neck. My heart gallops painfully in my chest, a tiny horse trying to burst through my rib cage. The music fades away as the song comes to an end, but I am still drowning in spiky hair and glimmering sweat. And lips, those barely parted lips.

Stop. I will the image from my head.

Me. Micah.

Kissing.

Impossible.

So then why do I want it so much?

Chapter 19

THERE IS A PROPER SEASON FOR MAKING ATTACKS WITH FIRE.

—SUN TZU, *The Art of War*

I suck in breath after breath of warm night air, waiting for my heartbeat to slow, waiting for my whole body to stop tingling.

What the hell *was* that? *Get a grip, Lainey. The idea is not to fall for your fake boyfriend.*

A handful of kids hover right outside the doors to the club. Two are smoking; the rest are clearly too young for the fourteen-and-over show. They're hanging around, peeking through the door of the club whenever someone goes in or out, probably hoping the bouncer will eventually take pity on them and let them in. One of the smokers whistles at me.

Ignoring him, I turn and wander half a block up the street, just far enough away to feel alone. This is a busy area of town, but it's after ten and all the stores are closed. The only things open are The Devil's Doorstep and Alpha, the pizza place across the street. Gathering my dress around me, I carefully lower myself to the rough sidewalk. I lean my head back against the dirt-encrusted glass window of a vintage clothing store and pull *The Art of War* from my purse. I need more ancient Chinese wisdom to make it through the night.

The clever combatant imposes his will on the enemy but does not allow the enemy's will to be imposed on him. Right. I'm supposed to be tricking Jason with this little charade. I'm not supposed to be tricking myself.

Micah ducks out of the club a minute later. I watch him spin a slow half circle as he tries to find me. Our eyes meet and I raise my hand in a partial wave. He ambles over and sits down next to me. Plucking the book out of my hand, he stretches his legs out in front of him and begins to read silently. "You brought your homework to the concert?"

"I'm actually reading that for . . . personal reasons." I stare straight ahead at my strappy sandals and the scuffed leather tops of his steel-toed boots. I catch glimpses of Alpha's patio through the space between the parked cars. A tall waiter with thick, blond hair ambles up to a table of women my mom's age. The way he walks reminds me of Jason—it's almost a swagger, as if he knows he's heading into territory where he will be universally adored. As he takes their orders, he pauses to put his hand on one's arm. The women burst into giggles the second the waiter disappears back into the restaurant. It's cute how much fun they're having, but it all strikes me as being a little fake.

I should know. I'm turning into somewhat of an expert when it comes to being fake.

Micah flips to the next page. He still hasn't said any-thing. I figure he's waiting for me to explain my behavior. Not going to happen. I mean, how mortifying would that be? Gee, I started getting into the music. Then I started getting into the way you were getting into the music. Then I started getting into *you*. And now I'm out here reading a warrior strategy guide to cool off. Nothing weird about that.

I could always lie—tell him it was too loud or too hot, that I was fanning myself with the book, but the more I watch the theater production going on across the street, the more the idea of any more phoniness makes me feel sick. Maybe if I sit here and say nothing Micah will think every-thing is fine.

"So," he says finally, setting *The Art of War* on the ground between us.

So is a word that can mean many things. Pretty sure this one means: "What the hell is wrong with you, freak show?"

I don't respond right away. I look straight ahead, trying to decide if the urge to kiss him has passed. It has. I'm back in control. He turns toward me and I catch of whiff of Red Lynx aftershave mingled with smoke and sweat.

"Are you okay?" Micah asks. Just when I'm thinking his concern is really sweet he says, "Did you have a stroke? This might be the longest I've ever heard you go without talking."

I try to force my face into a frown but my lips curl up at the edges. I can't help it. Even when he's teasing me, he's still kind of funny. "It's just a little overwhelming, you know?" The words fly out of my mouth almost without thinking.

Super. I sound like I've never been to a concert before. I steel myself for the barrage of scorn I know is forthcoming.

But all he says is, "Do you hate it? We can go."

"I love it," I say. "Or that song, anyway." He looks a little surprised. I should take this as my cue to shut up, but I keep talking. "It felt unreal. Like I was dreaming or on drugs or something." I shake my head. *Could I be more lame?*

Micah looks up at the sky. It's hazy and gray, the smoke from a nearby factory lacing together with feathery clouds. "I know what you mean," he says, passing up a second opportunity to rag on me mercilessly. "That whole mix of classical music and guitar and shit gets inside of you. I always feel like I'm floating through space or breathing underwater."

That is an excellent description of how I felt.

"I'm surprised you like this group," I say. "Pianos? Violins? I thought you only listened to hard-core punk and screaming death metal. You know, music to murder by."

"Well, they do harder stuff too." Micah nudges my foot with his steel-toed boot. "Hmm. Music to murder by, eh? That would be a cool name for a band."

I laugh. "I know, right?"

He punches me lightly on the leg. I flinch. He turns to look at me and I focus on the waiter across the street, memorizing his gait as if there's going to be a test later. "No, seriously," Micah says. "I think we need to form a band, just because you came up with that. Can you play anything?"

"Um, I can sing." If karaoke counts.

"Lead vocals for Music to Murder By. Let's hear it."

"What's our song called?" My mouth is still forming words independent of my brain.

"'Destructor.'" He says this in a low, booming voice, stretching the final *R* sound into a growl.

I let out a crazy half-screech, half-snarl, stretching it out for about ten seconds. My impression of what a song called "Destructor" would sound like.

A couple of the kids in front of the club look over. One of them puts his fingers in his mouth and whistles.

Micah holds his fist out for a bump. "Look, our first fans! Why, Glinda Elaine Mitchell. I didn't know you had it in you."

I cringe. Ever since I was old enough to know that my mother named me after the good witch in the *Wizard of Oz*, I've been trying to forget. Aside from the occasional substitute teacher, no one calls me "Glinda." No one. "Don't call me that," I say, tapping my knuckles against his. "Ever."

He holds his hands up in fake surrender. "The girl is feisty tonight."

"The girl is always feisty."

"So I'm learning." Micah picks up *The Art of War.* He clears his throat. "'*There are five ways of attacking with fire. The first is to burn soldiers in their camp; the second is to burn stores; the third is to burn baggage trains; the fourth is to burn arsenals and magazines; the fifth is to hurl dropping fire amongst the enemy.'* This is some serious shit." He smiles. "Should I be worried?"

"I'm actually using it to strategize," I blurt out. "You

know, to win back Jason."

I'm expecting Micah to burst out laughing but he just nods to himself. "How Machiavellian of you."

"Leo said that too. It was Bianca's idea. She's definitely the brains of the operation."

"I assume you and Bee aren't burning any soldiers or stores?" Micah asks with a gleam in his eye.

"Some parts of it are more relevant than others," I admit.

He tosses the book to me. "Well, show me what you got."

I show him my highlighted passages and tell him about some of the stuff Bianca came up with, like being deceptive and attacking from a position of power.

"Fall like a thunderbolt, huh?" he says.

"Right. When the moment comes, be bold. Decisive. Strike with power."

"Got it." The top ten list is tucked in the back of the book. Micah nods again as he goes through the strategies.

"Do you think it's crazy?" I ask.

He laughs lightly. "I think it's highly organized, and maybe a little scary. But I also think we're missing an excellent show." Rising to his feet, he holds his hands out toward me.

Tucking the book back into my purse, I grip his fingertips gently and scramble back to my feet. The image of him with his head back, eyes closed, swaying to the music flashes into my head ever so briefly. My face is flushed. My whole body still feels hot. My chest expands as I inhale a huge breath of air. *Get it together, Lainey.*

When we get back inside, the main act is getting ready to take the stage. I can see two of the members of Arachne's Revenge—the drummer and the guy with the dreads—sitting over at the T-shirt table. The lead singer is working her way through the crowd toward the stage. When she gets closer, I see she's not as old as she looked under the lights.

To my surprise, she doesn't veer off to grab an open space at the front of the stage. Instead she makes her way over to us. And then she wraps her hands around Micah's head, covering his eyes with her fingers. She leans in close to whisper in his ear.

Micah removes the girl's hands from his eyes and turns to give her a quick hug. It's the same kind of hug I gave Leo in the car, more of a pat on the back with lots of space between the torsos. "Hey," he says.

Hey is another word that can mean many things. As I watch this awkward embrace, puzzle pieces start snapping together in my head. Could it possibly be . . .

"I'm Lainey," I say brightly. The girl and Micah both turn to look at me. Micah opens his mouth to say more, but the lights drop again and the crowd begins to cheer as the four guys from of Bottlegrate run out onstage. They're older than Arachne's Revenge, probably late twenties to early thirties.

People behind me press forward, pinning my body against the stage. A strand of my hair gets tangled around something and my eyes water as individual hairs snap loose from my head. The lead singer of Arachne's Revenge wraps her hand around my arm, pulling me to the side of the crushing crowd.

"Thanks," I say, rubbing my scalp with one hand. I swear if I end up with a bald spot I'm going to charge Micah hazard pay.

"No worries." She leans in close to me and I notice she's wearing jet-black fake eyelashes. Despite the noise, I hear her next words like she's shouting them through a megaphone at church. "Nice to meet you. My name is Amber."

Chapter 20

"That's Amber?" I mouth, once the leggy blonde girl disappears back into her throng of bandmates. They're all sitting at the T-shirt table now, doing their best to look unimpressed by the headlining band. The lead singer of Bottlegrate launches directly into a hard-core cover of an old pop song without even stopping to greet the crowd.

Micah reads my lips. "Yeah."

I cup my hands around his ear. The warmth of his skin makes me tremble. "How come you didn't tell me Arachne's Revenge was her band?"

He says something I can't make out. The guitarist and the bassist walk circles around each other on the stage. I step even farther off to the side, to the point I'm almost hiding behind a stack of amplifiers. At least I'm not in danger of being crushed or trampled.

Micah brushes my hair back from my ear and repeats

himself. "I said I wanted to see if you liked the music before you knew who she was." His breath makes the blood rush beneath my skin.

"They're okay," I say. I sneak another peek at her, envying the laid-back style of her kimono and combat boots. "She's actually way more normal than I imagined."

"Told you so. Also, everyone says that if they meet Phoenix first."

"So why did you two break up?" I ask. Then I see Amber lean over and bite on one of her bandmate's dreadlocks. He turns his face toward hers and both of them collapse into a fit of laughter. "Oh."

Micah's pale skin gets even whiter. "She says she's not dating any of them. She just doesn't have time for both me and her music." He stares at Amber and Dreads Guy.

I watch him watch them. It's painful. In my head I see Jason and Alex kissing against Jay's Mustang.

The first song ends. Micah manages to rip his gaze away from the T-shirt table, like the end of the music has broken a spell. His jaw tightens. His eyes glow almost golden in the stage lights. "I'm not sure if I believe her."

I don't know what to say to this, so I don't say anything. Part of me wants to hug him. Not an awkward Leo hug or a let's-make-someone-jealous hug—a hug that says I get it. That I know exactly how it feels to see the person you love with someone else. But that's not what our agreement is about. We're not using each other to feel better about getting dumped. My job is to be his ally. To help him level the battlefield and then aid in his attack. That's going to take time. Like Bianca said: wars aren't fought in a day.

I try to focus on the concert. Bottlegrate puts on an amazing live show. The guys are constantly laughing and joking with the crowd. I recognize a couple of their songs from the ride to Mizz Creant's and find myself bobbing my head and singing along. Halfway through the set, the guitarist does a guitar solo where he ends up lying down on the stage, his fingers flying like lightning across the frets. The crowd explodes with cheers and whistles. I clap along with everyone else. I can't believe how much fun I'm having.

Micah, however, is not having fun. After about two more songs of him looking over at Amber every five seconds, I reach out and give him an awkward pat on the shoulder. "I'm sorry," I mouth at him, gesturing toward the side of the club with my head.

He cups his hands around my ear but still has to yell in order for me to hear him. "No, I'm sorry. I dragged you here. I shouldn't be ignoring you."

"It's fine," I say. "But we can leave whenever you want."

"Let's go." Micah wraps his hand around mine and we squeeze through the crowd. His touch is friendly, almost protective. It doesn't elicit the same shock waves I felt earlier. Somehow, meeting Amber and seeing Micah in pain has neutralized things. I'm refocused on our battle.

He drops my fingers as we head around the building to the gravel parking lot in back. He shakes his head as he unlocks my car door. "Maybe this was a bad idea. I don't think I'm ready to see her, especially not with some other guy."

As he turns around, the fluorescent lights of the parking lot illuminate his hunched-over form, his head lowered in defeat. This time I give in to the urge. "Hey." I reach out for him. "Come here." Leaning in, I loosely wrap my arms around his neck.

His body goes tense as he straightens up, but his hands end up in the vicinity of my waist. "I'm not a girl, Lainey," he mutters. "All my problems can't be fixed with a hug."

"I know that." As I release my hold on him, I brush my lips against the wedge-shaped scar on his temple.

He backs away. "What was that for?"

I shrug. I'm not even sure myself. "You looked so sad. I just . . . feel sorry for you."

"I don't need you to feel sorry for me," Micah says in a shrill voice. His lips curl into a smirk as he heads around to the driver's side.

It takes me a second to realize he's imitating something I said to him the day Jason broke up with me. I slide into the car and pull the door shut behind me. "Do you remember everything people say so you can use it against them?"

"I try." He stares at me for a moment, but doesn't say anything.

"What?" I make a big show of fumbling for my seat belt so I can escape his penetrating gaze.

"Tsk-tsk. Breaking your own rules, Lainey Mitchell," he says.

I click my seat belt into place. Wow, he's right. He looked so alone and vulnerable there for a second that I didn't even think about a kiss on the cheek being a technical infraction of my "absolutely no kissing" rule.

"Uh . . . sorry?" I offer, a blush creeping into my cheeks. "It was a random impulse. It won't happen again."

Micah glances over at me as he starts the car, a smile still playing at his lips. "You're kind of cute when you get all flustered." Then, before I can formulate a response, he plugs his phone into the stereo and cranks up the volume. As we pull out onto the road, he turns the music down slightly and starts talking about how it was the instrumental song "Wake Up Dreaming" that got Amber and her band noticed by a studio executive. "She never thought her classical violin training would come in handy with the band," Micah says. "Everything happened so fast for them. By this time next year they might be playing venues all over the US." His voice goes tight with grief. It's obvious how much he cares about her.

"It was so intense, the way you got into that song," I say. "Like you were the only person on the planet."

"It's definitely one of my favorites." He slows the car to a stop in front of my house a couple minutes later.

I unlock my door and slide out. Then I stop for a second and lean back through the open window. "You were kind of nice to me tonight."

Micah shakes his head. "Was not."

"I think you were," I insist.

"If you say so. I'll try harder to be a dick next time. After all, that is what you like, right?"

I purse my lips. "Jason isn't a dick. He just found some other girl he likes better." It's the first time I've actually put that thought into words. It hurts, but it's also freeing, like I've confessed a secret that's been slowly squeezing me to death.

Micah runs a hand through his mohawk. The humidity has mostly flattened it. "And then he dumped you at your job, in front of your friends."

"He probably figured it was the one place I wouldn't make a scene."

"Do you do that with everyone?" Micah puts the car in PARK and leans toward the passenger-side window.

"Do what?"

"Make excuses for their shitty behavior?"

My eyes widen. Do I? "I have no idea," I admit.

"It's kind of a nice quality," he says. "But it'll probably set you up to get hurt a lot."

The way he says the last part makes me think we might not be talking about me anymore.

I'm about to ask him for clarification when I notice his gaze has drifted slightly lower and he can totally see down the front of my dress.

I back away from the window and adjust my neckline so I'm safely covered. "Perv." I frown.

He grins, not at all embarrassed about being caught. "Like I said, I'll try to be more of a dick from now on."

"Good start." I turn around and head for my front door.

"Why do you want him back anyway?" Micah shouts after me. "You really don't think you deserve better?"

"I don't want better," I say, walking closer to the car. "I want my life back, with my boyfriend who likes the same things I do. I want the senior year I've been planning for since I started dating Jay. Homecoming. Prom. Soccer championships. Even graduation. Do you know how many times I've imagined all of those things?" I can hear my voice rising in pitch. I need to calm down before I wake one of my parents. "But I never imagined them without Jason. Nothing will be the same without him."

Micah nods slowly. "I know what you're saying. I guess I'm just wondering how we know when to give up and move on."

I shake my head. "Not yet. I'm not ready to quit fighting."

Chapter 21

KNOWLEDGE OF THE ENEMY'S DISPOSITIONS CAN
ONLY BE OBTAINED FROM OTHER MEN.

—SUN TZU, *The Art of War*

I dream the same dream all night. It's the first day of senior year. I'm at my locker when the lights fade and rock music starts to pulse from the intercom speakers. Micah appears in front of me, out of nowhere. He reaches out to touch my hair but it feels all wrong, like an alien has taken over his body. And then I notice he's wearing Jason's soccer uniform. I push him away and he floats backward across the hall. Two girls dressed all in black look up from where they're seated cross-legged on the floor, no doubt copying each other's homework. Ebony and Amber. Neither of them even go to Hazelton High, but you can't argue with a dream. Ebony pulls a plastic-looking gun from her purse and points it at me. I recoil backward against my locker as a teal paintball explodes across my chest. "Matches your streak," Ebony says. She, Amber, and Micah all start to melt into the wall behind them. As they disappear, the lights come back and the music fades. I'm standing in the hallway all alone, covered in paint.

Not real, I tell myself, but the dream starts again. And again. It's on infinite repeat and no matter what I do, I can't find my way out of the loop.

Until my phone chimes with a message.

I sit up, relieved to be in my room, relieved not to be covered in teal paint. The previous night plays in my head like a song. The concert. The swirly blue lights. The almost irresistible urge to throw myself at Micah.

And then the dream.

Rubbing the sleep from my eyes, I check my phone to see who saved me. Bianca—of course.

Her: Did you survive the night?
Me: Yeah.
Her: Yeah? That's all you have to say?

I pause, then type out:

Have you ever liked someone who was totally wrong for you?

My thumb hovers over the CANCEL button. I reread the text a few times and finally press SEND. I need Bee's help. Even if she's never felt attracted to someone completely crazy, she'll be able to help me make sense of it all.

Her: What do you mean?

I start texting her back and then cancel the message and call her instead. "It's Micah," I blurt out, as soon as she picks up. "I can't stop thinking about him. I even dreamed about him. It's freaking me out."

"Oh," she says. "That's . . . surprising. You want to go for a run and talk about it?"

"Yes." Perfect. Between Bianca's cool head and the calming influence of a good, long run, I can get a handle on these runaway feelings before they mess up the whole plan.

We do our usual loop through town and collapse under the oak tree at the park across from my house. "So you actually wanted to kiss him?" Bee's pupils dilate as she waits for my reply.

"Ohmygod." My heart is racing and my face feels hot. I don't know if it's from our run or from thinking about last night. "It was more than wanting. I was, like, possessed. I had to get out of there or I would have attacked him right in the club." I roll over on my side to look at her. "Honestly, I sort of kissed him on the cheek."

"What?" Bee gasps.

"I don't know. He looked sad. It felt like the thing to do. And before you ask: no, I wasn't drunk. I had one beer." I cover my face with my hands for a moment. "What is wrong with me?"

"Well, do you like him?" Bee blots her forehead on her sleeve. She reaches up to catch a leaf that's fluttering in the air above her.

"You mean *like him,* like him?" My bangs are drenched with sweat. I push them back out of my face, feeling the sting of sunscreen as it makes its way into the corner of my eyes. "I guess he's cool and all but I don't really know him." I'm kind of dodging the question. *Do I like him?* When I asked him to be my fake boyfriend that didn't even seem like a possibility.

"So you're just physically attracted to him?"

"I guess so," I say. "Dude, that sounds so bizarro. I'm into athletes, you know? Like Jason and Caleb Waters. Micah is the total opposite of what I always thought I wanted."

"But," Bee prompts after a few seconds of silence.

"Okay, sure, he's funny," I continue. "And he's got great eyes and a nice smile when he busts it out." I exhale deeply. "And he might have said I was cute."

Bee makes a squeaking sound.

I keep talking. "But still. Micah and I have nothing in common. The whole universe would probably spin out of alignment if we started dating for real. I mean, what would we even do together?"

"I can think of one or two things," she teases.

"Stop it, Bianca. I mean what would we do *besides* that?" I see Micah's barely parted lips in my head. The ridge of muscle. The gleam of sweat. "And now I'm thinking about it. Please fix me."

"Maybe it's just a bad-boy thing," she offers. "Didn't he get arrested last year?"

"Yeah. But since when do I have a bad-boy fetish?"

"You're kidding, right? Jason is a bad-boy poster child. Cheats on tests. Skips class whenever he wants as long as it's not soccer season." She pauses. "Gets caught with weed in his locker?"

Okay, so maybe Jason is a little rough around the edges, but it makes him more interesting than someone who follows all the rules. "You think that's all it is?" I ask hopefully. "I'm just attracted to parts of Micah that remind me of Jay?" It's a struggle to wrap my head around the idea of them having *anything* in common.

"Or maybe you're still feeling bad about the breakup and this is a way to feel better about things," Bee says. "Maybe you're lonely and you just want to be with *someone*."

"What? Like that old song? If you can't be with the one you love?"

"Then love the one you're with," she finishes. "They wouldn't write songs about stuff if it wasn't a universal experience." She looks over at me. "Or maybe this is just about winning. What does Micah's ex-girlfriend look like?"

"She gorgeous," I admit. "Stylish. Cool. Some kind of musical virtuoso. She even seemed nice."

"So maybe you don't want Micah, but you don't want her to have him either?"

I cover my face with my hands again. "I am the worst battle partner ever."

Bianca pats me on the shoulder. "Here's the only thing

that matters. Let's say you act on this impulse with Micah and it works out—"

"There's no way." I peek through my fingers as I cut her off. "Can you imagine what everyone at school would say? What Kendall would say?" It sounds lame, like I care what everyone else thinks. But the reality is that *everyone* cares about what *some* people think.

Bee snaps her fingers in my face. "Forget them all for a second. Let's say it would work out. If Jason decided he wanted you back once you were with Micah, would you go back to him?"

It only takes me a few seconds to respond. "Yeah."

Bianca nods to herself. I don't know why I was expecting her disappointed look. Maybe because it seems like I gave the wrong answer. But that's crazy. Why am I lying here feeling bad about potentially blowing off a guy I'm not even dating who doesn't even like me?

"That's what I thought," Bee says. "So don't mess with him just because you're lonely. He deserves better than that."

First Leo. Now Bianca. Everyone is so sure I'm going to steal Micah's heart and then trample it. "You're right." I think of Kendall and her "fan club members," her so-called "slumming phase." "I don't want to use a guy I'm not interested in just to feel better about myself."

"Are you *sure* you still want Jason?" Bianca asks. "Maybe this is your brain's way of telling you there are other guys out there."

"I think this is my brain's way of panicking because our plan isn't working," I say. "I want Jason. No one else fits with me like him."

"Why are you so sure of that?"

"I don't know. Being with him always made me happy. We could talk about anything. Laugh about anything. He always made me feel like I could be me." I look up at the giant tree's leafy branches. A few leaves are starting to morph from bright green to yellowish even though it's only the end of June.

"Really? Isn't he the one who told you to get a tan? That doesn't sound like letting you be you."

I frown. "It's not like he forced me or anything. He just said I looked better with more color."

Bee snorts. "And also with stick-straight hair?"

"Bianca," I say, shocked. "Be fair. Jason never cared about my hair. Kendall was the one who got me started flat-ironing." I pet my sleek ponytail. "And she was right. It looks way better straight."

"It looks fine either way. If anyone needs flat-ironing, it's me."

I shake my head. "No way, I love your monster waves."

Bee looks serious. "All I'm saying is, those things you think you can only get from Jason. Maybe you can get all of them and more from other guys."

I reach out and give her hand a squeeze. "I know you're trying to help," I say. "But my heart wants what it wants, even if it doesn't make sense. Don't give up on me, Bee. I can't do this without you."

"I would never quit on you," she says. "But there's nothing wrong with you deciding to quit, all right?"

I nod. My phone buzzes in the pocket of my running shorts. I slip it out and shield the screen with one hand so I can see who's calling. It's Leo. Sitting up, I dislodge a few blades of grass from my hair before answering. "Hey. What's going on?"

"I've got some information about your pal, Alex," he says. "We should meet up so I can fill you in."

"What? How did you get info about Alex?"

"Didn't Bianca tell you?" he asks.

"Uh . . . no." I turn toward Bee. "Why does Leo have info on Alex?"

She covers her mouth with one hand. "I completely forgot," she says. "He and I were talking Sun Tzu at work and I mentioned how I've been trying to engage in a little espionage for you but Dad's been out of town a lot and my mom keeps asking me to watch Elias and Miguelito all the time. Leo volunteered to do a little spying."

"Oh." I still think it's odd how Leo wants to be part of my "army," but, hey, seize all opportunities, right? "What kind of info?" I ask Leo. "Don't keep me in suspense."

He clears his throat and pauses for emphasis. "Let's just say Jason isn't the only guy Alex is hanging out with."

Pay dirt. Thank you, Dead Chinese Warlord. "Where do you want to meet?"

His voice breaks up for a second and I hear the bleat of a

car horn. "I'm actually heading toward Denali right now. I could meet you there."

"Sure. I can be there in fifteen minutes." I fill Bianca in about what Leo found out.

Her eyes widen. "Jason doesn't strike me as the type who would share," she says. "Let's go. I want to hear the whole story."

Chapter 22

BE SUBTLE! BE SUBTLE! AND USE YOUR SPIES FOR EVERY KIND OF BUSINESS.

—SUN TZU, *The Art of War*

When we arrive at Denali, Leo is sitting at our usual table. Instead of his standard baseball cap, he's got his haired spiked up like he did the night of the play. He's drinking a chocolate shake and skimming through a biography of some old football coach.

"Did you find that book here?" Most of Denali's bookshelf consists of paperback romances with long-haired guys dressed like pirates on the cover. I have a sneaking suspicion they once belonged to my mother.

"Yeah." Looking up, Leo marks his place and closes the cover. "Oh, hey, Bee," he says.

"Hi, Leo." She slides into the chair across from him.

Dropping my purse on an empty seat, I sit next to Bee and look expectantly at Leo. "So let's see what you found out about Alex!"

"Not so loud," he says in a hushed voice. "People might overhear."

Bianca giggles. I'm thinking Leo is taking his warlord role a little too seriously. I make a big show of glancing to my left and my right. On one side, a group of four guys is embroiled in some kind of role-playing card game. Shiny cards featuring elves and dragons are splayed out across their table. On one other side, Monochrome Girl—today in a rainbow of pinks and reds—is bent over her laptop, one hand curled around a skinny chai, one crimson ballet flat tapping to the beat of whatever she's listening to on her headphones. "No one is paying any attention to us," I say. "We're high school kids, remember? No one thinks we're doing anything worthwhile."

"Little do they know," Bee says, leaning in toward Leo.

He pulls out his phone and swipes his finger across the screen. "Okay. I followed Alex from the fire station to some guy's house."

I nod slowly. "Nice. And you got pictures? Did you go all superstalker and peek in her windows or something?"

"I didn't have to." He sips his shake. "I waited around and they both came back out of the house and got in his car. I could tell by the way they were dressed they were heading someplace fancy." He winks. "That's when I went all super-stalker. I followed them to the restaurant."

"You sure she wasn't just eating out with her brother?"

"At Tony's?"

Bee whistles. "*The* Tony's? Downtown? Wow." Tony's is the kind of place where the bill runs triple digits and you have an entire team of trained servers taking care of you.

Leo slides his phone across the table. There's Alex, in all of her flame-haired glory, sitting across from a guy who looks to be in his mid-twenties. Next pic: they're holding hands across a white-linen tablecloth. Next pic: they're kissing.

"I'm hoping that's not her brother," Leo says.

"These are amazing," I say. "I'm sending them to my phone." The hummingbirds start fluttering around in my stomach again as I transfer the pictures one at a time. So the girl who stole my boyfriend has her own boyfriend, eh? Serves Jason right. Maybe once he feels the sweet burn of rejection he'll figure out he walked away from a good thing. But how can I get the information to him without admitting I had her followed? "What do you think I should do with them?"

"Nothing right this second," Leo says. "Don't try to force the issue. Do like Sun Tzu. Wait for the right moment."

"Right," Bianca chimes in, arranging her braid over her left shoulder.

"But what if the right moment never comes?" I check my phone to make sure the files all transferred and then slip it back into my purse.

Leo runs one finger around the rim of his glass. "Then maybe it's not meant to be." He glances from me to Bianca before continuing. "I think that's what I decided about Riley. I'm done trying to win her back."

"What? Why?" I've been looking forward to hanging out with him again. It's not only about the money. Helping him makes me feel good, like I'm doing something important for once. Not to mention, I'd never know how much I liked plays if it weren't for him. My first order of business when school starts will be to switch into Karlsson's Intro to Acting class.

"I don't know. I went to another cast party and we had a good talk. She's not dating anyone right now but she seems really happy on her own." Leo leans back in his chair. "And she's right. We are going to be living in radically different worlds next year."

"We could do another date," I say. "Maybe if she saw you with me again . . ."

"Nah. If the only reason she wants me is because she doesn't want anyone else to have me, then I don't think it's going to last anyway."

"But that's kind of the whole idea of *The Art of War* plan, right?" I drum my fingernails on the table. "Scam someone who quit wanting you into wanting you again for the wrong reasons? That doesn't mean the wrong reasons can't become the right reasons again, does it?"

"I think you're really smart." Bee smiles at Leo. "Sometimes it's easier to fight for the wrong thing than to recognize it's time to let go."

I clear my throat. "Somehow I feel like that's directed at me, Bianca."

She toys with the end of her braid. "Not necessarily," she murmurs. "But I think even you should be open to the possibility that what you want might not be what you need."

"Well, sorry to disappoint you, but I *know* what I need." I yank my ponytail holder out of my hair and let it fall around my shoulders in soft waves. "And I'll miss hanging out with you, Leo, but Bee's right. You're a really smart guy. You'll find someone else."

His voice goes flat. "Thanks."

"No, seriously. Don't downplay it. It's your thing. You have to work with what you got, you know? Don't hide the things that make you unique or you'll end up . . ." I think about the day I walked into work with Bianca and neither Micah nor Leo even registered my presence. "Invisible," I finish.

"Pretty sure you could never be invisible," Leo says. "But you're right too. Trying to be someone else doesn't fool anyone for long."

The wind chimes do their clunking thing and Coach Halstead, the Hazelton girls varsity soccer coach, and his wife wander into the shop.

"Look." Bee angles her head toward our coach. "I'm going to go say hi."

"Be right there." I turn back to Leo as Bianca grabs her purse and scampers across the shop. "We'll still be friends, right? If it weren't for you, I'd still be wishing on planets."

"Of course," Leo says. "My astronomy knowledge is forever at your beck and call."

"I'm giving your money back too," I say. "All of it. I'm sorry I wasn't more help."

"You don't have to." Leo glances around furtively and

lowers his voice. "I've been talking to this new girl, actually. I might not have had the courage to if you hadn't given me that pep talk the night of the play."

My eyes light up. "Awesome. Did you ask her out?"

He holds up his hands. "No, I'm not ready for all that yet. But getting to know her is making things hurt less. Not like she's replacing Riley or anything, but just the idea that there's more than one person out there for each of us."

I nod. It's really similar to what Bee said. Maybe Jason hasn't called because it's not meant to be. I should ask my mom to do one of her tea-leaf readings about it. Not yet though. It's my turn for a fake date. Maybe the second one will turn out better than the first. I'm not ready to accept that things are over.

"Well, let me know if you change your mind." I glance over at Bianca. Coach Halstead has made his way up to the register, and his wife has found them a table near the front window. Bee appears to be explaining some of the menu choices while Ebony waits patiently to take his order. "I'm going to go say hi to them."

Leo gives me a little wave and then goes back to his book. I bound over to the register. "Hey, Coach," I say. "Welcome to the coolest coffee shop in town."

Ebony bites on her tongue ring as she rolls her eyes. "No thanks to you," she mutters under her breath.

As usual, I ignore her.

"Mitchell." Coach smiles. "Staying in shape this summer?"

"You know it." I sling an arm around Bianca's shoulders. "We just got done running in fact."

Coach orders two caffè lattes and a Death-by-Chocolate-Moose brownie. Ebony takes his credit card and swipes it. "Well, keep it up and don't lose focus," he says as we move down the line to the end of the counter. "I've had a few colleges inquiring about both you and Kendall Chase." He flashes Bianca an apologetic look. "There's nothing that says they might not notice you too," he adds kindly.

"No problem," she says. "I'm going for a nerdier academic scholarship. Soccer is just a hobby for me."

"What kind of colleges?" I ask, my curiosity piqued. I shift my weight from one foot to the other.

"Mostly local ones, so far," he says. "But that could change. I expect to see you on a select team for the fall, right?"

"I should be playing for the Archers again."

"Good," Coach says. "They're a solid organization."

Ebony sets a brownie and two steaming eco-mugs on the counter. "Maybe one of you can help him carry those?" she suggests.

"Got it," I say.

Coach grabs the plate with the brownie and one of the lattes and I grab the other one. We head over to the table where his wife is browsing through the latest issue of the *Riverfront Times.* She looks up with a smile as I set the cup gently on the table.

"Erin, you remember Lainey Mitchell, right?" Coach

says. "She's one of my star forwards."

"Of course," his wife says. "Winning goal at state, right?"

I smile so wide that my face actually hurts. It is so awesome to be reminded of that moment right about now. "Nice to see you again," I say. "Let me know if you guys need anything."

"Will do," Coach says. He calls after me as I head back to Bianca and Leo, "I meant what I said, Mitchell. Don't lose focus. Your whole future could be riding on it."

Chapter 23

HE WINS HIS BATTLES BY MAKING NO MISTAKES.
—SUN TZU, *The Art of War*

Coach Halstead's words weigh heavy in my brain for the rest of the afternoon. If it weren't for the breakup with Jason, I'd be playing competitive soccer this summer. Sure, just a recreational league, but better practice than one-on-one with Bianca. Maybe if we get back together, Jason will let me sub in for the remaining games.

Keeping the Alex pictures under wraps is killing me, but I know Leo is right. Sooner or later, an opportunity will present itself. When it does, I'll seize it and fall like a thunderbolt. In the meantime, I'm going on another fake date with Micah, to Beat, Hazelton's only teen dance club.

I peek my head into the study. My mom is tapping away on her laptop. Today, she's got her hair done up into two reddish-brown braids that are graying at the roots.

"Going out, Mom," I say.

She looks up from the screen. Her eyes trace the hemline of my T-shirt dress. "With whom, may I ask?"

"His name is Micah. I know him from work."

My mom smiles. "Ah, that nice mohawked boy your father is afraid of."

I laugh. "Yeah. There's nothing to be scared of, though. I promise."

"Is he the one who took you to the play?"

"No, that was a different guy."

"Different," she murmurs. "Lots of changes this summer. I can barely keep up with who you are anymore."

Me neither, Mom. Me neither.

"I know it can be tough," my mom continues, "splitting with your first love. I remember when the first boy I was intimate with broke up with me—"

Oh. No. No, please. "Wow, look at the time," I say brightly. I ram my fingers in my ears and head for the door but she follows me into the living room. And out the front door.

"I had no idea things could be so much better. I thought he was the only one in the world. But then when your father and I got together, things felt completely different—"

Please God, kill me dead. "Lalalalalalalala," I sing, heading across the dewy front lawn as fast as my strappy sandals will carry me. The last thing I want to hear about is my mom and dad's sex life.

Mom pauses at the end of the sidewalk. "Anyway, I'm not naive. Just be sure you continue to be safe, okay?"

I stop so quickly I almost pitch forward and land facedown on the driveway. "Wait, what do you mean *continue to be safe*? Are you saying you think Jason and I . . ." I can't say it. I cannot say the words "had sex" in front of my mother.

"Lainey. I have a PhD." My mom winks. "You have to be smart to get one of those."

"But if you knew, why haven't you freaked out?"

"The smart thing again," she says. "And I might have found your stash of birth control pills when I was putting away your laundry. You do understand those don't protect against—"

"Yeah. I got it, Mom." Crap. I knew my underwear drawer wasn't a good enough hiding place. Kendall and I went together to a local clinic to get pills at the beginning of tenth grade. I never told my mom because it never occurred to me she'd be okay with me sleeping with Jason.

"I'm *not* okay with it," she says, reading my mind. "I'd prefer you wait until you graduate . . . from college. But you're an adult now, and I know there's nothing I can do that will change your mind. Just be smart, and safe, and know that your mother is here if you want advice from a boring old lady." She clears her throat. "With a PhD."

I surprise both of us by backtracking up the driveway to give her a quick hug. "Don't worry, Mom. Jason is the only guy I've ever, you know, and I don't think that'll be happening anymore. Micah—we're not. Trust me."

My mom exhales a big breath of air. "Oh, good. I'll call the nunnery and see if they'll still take you."

"Funny." I tug on one of her braids. "By the way, I don't think senior citizens are supposed to be rocking pigtails."

Mom slaps my hand away. "Senior citizen? I'm forty-six."

"Fine. Elderly people," I say with a gleam in my eye.

My mom smiles. "One day you'll be old and gray too," she promises.

I shudder as I point my keychain at the Civic and unlock the door. "No way. They're going to perfect that serum that keeps people young before I get old."

"You and your brother are the serum that keeps me young." She reaches out to brush my hair back from my face. "It's good to see you smiling again."

After talking to Bianca, I realize I may have gotten a little too flirty with Micah at The Devil's Doorstep. My plan is to pull back on this date so I don't give him the wrong idea. No more breaking the rules.

He's home alone when I arrive to pick him up. "So where are you taking me?" he asks.

I stand in the living room with him, wondering where Trinity is tonight. "Oh, nowhere special. Just a little place called Beat."

Micah scrunches up his face like he smells something rancid. "This is what I get for being nice," he says. "I hate dance clubs. The music is always complete crap. Can I refuse?"

"Of course you can refuse." I give him my best doe-eyed look. "But I suffered through a whole night of what *you* call music."

He's not buying it. "You ended up *liking* what I call music," he says. "Pretty sure I know I don't like to dance."

"Don't like it? Or don't know how?" I pause, biting back a laugh at the thought of Micah tearing up the dance floor to the newest hip-hop beats. "Look, you don't have to dance with me. Just lean up against the wall and look bored."

"Okay." He nods at me. "Do I have to dress like a douche-bag?"

"You can wear that," I say charitably. He's wearing a pair of jeans with both knees ripped out and a black Hannah in Handcuffs T-shirt that hugs his slender frame. His silver anarchy pendant lies flat against his chest and the barbell through his eyebrow reflects the overhead light. He does have sort of an edgy bad-boy thing going on with the mohawk and eyebrow piercing. Plus I have to be honest, I'm starting to like his hair. Every other guy I know will be working the same part-spiky, part–bed head, all-boy-band look.

"Is what's-his-face going to be there?" Micah unearths a pen from a coffee table cluttered with magazines and scribbles his mom a note.

"I couldn't exactly call him and ask," I say. "But tonight is a full-moon party. Everyone who is *anyone* will be there."

Beat is a square, flat building that somebody decided to build in the abandoned lower parking area of the Hazelton Mall. Micah mutters something about getting epilepsy as we pass through the front door and into the main room of the club. Streaks of colored neon slash across a field of smoke so thick I can barely make out the clusters of gyrating bodies.

On the big screen, a popular hip-hop music video is playing, but somehow the club has jacked up the color scheme so the singer's skin is purple and the sky is green.

We stand right inside the door, watching the disembodied forms of the dancers move rhythmically in the haze. Some of them are dressed up like werewolves. A handful of Hazelton High recent grads push in behind us. The girls giggle as the guys in the group all burst into spontaneous howling. The DJ whistles and flashes a giant full-moon symbol on the ceiling of the club.

"You have got to be kidding me," Micah mutters.

We move out of the doorway, against the near wall. It's cinder-block gray, graffitied with glow-in-the-dark spray paint. The whole club is just a wide-open square with a few card tables in one corner and a bar where you can buy sodas and packaged snacks. The far side of the room has a door that leads out onto a patio. There are a lot of people going in and out, I guess to check out the full moon. Micah waves a hand in front of his face as the smoke machine makes a belching noise and a thick ribbon of haze billows out.

He leans close to me. "You didn't say anything about getting cancer," he yells over the pulsing music. "Pretty sure that smoke is toxic."

"Gee, that'd be a real convincing argument if you didn't spend half of every shift outside the back door puffing on cigarettes."

I expect a snappy retort but to my surprise he smiles, like I've one-upped him and he knows it. I lead him through the smoke and we sit across from each other at one of the card tables.

"Fancy." He wobbles back and forth in his chair to show me the legs are uneven.

"Yeah. They spend all their money on the lights and smoke."

"They definitely don't spend it on the sound system," he says as the recording cuts out and a burst of static pulses through the speakers.

I search the lingering fog and quickly spot Jason in his standard knee-length shorts and backward hat. He's one of the only boys actually dancing. Alex is standing a couple feet from him, wearing a strapless red dress that's so low cut she'll probably flash nipple if she leans over. I suddenly feel completely frumpy in my T-shirt dress.

"Did you find him?" Micah asks. He squints.

"Yeah. And his new girlfriend." I angle my head in their direction. "The one who's about ready to fall out of her dress."

"She looks all right, but I'm not really into girls with huge boobs." Micah furrows his brow in concentration as if he's giving the matter a great deal of thought.

"That's crass," I say. "But sweet in a messed-up kind of way."

"Sorry. It slipped out." He fiddles with his barbed-wire bracelet. "So what's her deal? Does she go to school with us?"

I tell him about Alex being nineteen, and then about

how Leo took pictures of her with some other guy. "What do you think I should do with them?" I ask.

"Not sure how you can get them to him without looking like a crazy stalker chick," Micah says.

"You think I'm a crazy stalker chick?"

"You're using an ancient war manual to try and win back your boyfriend. I think you're a girl who will do whatever it takes to get what she wants," he says. "Hey, at least you're committed."

I turn back to Jason and Alex. The music has speeded up. Alex and her breasts are bouncing up and down and a wardrobe malfunction appears imminent. Maybe it's just me, but after you reach a certain degree of ginormousness, strapless anything seems like a bad idea. "We've got to get closer to them or they're not going to see us. Dance with me for one song." I give Micah my best pleading face.

He points to his ear. "Do they play anything here that doesn't completely suck? I can't dance to this shit, Lainey. I don't even know any of these songs."

Right at that moment, the DJ hollers something about taking it down a notch. A popular slow song starts to play. It's the kind of song that you can hear playing on six different radio stations simultaneously. Micah has to know it. And every guy can slow dance, right? I watch for a second to see if Alex and Jason are going to keep dancing. They do.

"Come on," I beg. "It's perfect. Just stand next to me and move back and forth."

Micah groans, but allows me to lead him out onto the

dance floor. We stay a few feet away from Jay and Alex. I
don't want it to be too obvious. For a second we stand there
in the smoke, unsure of how to join ourselves together. Our
hands bump as we reach for each other. His fingers are
warm. Eventually both his hands end up on my waist, and
mine around his neck.

I keep a small slice of space between our stomachs and
chests, but even still there's no way to really assume this
position without being very close. I end up pressing my
cheek to his temple, mostly so I don't have to look at him. I
angle my nose away so I'm not exhaling directly into his ear.

"Your hair smells good," he says.

Random. He must feel as awkward as I do.

I watch Jason and Alex over Micah's shoulder. There's no
awkwardness there. If they dance any closer, Alex is going
to need a pregnancy test.

"Relax already," Micah says. "Stop staring at them."

"How do you know—"

"I can tell. Your whole body is stiff. It's like I'm dancing
with the Tin Man."

"Oh, so now you're a dancing expert?" I murmur, leaning back slightly.

Micah pulls me in close again. "I didn't say I *couldn't*
dance. I said I don't *like* to."

Jason leans down and starts kissing the side of Alex's
neck. Her hands slide under the back of his T-shirt. This
time even I can feel my muscles turn to metal.

"Tin Man," Micah whispers.

I resist the urge to punch him in the gut. He rotates us
so I can't see Alex and Jason anymore. I close my eyes and
try to feel the music as it moves through me. Gradually the
stiffness fades away and we move closer together. Micah is
so warm. I try to relax my whole body, one muscle group
at a time. I pretend his arms are the only thing keeping
me from collapsing to the floor. My fingertips accidentally
brush against the tail of his mohawk. It's soft, yet spiky. I
reach up and run my other hand through the full length
of his strip of hair, my fingernails gently grazing his scalp.

Micah's steel-toed boot comes down hard on my bare
toes. I yelp and stumble backward, losing my hold on Micah
and bumping into someone else. I'm afraid to even look
behind me, but I do.

I hit Jason. It figures. He turns around, probably to
cuss out whatever klutzy bastard slammed into him, but his
mouth snaps shut in surprise when he sees It's me.

"Hey, Lainey," he says, his eyes flicking back and forth
between me and Micah. "What's going on?"

Chapter 24

THUS ONE WHO IS SKILLFUL AT KEEPING THE
ENEMY ON THE MOVE MAINTAINS DECEITFUL
APPEARANCES, ACCORDING TO WHICH THE ENEMY
WILL ACT.

—SUN TZU, *The Art of War*

I stand there, speechless, thankful at least that the flashing lights and smoke are probably obscuring my blush.

"My fault," Micah says. "I told her I sucked at dancing, but you know women. They don't take no for an answer." He holds out his hand. "I'm Micah."

"Jay." Jason gives Micah his trademark bone-crushing handshake.

I hadn't exactly planned for the two of them to formally meet, and it is every bit as weird as you might imagine. Both of them turn to look at me.

"Right," I fumble. "This is, um, Micah." *Smooth.*

"Yeah, we've covered that," Jason says, his voice going flat. He lifts his baseball cap off his head and runs a hand through his thick, blond hair, replacing the cap at a slightly skewed angle. Very suburban gangsta.

"I'm Alexandra," the EMT formerly known as Alex pipes up.

I had almost forgotten she was there. All three of us turn to face her. She leans toward me and her teeth glow bright white under the club's iridescent lighting. For a second, I think she's going to try to shake my hand. I quickly cross my arms behind my back.

"This is Lainey," Jason says. His eyes meet mine but then he looks away. "She's . . . my sister's friend."

I drop my eyes to the floor. Is that how Jason thinks of me now? As his sister's friend? I'm tempted to say something smart, like how I wasn't his sister's friend when we were hooking up all over his dad's condo a few weeks ago, but that would totally blow my act with Micah so I bite my tongue.

"Nice to meet you," I force out. And then I just stand there, mute, shifting my weight from one leg to the other. Even the Tin Man probably would have had more to say. All I can think about is how Alexandra is different from me. What does she have that I don't? She's a little older, but Jason never expressed an interest in older women. She's shorter than me, definitely curvier, which I know he likes. But were her looks enough to lure him away? Or was it something else, something I can't see?

"Nice running into you—literally." Jason sounds like he means it, but I am still stinging from being called his sister's friend.

"Yeah. Sorry," I say. The song ends and the video screen lights up with a popular hip-hop song from a few years ago.

"Sweet." He spins around and moves his body to the beat. For a white guy, he's got rhythm.

Alexandra grabs him by the hand. "Come on. I love this song," she says.

"Later." Jason lets Alexandra pull him out into the middle of the smoke and lights. He does his spin-around thing again and she goes through a series of dance moves that look like part of a pom-pom-girl routine.

"I think that went well," Micah says.

He's trying to be funny, but I don't laugh. Instead I second-guess my decision not to punch him in the gut. "Yeah. Thanks for making me look like a complete idiot."

My eyes water, but I refuse to cry in front of Micah or Jason. Or Alex. Alexandra. Whatever. I wish Bianca were here. Pushing past him, I fish my phone out of my purse as I head for the front door. Beneath the pulsing beats, I'm pretty sure I hear Micah's combat boots tromping after me.

The night is warm but the rush of air that hits me as I cruise through the doors feels cool after the packed, sweaty club. I form my hair into a ponytail with one hand and fan the back of my neck with the other. Leaning up against the building, I text Bee.

Are you there?

She doesn't respond. Maybe she's working or asleep already. I consider trying Kendall. She's probably awake, but use of her phone is so restricted on *So You Think You*

Can Model there's no chance she'll pick up. I start to put my phone away and then wonder what time it is in Ireland. Pretty sure it's already the next morning there. Maybe my brother is up early. I send him a quick text:

Hey, how's it going?

Steve calls back right way. "Lainey?" His voice is half sleep and half worry.

"Sorry, did I wake you?"

He laughs under his breath. "It's five fifteen in the morning. Yeah, you woke me. What's going on? You okay?"

I slump back against the building. Damn it, I can't do anything right tonight. "Sorry, Steve. I thought the time difference was bigger. I thought maybe you'd be at breakfast." My voice wavers a little. A rogue tear trickles down over my cheek.

"No big deal." He yawns. A moment passes. "Are you crying?"

"Not really. I just saw Jason with his new girlfriend and I'm wondering what's wrong with me." I wipe the tear away, almost like I think my brother can see through the phone. Another one quietly takes its place.

Steve is completely awake now. "There is *nothing* wrong with you," he says firmly. "Forget about Jason. Find a better guy. One who doesn't make you feel like crap."

If only it were that easy. "I'll try." I sniff. "What about you? Did you find a pretty Irish girl to bring home to Mom?"

"Ha! You know she emailed me the other day about my tea leaves. A forked path. A big decision." He chuckles. "That could be the fortune for every single person for every single day of their lives."

"I know, right?" I smile through my tears. "Thanks. You always make me feel better."

"Likewise," Steve says. "Seriously. You're a superstar. Any guy who doesn't see that is too stupid to date you."

They're nice words, but he's my brother. He's not exactly objective. Still, I appreciate the effort.

"Speaking of stars," I say. "Did you know that one we used to wish on was actually Venus?"

"Yeah, I learned that last year in Intro to Astronomy," he says. "Explains why we never got any snow days, huh?"

"How come you didn't tell me?"

"I don't know. I guess it was one of those cool childhood memories I didn't see the point of messing up for you." He yawns again. "You sure you're okay?"

"I'm fine. Get some more sleep. Love you." I hang up and slide my phone back into my purse.

"Hey." I flinch at the sound of Micah's voice. He's standing a few feet away, the mix of shadows and fluorescent parking lot lights distorting his features. "Sorry. I didn't mean to eavesdrop but I didn't want to interrupt your conversation."

Instead of responding, I blot at my eyes with the back of my hand. A rush of emotions tunnels through me as my brain replays what happened inside Beat. Jason. Alexandra.

My sister's friend. Any strength I got from talking to my brother disappears instantly, like a kite snapped from its string and stolen away by the wind.

Micah leans against the wall next to me and pulls out his cigarettes. "Do you mind?"

I shake my head. I can't talk, because if I do I'll cry.

A moth buzzes around his head and he swats it down to the concrete. He flicks his lighter and I stare at the small flame. As he touches it to the tip of his cigarette, the end glows bright orange. Then the lighter flame winks out and something else seems to vanish with it. Jason. Maybe part of me always knew he was gone, but I never let myself believe it.

Until now.

I stare down at the fallen moth. It takes a few tentative steps toward a sidewalk crack, stunned but not injured. I think I'm ready to give up. My brother is right—there's nothing wrong with me. There doesn't seem to be anything wrong with Alexandra either. If Jason likes her better than me, maybe I should let it go. She might be really cool or she might be a dumb bimbo, but either way he's with her now, and not me. Maybe it's all decided, like my mom with her tea leaves. Maybe it's pointless to fight the universe. I try to swallow the sob that is working its way up my throat.

Micah turns away to exhale a puff of smoke. He turns back to me and instantly sees the emotions on my face. "Lainey." He drops his cigarette to the ground and crushes it under his boot.

Tears fall from my eyes. "I think I quit," I whisper. "I think maybe it's over."

"Come here." Micah puts his arms around me and pulls me in close, but I'm so tall in my platform sandals I end up crying mostly into the tips of his mohawk. I try to slouch down but then I'm crying directly onto his pierced eyebrow and that's no good either.

He doesn't seem to mind. He strokes my hair with one hand and pats my back with the other. "We should go," he says. "You don't want people to see you like this."

He doesn't mean people. He means Jason. "I don't care," I choke out. "Let him see what he did to his '*sister's friend.*'" Another storm of tears spews forth.

"You do care," Micah insists. "You care more than anyone I know, even when you shouldn't." He turns me toward the car but my legs are rubber, my feet stuck to the ground. "Hold on to me," he says. Bending down, he loops one arm beneath my knees and picks me up.

I try to tell him to put me down before he gets a hernia or something, but my words get lost in the spot between his chin and his neck. He carries me easily across the parking lot, like I'm made of feathers. The next thing I know, I'm tucked safely inside the passenger seat of the Civic, still crying, and Micah's sitting across from me, the keys dangling from the ignition.

"Do you want music?" He's got his phone out and is swiping at the screen.

"Do you have some kind of crying-girl playlist?" I wipe at

my eyes. "Why aren't you telling me to stop, like every other guy would?"

"Sorry. You didn't come with an owner's manual," he says. "Besides, I'm not big on telling people what to do." He reclines the driver's seat of my car and looks over at me. "Is there anything *I* can do?"

I shake my head. Gradually my tears dry up, my sobs become sniffles. "Things are never going back to the way they were, are they?"

"Maybe not."

"But we're wedding cake people," I say, more to myself than to him.

"What?"

I sniff. "Me and Jason. We're like those little people on top of a wedding cake."

"Made of plastic?" Micah's lips quirk into a smile.

"Quit trying to be funny."

"Sorry." He falls silent.

"You should be. Did you do it on purpose?" I ask. "Run me into him?"

"No," Micah says. "Why would I do that?"

"I don't know. To force the issue, I guess. It's like something Kendall would have done."

He whistles long and low. "I am many things, but I am *not* Kendall Chase."

"So what? You got klutzy all of a sudden?"

"You really want to know?" He glances sideways at me.

My heart thuds against my rib cage. Maybe I *don't* want

to know. No, I do. Knowledge is power. Not sure if I got that from Sun Tzu, but I know he'd be down with the idea. "Yeah. I want to know."

Micah is looking straight ahead again, staring out through the smudgy windshield. "The way you touched my hair. It kind of . . . turned me on."

I make a sharp, bitter sound, part laugh and part bark. "I don't believe you," I say. "You've made it perfectly clear you're not into me. That's the whole reason our little arrangement works." For a second, I consider telling him about the way I felt at The Devil's Doorstep, that some part of me is attracted to him. But no, I've endured enough humiliation for now. I don't need to add more rejection to the night's list of disasters.

Micah doesn't say anything. His fingers tap out an imaginary beat on the Civic's steering wheel. "I never thought of you as my type," he says finally. "But that doesn't mean you're not hot."

My face gets warm, even though I'm sure he's only saying it to make me feel better. "Thanks," I whisper.

"Don't act like you don't know. The whole school thinks you're hot."

It's funny. Kendall always says beauty is mostly a state of mind, that if you act like you're pretty, everyone will believe it. Getting dumped has made me question everything I used to think. Maybe my whole high school existence has been nothing but theatrics.

"I don't feel very hot right now," I admit.

Micah pokes me in the shoulder. "Come on. You got those legs and that smile and that shiny hair."

I bury my face in my hands. As much as I want to hear the things he's saying, I feel like the world's biggest loser. How lame am I that Micah has to take over where my brother left off? It's like I need a full-time personal cheerleader or something.

"Sorry. I sound like such a lame-ass," Micah says.

I peek at him through my fingers. "Why are you being so nice?"

"I guess I'm just a nice guy. Don't tell anyone, okay? It'll wreck my rep."

Letting my hands fall to my lap, I lean across the center console until my head is resting against his shoulder. "Sorry about your hair. I don't know what it is. I've wanted to touch it since that first day at Mizz Creant's." I exhale hard. "And now *I* sound like a lame-ass."

Micah laughs under his breath. "All the ladies love the mohawk." Turning to me, he lowers his chin so the top of his head is in my face. "You can touch it, now that I'm prepared."

"Seriously? Like a pity grope? No thanks," I say drily, trying to ignore the fluttering in my chest.

"Touch it," he whispers. "You know you want to."

"Shut up."

He gives up and leans back in his seat. "My sister cuts it and dyes it for me. She could give you a matching one if you're game. Think of how scary you'd look on the soccer field."

"I'll pass." I rest my head back against seat and look through the windshield again. Beyond the rows of parked cars I can just barely see Venus, low on the horizon, unblinking.

"Are you going to be okay?" Micah asks.

"Yeah, except I wish I could forget this night ever happened." I glance over at him. His hazel eyes glow softly in the dim car. He's been so cool to me. It would be easy, too easy, to let him make me feel better. Suddenly I am dying for any kind of closeness. "Do you want to go get drunk or something?" The words fly out of my mouth before I have time to even think about them.

Micah's lips twitch, and then his mouth curls into a slow grin. "Tsk-tsk, Lainey Mitchell."

"What?" I fiddle with the hem of my T-shirt dress.

"I'm sensing that might involve more rule-breaking." He reaches over and pats my bare leg. "And as fun as that sounds, it's probably a bad idea."

He's right. I started out the evening trying not to be a flirt and here I am offering him . . . I don't even know what. I hear Bianca telling me not to mess with him just because I'm lonely. She's right. Micah's right. Everyone is right, except for me.

His phone buzzes in his pocket. Pulling it out, he glances down at it but doesn't answer. It buzzes again. And again.

"Who is it?" I ask, curious.

"Amber."

"Aren't you going to answer it?" I am eager to salvage

any part of this night, and also to erase that ill-advised "go get drunk" suggestion. I might as well refocus on the plan.

"I can call her back later. You know, deception, not being too aggressive, all that crap. That is what the strategy guide calls for, right?"

"Something like that. Did you get yourself a copy of *The Art of War*?"

"I read it online. His voice softens. "Let's get out of here. You chill. I'll drive."

My voice speaks independently of my brain again. "Can I have a hug?" I cringe at how much I sound like a five-year-old, but you never realize how much you miss little things like hugs until you stop getting them.

He looks over at me. "Now that sounds like a much better idea."

Micah pushes a long piece of my bangs back from my face as I slide halfway onto the gearshift and throw my arms around his neck. This time I don't bother keeping any space between our bodies. I drink in his warmth and the faint tickle of beard stubble against my cheek.

He makes a strangled sound. "Try not to crack any ribs."

As we let go, his barbed-wire bracelet catches on my hair. He stiffens. A strand pulls taut.

"I got it." I reach up and untangle the bracelet from my hair. As I lower Micah's wrist, I can see his third tattoo hiding underneath the bracelet—a hangman's noose.

He catches me staring and adjusts the bracelet to cover most of the tattoo. "That's the logo for my dad's old band,

Hangman's Joke. It was my first tattoo, but teachers kept giving me crap about it, asking if I wanted to hurt myself, did I want to hurt other people, all that bullshit. It was like fifth grade all over again, so now I keep it covered."

Fifth grade. I can still remember what my desk looked like, how someone had carved an *F* in the lower-left corner, how there was a face hiding in the wood grain that reminded me of that painting *The Scream*. Looking down was so much easier than looking at Micah. "I never told you how sorry I was about your dad," I blurt out.

Micah doesn't say anything. He just stares at his wrist.

I think about what it must have been like for him to watch his dad bleed to death on the floor of a convenience store. "I've never really had a reason to be sad," I say. "Never lost anything."

"What about your precious Jason?" Micah snaps his head around to face me.

"That's different," I say. "It's not like Jason died. It's not like I can't ever see him again. Plus losing a boyfriend is not like losing a parent. I know I'm lucky to have both of mine."

He nods slowly. "Yeah. It sucks," he says. "I was the one who asked to stop at the store on the way home. I was . . . thirsty." His voice cracks. "I try not to blame myself, but most of the time I still do."

"Micah. You can't—"

He looks away, toward the side window. "I don't want to talk about it."

"Okay. Tell me about your other tattoos," My fingers

graze the pyramid tattoo on his bicep. There's an eye float-ing above it, like the symbol on the back of a dollar bill.

He pulls up his sleeve so I can see better. "My dad had this same tattoo. His favorite singer used it for an album cover. The guy got diagnosed with schizophrenia after his first big hit and lost everything. He was even homeless for a while, but then his brother helped him get the medicine he needed and he went back to performing." Micah looks down at his arm, the beginnings of a smile on his lips. "Dad always said it was the most inspirational story ever. Used to keep him going when times were tough."

"And this?" I reach out to trace the overlapping circles on the side of his neck.

Micah's smile widens. "It's a trinity."

Duh. "Wow, you guys must be really close."

"That's the one good thing that came from everything, I guess. Trin was only eight years old when Dad died, but she took care of me and my mom when we couldn't take care of ourselves." Micah shakes his head. "The mom. The new 'man of the house.' We were supposed to be the tough ones, but we both kind of lost it. The baby sister had to keep everyone going. We're all so close now. I would die before I let anybody hurt either of them."

The door to the club opens with an abrasive squeak and Jason stumbles outside with Alexandra. As they cross the pavement toward us, they pass through a circle of fluores-cent parking lot light. I notice that she's wearing his hat and he seems to be wearing some of her lipstick.

"Now it's definitely time to go." Micah starts the engine just as Jason and Alex pass in front of us. Jay glances over and I can tell he recognizes the Civic, even if it's too dark to see inside the car. If I had my warrior face on I'd be all over Micah, steaming up the windows, really putting on a show. But it feels like we became friends tonight and I don't want to wreck that by being phony.

I'm done with pretending, at least for now.

Chapter 25

WHEN ENVOYS ARE SENT WITH COMPLIMENTS IN
THEIR MOUTHS, IT IS A SIGN THAT THE ENEMY
WISHES FOR A TRUCE.

— SUN TZU, *The Art of War*

Micah drives my car back to his mom's apartment and shuts off the engine. He leaves the keys in the ignition and we both get out and stand by the driver's side, unsure of how to say good-bye. When you share feelings with someone, or secrets, it adds a layer of complexity to even the simplest things.

"Thanks," I say finally. "For being so cool."

"It's what I do best," he says. Then his smile fades. "Sorry things didn't go better for you."

"It's okay. Maybe it's just not meant to be."

Micah touches his fist to the bottom of my chin. "Chin up. We've still got three more dates if you want. I'm looking forward to seeing what other excruciating events you've got planned for me."

"But you and Amber are talking again."

"Nothing's definite yet," he says. "And I have to play it

cool, right? Isn't that what Sun Tzu would say?"

"Maybe not in those exact words, but yeah."

"Also, we made a deal. Five dates." He shifts his weight from one foot to the other. "You can have all five if you want, no matter what happens with Amber."

"Seriously?" It's awesome that he's willing to honor his side of the bargain, even if he doesn't need me anymore, especially considering the torture I just put him through at Beat. I can't believe he put up with me crying on him since it's obvious he doesn't think Jason is worth crying about. "You are a stand-up guy, you know, for being kind of a freak," I joke, trying to lighten the moment.

He nods slowly. "And you are actually kind of sweet, for being a mean girl."

I smile. Maybe the first real one all night. "Lies. All lies." Just as I'm trying to decide if I should hug him good-bye, his phone buzzes again. "You'd better answer that," I say.

"Yup." Micah starts composing a text to Amber as I slip into the driver's seat. He gives me a wave as I pull away from the curb.

I barely remember driving home. I keep replaying everything that happened in my brain. Jason and Alexandra. My brother. Micah. I'm still thinking about everything a half an hour later when my phone rings.

It's after midnight.

It's Jason calling.

I stare at the display for a few seconds. Am I supposed to answer? Let it go to voice mail and then call back? How many texts and calls from Amber did Micah get before he responded? Dropping my cell onto the bed, I flail in my purse for *The Art of War* for a few minutes before I realize the futility of looking for advice on phone etiquette in a book written, like, a zillion years ago.

The ringing stops.

And then starts again.

Be decisive. I answer. "What's up?" I ask warily. For some reason I'm nervous instead of ecstatic.

"What's up with *you*, Lainey?" Jason asks.

"Nothing." It comes out sounding like a question. I sit cross-legged on my zebra-print comforter. Caleb Waters smiles down at me from the wall behind my bed. I bet Caleb treats girls way better than Jason does. Probably never introduces his ex as "his sister's friend," anyway.

"It was cool to see you at Beat tonight." Jason says. "It's good you're getting out."

"I've never stopped getting out," I say sweetly. "I've just been going different places. Trying some different things."

"Trying some different things, huh?" Jason voice is laced with sarcasm. "Just be careful, okay?"

Be flexible. Be deceptive. I should be flirting or being coy or making it sound like my thing with Micah is serious. But it's like I've been transported back to Denali, to the beginning of summer when Jason dumped me. I feel pissed, so mad that controlling the hurt and anger isn't even a possibility. *Don't have a hasty temper.* No. Screw that. I've been restraining my temper all summer. There's nothing hasty about this. "Your concern is touching, but how careful I am isn't really your business, is it?"

"Am I not allowed to be worried about you?" he asks. "That's the same kid from the baseball game, right? Didn't he get arrested last year?"

"Didn't *you* get arrested two years ago?"

"Yeah, but the charges were dropped." I can practically hear Jason rolling his eyes.

"Oh, so I shouldn't hang out with him because he doesn't have a rich mom who paid to get him off the hook?"

Silence. Touched a nerve.

"Sorry," Jason says finally. "I just don't want to see you get hurt."

I pound a fist into my pillow. "Then you shouldn't have hurt me." Seriously. Where does Jay get off thinking he can kick me to the curb and then pass judgment about the next guy I date?

Fake-date. Whatever.

"I know. I was an asshole. I'm not going to make excuses. I'm sorry. I hope you forgive me eventually."

"Why do you even care if I forgive you, being that I'm just your *sister's friend?*"

"Bad choice of words, huh? I figured it would be more awkward for you if I told her you were my ex-girlfriend." Jason exhales deeply. "I didn't mean to offend you. I get it if you hate me." He pauses. "But I miss you."

I flop down on my bed and stare up at the ceiling. "You *miss* me? What does that even mean, Jay?"

"It means I want to see you. My soccer team is down a girl this weekend. Come fill in for us."

Now he wants me to be on his team? A few weeks ago, I was looking forward to a whole summer of soccer and fun and hanging out as a couple, but he didn't want me around. And the moment I finally think I'm starting to get over him, he invites me to come play? Tears push against my eyelids. "I'll think about it," I say quickly.

"Saturday. Eleven a.m. Forest Park."

"Maybe. I might have to work." I don't, but he doesn't know that. Maybe I'll pick up an extra shift. There's a first time for everything.

"You'll be there," Jason says, his voice suddenly brightening. "I know you can't resist a soccer game."

"Maybe," I repeat. "Bye." I hang up the phone and toss it onto the other side of my bed. It takes me a few minutes to process what just happened. Jason called. He definitely seemed jealous, even if he pretended it was all about being protective. And then he totally hit me in my weak spot. Even though I'm mad at him, I'm dying to play soccer. Suddenly I feel like I'm at the bottom of the mountain again.

Of course, I *could* skip the game, but I'm not supposed to prolong this battle. I'm supposed to be seizing opportunities as they arise. *"If the enemy leaves a door open, you must rush in,'"* I mutter.

I flounce down at my desk, log on to the internet, and find the webpage for the Forest Park coed league. Jay's team—the Red Flyers—has three wins and three losses. I scan the roster. I recognize a few names from the Hazelton boys team and one girl who plays varsity. The other girls listed are strangers, but none of them are Alexandra.

Jason plays forward with Dan Spencer and Jaime Martinez, who is probably more effective in the backfield. The Red Flyers could definitely use another strong player on the front line. I'm going to go. I log off the web and close my laptop. Resting my head on my arms, I try to make sense of everything—of why Jay called, why I was more hurt and angry than ecstatic, why I really want to play soccer with him this weekend. Across my room, I catch sight of my jewelry box perched on the top shelf of my dresser.

I go to it and undo the tiny golden clasp. The soccer ball pendant sits on a bed of red velvet. I pick it up, my fingers tightening around the cold chain. Closing my eyes, I relive that entire night—the party, the way Jason sneaked me into his bedroom, the way he touched me so gently. The way how when I started to get anxious about losing my virginity, he made some stupid joke about how sex was like us running a tricky formation together. We both laughed at that and then everything seemed like less of a big deal.

"What happened?" I whisper, my fingers still wrapped about the chain.

And then my phone rings again. It's Kendall.

I drop the necklace back onto the velvet. "Hey," I say, swallowing back a rush of emotion. "Aren't you up way past your official TV-star curfew?"

She ignores my question. "My brother said you replaced

him with a whack job." Each word is a cube of ice clinking into a glass. "Were you going to mention that to me at any particular point in time?"

And here we go. "Micah's not a whack job," I say. "And he's not a replacement."

"I see." Kendall is quiet for a moment. "Because, and I'm quoting, Jason said you were slow dancing with some loser with a mohawk. He said you two were all over each other."

"We were *not* all over each other," I insist. "And who cares if I hang out with a guy who has a mohawk. It's just a style."

"More like a lack of style."

I don't answer for a second. It's the exact same thing I said about Ebony's baldness a few weeks ago. I'm wondering whether I got the phrase from Kendall or she got it from me. I have a sneaking suspicion that I'm the copycat.

"Whatever, Kendall," I say. "We're just friends, okay?"

"What about the non-mohawked guy posting pictures of you two on the internet? Also just *friends*?"

She must be talking about the picture Leo took the night of the play. But how did she see it? I'm pretty sure she's not allowed to get online until after the taping of *So You Think You Can Model* finishes up.

"Yeah. A guy I work with."

"Lainey, you're not going Slutsville on me, are you? I get it if Jason bailing on you made you crazy, but promise me you won't get knocked up by some loser, okay?"

This is actually as close to worrying about someone as

Kendall gets. She's gone a whole three minutes without mentioning herself. I can even sense an undercurrent of concern beneath her crass words.

"I promise," I say.

"Good, because there is no way the student body is going to elect me president if my VP is preggo."

So much for concerned. I should have known. Only Kendall could make my breakup more about her than me. She has all these senior-year plans for us. Cocaptains of the soccer team. President and VP of the student government. It all sounds like a lot of work, but she likes to be in charge of things, on and off the field. I know she's learning it all from her mom, but Kendall's utter self-centeredness is really starting to get on my nerves.

"Well, I'm not planning on getting knocked up," I say tersely. "But you could always ask someone else to be your VP if you're so worried."

"You don't mean that."

Actually, I might. "Did you find out what the story is with Jason and his EMT friend? Alexandra?" It's a bit of a struggle to say her name.

"He didn't really say much about her, except that it's nothing serious." She pauses. "He totally wants you back, Lainey."

"He said that?"

"More or less. He's just afraid you're going to blow him off for Mohawk Boy so he's using soccer to get close to you."

It is a total Jason move to try and fix everything with

soccer. "We'll see how Saturday goes," I say warily.

"What should I tell him in the meantime?" Kendall asks.

According to Sun Tzu, the best spies are the ones located inside the enemy camp. "Tell Jason I'm really into this new guy. That he makes me realize Jay was all wrong for me. Tell him I refused to give you the dirt on how serious things are between us."

"Ick." She makes a gagging sound. "You're asking me to lie to my brother?"

"Is lying a problem for you these days?" I ask. "If Jason thinks I'm really getting over him, it'll push him to make a bold move, or at least decide for sure what he wants."

"Good point," Kendall says. "You'll have him back in no time. There's nothing more intoxicating to Jason than a girl who doesn't want him."

Chapter 26

IF EQUALLY MATCHED, WE CAN OFFER BATTLE.
—SUN TZU, *The Art of War*

The next day at work, I end up right behind Micah at the time clock. I fill him in on the conversations with Jason and Kendall.

"Sounds like last night worked out better than you thought," he says. "I've got to work at the Humane Society on Saturday morning, but afterward I can be a proper fake boyfriend and come watch you play." The time clock beeps and he slides out of the way for me.

"Perfect. What about Amber?" I ask, punching in my ID number.

"Definitely not going to come watch you play." Micah tucks his hands in the pockets of his baggy cook pants and waits for me.

"Ha-ha. How'd it go after I left?"

"Okay, I think." We head toward the back together. "We texted for an hour. She wants to meet up someplace soon to talk."

I leave Micah among the cutting boards and condiments

and toss my purse in my locker. As I'm heading back to the front, I pause and watch him wipe down the salad station.

"That's a good sign, right?" I peek up toward the register. Bianca is manning the front alone, but there's no line. She can hang for a few while Micah and I trade info.

"I'm not getting my hopes up." He yanks a paper towel from the dispenser above the sink and starts writing himself a to-do list on it. Caribou Cookies. Banana bread. Pizza dough.

"Why not?"

He shrugs. "I've been thinking that when people break up there's usually a reason, and whatever it is, it's still going to be there even if we do get back together." He grabs a pair of warped, silver sheet pans and lays them out on the counter.

"You're having second thoughts?" I can hardly believe it. "Dude, you sound like Leo."

Micah grabs a deep silver bowl from beneath the electric mixer. "Yeah? Well, Leo is one of the smartest people I know."

"But you've been pining away for her. And now she wants to meet up and you're having doubts?" For a split second it occurs to me I had these same thoughts about Jason. But I didn't, not really. I was just mad at him. Amber didn't dump Micah in public. She didn't blow him off for some other guy. He's not angry with her. His situation is totally different.

Micah disappears into the walk-in cooler without answering. He comes back with a carton of eggs and a stick of butter.

"Are you just afraid you'll mess it up again?" I persist.

He stops unwrapping the butter long enough to give me a hard look. "Maybe," he says. "Or maybe I only miss the *idea* of her—"

Footsteps approach from the front. Micah and I both turn toward the sound. Bianca slides around the corner into the prep area with a magazine in her hand. She skids to a stop when she sees us. "Sorry, am I interrupting?"

"No," Micah and I say simultaneously.

Bee's eyes widen. "Wow, you two are becoming the same person."

I frown. "Highly unlikely."

"Yeah, I find that insulting," Micah adds.

Bee holds the magazine out in my direction. "I was just wondering if you saw this interview with Caleb Waters. My mom subscribes to *Hollywood Insider*."

"Lame," Micah mutters under his breath. He tosses a stick of butter into the mixing bowl and flips it on low speed.

"Whatever." Grabbing the magazine, I scan the article and accompanying pictures. There's nothing here that I haven't already seen online.

Micah adds two cups of sugar to the mixer and then disappears into the walk-in cooler again.

"I'm going to grab some gum out of my purse and then I'll be back up front, okay?" Bianca heads toward the lockers.

"I'm going up there right now." Tucking the magazine under my arm, I head out to the front.

Bee joins me a few minutes later. "So what's Micah's problem?"

I shrug. "Too much angry music, probably." I grab Bee's hands and spin her around in a circle. "Guess what. Things might be finally coming together in the old war on Jason." I give her a condensed version of the disaster at Beat, and then my phone calls from Jay and Kendall last night.

"He talked to you and immediately called his sister for more information? That sounds highly promising."

"Micah is going to come to the game on Saturday," I say. "You should come too. Maybe you can sub in with me." I have no idea how many players Jason has on his team, but I'm going to be nervous and it would help to have Bianca there with me, even if she only ends up watching from the stands.

"I can't. I'm going hiking with my family that day."

"Can you cancel?" I ask. "Come on. Wouldn't you rather play soccer?"

"Not this time. We're going out to Elephant Rocks State Park and my mom has been looking forward to this trip forever." She toys with the end of her braid. "You don't need me anyway. It sounds like you and Micah have things all figured out."

I reach out and give her braid a friendly tug. "I always need you, Bee."

Chapter 27

LET YOUR PLANS BE DARK AND IMPENETRABLE
AS NIGHT, AND WHEN YOU MOVE, FALL LIKE A
THUNDERBOLT.

—SUN TZU, *The Art of War*

When Saturday morning rolls around, I spend a ridiculous amount of time getting ready for the game at Forest Park. Jason texted me and said to wear black shorts and that he'd give me a shirt when I get there. You'd think it'd be easy then—cleats, shin guards, socks, sports bra, ponytail, done.

I don all of these items and check myself out in the mirror. I sigh. I might as well be a boy. It's hard for me to look hot playing soccer. I trade the ponytail for a pair of fish-bone braids, pinning my bangs back with bobby pins so they won't flap in my eyes and distract me. My Jersey-shaped blotch of freckles stands out like some old lady's liver spots. I dot a bit of concealer over the mark and then line my eyes with brown pencil. It's going to have to be good enough. There's only so much makeup I can get away with wearing before it'll be obvious to everyone that I'm trying to look good for Jason. *Be deceptive,* I tell myself. Today has to be all about soccer.

Forest Park is home to the zoo, several museums, a lake, tennis courts, and lots of sports fields and picnic pavilions. I turn into the main entrance and wind my way past Art Hill, where kids from nearby Washington University go to play guitars, sunbathe, and snuggle together on blankets.

A siren shrills from behind me. Pulling over, I watch a bright red ambulance roar past. It's probably on the way to the big city hospital just outside of the park where Bianca's mom works.

The soccer fields are located around the corner from the tennis courts. As I pull up, there's a huddle of players in red on the near side of the field and a sprinkling of players in yellow on the other side.

Jason stands in the middle of the red players, towering over most of them, his sandy-blond hair blowing in the wind. I check the stands for Alexandra, but she's nowhere to be found. Slowly I approach the team, looking for anyone familiar. Dan Spencer is there, and Matt Clifton from the Hazelton boys team. And there's Jaime Martinez, another varsity starter. But no one I would call a friend, and at least ten people who are complete strangers. I wish Micah were here now instead of showing up later after his community service. I'm kind of used to having him around during my "battles."

Jason sees me crossing the field and breaks free of the

huddle. "I knew you'd come." He strides up to me, a red shirt balled in his hand. "Here."

I take the jersey. It's a number 5—the number I've worn since freshman year. The shirt is new. He either just had it made or ordered it for me at the beginning of the summer and never let anyone use it. "Jay." I look up at him. "Any old T-shirt would have worked."

"I've been saving that for you." His face is perfectly neutral but there's a softness in his voice I haven't heard in a while.

"Thank you." I slip the jersey over my tank. It fits perfectly. It feels right. All of this feels very right. "I don't know what to say."

He angles his head toward the opposing team. "Say you're going to help kick these guys' asses."

We both turn around to check out the Yellow Jackets. There are only fourteen players and six are girls. They're down on the ground doing sit-ups with varying degrees of success.

"Look at all the chicks. We should be able to beat them blindfolded," I joke.

"Yeah. Girls can't play soccer," Jason says. "They ought to be at home baking bread and doing woman things."

I grin. "You're such an asshole."

"I know." He holds out his hand for a high five. I go to slap it, but he grabs my fingers and squeezes them as he pulls me in close. "I'm glad you came."

And just like that, any doubts I had melt away. Everything

I love about Jason is amplified on the soccer field. At school he might be a class clown or a troublemaker, but when he puts on his uniform, he becomes the kind of guy that everyone is in awe of. His walk, the fit of his jersey, the way he doesn't stop fighting until the last whistle is blown—it all says "champion." It's the way I want people to think of me when I play.

It occurs to me that he's waiting for a response. "Yeah. Me too," I mumble. *Real smooth, Lainey.* It's like Jason's proximity has transported me back in time. Good-bye, Dead Chinese Warlord. Hello, Tongue-tied Freshman.

He claps me on the shoulder. "Come on. Let's figure out where you're going to play."

Jason drags me back to the huddle and announces that I'll be starting as striker with him. An Indian kid I don't know looks less than thrilled at this, but agrees to switch from striker to winger forward. One of the winger forwards switches to left halfback, which is apparently the spot that's actually needing to be filled today. There are only three girls here, including me. League rules require at least two girls on the field at all time. It's going to be a tiring game, but I'm up for it.

We split into lines and run some practice formations against our goalie. Doing drills with Jason reminds me of how perfect we are together. We've played together so long we know exactly how to anticipate each other's moves. I know how far to lead him on a pass. He can adjust for how fast I run, for the length of my stride.

The referees show up and both teams head for the side-lines. The Yellow Jackets now have twenty players. That's more than we have. I notice they're wearing real jerseys, not flimsy T-shirts with numbers printed on them. They seem much tougher than they did when Jason and I were joking around. The hummingbirds take flight in my gut, but it's a good kind of nervousness.

I channel it. It will make me run faster, kick harder.

It will make me invincible—for the next hour anyway.

When the refs call for captains, Jason and I break away from the team for the coin toss. The Yellow Jackets send two girls to midfield.

"You call it," Jason says.

"Me? Really?" Jay has never let me call a coin toss before.

"Yeah, you really." He looks me up and down. My heart flip-flops in my chest. I can't believe *The Art of War* plan suddenly seems to be working. I can't believe I might come from behind and pull off a victory.

I call heads. We win the toss.

The refs look expectantly at Jason, but again he defers to me. "What do you think? Ball or direction?"

"We'll take the ball first," I say. It's an aggressive strat-egy. Usually Coach Halstead wants to give away the ball so we can start with it in the second half, but I'm ready to attack.

The rest of the team take their places. Jason and I stand together at midfield, waiting for the ref to blow the whistle. He grins at me. "This is where you belong," he says.

He's right. I'm just glad he finally realized it.

The whistle sounds. I pass the ball to Jay. He passes it out wide to Jaime Martinez and I take off running down the field.

The next fifteen minutes are a blur of shouting and colors, the sound of my heart pounding and my breath exhaling hard into their air. Twice I end up on the ground when a Yellow Jacket tries to steal the ball. The second time I am awarded a free kick. Running as fast as I can, I launch the ball toward the goal. Jason races up the field. He dodges a defender. His left foot connects with the ball and it rockets into the back of the net. 1–0.

I scream and run toward him to celebrate. Everyone is patting him on the back. He picks me up and spins me in a circle. I squeal with laughter.

"Put me down." I flail my arms and pretend to be struggling.

"Not until you say we make a good team."

I touch the dimple in his left cheek. "I've always thought that."

But then I see our crowd of onlookers in the stands behind Jason. Alexandra isn't there, but it's easy to pick out Micah in his black-on-black outfit. He's sitting all alone. I lift one hand in a greeting and he waves back.

Jason puts me down.

A girl with a dark brown ponytail comes in to relieve me. I grab my water bottle and take a seat on the bench, blotting my sweat with the back of my hand. My left knee is dirty and skinned from where I fell. I pour some water over it and wince. Spots of blood bloom like tiny flowers in the torn flesh.

"Hey." Micah is winding his way through the sparse crowd that is spread out on the bleachers. He hops down to the grass. I meet him at the edge of the bench, my water bottle still clutched in my hand. "Nice kick," he says.

"Thanks." My smile feels almost big enough to split my face in two. "But Jason did the hard work."

Micah rubs at the scar on his temple. "That was some celebration you two had. Let me guess. The old 'We make a good team' line?"

"How did you know?"

He glances at the field. It's almost halftime, and Jason hasn't taken a single break. As we watch, he steals the ball from a girl in yellow, dribbles down the field, and launches a rocket at the upper-left corner of the net. The Yellow Jacket goalie just barely gets a hand on it, blocking it back over the crossbar. Jason looks over at the bench before he jogs out to take the corner kick.

"Maybe he's using the same playbook," Micah says.

"Jay's not the type to read ancient Chinese literature," I say. "Or any literature. Besides, we *do* make a good team, on the field at least. I almost forgot how good."

But is that enough? Five minutes ago I was thrilled at the thought of diving back into Jason's arms, but now Micah is here warning me and his words make sense. And there's something else. Getting back together with Jay would mean not hanging out with Micah anymore, and that thought makes me . . . sad.

"Just don't let him beat you at your own game, okay? I'd keep playing it cool. Keep the upper hand."

"Right." I hold my hand out and Micah gives me a high five. "It's better to be the one at the top of the mountain," I murmur.

At least I think it is.

I sub back into the game a few minutes later and stay through the end of the half. It's still 1–0. The Yellow Jackets tie it up on a breakaway goal in the second half. At this point, I'm running from one end of the field to the other, playing more defense than any striker forward ought to be playing. I can't help it. It feels so good to be in the game.

Matt Clifton saves a shot on goal and drop-kicks the ball in my direction. I dribble up the field, outmaneuvering two of the other team's defenders. I pass the ball to Jason who sends it across to our right wing forward. The defense kicks the ball out of bounds and we get a corner kick. Jason goes to take it. I position myself in front of the goal, dancing back and forth as I vie for position with one of the Yellow Jacket fullbacks.

It's a beautiful kick—high and strong, and it's coming right at me. The other players, the shouting, the movement, they all fade into the background as I keep my eyes locked on the ball. Angling my body just slightly, I propel all five feet and eight inches of myself into the air at exactly the right moment—I think, I hope—and the crown of my head connects squarely with the ball. The players around me all turn to watch as it arcs through the air, just missing the tips of the goalie's right glove before landing in the back of the net.

The Yellow Jackets deflate as I shriek with joy, their chins dropping low, some of them giving their goalie a disgusted look. The Red Flyers run toward me as a group. I get bombarded with hugs and high fives.

Jason is all hands and chest and sandy-blond hair as he picks me up and spins me in a circle again. "You are a champion," he says. "You're going to be our MVP for that header."

"I couldn't have done it without your perfect kick," I say. "That was even better than Kendall."

"Heh." Jason's eyes gleam. "Don't let her hear you say that."

We head back to the midfield circle where the other team's strikers are ready to put the ball in play. Frustrated, they seem to have abandoned strategy in favor of just kicking the ball toward our goal as hard and often as possible. Our midfielders and defenders easily intercept the ball repeatedly, sending it back toward the Yellow Jacket goal in smooth, calculated attacks. It makes me think of *The Art of War*, and I can totally see how sports teams could use the book to develop strategy.

When the final whistle blows, I am so giddy I turn an impromptu cartwheel on the midfield line. I glance over toward the stands. Micah gives me a thumbs-up. The Red

Flyers line up to slap hands with the Yellow Jackets and say "good game." Some of the players sound like they mean it more than the others. Afterward Jason stops to talk to a couple of the guys about next week's game. I turn back toward the stands where Micah is waiting for me.

I jog over to him, grinning like an idiot. I am sweaty and dirty and slightly bloody, but I don't care. Almost nothing feels better than playing my heart out and winning a soccer game. We stand face-to-face, eye-to-eye.

"Nice job," he says. "You didn't tell me how good you were."

"You think I'm good?" Okay, whatever, I know I'm good, but it still feels awesome to have other people verify it.

"Well, I don't know jack about soccer, but you looked good to me." Micah tugs on one of my braids. "These are cute, by the way."

"Thanks." I blush. "Sorry if it was boring for you."

He steps closer to me, so close we're almost touching. "It wasn't boring for me at all." Gently he pushes my braids back over my shoulders. His hands feel warm, even on my flushed skin. His fingertips linger on my jawbone.

"Micah?" I say.

"Wait." He's not looking at me. He's focused on something over my shoulder, something off in the distance.

"What are you looking at?" I start to turn.

His hands drop to my waist. I can feel his individual fingertips through the thin fabric of my jersey. A tremor moves through me. "Don't turn around," he says. His lips quirk into a smile. With no warning at all he leans in and kisses me. Quick and light, like a leaf falling from a tree. But definitely a kiss.

On the lips.

It happens so fast I don't even have time to close my eyes. The ground wobbles beneath my feet and I can feel the blood rushing to my face. I reach out for his arm to steady myself.

And then—perhaps because I didn't punch him—he kisses me again, just a tiny bit longer, and this time I do close my eyes. It's like going down one of those big twisty slides—a little bit of fear, a little bit of dizziness, over way too quickly. When we break apart, my lips still pulse with Micah's heat. I resist the urge to lift a hand to my mouth. Thankfully I am already red from all of the running.

"Um. Whoa." I have been reduced to single syllables.

"Sorry," he murmurs. "I think maybe this is your 'fall like a thunderbolt' moment. My turn to break the rules."

Chapter 28

"So I'll talk to you later," Micah says loudly.

"Wait. What?" My brain is still short circuiting. Around me, time is moving forward but I'm living thirty seconds in the past. Micah kissed me. On the lips.

Twice!

He lets go of my waist. "Now you can turn," he whispers.

"Huh?" I'm still fixating. Lips. Pulsing. Heat. The sun reflects a zillion colors of green and gold and brown in Micah's eyes.

He cocks his head to the side and gives me a long look. "Damn, girl. If I didn't know better, I'd say you enjoyed that." He pats my cheek with one hand and then starts walking toward the street. "Talk to you soon."

I watch him slide into the Beast and fire up the engine. I turn around and look blindly for the Civic. Jason is just a few yards away from me, making a big project of putting the soccer balls and water cooler in his trunk of his Mustang. He must have been watching us. That's what Micah saw. *That's* why he kissed me.

Relief surges through me, mingled with fondness for Micah. He's definitely going all-out to help me win back Jason. Not that kissing me should be torture or anything, but for a second it felt like more than just part of our plan. I shake the idea from my head but I can still feel the blush blooming in my cheeks.

I pass Jason on the way to my car and give him a half wave. "Thanks for inviting me to play, I had fun."

"Thanks to you we'll probably make the play-offs." He shuts his trunk and leans against the back of it. "The whole team wants to know why you're only an alternate. I had to tell them how stupid I was."

I pause. This could be enjoyable. "How stupid were you again?"

"So stupid I pushed away one of the only good things that's ever happened to me." Jason says it lightly, like he's teasing, but I can sense the feeling behind it.

"Jay, I—"

Our eyes lock, and just like that, the moment passes. "Forget it, Lainey." His face brightens. "I think we'll probably have an open spot in two weeks if you want to fill in again."

"Yeah," I say. "I'd like that."

"Cool. Talk to you soon." He lifts himself over the side of his convertible without even bothering to open the door. He revs the engine. Rap music blares from the speakers. Sliding on his sunglasses, he pulls away from the curb.

"Wait," I shout. "What about your shirt?" I slip the jersey over my head and make like I'm going to toss it at him.

Jason puts his Mustang in PARK right in the middle of the road. He hops out of the car and walks over to where I'm standing on the sidewalk.

I hold the shirt out toward him. "What are you doing, crazy? You're going to get a ticket."

"Nah." He takes the shirt from my hands and lets the folds fall out. Stepping close to me, so close that I can smell the mix of sweat and aftershave, he slides the jersey back over my head, slowly working each of my arms through the sleeves.

"What are you doing?" I repeat, this time slower, my voice trailing off at the end. My heart pounds violently. All I can think about is the feel of Jason's hands on me, the pressure of his fingers on my back and arms. My breath catches in my throat.

"Something I should have done a while ago." He leans back and nods at his handiwork. "This is your jersey, Lainey." His hands linger for a moment on my waist. "It's always been yours." Without another word, he spins on his heel and heads back to his car.

All I can do is watch him leave.

The next day at work, Micah doesn't mention the game, or his blatant violation of our no-kissing rule. I still can't believe he kissed me! My brain is playing a strange game of tug-of-war. Micah's lips. Jay's hands. Micah's lips. Jay's hands. I'm a complete mess.

I'm hanging out in the prep kitchen since there's no one at the counter. I focus on Micah's to-do list as if I know the first thing about prepping quiche or mixing bread dough.

"You know that band from The Devil's Doorstep you pretended not to like but secretly liked a lot?" he asks. "The show I made you leave early because I was being a big lame-ass?"

Bottlegrate. They were pretty good, I guess. I don't really remember much about that night besides fantasizing about kissing him. "Um . . . maybe?"

He pinches the edges of his quiche crust and then begins to ladle filling into the center. "They're doing a show on Tuesday night, part of Fair St. Louis, this stage right in front of the Arch. You want to go?"

Fair St. Louis is the city's big Fourth of July celebration. Half the metro area usually turns up. When I was little, I used to watch the fireworks on TV with my family. The last couple of years I've spent Fourth of July with Jason.

I can't believe the summer is almost half over.

"What about Amber?" I ask.

Micah slides the quiche into the oven. Then he consults his list and pulls a mixing bowl out from beneath the long, silver prep table. "Arachne's Revenge isn't going to be there."

"No, I mean, why don't you ask her to go?" I glance up at

the front counter. No customers.

"Amber is probably already going with some friends. And she already agreed to get together next week. I need to take it slow or I'll just scare her off again, right? No stupid haste? Don't attack from an inferior position? The art of this or that?"

Right. "So is this one of our dates? Are we going to try to find her and her friends? Because I'm thinking that might be tough in the crowd of eleventy million people."

The shine fades from Micah's eyes. "I don't care if we count it or not. I just wanted to make up for being a idiot that night." I sense him shutting down, wishing he'd never brought it up.

I wish he'd never brought it up either. I've been telling Bianca and Leo that they're wrong, that there's nothing going on with me and Micah, that he doesn't like me like that.

But then why is he asking me to hang out? And why do I want to go? *Why did he kiss me?* No, no, no, that was just part of the plan. My "fall like a thunderbolt" moment, like he said. Still, I can see it only too clearly, the two of us kicking back on the handwoven Guatemalan blanket floating around in the trunk of my brother's car. The sun would go down and the stars would come out. Then wind would blow off the Mississippi. I'd get shivery. Micah would sit close to me. I'd zero in on those barely parted lips as he sang along with the music. Later there'd be fireworks, real ones and . . .

You can't have them both, Lainey. I'm scared about messing stuff up with Jason so I'm trying to secure a backup. Micah is not a consolation prize. He deserves someone who is crazy about him—someone like Amber. "I can't," I say. "I think I'm busy."

His mouth forms into a hard line. "Another soccer game?"

"No." My voice falters. "I have this thing."

Shit. So not smooth.

He looks at me hard. "Right," he says, his voice heavy with sarcasm. "A thing."

Cal wanders out of the manager's office and heads toward the back hallway, no doubt on the way to smoke his eleventh cigarette of the day. "I have a thing too," he says, grabbing his crotch.

"You're disgusting," I say.

"That's not what you said last night."

I make a face. "You wish."

Cal laughs, but he doesn't deny it. After he's gone, I shudder. "I bet that beard is a violation of county health codes."

Micah twitches. "I don't think he's shaved in the two years I've known him. He's probably got endangered species living in there." He pauses. "Or at least half a sandwich stashed for later."

"Ew." I smile.

Micah grins back at me. He touches my teal streak. Some of the hairs have broken off and others are beginning to look a bit straggly from being repeatedly washed and flat-ironed. "You should have my sister redo this."

"Good idea." Suddenly hanging out with Micah doesn't seem like that big of a deal. Now that he's talking to Amber again and I'm talking to Jay, it isn't like we can't stay friends. "You know what? I changed my mind," I say. "I haven't been downtown for the fair in a couple of years. I want to go with you."

"But what about your thing?" Micah asks with mock seriousness. "I wouldn't want you to fall behind on your thingage."

"It can wait," I say. So what if Micah said I was hot and I also find him a teensy bit attractive? That doesn't mean we can't control ourselves. He also said I wasn't his type. Amber is better for him. I know this. Just like I know that Jason is better for me. Everything is working out perfectly. As long as Micah and I stick to the plan, what could really go wrong?

Well, for one, I could get a zit. It's after lunch on Fourth of July when I notice a red bump forming on my forehead. It's probably from all the exfoliating I've been doing to try to fade my giant freckle tumor.

I head into the living room and sit cross-legged on the sofa. I flip through our limited selection of basic cable channels, my disgust growing with each click of the remote. *Click.* Reality TV about housewives that spend too much money and get drunk all the time. *Click.* An episode of *Happy Cheetah.* I hover there for a few minutes until the channel cuts to a commercial. *Click.* An '80s movie with some frizzy-haired guy as the lead that my mom probably still thinks is hot. Boring. I rub the zit on my forehead again. It feels like it's doubled in size.

"Don't pick," my mom says, floating into the room with a handful of mail. She drops the latest issue of *Celebrity Tattler* magazine on my lap. "I don't know why you waste your time reading this junk."

"You read tea leaves," I say. "You don't get to judge."

"Ooh, that reminds me. Have you found any new love yet?"

I totally forgot about Mom's tea-leaf reading from last week. She *is* usually right about these things. If Jason and I got back together, would that count as new love? I'm thinking yes, but I don't want to jinx things. I hold up the *Tattler*. There's a special promo for *Flyboys* on the cover. "I didn't tell you about me and Caleb Waters?"

"He is dreamy," she says. "When you two get married, can your father and I live in the servants' cottage?"

Dreamy. My mom is so old it's hilarious. "Um, no," I say with fake disdain, "because then where will the servants live?"

"Speaking of servants," Mom says with a sparkle in her eyes, "I'm sure your father could find something for you to do around the shop. You look a little bored."

"Extra work? On a holiday? Thanks, Mom, but I'll never be that bored," I say. Right on cue my phone buzzes.

It's Jason.

Chapter 29

DO NOT REPEAT THE TACTICS WHICH HAVE
GAINED YOU ONE VICTORY, BUT LET YOUR
METHODS BE REGULATED BY THE INFINITE
VARIETY OF CIRCUMSTANCES.

—SUN TZU, *The Art of War*

I slip into my room with the phone. "What's up?"

"What's up?" Jason asks incredulously. "It's Fourth of July—that's what's up. What are you doing tonight?"

I flop down on my zebra-print comforter. "I'm going to the fair."

"Downtown? It's too hot for that. I have a better idea."

"What's that?" I ask.

"A pool party. Why sweat your ass off with two million strangers when you can kick back in the Chase pool?"

"I don't know. I—"

"Come on, Lainey. Mom is out of town. The house is all mine. You love my parties."

I used to anyway. Back when they all ended with me and Jason in bed together. Watching him drool all over Alexandra might not be quite as fun. But she wasn't at the soccer game, so maybe she won't be there. Still, my first instinct is to blow him off. Then I think about *The Art of War* again, about seizing opportunities and rushing forth like flood-water and how no one benefits from prolonged warfare. Drawing things out just makes everyone tired. And weak.

I hate feeling weak.

"You can bring that Micah guy if you want." Jason pauses. "Not going to lie, though. I'm hoping you don't."

Micah. I'm technically supposed to go to the Bottlegrate concert with him tonight. But if I'm going to get back together with Jason, this party would be the place to do it. He'll be drinking. I can wear something sexy. He just saw another guy kiss me. It will capitalize on all of his weak-nesses. And who knows what happened for him to invite me to a party? Maybe he and Alexandra are fighting. I shouldn't let that opportunity pass me by.

"I'll try and stop by," I hedge.

"Whatever. Cancel your plans and get your ass over here around eight," Jason says. "Because I know you love sur-prises and I have a surprise for you."

Okay, so now I'm dying of curiosity. Jason was never the kind of boyfriend who surprised me. Sure, he bought me presents, but he always let me pick out stuff so he didn't have to risk disappointing me. I can't think of a single thing he ever surprised me with. Well, except for our breakup.

"I'll try to make it, but no promises." I smile to myself. Let him wonder.

"Okay. See you later, I hope."

I hang up with Jason and bury my face in my pillow. "What now?" I mumble. I need help. I call Bianca. As usual, she picks up right away.

"What are you doing today?" I ask.

"I'm at a church picnic," she says. "They've got thirty different types of chili here. You should come check it out."

"No way. That makes me sweaty just thinking about it." I pause. "Hey, I need to ask you a question." I tell her about sort of having plans with both Jason and Micah. "What should I do?"

"Well, it's simple. Who would you rather spend Fourth of July with?"

I think about Fair St. Louis and the Bottlegrate concert: Stars. Music. Fireworks. Micah. Then I think about Jason's party: the chance to finally achieve what I've been after for the past month.

"The fact that it's taking you this long to answer is interesting," Bee says. "Did something happen with you and Micah?"

I blush. "He sort of kissed me at the soccer game," I say. "But not seriously. It was part of the plan, you know? He was just trying to help me make Jason jealous."

Silence.

"Bianca? I'm sorry I didn't tell you, but you were gone all weekend with your family and—"

"No. It's fine. I'm just processing," she says. "Was this unserious kiss so amazing that you're having second thoughts about Jason?"

"No," I say quickly. "I mean, it was nice, but just kind of a quick peck." Okay, two. Whatever.

"So then what are you thinking?"

I let it all spill out. "I feel like I should go to Jason's," I say. "Jay and I make sense. Micah and Amber make sense. This is what we've been working toward all summer. Why screw it up now?"

"Because you and Micah like each other." She continues before I can protest. "If he kissed you, he *likes* you. And I can tell you like him back. So why are you trying to avoid him?"

"I'm not trying to avoid him," I whine. "But if I go to the concert, something will happen. Things will change and I'm not sure I'm ready for that. I kind of like what Micah and I have right now. I don't want to mess it up."

"Hang on." Bianca says something to her mom and then comes back on the line. "I have to go, but I'm working tonight so I'll be around to hear about whatever it is you decide." She pauses. "But consider this: what you and Micah have right now is *fake*. One way or another, you're going to have to give it up eventually."

She's right. I don't want her to be, but she is. And I still don't know what to do. I know what I'm getting into with Jason. I feel like there's a chance it could work. Micah—no, that just feels unreal and impossible, like trying to be someone I'm not. What if I'm just sabotaging myself? What if I go with Micah and then wish I'd gone to Jason's party? I don't want to be that girl. I don't want to mess things up with him and Amber either.

Maybe I should ask Micah what he thinks. I send him a quick text explaining that Jay just invited me to a party. I don't tell him I spent the last ten minutes obsessing about what to do. If he seems pissed about me bailing on him, then I'll go to the concert. If he doesn't seem to care, I'll go to Jason's.

Micah calls me a few minutes later. "Nice work, Warrior Girl," he says.

"So you won't be mad if I go? I don't want to cancel on you at the last minute."

"No worries, Lainey. It's a free concert. I'm sure I'll run into some people I know. Maybe I'll do like you suggested—give Amber a call and see if I can meet up with her."

It's exactly what I was hoping he'd say. "You are the best, you know it?"

"I hear that a lot." He laughs lightly. "You'd do the same thing for me."

He's right. I would understand if he bailed on me for Amber. I mean that's the whole basis for our relationship.

Friendship. Agreement. *Not* relationship.

I hang up the phone and start going through my closet in search of the sexiest thing I own. Near the very back, I find a killer sundress I bought a year ago on a sale rack and never wore. It's turquoise, one of my best colors. The bottom is trimmed in feathers and the shoulders split into spaghetti straps that weave a crisscross pattern across my upper back. It's totally to die for.

Totally to die for. I can almost hear Micah mocking me.

Smiling to myself, I jump in the shower and start shaving and exfoliating and deep conditioning everything. Tonight, I have to be perfect. Everything has to be perfect.

He wins his battles by making no mistakes.

The hummingbirds start sparring in my stomach as I jump in the Civic and cruise over to the Chases' two-story Italian villa. Cars line both sides of the street. A clothesline weighted down with paper lanterns hangs across the front of the screened-in sunroom, and the lawn is brimming with jocks, preppies, honor students—everyone who is anyone at Hazelton High. I pass a handful of guys from the soccer team who are reclining on the grass, passing around a flask.

Jaime Martinez holds it out in my direction. "'What's up, Superstar?" he asks. "You playing in our game next week?"

"Maybe," I say, heading inside. My eyes scan the crowd for Alexandra's flaming-red hair. I don't *think* Jason would have invited me if she was going to be here, but you never know. One glimpse of her boobaliciousness and I'm out of here.

I nod to a few people as I make my way through the cavernous living room. I notice that Jason didn't bother to pack away any of his mom's prized sculptures. Her collection of Asian-inspired pottery and white marble angels are arranged on a series of built-in shelves next to the fireplace. All that crap will be broken or stolen by sunrise, I'm sure of it.

A girl named Tamara from the JV soccer team grabs my arm as I head into the dining room. "If you're looking for Jason, he's out by the pool."

"Thanks."

Tamara keeps talking but I'm done listening. I squeeze past four guys from the football team playing some kind of drinking game with dice and cards and head toward the back of the house, through the kitchen, and out onto the deck.

For a second I just stand there, looking down at the chaos. The in-ground pool is lighted from beneath. The surface glimmers, casting distorted reflections of the three couples hanging out in the water. One of the girls is in danger of losing her bikini top, but she doesn't seem to care. A pair of sophomore boys sit on lounges nearby, probably hoping for a show. Beer bottles and plastic cups bob in the deep end.

Other couples are snuggling on chaise lounges. Jay's pal Dan Spencer is sitting with his feet dangling into the water, chugging straight from a bottle of Jack Daniels. As I watch, he bends over and spits on the lawn. He belches, wipes his mouth, and takes another slug of the whiskey. The bottle falls from his hand and spills out onto the concrete surrounding the pool. A girl sitting on the nearest lounge wrinkles her nose and moves to a chair on the other side of the backyard. I can't tear my eyes away from the puddle of liquor. In a few minutes, it'll probably start running into the deep end.

I've been to tons of Chase parties in the past couple years, but I don't remember them being like this. I don't remember them much at all, to be honest. Maybe it's just because I haven't had anything to drink, but as I look down at my classmates, it's like I'm viewing my life through a magnifying glass. Suddenly I can see everything, and it skeeves me out to the point where I almost leave. Is this what I wanted for my epic summer? Hanging out with my friends, all drunk and oblivious? What am I even doing here?

But then I see Jason, sprawled out on a lounge at the far end of the pool. I think of him picking me up after I scored my goal, of the soft pressure of his hands as he put the soccer jersey back on me. I'm too close to everything I want to turn back now. I adjust the straps of my dress and smooth the feathered skirt before making my way to the stairs leading down onto the lawn. As I get closer, I see he's talking to the person on the lounge next to him. They have their heads together, laughing. It's a girl, but it isn't Alexandra.

Chapter 30

FORCE HIM TO REVEAL HIMSELF, SO AS TO FIND
OUT HIS VULNERABLE SPOTS.

—SUN TZU, *The Art of War*

"Ohmygod, Kendall!" Flying down the wooden steps, I hurry across the yard and launch myself toward her with open arms. "When did you get home?"

She embraces me lightly. "Laineykins, I missed you so much."

Jason smiles lazily from the next lounge. "I see you found your surprise," he says. "I'll be back. I'm going to go turn Dan on his side so he doesn't choke to death on his own puke."

"Nasty." Kendall waves her brother away and then turns back to me. "I haven't been home for too long," she says, maddeningly vague. "I took your advice and quit."

"But why?" I ask. "I figured you'd want to stay there as long as possible just to avoid your parents."

"Those people were worse than my parents. They had a million rules. It was like model boot camp, I swear." Kendall makes a gagging sound. "And my mom will be in Chicago for the next few days. It'll be almost time to go to Costa Rica by the time she's back."

I gave up on going to Costa Rica once Leo stopped pursuing Riley. I pretty much knew I was never going to save enough money. No big deal, though. Things are looking up with Jason, even without a deserted beach. "But what about the prize money?"

"I wasn't going to win," Kendall says. "The producers hated me. I'll figure out something." She tosses her hair. "I always do."

Her formerly long-flowing locks have been razored into a shaggy bob. It looks good—very high fashion. "I like your hair," I say, reaching out to touch it.

She snickers. "Speaking of hair." She captures my teal streak in between her thumb and first finger and runs her hand down the length of it. "Have you been playing dress-up?"

"A friend did it for me," I murmur. Leave it to Kendall to make fun of anything different.

Jason walks back up. He hands me a cup of beer and plunks down next to me on the lounge.

"I just remembered something I have to go do," Kendall says with a wink.

"If it's Dan, you'd better hurry," Jason says. "He's about to pass out."

Kendall gives her brother the finger and then sashays off toward the other end of the pool.

"Nice dress," Jay says. His eyes rove over my entire body,

lingering on my long, bare legs peeking out beneath my feathered skirt. He's looking at me the way he used to, and I find that both exciting and terrifying.

"Thanks." I set the beer down next to my lounge. I need to keep my emotions under control, and getting all wasted isn't going to help with that. I channel my inner warlord. *Exploit your enemy's weaknesses.* I slide my skirt up ever so slightly, letting another inch of tan skin peek out. "Where's your girlfriend from Beat?" I ask. "The redhead?"

"Who knows?" Jason shrugs. "She's not my girlfriend. She's just a girl." His big hands start to fiddle with my overlapping spaghetti straps, pulling them down one at a time over my shoulder.

His touch feels new and familiar at the same time. *She's just a girl.* What does that even mean? They broke up? They're not exclusive? I want to ask, but I don't want to ruin the moment. I tell myself it doesn't matter what happened to her. All that matters is that I'm here and she's not. Jason finishes pulling down the straps on my left side and moves to the ones on my right.

"Stop," I say.

"Why?"

"People are staring at us."

I scan the area around the pool. Partially Topless Girl is now completely topless and the sophomore boys are snapping pictures with their phones. I should go over there and tell them to knock it off, but the damage is unfortunately already done. She is seriously going to regret drinking tomorrow. The rest of the partygoers outside are paired up on lounges or passed out. Pretty sure no one is even *looking* at Jay or me.

"You're just saying that so I'll take you upstairs," Jason says.

"Uh-uh," I say. *Very convincing, Lainey.*

"Yuh-huh," he says back. He smiles. A real one, with dimples. He slides one more of my spaghetti straps off my shoulder. "Hey. I've got a great idea. You want to go upstairs?"

I hesitate. Everything still feels a little off, but it's probably because I'm the only one who's sober. Or maybe because I haven't been alone with Jason in over a month. I'm just nervous. *Seize opportunities. Seize opportunities. Seize opportunities.* It's weird. I wouldn't have imagined I would need to psych myself up for this moment. It's about as opportune as it can get.

Jason takes my silence as a yes. "Drink your drink. I'm going to fish a couple beer bottles out of the pool and tell those guys to stop taking pictures of that drunk chick. Be right back."

Ignoring the beer, I watch Jason make rounds and clean up for a few minutes. Then I get up from the lounge. By now, the sophomore boys have scattered and the pool is empty. Jay motions to me. He leads me into the house, through the crush of tangled bodies, some dancing, some standing around, some smoking.

We wind our way up the spiral staircase and then down

the long hallway that leads to his room. I feel almost like I'm watching the scene unfold from outside my body. My fingers are interlocked with his as he pulls me toward a moment that's going to change everything. We are ten steps away. Five steps. I can't decide. But then I do. I should turn back. I should leave.

But the girl behind Jason keeps walking.

The door opens with a squeak. His room is dark except for a hazy circle of light cast by a halogen lamp in the corner, but I can see plenty. There's the same queen-sized bed, the same broken frame supported by a couple of old school books that Jason was probably supposed to turn in years ago. The collection of soccer trophies still sits on the upper shelves of his dresser, coated in a layer of dust. Baseball caps hang on a wooden coatrack he made in woodshop, only he has more hats than hooks so the caps are layered two or three deep, some of them having fallen to the floor below.

Dusty trophies. Baseball hats. These are things I would normally not notice, but for some reason I can't tear my eyes away from Jay's fitted Cardinals cap, from the stitches that are coming loose on the left side of the logo.

I remember him fiddling with those stitches a few months ago. Last semester: time of the state championships, the Hazelton Forest commercial. Last semester was perfect and it's all preserved right here. There's even a picture of us from prom still wedged in the frame of his dresser mirror.

Jason presses me up against the wall and kisses me. "I

thought you would never forgive me," he mumbles into my hair.

His breath reeks of alcohol, but his kisses do all the same things they have always done to me. Tremors. Warmth. My eyes fall shut. I reach out with my mind and try to grab hold of last semester.

He tugs on my teal streak. "You really are trying to become a different person this summer, aren't you?"

My eyes flick back open. I don't bother telling him it's fake. Let him sweat it. "I like my streak," I say. "It fits me."

"No it doesn't." Jason grins at me—another dimpled smile. "People don't change, Lainey. You are who you are. We both are."

I slide out from between him and the wall. "Maybe I'm just now figuring out who I am."

"Yeah, right." Jason sits on the edge of his bed and pats the spot next to him. I sit. The dim light reveals his blood-shot eyes. I wonder if he will remember any of this when he wakes up tomorrow. He leans in to kiss me again, and once more I reach out desperately for the past. I go through memory after memory, looking for reassurance that nothing has changed, but it's like flipping through a book of stories I've outgrown.

Everything has changed.

Micah's face flashes before me. His lips on mine. I push him away, into the darkness. There's not enough room in my head right now for anyone but Jason and me.

Jay lays me back on the bed. His hands stroke the fabric

of my dress as his beard stubble scrapes across my face, almost abrasive enough to draw blood. I clench my jaw. He pulls back, lifts up, looks down at me. The lamp back-lights the curl of his hair, his broad shoulders. Everything that meant so much to me now feels like nothing but outlines and shadows.

"What?" he asks.

"What happened to Alexandra?" What I really mean is: *what happened to us?* I roll out from under him so we're lying side by side.

Jay looks over at me, brushes a lock of hair back from my face. "Nothing happened to her."

"Do you know she was seeing someone else?" I ask. "I saw her not too long ago with this guy at a restaurant." Almost the truth.

Jason sighs. "I think she was seeing lots of guys. Who cares? We were never really together."

So much for the use of spies. So much for the right moment. "She's just some girl that you screwed for sport?"

"Basically," he admits. "We started talking during one of my first ride-alongs about how she and her boyfriend had broken up because he wanted to get engaged and she wasn't ready. She said she needed more time to play and have fun."

"How fortunate for her that you came along," I say bitterly.

He sits up. "I hate that I hurt you, Lainey. I thought about my parents having kids so young and my mom being a royal bitch to my dad and it all made sense, you know?

Keeping things casual." He runs a hand through his hair. "I got scared and I messed up. I guess I just needed to escape from my life."

I push myself up off the bed and pace back and forth. "Oh, like a little vacation." I rake my fingers through the feathers of my skirt. One of them flutters to the thick carpet. "I didn't realize being with me was such a job."

"You know, a lot of guys would have just cheated on you," he says. "Don't I at least get points for not doing that?"

My eyes turn to slits. "You dumped me at my parents' coffee shop, in front of everyone. No, you don't get points."

Jason sighs again. "You're right. I'm an ass. I felt like if I didn't end it, it was only a matter of time before I *would* cheat on you. I didn't want to be that guy so I just snapped. I was selfish. I was stupid. But I'm trying to tell you I'm sorry. I want you back."

Like the rest of the Chase clan, Jason isn't used to apologizing. I know this is hard from him, that he wouldn't be saying all of this to me if he didn't really care about me. But it pisses me off that he thinks he can just invite me to a party and I'll come running back to him. "What about the next time you need a vacation? What then?"

"There won't be a next time, I promise."

"How can you promise something like that?" I whisper.

"Because look at us. I got scared and pushed you away and we ended up right where we started. We belong together. Could it be more obvious?"

We belong together. For so long I believed those words.

All I wanted was to hear that Jason felt the same way. And now he's saying all the right things but he's acting like the randomness of the universe reunited us. No. Not true. I waged a freaking ancient Chinese war to get him back.

And it worked.

And I *should* feel vindicated. Triumphant.

But I don't.

Because something is different.

Something is missing.

"Why?" I ask. "Why do you think we belong together?"

Jason's lips quirk into a smile. He thinks he's got me. He has no idea that I am empty, a hollow girl in feathers, preparing to fly away.

"You know." His grin deepens. "We're both hot. We're both cool. The whole soccer thing—we hang with the same crowd of peeps." He winks. "We have *chemistry.*"

"Seriously? That's enough for you? Isn't that a little . . . shallow?"

"It is what it is," he says. "So we're shallow. So what? It's not like I'm only into your looks. You're fun to be around. I want to spend senior year with you. You and my sister. The three of us could get up to all kinds of craziness."

"Yeah, "I say. "I wanted that too. But now I want more."

"What? Like a promise ring?" Jason's shoulders slump slightly as he realizes that I'm pulling away. "We're too young for that shit."

I shake my head. "It's not about rings or promises. It's about . . . something that actually matters."

"I don't get it." He rubs his eyes.

"I know you don't. And that's why I can't do this right now." I bend down and give him a kiss on the cheek. "I'm going to take off."

His jaw tightens. "Fine. Go think about it if you have to. You'll be back. I know you will."

That's probably the exact same thing his mom said to him when he moved out of this house. Here's hoping they're both wrong.

Wordlessly, I head for the bedroom door. I hurry back downstairs even though I know Jason is not going to come after me. Chases do not follow or beg. Excessive pride is coded into their DNA.

The party is still in full swing. I twist my way between the hordes of sweaty, dancing bodies. Someone knocks into me from behind, spilling what feels like half a beer down the back of me. Super. The perfect end to a perfect night. I think I hear Kendall calling my name as I make it to the front door, but I don't turn back. The night wind streams my hair out behind me as I head down the block to where I parked. I slide into the car, punch the door lock, and sit there for a few moments, waiting for tears that never fall.

Chapter 31

ENERGY MAY BE LIKENED TO THE BENDING OF A
CROSSBOW; DECISION, TO THE RELEASING OF A
TRIGGER.

—SUN TZU, *The Art of War*

I need to talk to someone, and that someone is Bianca. I peel into the Denali parking lot, practically bringing the car up onto two wheels as I turn the corner.

As I hurry across the pavement, I adjust the overlapping straps on my shoulders, trying to cover up my bra. Plunging through the front door, I expect to see Bee's kind eyes looking back at me from behind the counter.

But it's Ebony.

"Nice dress, Lainey." She rolls her tongue ring across her lower lip. "How are things on the corner?"

"Where's Bee?" I ask, skipping past a snarky comment about how I almost didn't recognize Ebony without her ass glued to her usual booth.

"She called in."

There's some kind of Tibetan chanting playing over the loudspeakers instead of the usual pop music. That means my dad is here. Crap. I didn't even see his car in the parking lot. I need to leave before he smells the beer soaking into the back of my dress and grounds me for a million years.

Too late. He appears from the prep area, probably because he heard my voice. I step back a couple of feet and do another quick rearrangement of my straps and hem, trying to make sure everything is covered. Two teal feathers fall to the hardwood floor.

Leaning on the counter, he peers at me over the tops of his glasses. "Post-traumatic dress disorder?"

"Funny, Dad," I say. "What's wrong with Bianca?"

"Not sure. She's sick. She said something about maybe eating some bad chili."

"Oh." I back slowly toward the door. "I just wanted to talk to her. I guess I'll catch up with her tomorrow."

My dad slips his glasses off and polishes them on his shirt. "Did you go to the fireworks?"

"Nah. I went to a party at Kendall's."

"Ah," he says, slipping his glasses back on. "So she's back in town? Well, I guess I'll see you tomorrow if you're asleep before I get home."

"Yeah, she's back. Sure, Dad."

I escape into the warm air and make it halfway across the dusty parking lot before I notice the Beast parked next to my car. What's Micah doing here? He's supposed to be at the Bottlegrate concert.

Instead, he's leaning up against my car smoking a cigarette. "Back from Jason's already?" he asks. "It's not even eleven. Must have been a lame party."

"Sort of lame." I point at his lit cigarette. "Thought you were going to quit."

"Still trying," he says. "Maybe by the end of summer. I'll put it out if you want."

"It's okay." A warm breeze cuts across the parking lot, ruffling the feathers of my skirt. "How was the concert?"

"Awesome." He inhales deeply and exhales over his shoulder.

"And the fireworks?"

"Very cool."

"Did you end up meeting Amber?" I'm not sure I want to know, but it would be weird not to ask.

"Yeah, we ended up going together," he says.

"So then why are you here?"

He blows another cloud of smoke away from me. "Because it's the only place around where I can get decent food this late?" He gestures toward the front door with his head. "You hungry?"

I'm about as far from hungry as a person can get. "No thanks. I was looking for Bee, but apparently she called in sick, so   "

Micah's eyes go dark with worry. "Is she okay?"

"Food poisoning, but it doesn't sound serious." One of my hairs sticks to my lip gloss. I can feel it tickling my mouth as I talk.

Micah dislodges the offending hair with a quick swipe of his index finger, and then looks me over slowly.

"What are you staring at?" I try not to fidget. The wind tugs another feather loose from my skirt. At this rate I'll be half naked by the time I get home.

"Are *you* okay?" he asks.

I cross my arms over my chest. "Yeah, why?"

"Well, for one, you reek of booze. Are you sure you should be driving?"

I feel the back of my dress. It's still damp. "Some idiot spilled a beer on me. I haven't had a sip all night."

"Interesting." Micah rubs at the scar on his temple. Behind him, a flash of gold punctures the dark sky, followed by a sharp popping sound. Fireworks. He turns around to look. "What else happened?"

"What do you mean?" Another burst of light—this one colored. Someone who lives nearby must be putting on quite a show for their neighborhood.

"You seem upset."

"Upset how?" I watch the falling embers of the fireworks dissolve into the night.

"Upset like maybe you discovered that the soccer guy you worship is actually a robot designed by the people who create boy bands." Micah takes another long drag off his cigarette.

What I mean to say is "I'm fine," but what comes out is "Jason and I are over."

Micah coughs hard, expelling little swirls of smoke from his mouth. "Why?"

I think about Jay and his lame reasons for us being

together and how everything I thought I wanted suddenly seemed irrelevant. How do things like that just change? My face scorches hot when I imagine how the night might have gone if I'd decided to drink or if Jason had been a little more persuasive. "You know what? It doesn't even matter. I'm pretty sure I'm not supposed to be with him anyway."

A tiny fleck of glowing ash falls from the tip of Micah's cigarette. The wind pulls it in an arc through the air, like a miniature shooting star. "Got someone else in mind?" he asks.

This simple, but not-so-simple question terrifies me. I know what it means, I think. But I'm not ready. I don't want to get hurt again. I don't want to hurt Micah either. It's hopeless. Me and him—we can't. We just can't.

"Lainey? Are you in there?" He waves a hand in front of my face.

"Sorry."

"No, I kind of like this new, quieter you." He's using that low voice again.

"I think I need a break from dating," I blurt out. I turn to unlock the car door with a click. I definitely need this conversation to be over.

Micah doesn't get the hint. He stays right where he is, effectively blocking me from leaving. "Oh yeah?"

"Yeah. It's been kind of a crazy summer." I jingle the car keys in my hand and he slides out of the way so I can open my door. He takes another puff off his cigarette, watching me as I slide into the driver's seat and fasten my seat belt.

He taps on the window and I roll it partially down.

"What's up?" I ask.

"Sorry it didn't work out with Jason. At the soccer game, it seemed like things were going your way." Micah's mohawk twists in the breeze, individual spikes of hair blowing forward into his face. He drops his cigarette to the ground and grinds it forcefully into the asphalt parking lot. His eyes meet mine, just for a second, and then he looks away. "Of course, sometimes it seems like that and then you find out it's all bullshit you made up in your head."

He bends down to pick up his cigarette butt and I put the car in PARK. I roll the window down the rest of the way. "Hey. You're not mad at me, are you?"

"Nope. I'm thinking you're probably right. We have had a crazy summer. Maybe you're not the only one who needs a break from dating."

Another burst of fireworks explodes across the dark sky, back-lighting Micah's frame as he turns and walks away.

Chapter 32

WHEN THE ENEMY IS CLOSE AT HAND AND
REMAINS QUIET, HE IS RELYING ON THE NATURAL
STRENGTH OF HIS POSITION.

— SUN TZU, *The Art of War*

I'm dying to tell Bianca what happened at Jason's party,
but she calls in sick again the next day so I'll have to
wait until later to fill her in. Leo apparently picked up
her shift and it's just the two of us out front—him on the
register and me making drinks.

I catch up on orders and then lean against the counter.
"Did you ask that girl out yet?"

"Shhh." Leo looks around nervously. "You're the only
one who knows about that."

"You told me but didn't tell Micah? Why?"

"I don't know." He wipes down the cash register with a
damp towel. "I'm waiting to see if anything is going to come
of it."

"Probably nothing is going to come of it if you don't ever
talk to her," I say.

"You guys telling secrets?" Micah passes by with a tray

of Caribou Cookies. I feel my lips curving upward at the sight of him.

"Lainey's giving me a pep talk," Leo says. "I think she'd make a good cheerleader."

"Thanks, Leo." I tap the brim of his cap so it covers his eyes.

"That's not really a compliment," Micah informs me with a grin. He seems to be in a better mood than he was last night.

"Dude. Those cookies smell amazing." My stomach growls.

Micah snaps the nearest cookie in half. "Oh, look, I broke one. Can't sell that." He offers the two pieces to Leo and me and then turns back to shut the pastry case.

"Micah, you are seriously the best." I turn to Leo as I nibble on the frosted cookie. "I'm going to take a quick break if you're cool up here for a couple minutes. I want to check on Bianca."

"Sure," Leo says. "Tell her I hope she's feeling better."

I follow Micah to the back where he returns to his prep list. Loitering in the doorway to the manager's office, I finish eating my Caribou Cookie and then slide out my phone to call Bee.

She answers on the first ring. "Hey. How's everything going?"

"Fine. I just wanted to see how you were doing. Everyone here says they hope you feel better."

"I do. Might become a vegetarian though." She sounds

cheery, but weak. "How are things? What'd you end up doing last night?"

"I went to Jason's." I watch Micah's knife blade fly as he slices mushrooms for the pizza station. "I'll fill you in on everything later." I lower my voice. "When I can speak freely."

"Sounds intriguing," Bee says. "I look forward to it. Tell everyone I said hi and that I'm sorry for leaving them short-handed."

Even when she's sick, she feels guilty about missing work. Sainthood. "Okay. We'll talk soon." I hang up the phone and head back to the register.

Leo gets off work an hour before my shift is over. "Hey," I say as he heads for the front door. "Hang on for a minute. I've got your money in my purse."

Micah glances up from the smoothie station where he's cooking himself up some kind of blueberry-chocolate concoction. He's always doing weird mixes of stuff. The other day I caught him blending pineapple and chili powder. He drank the whole thing without gagging too.

"It's all good," Leo says over the whir of the blender. "We had a deal."

I shake my head. "I wouldn't feel right. I shouldn't have let you pay me in the first place." I head to the back and grab the stack of twenties out of my purse. I count the money to make sure it's all there as I return to the front counter. "Here." I toss Leo the wad of bills.

Leo shoves the money in his pocket. "Cool. Thanks. I've got to get to my other job. See you guys." He waves and then disappears out into the sun. Through the window, I watch him cross the parking lot.

Micah finishes blending and gives me a long look.

"What?" I ask.

He shakes his head, topping his grayish-brown smoothie with a dollop of whipped cream. "I didn't say anything."

My phone buzzes in my pocket. I swipe at the screen. Kendall. No thanks. The phone buzzes again. And again. I pick it up and hit IGNORE. She calls back. Relentless. I swear.

"I can watch the counter if you want to get that," Micah says.

I sigh and walk toward the front door where he won't be able to hear every word I say. "What?" I snap into the phone.

"What happened last night? Jason said you guys got in a fight and then you ran off."

"I did not run off." I lower my voice and cup my free hand around my phone. "We started to hook up but then it felt weird so I left."

"Weird how?"

"I don't know. It just did."

She scoffs. "Probably because it's been a while for you two. He seems pissed. I'm not sure if he's going to give you another chance."

"I don't think I want one," I say coolly. I can't believe I used to think Kendall was so smart. In a way, I'm glad she left town this summer. It gave me the space to think, to fig-ure out what was important to me.

She changes the subject abruptly. "Come out tonight," she says. "Let's go dancing."

The door swings inward and a pair of girls in plaid skirts and St. Martin's windbreakers enter. One of them has a thick braid like Bianca.

"Where? Beat?" I watch the girls ponder the menu on the wall.

"Sure," Kendall says.

Micah looks over at me from the cash register. He can make drinks but I'm not sure if he's ever been trained in ringing people out. I need to go help him. "I don't know, K. I'm kind of tired. And I don't think I can deal with your brother again right now."

"Come on," she wheedles. "Jason won't be there on a Wednesday night, I promise. He said something about going to Pin-Up Bowl. You totally owe me after skipping out on our party without even saying good-bye. My Jeep's run-ning all crazy and I'm afraid to drive it. If you don't come get me, I'll be stuck home doing nothing."

I sigh. God forbid Kendall be stranded at home on a Wednesday night. I know I'm being manipulated but some-times it's just easier not to fight with her. And I could use a distraction of the non-boy variety. "Okay, I'll go. But I have to get back to work now."

Slipping my phone in my pocket, I rescue Micah from the register and he brews espresso for two cappuccinos while I make change. "Big plans?" he asks wryly.

"All my plans are big," I say. "You? What was that about last night? You seemed kind of down when I left. I thought you and Amber had fun at the concert. Did I misunderstand?"

Micah pulls a rag out of his back pocket and wipes at an invisible spot on the espresso machine. "No. We had fun. We're supposed to do something tonight too. I guess I'm just worried about rushing back into things." He froths milk and finishes the girls' drinks, setting them gently on the far side of the counter.

"Well, I hope it works out. I'm happy for you," I say. I'm trying to be happy, I really am. But it's hard to ignore the voice in my head that's telling me if only I hadn't been so stupid it could have been me and Micah having fun at the concert last night instead of him and Amber.

The girls take their drinks and Micah attacks a splash of milk on the counter with his rag. "I guess that's it for us then, huh?"

"What do you mean?" A tiny crack opens up inside of me. *You can still win,* the voice says. I shush it. Enough with *The Art of War.* Enough with winning. People aren't prizes. They're not foreign territories or the spoils of victory or whatever Bianca said I should equate them to. Micah clearly wants Amber or he wouldn't still be strategizing to win her back. And she's better for him. She knows how she feels and isn't afraid of it. They like the same stuff. For once in my life, I'm trying not to be selfish.

Why does it have to be so difficult?

"You're giving up on Jason. Amber and I are probably getting back together. . . ." Micah trails off. There's a hardness in his eyes.

"You know, we could always hang out as friends," I suggest. "If being seen with a girl jock won't damage your rep."

His expression relaxes. "I might make an exception, for you."

"You better," I say. "Besides, by my count, you still owe me a couple of dates, and I reserve the right to collect on those when I have a sudden craving for screaming music or torture breakfast food."

"Deal," Micah says. Then he smiles. "Tell the truth. I'm more fun than that douchebag Jason, aren't I?"

I smile back at him. "Maybe."

Chapter 33

IF IT IS TO YOUR ADVANTAGE, MAKE A FORWARD
MOVE; IF NOT, STAY WHERE YOU ARE.
—SUN TZU, *The Art of War*

Beat is much less crowded during the week. There
are only about fifty people here. Thankfully none
of them are Jason.

"I can't believe I let you drag me here," I tell Kendall.

She pulls me out into the smoky haze. "You like dancing," she insists. "This will make you feel better."

The weird thing is, I don't actually feel too bad about
everything that's happened. I'm happy. Micah is happy. Leo
is happy. So what if only one of us got our ex back? We all
had fun, and I made a couple of new friends in the process.

The video screen is pumping out a skewed version of
a rap video. The bass reverberates through the floor, the
music cutting out occasionally. A handful of people are
moving to the beat. I can only see the occasional flash of an
elbow or head through the fog.

"Don't think of this Jason thing as an epic fail." Kendall
grinds up against me. "If you're really done with him, we'll

just have to find you someone else suitable."

I barely hear her. The smoke is filtering away. Across the dance floor, a girl with ripped jeans and long, blonde hair is swinging her hips to the music. Amber. And shuffling his feet next to her is Micah.

Kendall follows my line of sight. "Mohawk Boy, she says triumphantly. "Micah something, right? You know, since I got back in town, several people have asked me what's going on with you two. I thought they were delusional, but maybe I was wrong."

"Nothing is going on with us," I say.

"Then why are you gazing at him like he's my brother and Caleb Waters rolled into one?"

I don't answer. I'm still staring. Amber tosses her hair back from her face. The song stops but she keeps dancing.

"I think I get it," Kendall says. "When Nicholas and I broke up, I hooked up with Dan Spencer the next weekend, just so I could feel better. Jason broke your heart and you did the same thing, right?" She takes my silence for agreement and keeps talking. "You have to let it go, Lainey. Think of it like a sexorcism, something you had to get out of your system."

"I didn't get anything out of my system," I say sharply. "Nothing happened." And for some reason that cuts me almost to the point of tears. Choking back a sob, I make for a folding chair along the nearest wall.

Kendall follows, flouncing down in the next chair. Her eyes turn to slits. "No freaking way. You are seriously into him. Why? Better yet, how?" She peers at Micah through the dwindling smoke. "Isn't he a total loner with no friends? How did you even start talking?"

"He works at Denali," I say. "And he has friends. Obviously."

Amber puts her hands on Micah's waist and twirls both of them around in a circle. Micah leans in to tell her something and she throws back her head and laughs.

Kendall scoffs. "More like accomplices. Jason heard he got expelled from middle school for attacking a security guard."

"It was elementary school," I mumble. "And he didn't get expelled. He just got homeschooled until the end of the year. No big deal."

Kendall scoots her chair close to mine, so close I can smell her jasmine perfume. "What about his arrest last year? Also no big deal?"

"No, but who even knows what he did?"

"Well, it probably wasn't overdue library books," she says. "Oh my God, Lainey. What is going on with you?"

Again, I feel like maybe she's worried about me. And then she keeps talking.

"What are people going to say if you go back to school as the girl who is pining after a criminal?"

"I seriously doubt most people would care," I say. But Kendall would. Of course she would. She was raised to believe that what matters more than effort or talent or heart is the way that people perceive you.

"I just don't want people to get the wrong idea," she mur-murs.

"Like I said, nothing happened. Remember what I was telling you on the phone? It was all a plan to win back our exes." I relay the high points of the plan, leaving out the part about *The Art of War* and how I actually fake-dated Leo too.

Kendall whistles. "What a diabolical scheme." She points at Micah and Amber. Their bodies are pressed tight together. "And look, it obviously worked for those two. Why are you being all mopey? You should be proud of yourself."

"It was mostly Bianca's idea. I told you she was smart." I swipe at the tear that hovers in the corner of my left eye. Micah and Amber *do* look happy. So then why do I feel like total crap?

"It's stuffy in here," I say. "I'm going to get a soda and sit on the patio."

"Cool, I'll come find you in a couple of songs. I need to sweat off a little more weight. My mom was überpissed about the pounds I gained in New York."

"Both of them?" I make a mock scandalized face. "You fat pig."

"I'm a solid one twenty." Kendall holds her hand up for a high five. "If you ask me, I look better than ever, but she's still monitoring my weight, so it's just easier to stay skinny until I can move out." She cruises off toward the middle of the dance floor.

I buy a soda from the bar and step out onto the back patio, being careful to keep my back toward Micah and

Amber until the door closes safely behind me. Seeing them together hurts even more than seeing Jason and Alexandra did. Which is a stupid way to feel, considering that I'm the one responsible for it. Well, me and Bianca. And Sun Tzu.

Five wobbly card tables are arranged in a semicircle out here, but I'm all alone. The night air is thick and humid. I sink down into a chair and think about the last time I came to Beat, about the way Micah carried me to the car and let Amber's call go to voice mail until he knew I was okay. My eyelids flutter closed. I can almost feel his hands on me. I can practically hear his voice.

"Who are you hiding from?"

I *can* hear his voice. My eyes snap open. Micah is standing right in front of me.

"Kendall," I say. "She's a little too energetic for me tonight."

He shudders. "Yeah, I'd hide from her too."

"She's not that bad."

"Yes she is," he says with a grin. "Where's she been all summer, anyway?"

"Shooting a reality TV show, if you can believe it."

He sits down next to me. "I believe it. They always need at least one mean girl on those shows."

"That's not nice." I punch Micah lightly in the thigh with my fist. He catches my hand, unrolls my fingers. "What are you even doing here?" I ask. I can't look at him. I can only look at his hand. On mine. My heart thrums in my chest. My mouth gets dry. "Thought you hated this place."

"I do. Amber wanted to come for some reason." He gestures back toward the club. "She just ran into some girl from her school. They're talking about violins. Blah, blah, blah."

I want to ask if he and Amber are officially back together now, but I'm afraid of the answer. "Did you come out here to smoke?"

"Nope. I haven't smoked all day," he says.

"That's awesome."

"Amber thinks it's crazy. She smokes at least a pack a day, not to mention a substantial amount of weed."

"Is that what you got arrested for?" I can feel beads of sweat forming on my forehead. I blot at them clumsily with my left hand.

"Her, not me. I don't smoke weed anymore."

I am still staring at my hand, at the way Micah has it pinned to his leg. If I fold my fingers just so, his will slip into the spaces between, and we will be linked. I have never wanted anything so much in my whole life. "So then what did *you* do?"

"You really want to know?" The low voice again. The one that makes me think of rainstorms and stained-glass windows and rock songs with violins.

"Yeah. Tell me," I say, even as I realize I don't care. I don't care about who Micah used to be. I only care about who he is now, about the cracks gluing themselves back together in my chest. Nothing else matters. Maybe I shouldn't do this. So what if he's attracted to me? Amber is right for him. But my fingers start to fold anyway. A surge of warmth rushes through me as Micah gently squeezes my palm.

And that's game over. I start figuring out how to make it work—Micah and me.

Kendall will never approve, but she'll have to deal. Or not deal. I don't care. I'm not worried about her. I'm worried about everything else—about messing things up, about getting hurt, about hurting him. But I have to try. The way I feel in this moment, that's worth fighting for. All those lines in *The Art of War* about choosing one's battles wisely suddenly make sense to me. Not everything is worthy of great risk and possible sacrifice.

Micah is.

I won't be a coward. I'm done worrying. This isn't reckless—it's real. Amber might have more in common with him, but that doesn't make her feelings worth more. This. This is my "fall like a thunderbolt" moment and I am not going to waste it.

"You remember how someone graffitied the old airport terminal?" he asks.

"Yeah." My chair squeaks as I inch closer to him. My heart is thudding so loudly I can barely hear my response. "The news people said it was gang members or something."

Micah rests his head against my shoulder. "It was me."

His hair smells like peppermint shampoo. Soft pieces of it brush against my cheek. "Seriously? Graffiti?" I don't know what I expected, but it wasn't vandalism. It's so random. "Why?"

He rubs his thumb back and forth over the pointy bone in my wrist. "It's hard to explain. Did you ever want to scream, but when you open your mouth nothing comes out? Like you have all this shit trapped inside of you and you'll go insane unless you get rid of it?"

"Stuff about your dad?" I want to look into his eyes, but our heads are too close and I refuse to pull away from him.

"About a lot of things," he says. "Like how terrible is it that I want to leave my mom and sister to go to college? They need me. I should stay, but I want to go. . . ." He shakes his head in disgust and his hair tickles my cheek again. "I've done such a crap job taking care of them. Even now, I can't do the one thing I know would make my mom happy and quit smoking. I feel like my dad would be disappointed in me."

"Micah, that's not true. Your dad wouldn't want you to give up your dreams, and neither would your mom or Trinity." I turn toward him slightly. Our faces are almost touching. I wish I knew what to say to make him feel better. "You can't be so hard on yourself."

I feel his mouth smile against my shoulder. "Sorry," he says. "Didn't mean to get all heavy. Now you have to tell me one of your secrets so we're even."

Well, I couldn't ask for a better setup than that. Here goes nothing. "I like you," I blurt out. And even though Micah doesn't say anything right away, even though tears form out of nowhere and I'm shaking and my heart is threatening to explode, part of me feels like I've just lost fifty pounds.

And then he angles his head toward me. "I like you too," he murmurs in my ear, his lips hovering dangerously close to my skin.

And then it's like the song from The Devil's Doorstep is playing again. "Wake Up Dreaming." But the only music is the sound of our breathing and I know that if I turn just a few degrees to the right that Micah will twist inward toward me, and our lips will touch. A real kiss, more than at the soccer game. A kiss we can't take back or justify as part of some silly plan.

I'm still shaking, but it's like someone else is controlling my body. She's telling me nothing matters except for the way I feel this second, how once I start kissing Micah I'm never going to want to stop. She's turning my head for me, slowly, tilting my chin ever so slightly. I can feel him sliding around to face me. Any second now . . . I reach my left hand up and skim it across the top of his mohawk. He exhales slow and hard, his breath condensing on my lips. I hear a rushing, a roaring in my ears. My blood, my heartbeat, pounding throughout my whole body.

And then someone coughs.

I spin around so fast that my chair slams into the flimsy table leg and sends the table skating a foot across the patio. Micah drops my hand like it's a tarantula. Amber is standing outside the back door of the club.

We are so busted.

Chapter 34

A KINGDOM THAT HAS ONCE BEEN DESTROYED
CAN NEVER COME AGAIN INTO BEING.
—SUN TZU, *The Art of War*

"Don't let me interrupt," Amber says. Her blue eyes are icicles, frigid and stabbing in the summer heat.

Before either of us can speak, she disappears. The door slams behind her.

"I have to go." Micah pulls away and I feel instantly colder. He scrambles to his feet and heads toward the club.

"Yeah. You do that," I whisper.

He hears me and pauses with one hand on the door. "I came here with her. I shouldn't have—I'm sorry." His voice is heavy with grief.

Regret.

As he disappears back inside the club, I crumple my soda cup with one hand and throw it against the side of the building with all my might. It bounces limply off the bricks and falls to the ground. I want to scream. I clearly don't understand guys. If Micah is so into Amber that he ran after her like a puppy dog, what was he doing out here holding hands with me? Is he no different from Jason? Am I just a "vacation" for him?

I rest my cheek on the metal tabletop. The tears come fast. Wrapping my arms around my head so that no one who comes outside will be able to see my face, I sob quietly into the fold of my elbow. Phrases about being decisive and long delays dampening my army's ardor float around in my head. But no, that's bullshit. Talk is cheap. If Micah wanted me, he would be with me and not Amber. He would have walked away from her the way I walked away from Jason.

The patio door squeaks open and then slams shut. Wiping my eyes on my sleeve, I sit up and try to pretend that I'm just tired or feeling sick, that I'm not some crazy girl crying at the dance club.

But it's Kendall, and she's a tough one to fool. She's at my side in a second. "Laineykins, what happened?"

I can't get into it with her because if I do I'll start crying again and she'll start telling me how Micah doesn't matter and then the tears might never stop. "It's nothing," I say.

"I saw him and that girl come inside. What did they say to you?"

"Nothing."

Kendall stares me down. "*Nothing* would not have made you cry."

I hang my head. "Just forget it, okay? It's over." It's so over. I don't know what I was thinking. That's just it—at some point I stopped thinking. I wasn't strategizing. I wasn't justifying. I was just responding to the situation. And it felt right. Except Micah came here with another girl. And now he's probably leaving with her.

"No. Screw that." Kendall is up and heading back inside the club. Good. I want her to go dance or something. Leave me alone. I want everyone to leave me alone.

Too late, I realize what her plan is.

"Kendall, wait."

I leap from my seat and clatter after her in my platforms, stopping just long enough to pick up my crumpled cup and toss it in the trash can outside the door. Inside, Amber and Micah are standing against the far wall. It looks like they're arguing, but the music is too loud for me to hear what they're saying.

Kendall is cruising across the dance floor, a skinny blonde missile, a tornado bent on destruction.

"Stop." She's not listening. I hurry after her, half limping, wishing for once I had worn more sensible shoes.

Amber wipes at her eyes, and Micah enfolds her in a hug. I die a little inside. I try to stop staring, but can't. I'm slowly losing control. I have been all night, but I don't care. I don't care about anything right this second.

Except Micah.

And the way he's got his hand on Amber's lower back as they head toward the exit.

Kendall reaches the two of them before they can escape out into the parking lot. Her hand clamps down on Micah's shoulder. I can only watch in horror as he spins around, a confused look on his face. She starts screaming. The music is too loud to hear what she's saying, but from the way she's tossing her head and waving her arms around it's not too hard to fill in the blanks. Amber's mouth falls open in shock.

For a moment, I consider sneaking past all three of them and out into the night. But no, I'm the cause of this scene, and even if Micah might have earned a little of Kendall's wrath, Amber doesn't deserve to be sliced and diced with her razor-sharp tongue.

I reach Kendall's side and tug on her arm. "Come on. Let it go, please." At least the club is dark. Hopefully Micah and Amber can't tell I've been crying.

Kendall glances over her shoulder and then pulls free of my arm. "I will *not* let it go. No friend of mine is going to get treated like shit by anyone, let alone some loser thug." She turns back to Micah. "She liked you, you asshole, and you made her cry."

I have no idea what Micah's response to this is, because I can't bring myself to look at him. I will probably never be able to look at him ever again. I wish I had walked on by like I first considered. Better than that, I wish the pulsing lights were lasers that would vaporize me.

"Please, Kendall." I try once more to steer her away. My eyes are still trained on the floor. "It's not worth it."

Now Amber is screaming too, calling Kendall a psycho-bitch, telling her to back off. Somewhere between them I hear Micah telling Kendall he's not afraid of her and that she shouldn't speak for me. Their voices encircle me like snares; they stab me like spikes. My head is throbbing from the smoke and the lights and the thudding bass. I barely notice a small group of people beginning to cluster around, hoping for an actual fight.

"I can ruin you, you know that?" Kendall shouts. "I can make sure that no one ever speaks to you."

"Stop it, Kendall. That's enough!" I give her wrist another vicious yank. "Quit being a bitch."

She looks at me in surprise, rubbing her wrist where I grabbed her. "No. It's not enough. No friend of *mine* is—"

Of course. Once again Kendall is making my problems all about her. "This has nothing to do with you," I say. This time she finally lets me drag her away.

"What has gotten into you?" she asks. "Did you really just call me a bitch? I was defending you, in case you didn't notice, since you seem incapable of doing it yourself."

The comment hurts but I'm in no mood to make an even bigger scene. "I told you to stop." I have to shout so she can hear me over the pounding bass. "He doesn't matter to me. I used him, okay? That's all it ever was." Of course the music picks that moment to cut out so my words explode across the club like a machine-gun blast. Micah and Amber are halfway out the door, but they hear every word. I can tell by the way Micah stumbles, just barely.

Nearby a voice I don't recognize yells, "Damn, that was cold, even for her."

Micah turns halfway around to face me. Once again I

wish the lasers would vaporize me on the spot. His eyes sear into mine, with what? Surprise? Hurt? Both. And then all of the expression fades away until he looks dead. More like a ghost than a real person. Everything goes blurry, like I'm watching the events unfold through a fish tank. I barely notice the pale circles, faces of people still staring at me, hoping for more theatrics. My eyes see only one thing, the dark outline of Micah's back as he disappears through the front door of the club, with Amber at his side.

Chapter 35

IF SLIGHTLY INFERIOR IN NUMBERS, WE CAN
AVOID THE ENEMY; IF QUITE UNEQUAL IN EVERY
WAY, WE CAN FLEE FROM HIM.

—SUN TZU, *The Art of War*

I'm supposed to work at Denali the next day, but I tell
my parents I'm sick. I can't face Micah. I have no idea
what he might do. Maybe he'll go off on me in front
of the whole coffee shop, reduce me to tears as Jason did
at the beginning of summer. Only this time it'll be worse,
because this time the whole crushing feeling will be totally
deserved. Or maybe he'll quit talking to me completely,
freeze me out like I don't exist.

I pull the covers up over my head. I want to go back to
sleep so I don't have to think about it.

A few minutes later, my mom pops into my room with
some mail. An issue of *Soccer Illustrated* and some letters
from college athletic departments that I should probably
open right away. But they're all small Division II and Division III schools and even though I should be glad anyone is
interested in me, it just feels like one more big, fat failure on

top of everything else.

"Just put it all on my desk," I say. "I'll look at it when I'm feeling better."

She stacks the letters neatly on top of the magazine and comes to sit on the side of my bed. Reaching out, she feels my cheek with the back of her hand. "You don't feel feverish."

"I have a killer headache and I'm really tired," I say. "And nauseous," I add for good measure, giving her my best queasy face.

"You're not pregnant, are you?"

"Mooom!" I blush, even though I know it's not a possibility. "Not a chance."

"Are you certain? Those birth control pills aren't 100 percent effective, you know."

"Positive," I assure her.

She kisses me on the forehead. "Good. I suppose you can stay home today, but I hate the fact that I'm not going to be here to take care of you."

"I don't need anyone to take care of me," I say. "I'm just going to go back to sleep."

Her face crinkles up. "Okay, sweetie, but call your father if you need anything. I'll be in meetings but he could always slip away from the shop for a few minutes if he had to."

"Sure, Mom." I roll onto my side so I'm facing away from her. The reality is, I've already been asleep for close to ten hours. More shut-eye is not going to happen. I wait until she leaves and then sit up in bed. For the first time all summer, I'm actually bored.

I send Bianca a text.

Me: Are you picking up my shift?
Her: Probably. Are you sick?

I start texting her about what happened last night but then give up and call her. She listens quietly while I run through the whole disastrous evening. Micah and Amber dancing. Micah and me on the patio. Amber catching us. Kendall going psycho-bitch on Micah. Me losing it.

"I blew it, Bee." My voice cracks. "I said all that stuff so Kendall would shut up, but the way Micah looked at me." I shudder. "It was like I was dead to him. And he and Amber looked pretty cozy leaving together." It takes everything I have to choke this last sentence out.

Bee sighs. "Oh, Lainey. You *really* like him, don't you?"

I grab a tissue from my nightstand at blot at my eyes. "Yeah, but I messed everything up."

"First of all, quit letting Kendall get to you," Bianca says firmly. "And second, just go talk to him. You told him you liked him and he said he liked you too."

"Yeah, but then I basically told half the school that he meant nothing to me."

"He's been hanging out with you for how long?" Bee asks. "I'm sure he knows how you get when you're upset. Just apologize."

"Maybe you're right," I say. "I'll think about it." After we hang up, I reread all of my text conversations with Micah, smiling at some of our sarcastic exchanges. But each time I start to type out an apology, I end up deleting it. Maybe I should just leave not–well enough alone, quit while I'm behind, save both of us the awkwardness of having to talk about what happened. What would be the point? Micah chose Amber. I should respect that, even though it hurts.

And then my phone rings. I'm praying it's Micah, that he received my messages telepathically or something, but it's my brother.

"Hey, Steve," I say.

"I heard you're sick. I just wanted to check up on you after our little chat last week. Still upset about Jason?"

"Believe it or not, he wanted me back and I turned him down."

"That's my girl," Steve says. "Plenty of other guys out there."

"Yeah, I kind of had one, but I managed to mess that up already."

"Holy crap." Steve chuckles. "You move fast. When I told you to find a better guy than Jason, I didn't mean in one day. You don't want to rush into a rebound thing."

"You're probably right," I say. "Maybe the best thing is to just spend some time alone."

Saturday, my dad really needs me at Denali. I go in, praying that Micah isn't working, even though I know he's scheduled.

My heart sinks like a rock when I see the Beast parked in its usual corner spot. I sit in the Civic for a few seconds, making extra sure there aren't any tears near the surface. *Stay in control. Stay in control. Stay in control.* I'm good. I can do this.

I breeze through the front door like everything is fine, like I'm coming off the most epic night of my life. Ebony and a new part-time girl are working the front. Neither of them even look up as I head to my locker in the back. I have to walk past Micah in the prep area to put my purse away. He's buried up to his elbows in bread dough, humming along to the music on his headphones.

Ebony gives me her spot at the cash register. For once I'm glad to be trapped out front. The new girl's name is Emma. Apparently she's the daughter of one of my mom's professor friends, but she doesn't even look old enough to have a job. Whenever we need anything from the back I send her to go get it. The longer I can go without facing Micah, the better.

"Is everything all right?" Emma asks after the fifth time I send her away. She curls a ribbon of black hair around one of her fingers as she studies me with concern.

"Everything's super." I plaster a fake smile on my face.

Eventually Emma is in the middle of ringing people out and I have to go back and ask Micah for some peanut butter cookies. I can barely choke the words out but he seems completely fine as he plates up a dozen for me, like he's coming off the most epic night of *his* life.

He doesn't go off on me *or* ignore me the whole day.

Instead he does something that manages to hurt even more. He goes back to treating me the way he did at the beginning of the summer: distantly, politely, like I'm a customer—one who orders a lot of blended drinks and doesn't tip. If he had any feelings for me, he's managed to turn them off, like flicking a switch. I wish I had that power. My whole summer would have been different if I could have gotten over Jason in a nanosecond. *But then you wouldn't have gotten to know Micah.*

Okay, maybe I don't want that power after all. But I want the pain to go away.

Leo doesn't seem to know what happened so he's still talking to us like we're all friends. "You read *The Prince* yet?" he asks, smearing tomato sauce on one of Micah's hand-tossed pizza crusts. "Deceit. Betrayal. Totally your thing."

Totally my life.

"No, I'm done with strategizing."

Leo sprinkles the pizza with shredded cheese. "So you gave up on your ex too?"

"Yeah. Turns out we're not as compatible as I thought." I swear I can feel Micah's eyes on me, but I'm too afraid to look up, too afraid I'll see him staring straight through me. "But thanks for all your help. If there's ever anything I can do for you, let me know."

Leo furrows his brow as he tops his pizza with sliced mushrooms and green peppers. "There is one thing." He puts the pizza in the oven. "Bianca. She's one of your best friends, right?"

I'm thinking right about now she's my only friend. "Yeah," I say, not really understanding where Leo is going. "She's off today."

"Is she dating anyone?"

"Oh." I force myself to smile. "So Bee is the girl you're interested in?" Now I get why Leo was so anxious to plot warlord style with us. I steal a peek at Micah. He's, like, four feet away but his music is so loud I can hear the tinny echo from his earbuds. He might as well be four miles away. "No. She's not." I struggle to stay focused. "You know, she's really smart like you. She wants to be a doctor. You should totally ask her out."

Leo looks mortified. "Is there any way you could maybe find out if she'd be interested?"

"Yeah, I can do that," I say. "But remember. We're talking about Bianca. If she's not interested, she's going to be so nice about it that you'll walk away feeling even better than if she'd said yes."

"I know. But I don't want to make her feel uncomfortable. Especially since we have to work together," he says.

"Right," I agree. "You wouldn't want things to be awkward at work." My eyes flick over at Micah again. He's scooping out cookie dough with an ice-cream scoop. The dough balls land neatly and evenly spaced on the warped, silver sheet pan. If he feels awkward, I sure can't tell.

Chapter 36

To secure ourselves against defeat lies in
our own hands.

—Sun Tzu, *The Art of War*

After work, I convince Bianca to meet me at Hallowed Grounds, Hazelton's *other* coffee shop, the one where no one knows me.

"So what do you think of Leo?" I ask, trying to be coy. Bee has never had a serious boyfriend. She's definitely been asked out, but she always refuses and ends up going to school dances with friends. I don't know if it's because she's so focused on getting a scholarship or because her overprotective family scares off any guy who shows an interest in her.

"Leo?" Bianca pulls the chopsticks from her bun and sets them on the red lacquer tabletop. She shakes her head once and thick waves of black hair cascade over her shoulders. She looks down at her iced chai. "I don't know. Why?"

"Because he likes you."

She giggles. Seriously a giggle, like we're back in sixth grade and the cute boy from Massachusetts who sat behind her just pulled on her braid. "Why would you even say that?"

"Ohmygod. You totally like him." My jaw drops a little. "How did I not know this? You loooooooove him!"

"Shh." Bianca's honey complexion is rapidly turning red. She takes a long swill of her drink. "I do not *love* him."

"But I can tell him you're interested?"

She looks up from her drink. "Are you sure he likes *me*?"

"Why? Because you're so hideous and unlikable?" I tease. "Of course I'm sure. He told me."

"I figured he probably . . . you know." She twirls her straw violently. The ice cubes clink together in the environmentally unfriendly plastic cup.

"What?" I feel like we're having a conversation in a foreign language where I can only translate every other word.

She looks up at me. Her eyes are soft and dark. Nervous. "Liked you," she finishes.

I almost choke on my drink. "No chance. He's a really cool guy," I say. "But it's not like that with us."

"What if it's not like that with you, but it *is* like that with him?" Bee asks. "I don't want to be the girl who gets used so some guy can get close to her popular friend."

"I swear, Bianca. He has never even flirted with me. Apparently he has liked you for weeks but is too shy to do anything about it."

"Really?" Her face lights up like a stained-glass window. Right then I know I will kill Leo if he ever hurts her.

"Yeah, really," I singsong. "If I had known you liked him sooner I would have let you be his pseudo-date. How come you never told me?"

"Well, I knew he was trying to get back with Riley. And also, I knew you'd pressure me into talking to him, even if I wasn't ready."

"Why would you say that?" I ask. I remember Kendall forcing me to talk to Jason during our freshman year, how terrified I was that day. Bee is making me sound exactly the same, which is not cool.

"Because that's your style, Lainey. And you think it works for everyone."

"That's not true." I am stunned that Bee feels like this. I had no idea.

Bianca's eyes narrow. "What about Shaun Demetz, sophomore year? You sent him a carnation-invitation to the Turnabout Dance and signed my name to it."

"You told me you liked him and I *knew* he would say yes." I huff. "Come on, Bianca. He does other people's math homework for fun. Were you really worried about getting rejected?"

"He gets paid for that," she says. "And it wasn't rejection I was worried about. I just wasn't ready to have a boyfriend and I didn't want to give him the wrong idea. I didn't want to have to blow him off afterward."

I try to remember what happened after the dance. "But didn't you guys go out for a while?"

"Yes," Bianca says. "Because I didn't want to hurt his feelings. But eventually I had to. Not everyone is always moving at fast-forward like you."

"Moving at fast-forward? I feel like I'm the one stuck on PAUSE while everyone else makes these epic future plans. You're going to Mizzou to be a doctor and Kendall wants to go back to New York. I've got nothing except soccer, maybe. I'm going to end up as that girl who peaked in high school."

"You'll have epic future plans someday too," Bee says. "You just have to figure out what you want to do. And if you don't get a scholarship, then you can play wherever as a freshman and try get a scholarship somewhere bigger the following year."

"You think?" I never thought about doing it that way, working my way up from a small school to a larger one. And then I realize I've made this conversation all about me. I have a feeling I do that a lot. "Forget it. What about Leo? You want me to tell him to hold off? He's a good guy. I don't want to see him get crushed."

Bee giggles again. "I'm not sure if it makes sense for me to start dating someone now, but I'll talk to him next time we work together. You know, if you and Micah would just admit you're still crazy about each other, then the four of us could all hang out."

"Micah is not crazy about me." I shudder. "He won't even look at me. He looks *through* me now. I'd say he even hates me, except that would require actual emotion on his part, and I'm pretty sure I don't rate that much."

She shakes her head. "I don't believe it. I bet he's miserable too. But if you want him, you might have to fight for him."

I let my head fall to the tabletop. "For the love of all that is dead and Chinese, please, no more fighting. This army needs a break."

"Forget *The Art of War*," Bee says. "Use 'The Art of Lainey.'"

I peek up at her. "I'm pretty sure that book will not be getting published anytime soon." But she's right. It's like I told Leo. I need to work with what I've got . . . even if I don't know exactly what that is. The good news is I can't really mess things up worse than I already have. "But what if I can't fix things?"

I fully expect Bee to go into cheerleader mode, to tell me I'm being dramatic, that everything is fixable. She definitely takes a Disney-movie view of the world most days. But today she surprises me. "At least you'll know you tried," she says. "And then we'll go run until you're too tired to hurt. And then we'll get ice cream." She smiles again. "But only one scoop."

Chapter 37

A week passes. It's Friday night again, maybe the first Friday night of the summer that I don't have plans. Kendall hasn't called me since the blowup at Beat. Pretty sure she's waiting for me to apologize for calling her a bitch. I'm still pissed over that crack about not being able to defend myself. Standing up for yourself is about more than flinging barbed-wire insults around. It's about picking your battles, knowing when to fight, knowing exactly what and who is worth fighting for. If only I had figured that out a little bit earlier.

I'm out in the backyard with my soccer ball. It stormed all day so the grass is wet and the ground is soft. Mud spatters up on my shins as I dribble the ball around a trio of weirdo totem poles my mom just got from some online hippie warehouse. They remind me of the tribal masks I hung up at the coffee shop. I swear there is no escaping the creepy leering faces around here.

I cut around the third totem like it's a defender and shoot the ball at the back door. Goal. I've been practicing soccer a lot. Maybe I *am* good enough to score a Division I scholarship. So what if it's not Northwestern? It would be cool to go to Mizzou with Bee. It's worth a try.

Things are almost back to normal at work. By normal, I mean how they were at the beginning of the summer, when Micah and I had nothing to say to each other. My insides feel like someone is processing them in the bean grinder every time we cross paths so I've been staying out front as much as possible. I tried to talk to him twice—I swear I did—but the first time I trapped him in the manager's office and he looked so uncomfortable that I just let him go. I remember thinking: *Do not pursue an enemy who simulates flight.* Yeah, it's like *The Art of War* has become part of me. Even when I'm not thinking about it, I use it.

The second time I ran into him outside after a shift. He was leaning against the Beast smoking a cigarette and I thought *maybe* he was waiting for me. But before I could even make it across the parking lot, he got a phone call. I could sense it was her—Amber. I passed him up, went straight to the Civic.

But he smiled when he answered his phone. I saw that much from the safety of my car.

Which I guess will be my brother's car again soon. As much as I'll miss it, it'll be good to have Steve back.

My phone buzzes on the picnic table.

911. Call me.

It's a text from Bianca. I'm pretty sure I've never gotten a 911 from Bee before. She just isn't dramatic like me. I call her back and she picks up on the first ring.

"Is everyone okay? Your grandmother?"

"No, no, everyone's fine," Bee says. "It's Leo."

"What about him?"

She swears in Spanish. "He's picking me up in two hours. We're going to Tony's."

"*The* Tony's?" I whistle. "Nice." I'm wondering if Leo is blowing all the money I just returned to him on one date. Talk about aiming to impress.

"I know," Bee says. "But it's our first real date and that place is so elegant. Everything I try on makes me look fat and my hair is extra huge since it rained earlier and I look so terrible I'm thinking about canceling."

She sounds close to tears. Bianca is always the one calming everyone else down. Who would've guessed she couldn't work the same magic on herself?

"Relax," I say. "Remember the dress you wore to the state championship dinner? The navy blue one with the sequined shoulder straps?"

"Yeah."

"Wear that."

A pause. Deep breath. "You don't think it's too short for a fancy restaurant?"

"Nah. Wear flats if you're worried about it."

"Good idea. Now if I only knew what to do about my hair."

"Why don't you come over?" I suggest. "I'll plug in my flat iron and we can tame it down a little."

"Really?" Bee sounds so hopeful. "Don't you have plans tonight?"

Plans. Let's see. Micah isn't talking to me. Kendall isn't talking to me. The two people who still *are* talking to me are going out for a romantic dinner together. My parents have a better social life than I do. "My plans are to live vicariously through you," I say. "I'll be waiting."

Bianca shows up about twenty minutes later in her navy blue dress. It hugs her curves in all the right places, but the humidity from the afternoon storm has made her hair twice as big as normal. I go after it with my flat iron, keeping the heat on low so it takes out some of the body but doesn't completely obliterate her thick waves.

"You are a lifesaver," Bee says, watching her hair return to normal size in the mirror. "Will you do my makeup too?"

"Sure." I dig through my top drawer where I keep all my cosmetics. "So. Tony's, eh? Pretty swank for a first date. I don't even think my parents can afford that place. Is that why you're so nervous? Thought you weren't even sure if you wanted to date Leo."

Bianca blushes. "Well, we've been talking on the phone for the past few days. You're right. He is kind of funny. And smart. And it turns out he's thinking about going to Mizzou too."

"Sounds promising." I highlight her eyelids with blue and gold shadow to match her dress. Then I line Bianca's upper and lower lids with deep charcoal eye pencil and hit her lashes with black mascara. I'm in the process of picking out a lip shade when I stop. She looks perfect. Radiant. There's no need to smother her in makeup so she's unrecognizable.

"You're finished," I tell her.

She crinkles her nose at her reflection. "No lipstick? No blusher? No bronzer?"

"Bronzer?" I laugh. "You're the most naturally bronze person I know."

Bee smiles. "I love it. I look like me. Only better."

"You're stunning," I agree. "But you could have gone in your running gear with no makeup at all and you'd still be stunning." My voice almost cracks. "You're always stunning."

"Lainey." Bianca's dark eyes turn liquid. "Are you really going to leave things like this with Micah? If you can't talk to him, why don't you at least text him?"

I slump my shoulders. "Because I'm afraid he won't text back."

"Aww." Bee throws her arms around me. "I feel bad leaving you alone when you're sad. Maybe we can go someplace more casual and you can come too."

"Dude," I say, swallowing back the lump in my throat. "This is your big date and you're letting me make everything about me. You are totally the best friend a girl could ever have. Sometimes I wonder why you don't just tell me to get lost."

Bee reclines back on my bed. "Elaine Mitchell. I've been your friend for ten years. You're family. Maybe I want to strangle you every once in a while, but I will never tell you to get lost, okay? I would miss you too much."

I pull her up off my bed and twirl her around in a circle. "The best. Seriously. Go enjoy your fancy dinner. I can't wait to hear all the *intimate* details." I wink. Bianca reddens again.

After she leaves, I flop down on my bed with my laptop and skim through a few gossip websites. I can't really get into them. I check my email. There's a message from my brother.

> Hey L—
>
> Wow. The summer has really flown by, hasn't it? I'm heading to London for the weekend to drink warm beer with some of my friends before we all head home. We've got tickets to a soccer game, oh wait, make that a football match, and I couldn't help but think of how much you would love it. I promise to take lots of pictures of whichever players the girls tell me are cute. I'd tell you who is playing but apparently there are a ton of football teams just in London and I can't remember the names. Here's hoping they have cheerleaders.
>
> See you soon,
>
> S

I click my laptop closed and dig through the magazines on the floor next to my bed. Last month's *Soccer Illustrated* has a feature on some of the London football clubs. I pore over the pictures, but none of the players are as cute as Caleb Waters. No one has his stats either.

The faded red corner of *The Art of War* peeks out from beneath the glossy magazines. I finally quit carrying it around, but like I said, the whole freaking book seems to be tattooed across my brain. Well, maybe not the whole book, but at least my highlighted passages. Maybe I should bring it up to work and hide it amongst the flowing locks and poufy-shirted pirotica, where no one else is likely to find it and become an obsessive warrior person.

Flopping down on my bed, I open to the very first page and start reading. I'm not sure why, if I'm just bored or if some little part of me is hoping I missed something, some secret little trick that will win back Micah. But the more I read, the more I realize there's a lot more to it than the simple top ten list Bianca and I made.

Certain passages stick out to me now, words that I skimmed past or interpreted differently the first time I read.

Part III:
> SUPREME EXCELLENCE CONSISTS OF BREAKING
> THE ENEMY'S RESISTANCE WITHOUT FIGHTING . . .
> THEREFORE THE SKILLFUL LEADER SUBDUES THE
> ENEMY'S TROOPS WITHOUT ANY FIGHTING; HE

CAPTURES THEIR CITIES WITHOUT LAYING SIEGE
TO THEM.

Two pages later:
HE WILL WIN WHO KNOWS WHEN TO FIGHT AND
WHEN NOT TO FIGHT.

Part VIII:
THERE ARE ROADS WHICH MUST NOT BE
FOLLOWED, ARMIES WHICH MUST NOT BE
ATTACKED.

Part XII:
NO RULER SHOULD PUT TROOPS INTO THE FIELD
MERELY TO GRATIFY HIS OWN SPLEEN; NO
GENERAL SHOULD FIGHT A BATTLE SIMPLY OUT OF
PIQUE.

Next page:
A KINGDOM THAT HAS ONCE BEEN DESTROYED
CAN NEVER COME AGAIN INTO BEING.

It's like I'm reading a whole different book. Maybe
Bianca missed the point. Maybe we all did. As much as *The
Art of War* looks to be about military strategy, I'm pretty
sure what Sun Tzu was saying is that the best plan is the one
that doesn't require marching into battle. That the true goal
of strategy is victory *without* having to fight.

But how does that apply to me? I'm fighting with almost everyone. Jason. Kendall.

Micah.

What do you do when you're knee-deep in battle and don't want to fight anymore?

Chapter 38

SUPREME EXCELLENCE CONSISTS IN BREAKING
THE ENEMY'S RESISTANCE WITHOUT FIGHTING.
—SUN TZU, *The Art of War*

You stop fighting. You fix things . . . or try anyway.

I'm going to start with Kendall because as scary as she is, she's way less scary than Micah. She shouldn't have gone all rabid pit bull on him, but she did it to defend my honor. Besides, I kind of miss her, and if we're going to be soccer cocaptains together this year we need to at least be civil.

She shocks me by apologizing as soon as she answers. "I shouldn't have caused a scene," she says, so loud that I have to hold my phone away from my ear. "I should have let it go."

"Where are you?" I ask. "Is this a bad time?"

"I'm at Jay's. He's got people over." I hear music and muffled voices in the background. "He says to tell you he misses you."

"That's sweet. Tell him I said hi. Look, I called to apologize too. I know you were only trying to help. I should have just admitted I liked Micah."

"Right." Kendall seizes on this information like she's just secured an airtight alibi for a horrible crime. "Why would you lie to me? None of that would have happened if you had told me the truth."

"Come on, K. You made it seem as if liking him would be social suicide."

"It probably would be," she says. "But you still didn't have to lie about it. I thought best friends told each other everything."

Which is total bullshit because Kendall tells me almost nothing. She didn't even tell me she was back in town. Besides, *I* thought best friends supported each other.

"I knew if I told you that you'd harass me and try to fix me up with other guys or your brother until I gave up on him," I say.

"Okay, you're right," she admits. "I would have tried to make you forget him. I mean, get real, Lainey. Dating is hard enough. Dating someone like that—it'd be überhard, like interracial dating used to be. All those questions from kids at school, the mean looks from people who assume you're acting out some prison role-playing fantasy. It'd be like that fairy tale with the princess who falls in love with the monster."

There's no reasoning with Kendall, but I give it one last try. "Uh, just because Micah isn't a pretty-boy soccer star doesn't make him a monster," I say. "And that fairy tale had a happy ending, in case you forgot."

"Let's stop arguing about this," she says brightly. "Mohawk

Boy will get over it eventually, or not. But who really cares? There are plenty of hotter guys without criminal records, and you shouldn't sell yourself short. How about we focus on the now, as in where I'm going to take you to cheer you up tomorrow night."

Classic Kendall move—if you can't beat them, distract them with something shiny.

"Which means what, exactly?" I ask.

"Epic party. A friend of a friend of a girl I met on *So You Think You Can Model* goes to Washington University. She's having a big welcome-back-to-campus thing. College boys, Lainey. You'll forget all about your slew of questionable choices this summer."

"The only questionable thing I did was make out with your brother after he dumped me," I say. "And isn't it a little early for the Wash U kids to be coming back to campus?"

"I think she plays tennis or something so she has to be back early for practice," Kendall says. "Even better. A whole party full of jocks. Say you'll go with me. I don't want to go alone."

"I guess," I say. But inside I'm kind of dreading it.

I'm at work when Kendall texts me the next day:

Her: You ready?

Me: I dunno K. Not sure if I'm up for it.

Her: Trust me. Tonight will be life changing. You get off at 7?

Me: Yeah.

Her: My jeep is in the shop. Apparently I trashed the transmission. If Jay drops me at Denali, can we take your car?

Me: Okay.

I'm too tired to even argue. Maybe she's right and I do need to get out. Maybe I need anything that will get my mind off Micah. Thankfully he left early today, so I only had to endure a couple hours of him treating me like a stranger.

Kendall sashays her way through the front doors right at seven. She's dressed in a skimpy sundress short enough to almost be illegal and platform sandals tall enough to definitely be impractical. The effect makes me think of "sexy circus performer." I watch as she heads across the front of the dining room toward an open booth.

She pulls her phone out of her purse and starts texting away while she waits for me. There are a couple of people in line. As I ring them up and help Ebony make their drinks, I see Kendall look repeatedly up at the clock on the wall and then back down at her phone.

By the time I clear the line, clock out, and flop down across from her in the booth, she looks positively irritated. "Took you long enough," she says. "I wanted to find someplace to get food before the party."

"You mean like a coffee shop?" I say, looking around.

"No. *Good* food."

Since Kendall's daily caloric intake doesn't usually break

triple digits, I have no idea what "good food" involves. I look down at my baggy capris and Denali T-shirt. "You have to at least let me run home and change."

"Tell me you didn't bring different clothes with you." Kendall inhales so deeply I can see her impossibly flat stomach puff outward ever so slightly. But before she can unleash her monster sigh, the coconut wind chimes do their clunking thing and Micah's little sister, Trinity, stumbles into the shop.

Her bangs are matted to her face with sweat and she's got a smudge of dirt across her left cheekbone. Her cargo pants are ripped up the left side of her leg—not the kind of cool, trendy rip that kids spend hours with a razor to achieve. The frantic "half my butt is hanging out" rip a girl might get if she was attacked by a mountain lion.

I jump up from the booth and hurry over to her. "Trinity. Are you okay?"

"Is my brother here?" she asks, slightly out of breath.

"He left around three," I say. There's a golf ball–sized welt growing out of her forehead and it looks like she's got blood between her front teeth. "What happened?"

"I'm fine." Trinity peers up at the clock on the wall. "Did Micah mention where he was going?"

I shake my head.

She glances down at her phone. It's got a big spiderwebby crack across the screen but the display is still functional. "He isn't answering his cell. Hey, if he comes back by here, will you tell him to call me?"

"Yeah. Of course. I—"

She spins on her heel and heads back out into the heat without waiting for me to finish.

Kendall slides out of the corner booth and clops across the wooden floor in her sandals. "All ready?" she asks brightly. "We can zoom by your house and grab a dress for you. You can change in—"

"Hang on a minute." I follow Trinity outside. She's kneeling by a mangled bicycle that's lying on the sidewalk. The front wheel is folded in a ninety-degree angle. She lifts the bike and tries to roll it next to her but it won't roll. She drags it a few feet and then gives up. Sighing, she drops the hunk of crumpled metal and starts to walk off in the direction of her apartment building.

"Trin. Wait," I say.

She turns around. Looks nervous. "Yeah?"

"Did you get hit by a car or something?" I ask, my voice incredulous. Her bike looks like it got hit by several cars. And then maybe a bus.

"It just clipped me. No big deal." She turns around and keeps walking.

I catch up with her in a few strides. It doesn't take much effort on my part since she's way shorter than me and limping. I grab her gently by the shoulder. "Dude, you need to go to the hospital. Can I call your mom for you?"

Trinity sighs. I can see her fighting back tears. "I tried her cell too. No answer. But dinner rush is still going on. She won't have time to check her phone until at least nine."

"Well then, let me take you." I can't even believe the girl got hit by a car and she's trying to brush it off like it's no big deal.

"I don't want to be a burden. Besides, I don't think the doctors can do anything without Micah or my mom there."

"Maybe not," I say, "but at least you'd be someplace safe in case you pass out." I point at the lump on her forehead. It's puffed out to the size of an egg. "You could have some kind of brain injury."

"I'm okay. It doesn't even really hurt that much."

"Probably because you're in shock." I lean in close to check Trinity's pupils. It's bad if they're different sizes, I think. Hers look normal. A fist clenches in my stomach. "Did the guy stop at least? Where did this happen?"

"A couple of blocks from here." She looks down at the hole in her pants, adjusting the seam to cover her underwear. "He didn't stop, but it was my fault. I didn't wait for the light."

"Bullshit," I say. "That's still a crime."

Kendall bursts through Denali's front door. She gestures wildly toward the parking lot. "Come on. Lose the street urchin. We've got places to be."

I suck in a sharp breath. "Ohmygod, Kendall. Rude much? She got hit by a freaking car."

"So call an ambulance, already," Kendall snaps.

"Forget her," I say, turning back to Trinity. "You've got two choices. Either you let me drive you to the ER or I call 911."

Trinity appears to consider the offer, but then she shakes

her head. "My mom can't afford an ER bill."

"It's fine," I say. "Kids are covered under state insurance when they're your age."

"Yeah, but you still have to pay something, right?"

"I'm not sure, but if so it's a lot less. Look, your head might be broken, Trinity. This isn't optional. Some things don't heal on their own."

She looks nervously over her shoulder at Kendall. Just the act of turning her neck makes her wince. "What about her?"

"Her head is definitely broken," I say. "Wait here for a second."

I backtrack to where Kendall is leaning against the front window of Denali. "We have to take her to the ER."

"Seriously?" Kendall sighs. I know she wants to refuse but she can't because she doesn't have a car and there's no guarantee Jason will come get her. If there's one thing that Kendall Chase does not do, it's take public transportation. "Today is the day you need to play hero? Why exactly can't you just call 911?"

Maybe she's right. Maybe I should call Trinity an ambulance. But then she'd have to go to the hospital all alone. No one deserves that. "Just come with us, okay? I'll wait with her to see a doctor and you can take the Civic to the party. I'll take the MetroLink down to the Forest Park station and meet up with you later."

"Fine." Kendall lifts her chin. "But I can't believe you're bailing on me for some middle school girl." She gives Trinity a glare that threatens to melt her. "Who is she?"

"It's Micah's sister," I say. "And she's a freshman."

"Oh. Now I get it." Kendall turns her scalding eyes on me. "You're still strategizing. Only now you're after Mohawk Boy instead of Jason."

"No, Kendall. Not everything I do has an evil agenda, okay? She's a nice kid and she's scared and she shouldn't have to be alone in the hospital," I say. "That's all there is to it."

The three of us head to the All Saints ER. I make Kendall triple-promise to be careful with Steve's car and reluctantly hand her the keys. Trinity and I head inside. Turns out Trin is right and the nurses and doctors can't officially treat her without parental consent, unless her condition changes and becomes a life-threatening emergency. They tell her not to eat anything, and to let one of the desk girls know if she's able to get her mom on the phone. We try her mom's cell phone again and also leave a message at the diner. Then we try to get comfortable in the waiting room. It's not happening. The thermostat is set somewhere between refrigerator and ice rink, and all of the plushy chairs are taken.

We sit next to each other on a hard bench with no back. Behind us, a pair of angelfish swim lazily around in a cylindrical aquarium. "How are you going to get to your party?" Trinity's pale face is a mess of bruises and worry lines. She traces the path of a fish with one trembling index finger.

"I can take the train," I say. "I'm not worried about it. I'm worried about you. I'll hang out until your mom or brother shows up."

She shakes her head. I notice her colored streaks are gone. I wonder if she got tired of them or if they got ripped out during her accident. "I'd feel better knowing I didn't mess up your plans." She looks down at the floor. "I don't want the most popular girl in school to hate me before I even set foot in Hazelton High."

I wave my hand dismissively. "Kendall? Her bark is worse than her bite." Privately I'm thinking the probability of Kendall even remembering what Trinity looks like over a month from now when school starts is less than zero.

"Still. The nurses are keeping an eye on me. You can go."

"Are you trying to get rid of me?" I make a pretend-outraged face. "Don't make me tell your brother on you."

Just the thought of Micah makes Trinity smile. "What happened to you guys anyway?" she asks.

My hair falls forward into my face as I look down at my lap. "It's a long story."

"Yeah, Micah told me you were never technically dating. But now it seems like you guys aren't even friends." Trinity picks at a loose thread on her pants. "He misses you, you know?"

I swallow back a lump in my throat. "Highly unlikely."

"You miss him too, don't you? I keep telling him that you do."

"Why would you even think that?" I raise my head. "I haven't seen you since the first time Micah and I hung out."

"Because I know how awesome my brother is. You'd have to be stupid not to miss him." She smiles her toothy smile at me. "You don't seem stupid. You should call him."

I turn away, toward the aquarium. It's my turn to trace the angelfish's path with my finger. "It's not that simple," I whisper. "Maybe everything is already decided. Why fight the natural order of things?" The fish ducks inside a plastic grotto. A cluster of bubbles shoots from the filter.

"I guess because some things are worth it."

I pull my eyes away from the aquarium, back to Trinity. Her cheek is turning purple and the lump on her forehead seems to have grown even bigger, but a faint smile clings to her lips. She's still thinking of her brother. She reaches out and touches my teal streak. "I can't believe you still have this."

"I know, right? It's getting a little raggedy. I'm going to need you to give me a new one before school starts."

She beams. "I think you should do red and black, to match your soccer uniform."

I nod. "That is an excellent idea."

The doors to the ER slide open with a hiss and Micah storms in, his face clouded over with worry. He crosses the tile floor in about three strides. "Trin." He kneels in front of her, examining the welt on her forehead. "I just talked to Mom and she's on her way. I am so sorry I didn't get here sooner."

He turns to me and my heart skips like a stone bouncing across a lake. But right as I open my mouth to say something,

Amber hurries in, the keys to the Beast dangling from her fingers. I guess that explains why Micah wasn't answering his phone. She must have forgiven him for that whole scene at Beat.

Amber makes a beeline for Trinity and wraps her in a hug. Then she sits down on the other side of her and pretends I don't exist. I spring to my feet so Micah can have my seat. "Looks like you're in good hands," I say tightly, flashing Trinity a smile as I practically run for the exit.

"Thanks, Lainey," she says. "We'll talk more about your new streaks."

"Deal." I am halfway to the door.

"Lainey?" Hearing Micah say my name twists my stomach into knots.

I skid to a stop. "Yeah?" I turn, but can't make eye contact. Instead I concentrate on a blotchy, brownish stain on the linoleum floor.

"You brought her in?"

"Yeah."

"Thanks."

"No problem," I choke out, turning back toward the doors. The fading daylight beckons to me. All I want to do is escape the frigid coldness of the ER and the sight of Micah and Amber together again.

Chapter 39

SO IN WAR, THE WAY IS TO AVOID WHAT IS
STRIKE AT WHAT IS WEAK.

—SUN TZU, *The Art of War*

I have to call my mom to pick me up. Once I'm safely
buckled into her passenger seat and she can see I'm
okay, she starts worrying about Steve's car.

She backs carefully out of the parking spot, waiting for
an elderly woman with a walker to pass behind us. "You
trust Kendall to drive it?"

"My options were limited," I say. "I said I would take her
somewhere and then canceled on her at the last minute.
She's not a terrible driver. She triple-promised she would
be careful."

My mom looks over at me as she puts the car in drive.
"You canceled to stay with a friend after an accident, Lainey.
You could have just told Kendall no."

"Kendall doesn't care about the why, Mom. She only
cares about the what."

"Sounds like she only cares about herself." My mom
turns out of the hospital parking lot. "Sorry," she says

smoothly. "She's your friend and I know she's had it kind of rough. I just hate to see you let someone take advantage of you. Not to mention, Kendall Chase may be seventeen going on thirty, but I'm not sure it's safe for her to be going to college parties by herself."

Crap. I didn't even think about that. "I'm supposed to take the train down and meet her."

My mom checks both mirrors before changing lanes. "I don't want you on the MetroLink at night by yourself."

"It's, like, eight o'clock, Mom." I scoff. "It's still light out."

"And what if you don't find her? Then you'll be heading back to Hazelton after dark, by yourself. People get mugged all the time, Lainey. You kids need to stop thinking you're invincible."

I slouch down in my seat. "But she's mad at me. She'll be even more mad if I don't show up."

"I don't care. Call her and tell her you're not coming. Tell her I grounded you for letting her take Steve's car if you want."

I give my mom a sideways glance. "You want me to lie?"

She winks at me. "You want me to really ground you?"

I call Kendall. She doesn't answer. I leave a quick voice mail telling her I won't be able to make the party and asking her to call me back. Then I try Jason.

He picks up right away. "Lainey," he says, like he's surprised to hear from me. "What's going on?"

"Your sister took my brother's car to some party at Wash U," I say. "I'm supposed to meet her but now I can't and she's not answering her phone. She's kind of pissed at me, so that might be all it is, but I feel bad leaving her by herself."

Jason swears under his breath. "Our dad coming to town has made her half crazy, I think. So far she refuses to even talk about him. Do you know where this party was supposed to be?"

"Like a block off campus on Pershing Avenue? She said it was being thrown by a friend of a friend of someone she met on *So You Think You Can Model.*"

"Okay. I'll track her down. Thanks for calling me."

"No problem. When you talk to her, tell her I'm sorry."

"Sure. Hey, we made the play-offs partially thanks to you," Jason says. "Games the next two Saturdays. Give me a call if you're interested in filling in."

"I am completely and utterly interested in filling in," I say. Maybe it'll be a little awkward playing with Jason, but if he's willing to give it a shot, so am I. "Let me just check my Denali schedule and get back to you."

"Sounds good. I'll make sure Kendall returns the car in one piece."

"Thanks, Jay. Bye."

"So are things back on with Jason?" my mom asks after I hang up the phone. I can tell she's curious.

"Nah. But hopefully we can be friends." I fiddle with the buckle of my seat belt.

She turns onto our street. "I see." She doesn't press me for details.

Which I bet is hard for her, considering that she prides

herself on being one of those "cool moms" who their kids can talk to. "Have I told you lately how awesome you are?" I ask.

She laughs. "Not in the last five years or so."

"You're pretty awesome." I watch the neighbors' houses roll by through the passenger window. A sheepdog frolics on one of the front lawns. A dog could be fun. Maybe if I do end up staying in Hazelton to go to college I could get one. That might make living at home worth it.

My mom swings her car around onto our driveway. My dad is out on the lawn watering his herb garden. He swears it has parsley, basil, cilantro, and oregano, but it all looks like the same leafy, green stuff to me.

"How did you know Dad was the guy for you?" I blurt out. These are normally the types of stories I avoid, but it occurs to me that as similar as my parents act sometimes, they've definitely got their differences.

My mom chuckles. She turns off the engine but makes no move to get out of the car. "Your grandparents were less than thrilled with my choice," she starts. "Everyone in my family had gone to college. Your dad was just a high school grad working at his family's business." She exhales long and slow. "I had my own worries, I admit."

Dad flashes an impish grin at us and turns the hose on the car, sending a thunderous spray of water against the driver's-side window.

"I can't imagine why." I snicker. "So what made you stick with him?"

She looks over at me and her lips quirk into a smile. "I wish I had a concrete answer for you. Like maybe I walked into Denali one day and saw your father cutting apart the plastic six-pack rings to save baby animals, and then in that instant I knew it was love." She pats me on the knee. "But it wasn't like that. I liked being with him, but there were things that scared me. Then one day none of it seemed to matter anymore."

My dad disappears into the garage. Mom glances over at me. "Nothing changed, and yet things were different." She shrugs. "Maybe I changed."

It makes me think of Micah and me on the patio at Beat—how all of my fears melted away in that moment. How nothing mattered except for being with him. Maybe it's too late for that, but it can't be too late for us to be friends. *I guess because some things are worth it.* I'm going to talk to him the next time I see him, even if it scares me.

I slide out of the car and shut the door behind me. "Dad really cuts apart the six-pack rings to save baby animals?"

My mom shakes her head. "No, I saw that in a movie once, but hey, a girl can dream."

Kendall shows up with Steve's car—in one piece—around eleven thirty. I'm already in my sweats and ready for bed when I see the headlights slow to a stop outside my window. I peek my head into the study and tell my mom Steve's car is fine and that I'm going to drive Kendall home. Mom is surrounded by notes and books as usual. "All right," she says.

"I'm heading to bed. Be careful."

I intercept Kendall on the way to the porch and steer her back to the Civic. She starts bitching before I even pull away from the curb. "I can't believe you called Jason." She slurs her words and I don't have to lean very close to her to smell the liquor on her breath. "He said if I wasn't home by midnight he and my dad were going to come find me."

"I was worried about you, for good reason apparently. I can't believe you drove my brother's car drunk."

She adjusts the passenger seat to make more room for her long legs. "I'm not drunk, Lainey. I just had a few shots. Big deal."

"Big deal? Are you kidding me?" I back down the driveway and turn out onto our street. "What if you got arrested? What if you got in an accident and killed somebody?"

Kendall tosses her hair back over her shoulders. "What if you stopped being so dramatic?"

"Okay then." I turn left out of my subdivision and head for the highway. "What if you simply wrecked my brother's car? He freaking loves this thing like a baby."

"This piece of shit is probably not even worth five grand." She stares straight ahead through the windshield. "He needs to get over it."

"No. You need to get over it," I say. "Just because you don't think something is worth caring about, doesn't mean the rest of us have to agree."

Her eyes narrow as she glances over at me. "Are we still talking about the car?"

The words strike like a whip, but this isn't about Micah, and I'm not going to let her bait me. "You know how cops are around here. They won't just write you the minor possession. You'll get a DWI too." I merge on to the highway. "Do you want to get arrested? I know you're pissed at your dad—"

"Stop trying to play therapist," Kendall says coolly. "You don't know shit about my family."

And that's Kendall, the girl who lectured me about how best friends should tell each other everything. And like I said, she never tells me anything. Never lets her guard down.

"I could though," I say softly. "If you would talk to me. I'm trying to be your friend here, K."

"If you were trying to be my friend, you would've come to the party with me tonight. Maybe I wanted to talk to you about my dad, but now I don't feel like it." Kendall flips the radio on and makes a face at the music.

Micah's music.

I turn it off. "Are you kidding me right now? You barely talk to me about your *mom* and you've been dealing with her for seventeen years. You don't confide in anyone ever, do you? Not even Jay. It must be so lonely." I shake my head. "I just think it's sad."

Something about the combination of "lonely" and "sad" ignites a fury in Kendall. "You bitch," she says. "You don't get to tell me what to do. *You'd* be sad and lonely if it weren't for me. No one but your fat little Mexican friend would even know your name."

"She is not fat," I say, feeling rage flare up inside me too. "And I have plenty of my own friends."

"Yeah. What a bunch of *winners*."

I take a deep breath and bite my tongue. Kendall is only saying this stuff because she's drunk and upset. But still, she doesn't need to be hateful toward people I care about, and it was beyond irresponsible of her to drive my brother's car all wasted. Maybe Micah is right. Maybe I do make excuses for people's shitty behavior. As I pull off the highway, I swallow hard and start to tell Kendall she's out of line, but she's not finished yet.

"You would be *no one* if it weren't for me. I introduced you to all the right people, made you go to all the right parties. Basically, I *made* you."

Did she? When I met Kendall, my entire wardrobe consisted of soccer shorts and sports tees. I was more freckles and braces than human. I spent my free time watching soccer on TV and hanging out with my brother. After she and I were the only freshmen who made varsity, Coach Halstead paired us up a lot and it felt inevitable we'd become friends. But nothing is inevitable with Kendall. It's all calculated, controlled.

Was she responsible for my popularity?

Maybe.

But I made the team on my own.

Was she responsible for my continued social climbing throughout sophomore and junior year? I think about the fashion advice, the parties, about her hooking me up with Jason.

Probably.

"You're right," I admit. "You made me. But in case you haven't noticed, I'm remaking myself. And I like the new me better."

"Good thing," Kendall spits out. "Because I will see to it no one else does. No one that matters anyway."

A few weeks ago these words would have terrified me, but now they just sound frail and pathetic. I turn to look at her as I pull into her subdivision. "I get it, you know? I feel for you having to grow up with no dad and a control-freak mom, but that doesn't give you the right to do and say whatever you want. You're better than this. I know it." I sigh. "But lately you've been acting just like your mom." It's a harsh thing to say, but it's true, and I can't hold back anymore.

"Take it back," Kendall demands. "Take it back or else."

I turn into her driveway and shift into park. Part of me wants to take it back. Part of me wants to apologize, to forget the hateful things she's said tonight. To just wash them away because she's obviously upset and I don't want to lose her from my life. But I didn't say anything wrong. She's the one who needs to apologize.

"Good night," I say.

Kendall unclicks her seat belt and slides out of the car. For a moment, she stands there, her face half rage and half shock as I pull the car door closed and back out of her driveway.

I'm actually trembling as I make my way through her neighborhood and back to the highway. It's like walking away from Jason all over again. Almost without thinking, I turn the car toward Denali. Funny how all roads seem to lead there.

I pull into the parking lot right after midnight. The lights are still on, but I can see through the window that the front of the coffee shop is empty. Everyone must be clocking out. Micah's car isn't here, but Bianca's is. Also Ebony's and Leo's. After having it out with Kendall, all I want to do is give Bee a hug and thank her again for being such an amazing friend.

I watch the three of them appear from the back and pass through the dining area. The door opens and Bianca steps out into the night. She looks insanely gorgeous in her Denali tee and long skirt. The wind blows shiny ribbons of black hair around her face. I start to call out to her, but then she opens her mouth and I can tell she's laughing, even though I can't hear it. Leo follows behind her. He takes her hand and she leans in close to him. There's no way I can disturb this moment.

Instead I wait until everyone has left and then pull out of the lot. The street is deserted. Only the whisper of wind and the reflection of the metallic lane markers keep me company. I know where I am driving, but I'm not sure why. Micah is not going to just be sitting outside at midnight waiting for me.

Sure enough, when I loop past his apartment building

there is no sign of life. The Beast is parked out front. I berate myself for being a stalker. Fine, I need to apologize to him, to see if we can at least be friends, but that doesn't mean I have to do it right that second. But I don't want to go home yet either.

I return to the deserted Denali parking lot and pull the Civic into Micah's usual spot. It's lame, but just being parked there makes me feel a little closer to him.

As I slouch down in my seat, my foot hits something on the floorboard. I bend down to grab it. It's Kendall's flask—I've seen her bring it to parties before. I twirl it around in my hands a few times before I uncap it and take a long swig. Whatever it is, it's too strong, but it numbs the heavy feeling in my stomach. Being friends with Micah is not going to be good enough. I should have just told him how I felt about him. So many chances—at The Devil's Doorstep, at Beat, at the soccer game, at Denali. So many lost opportunities because I couldn't figure out what I wanted, because I was scared. I close my eyes and see Micah and me out on the back patio at Beat, his head on my shoulder, his fingers rubbing the pointy bone in my wrist. *I like you too.* Why would he say that if he was getting back together with Amber?

I take a few more sips from Kendall's flask without really thinking about it. The steering wheel starts to blur before my eyes. Shit. What am I doing? I just yelled at Kendall for drinking and driving. Now I'm stuck here, unless I want to walk home alone in the dark. *Smart, Lainey. Real smart.*

Oh, well. I'm in no hurry to get home anyway. I'll just

hang out here in the car for a little while, until my head clears. I recline my seat and get comfortable. My eyelids flutter closed. I'll just rest my eyes until the whole world stops spinning. I won't actually go to sleep.

Only I do.

Until someone yanks my car door open with such force that I almost tumble out into the parking lot.

Chapter 40

O DIVINE ART OF SUBTLETY AND SECRECY!
THROUGH YOU WE LEARN TO BE INVISIBLE.

— SUN TZU, *The Art of War*

I clutch the steering wheel to keep from spilling out onto the pavement. My heart thuds against my rib cage. The sky is a grayish purple, like the sun is preparing to rise. Micah slams my door and walks around the front of the Civic, sliding into the passenger seat next to me. "Jeez, you're lucky your dad didn't find you or he would've called 911. You looked dead."

I stare blankly at him, taking in his black-on-black attire. His hair is flat in places like he's been wearing a hat. What is he doing in my car? What is he even doing awake at—I check the clock on the dashboard—5:31. Am I dreaming?

He rests the back of his hand against my face, and then rotates his wrist and slaps me gently on the cheek. "Are you in there? Do I *need* to call 911?"

Wait. 5:31? "Shit." I pull out my phone and check my messages. None. If my parents wake up and realize I never came home, they'll freak. "One second." I rattle off a quick text message telling my mom I fell asleep watching movies at Kendall's house and that I'll be home in a little while.

Turning back to Micah I take a deep breath and blurt out the words I've been trying to say for almost two weeks: "I'm sorry about what happened at Beat."

He runs a hand through his mohawk. "Me too," he says.

"I didn't mean those things. I meant what I said on the patio." I catch a glimpse of myself in the rearview mirror and realize I have no makeup on and that the humidity has turned my hair into a mess of frizz. Oh, well, there's no hiding the real me now. "I spent weeks trying to convince myself there was nothing more than ancient Chinese strategy between us and that night everything changed for me," I say. "And I thought you felt the same way. But then you trotted after Amber like an obedient puppy." I clench my hands into fists. My fingernails cut crescent moons into my palms.

"I know what it looked like, me going after her like that," Micah says. "I shouldn't have been there in the first place. I only went because I knew you'd be there."

"Wait. Are you saying you only brought her there to make me *jealous*?" I ask. "You tried to *Art of War* me?"

"Something like that," he says. "I was pissed that you'd rather date no one than date me, and I figured if the strategies worked for Jason and Amber they would work for you too. But then after that whole screwed-up night, I decided you were probably right about not rushing into something new."

So where does that leave us? I can't quite bring myself to ask. I glance over at him. "I can't believe you tried to use my own strategies against me."

Micah rubs at the scar on his temple. "It was a shitty thing to do, and it wasn't fair to you or Amber. I treated both of you like crap that night."

"You did," I say. "You, the guy who told me to stop making excuses for people's shitty behavior."

"So don't make excuses. I apologized to her. And now I'm apologizing to you. I'm sorry, Lainey." He exhales deeply.

I barely hear him. I am focused on his barely parted lips. I don't know what this means, him being here with me, him saying these things. I know what I want it to mean, but I'm afraid to get my hopes up. "Was it all fake to you?" I blurt out. I look down at my lap and then back up at him. "At Beat, you said you liked me. Was there a *but* in that sentence? I mean, is there something wrong with me?" My voice fades to a whisper.

His lips curve slightly. "Oh, Glinda Elaine, there are so many things wrong with you. I don't know where to start."

I frown. My head feels like the drummer of Arachne's Revenge is practicing a new solo behind my eyes. One with lots of cymbal clashes. "How do you even remember my real name?" I fumble in my purse for some ibuprofen.

"I was in your grade school class for five years. You used to practically crawl inside your desk every time a sub took attendance."

I shake the little white bottle of pills but I can't seem to line up the arrows well enough to get the cap off. I curl my fingers tight around the pill bottle and yank with all my might. "But that was forever ago. I can barely remember what I had to eat last night."

"Well, it's a hard name to forget," Micah quips. Then, seeing my face crumple, he reaches out and quickly snaps the top off the ibuprofen. "We used to get along. Don't you remember?" He shakes two pills out into my palm. "I thought you were kind of cool back then. Back when you were still Elaine Mitchell. Before you became Kendall Chase's clone."

I can't dry-swallow the pills so I have no choice but to wash them down with another swig of whiskey.

Micah takes the flask away from me and caps it. "That's probably enough of that."

The whiskey burns my throat. "I am not Kendall's clone," I say. "Not anymore."

But I was. *I made you.* She told me what to like and who to be, and I let her. Once I got popular, well, who walks away from the feeling that everyone else wants to be you? Not me, apparently. The worst part is, like a true clone, I was a lower-quality replica. Not quite as pretty, not quite as popular, not quite as good at soccer.

Micah reads my thoughts from the expressions flitting across my face. "Glad to hear it."

I want to reach over the center console and hug him, but I'm afraid to. "I messed everything up, didn't I?"

"With Kendall?"

"With you."

Micah pushes a chunk of hair back from my eyes. His

touch makes me tremble. I bury my shaking fingers in my lap. "You didn't mess things up with me, Lainey. I'm glad I found you."

"What are you even doing here so early?"

"I couldn't sleep so I went for a drive. I saw your car on the way home. I've been meaning to thank you for being so cool to Trin. She told me everything you did for her yesterday."

"Is she okay? I could not believe she was going to walk home with that baseball-sized knot on her head."

"Girls. No common sense." He laughs under his breath. "She had to give a report to the cops, which was kind of scary for her, but her X-rays and CT scan came back negative, and once she got some pain medicine she said she was awesome-sauce, whatever that means."

My lower lip wavers. I tighten my jaw and bite back a couple of tears. "I'm glad."

"Me too."

"Sorry I ran off at the hospital. I just saw you and Amber together and kind of lost it."

Micah furrows his brow. "Right. Yeah, we were grabbing a bite to eat after finishing up at the Humane Society when I got the message. Trin and Amber are pretty tight so she wanted to come along." He yawns. "But I didn't find you to talk about my sister or Amber. I found you to apologize."

"You did already," I remind him. Inside I am replaying what he just said over and over. Does that mean Amber was only with him as a friend? I should just ask him, but I can't.

I can't handle the answer if it's not what I want to hear. I'll start crying. I don't want to do that to him again.

"I'm not finished apologizing. There's something I want to show you. Pretty sure you're going to think it's"—he pauses and makes his voice high-pitched and girly—"totally to die for."

"Oh yeah?"

"Yup." He sniffs. "But we're taking my car. This thing smells like a distillery."

"I didn't drink that much," I insist. "I think I spilled some."

"Didn't you use that same line last week with me?" He snickers. "I'd start working up a better story for your parents."

"No, last week someone else spilled beer on me. This time—"

"Whatever." Micah winks. "Get your alcoholic ass out of the car."

I feel like I lose another fifty pounds as I slide out of my brother's car and settle into the passenger seat of the Beast. I can't believe Micah and I are talking again. I swear if I get another chance I will not mess things up. My heart is beating so fast it's practically vibrating. *Get a grip, Lainey.*

As Micah turns out of the Denali parking lot, he fishes his phone out of the center console with one hand while he holds the steering wheel steady with the other. He hooks his phone into the stereo, swiping blindly to find his music.

"Let me help." I reach over and skim through the options

on his phone until his music library appears. He's got a bunch of playlists. I start to read the labels aloud. "Denali. Driving. Gym." I snort. "Gym? Really?"

He makes a fake-offended face. "I work out every once in a while."

"Oh yeah?"

"Okay. More like once a year," he admits.

I keep scrolling. "Car trips. Sleep." I pause. The next playlist is called "Dad." I'm about to ask him if it's his dad's actual music when the next list pops into view.

My throat feels like I swallowed a big spoonful of sand. "What's on this one called Lainey?" I ask, keeping my voice light.

Micah doesn't look at me. "I made it after we went to Mizz Creant's," he says. "It's stuff I thought you might like. I figured since we were going to be hanging out . . ."

"That's awesome. I want to hear it all." I start the Lainey playlist. The first song is by Bottlegrate. I hum along, wishing I'd gone to the concert with Micah instead of Jason's party, wishing I hadn't been so clueless. Micah and I could have gotten together that night, if I hadn't been so unable to figure out what I wanted. And now I don't know where we stand.

He navigates through the main streets of Hazelton and pulls the car into the gravel parking lot behind The Devil's Doorstep. A can of blue spray paint rolls out from under the front seat. I cough meaningfully and point at the can with my foot. "Went for a drive, you said?"

"What?" he asks. "You're not the only one who's had a rough time of it lately, you know?"

"Where are we going?" I look around at the deserted parking area. "I'm assuming the club isn't open."

"Nope. We're going the rest of the way on foot." Micah shuts off the engine and opens his door. "It's a surprise."

I follow him past the back of The Devil's Doorstep, down an alley, and through an abandoned lot. The lot backs up to a strip of trees that runs adjacent to the unused part of the airport. Looking up, I can see the clearing where Bianca and I stopped when we were jogging. It's deserted. "What kind of surprise?"

Micah ignores me. Beyond the trees, a fence stands about ten feet high. A NO TRESPASSING sign hangs crookedly from one of the support poles. A swarm of gnats buzzes around my face.

"How are you at fence climbing?" he asks.

"Not bad, actually. My brother and I used to practice flipping over our backyard fence when we were little." Of course that's only about half as high as this one. Then again, I was probably half as tall as I am now. "You're taking me to the airport? For what? Some therapeutic graffitiing?"

"Maybe."

"You're still on probation, aren't you?"

"Yup." He sticks the toe of his boot in one of the diamond-shaped holes of the chain-link fence and begins to make his way to the top. The sun starts to rise, painting the sky a brilliant pinkish color.

I point at the sign. "You know this is illegal, right?"

"Yup. Would you trust me if I told you it was worth the risk?" Micah drops to the high grass on the other side of the fence.

I scale the fence gracefully and land next to him. I'm suddenly glad I'm in my sweats instead of whatever dress and heels combo I would have worn to the Wash U party. "I guess, but I'm not the one on probation."

Micah wraps his hands around my neck and pretends to strangle me. "Just stop talking for five minutes, okay?"

He leads me across a dead runway, the cracks in the cement so deep they might go all the way to the center of the earth. We pass a pair of cargo hangars as we near the wall of the abandoned terminal. It looks like Micah's already done his painting for the day. A pair of fading nooses have been repainted in bright blue, the words *Hangman's Joke* suspended between them.

"Micah," I say softly. I wonder why he does it, if it's a symbolic way for him to keep his dad alive.

He shakes his head. "Not that. This." He ducks down against the wall of the terminal and waits for me to do the same. We hug the cold metal as we creep our way around to the other side. There are a lot of trucks and trailers parked on the adjacent runway.

"What the—?" And then it hits me. These are movie trucks and trailers. *"Flyboys?"* I practically shriek.

Micah clamps a hand over my mouth. "Shhh, they'll hear us."

We sneak closer and duck down behind a baggage transport truck. Black-clad Hollywood types with laminated badges around their necks mill between the rounded silver trailers. A couple bald guys are busy opening a bunch of black cases. They start building a weird scaffolding of metallic ladders and round, fuzzy things that must be microphones. I swallow hard. It's not even seven a.m. yet, probably too early for a big star like Caleb Waters to be filming. But I swear, if he saunters out of one of those trailers I will totally faint.

"I can't believe this," I whisper. "I can't believe you found this. I can't believe you brought me here."

"It is a risk, I guess, bringing the girl I like to see the thirtysomething washed-up athlete of her dreams," Micah says with a teasing grin. "But I figure if you observe us side by side, it'll be obvious who is superior."

"I'm serious, Micah. This is amazing. I wish Bianca could be here." I fish my phone out of my pocket. "I've got to get pictures for her."

"I'm serious too. That guy is old."

"He is not that—" I stop. "Did you just call me the 'girl you like'?"

Micah ruffles my unbrushed, un-flat-ironed hair, and warmth surges through me. "We can talk about that later."

Part of me wants to talk about that right this second, but we're only a few yards away from the crew and if they get any closer they might overhear us. I lean in and brush my lips against Micah's cheek. "Seriously life-changing moment," I whisper.

"I thought you might think so," he whispers back.

I recognize a couple of the actors who play smaller roles in the movie. A truck tows a commercial plane down the runway—a smaller one with collapsible steps instead of a jet bridge. I start snapping pictures of everything. Bee is going to be sad that she missed this, but at least I can show her as much as possible. The actors take their places on the stairs leading up to the plane. And then I see him.

Caleb Waters.

He steps out of a trailer wearing aviator sunglasses and a pilot's uniform. Immediately I turn my camera on him. Bianca is going to die.

The wind blows Caleb's hair forward and I hear someone else yell for him to put his hat on. A woman in pointy glasses runs over with a blue pilot's hat. A pair of big, burly guys without necks pace back and forth a few feet away. Bodyguards, no doubt.

I zoom in on my phone and snap a picture of Caleb.

And then it rings.

Chapter 41

WHEN THERE IS MUCH RUNNING ABOUT AND THE
SOLDIERS FALL INTO RANK, IT MEANS THAT THE
CRITICAL MOMENT HAS COME.

—SUN TZU, *The Art of War*

Oh no. My mom. It figures.

No Neck One and Two pivot in unison.

"Shit. Come on." Micah's wiry frame is already streaking from the transport vehicle back around to the far side of the terminal. Damn, he's fast. He's like a black blur. I take off after him.

I hear a shout. Looking over my shoulder I see the entire cast and crew staring. No Neck One and Two are running toward me. They're a few yards behind me. Micah is almost halfway to the fence already.

"Stop right there," No Neck One says. Boy, does he sound pissed.

I sprint toward the fence. Micah glances back over his shoulder.

"Keep going," I holler. I'm so glad Bianca and I did all that running this summer. I'm flying. I put a few extra feet of distance between myself and the security detail.

Micah stops at the fence and turns to wait for me. "Come on. You can do it."

I lengthen my stride. I don't look back. I can't. I keep plunging straight ahead, toward Micah. Toward freedom. He laces his fingers together and holds out his hands to give me a boost. I don't think I need it but the gesture makes my heart tense up and then go weak. If Micah gets caught trespassing, he'll be in violation of his probation. He risked everything to indulge me in some silly celebrity fantasy and now he's risking everything again so I don't get caught.

My right foot lands in Micah's hands. I hear him grunt as I lift off and manage to grab the top of the fence. I twist my body around and fall to the ground on the other side. Micah's halfway up the fence but the beefy guys have caught up to us. One of them has Micah by the ankle. He kicks out with his foot.

"Let him go!" I yell. I grab a stick from the edge of the trees and poke at No Neck Two, who now has hold of Micah's jeans. The guy swears. Micah wriggles out of his grasp and falls to the ground beside me. We take off running, back through the trees and down the alley. All the way back to the parking lot of The Devil's Doorstep where the Beast is parked.

I skid to a stop in front of the car. I'm hyperventilating, half from the run and half from the shock of almost getting caught.

"I thought we were going to get arrested," Micah says.

His hands are shaking so bad he can barely get the car doors open. We both slide into the Beast and press the door locks.

I slink down in my seat, even though the parking lot is still deserted. "I thought we were going to get pounded into a pulp! Those guys meant business."

"Who the hell was calling you this early?"

"My mom, of course. We Mitchells have impeccable timing."

"Is she going to be pissed that you didn't answer?" he asks.

"Probably, but who cares? I saw Caleb freaking Waters. How cool is that?" I scroll through the photos on my phone. "And I've got pictures! Bianca is going to die when she sees these."

"You two have issues," Micah teases. "But I'm glad you enjoyed it since I almost had a heart attack."

Smiling, I shush him just long enough to listen to my mom's voice mail message.

"Lainey. Hi, I know you said you were at Kendall's, and you probably just fell back to sleep, but I did a reading for you with my breakfast tea and the leaves indicated you might be in some kind of danger. I know you're not a believer like me, but I just had to call once more and check on you. Please humor your mom and call me back when you get this."

I quickly call her back.

"Lainey!" My mom sounds out of breath when she answers. "I'm so glad you're all right. Are you still at Kendall's?"

"Uh, I actually went by Denali and ran into Micah so we're just talking right now." I feel a twinge of guilt, even though technically everything I said was true. "I'll be home soon."

"Promise me you'll be careful."

"Promise. Love you." I turn to Micah as I slide my phone back into my purse. "You will not believe this," I say. "You know how my mom reads tea leaves? She just did a reading for me and it indicated I was in danger."

His jaw drops a little. "That is creepy." He slides the key into the ignition and turns the Lainey playlist back on. It's one of the Bottlegrate songs we heard at the club. The frantic drumbeat perfectly matches my pounding heart.

"I know. That dude had you by your jeans . . ." My mind starts replaying the whole adventure like I'm watching a movie. A really amazing movie, where the lead actor is neither tall nor tan, but is still an insanely hot hero guy. I turn toward Micah. "Thank you. I still can't believe you did that for me. You could've gotten in so much trouble."

He shrugs. "Hey, big risks, big rewards, you know?"

I can't stop staring at how the rising sun back-lights his slender form, at how his mohawk casts a funny shadow on the dashboard. I reach out for him without thinking, running one finger across his pierced eyebrow and then the back of my hand along his jaw. "What sort of rewards were you hoping for?" I ask softly.

Micah reaches up and curls his hand around mine. "This is enough." His voice catches. "Seeing you so excited."

My whole body goes weak. "What if it's not enough for me?" My other hand cups his chin, a hint of beard stubble prickling against my fingertips. I lean toward him, aligning my face with his. My chest caves with each breath.

His whole body is radiating heat. Even though I've been kissed hundreds of times by Jason, somehow this moment feels different, as if no one has ever touched me. I let my eyes flutter closed. I know exactly how far Micah is away from me. I know exactly how many seconds it will take for our lips to meet.

Our foreheads touch first. The song ends and a new one comes on. "Wake Up Dreaming"—the song Amber's band was playing the night I first wanted this to happen.

Micah reaches out and turns the volume all the way down.

"Leave it on," I say.

He turns it halfway back up. The violins meld with the guitar. My heart does a somersault in my chest.

"I have to tell you something." His words mix with my breath.

"Yeah?" My eyes are still closed.

"I never got back together with Amber, okay? I thought about it, but I realized I was just thinking the same as you— like why fight the natural order of things?"

"Trinity told you about that little conversation, huh?" I slide my hand around to cradle the back of his neck. So close. The music starts to build.

"She's my sister. She tells me all kinds of stuff." His

cheek grazes mine. Our noses brush. "And then I didn't want to rush into a rebound thing."

"Me neither." The violins and guitars swell to a crescendo. Once again, every beat is punctuated with the image of Micah and me kissing.

"But then I realized I'm not rushing, if I've wanted this for weeks."

My heart feels huge in my chest. "Me too," I say. And then: "Shh."

"Sorry, I just want to make sure I don't mess this up."

My eyes flick open for a second. I grip Micah's neck and pretend to strangle him. "Just stop talking for five minutes, okay?" I let my eyelids fall shut again. Without waiting for an answer, I close the distance between us.

I can feel Micah smile as our lips finally meet. Soft. Warm. He squeezes my fingers gently. His other hand tangles itself in my hair. My whole body trembles. I exhale hard against his chin.

"Damn, girl," he murmurs, tightening his hold on me. His tongue tastes my lips and then finds the inside of my mouth.

I press myself toward him, willing him to kiss me harder. And he does. The Beast's gearshift threatens to poke a hole in my hip, but I don't care. The car starts to fade away. The whole world goes hazy. Micah lifts me over the center console until I'm half in his lap. We stay locked together until we both run out of breath.

Then he kisses his way up my jawbone and flicks his

tongue across my earlobe. "I hate to bring this up, but your mom's not going to call the cops or anything if you don't show up at home soon, is she?"

"Nah." I wrap my arms around his neck and adjust myself so we're both comfortable. "I figure I've got at least a couple hours before she starts worrying again."

"Mmm." He trails his lips down the other side of my neck. "I like the sound of that, as long as you're sure you won't get grounded."

"Who cares?" I twine my fingers in his mohawk. "It'd totally be worth it."

"You are the biggest rule-breaker ever." Micah shakes his head and then pulls me close again. Our mouths move hot against each other as his hands explore my face and hair and back. I don't know how long we kiss, but when we finally break apart, the music is over, the windows are white with fog and the soft drumbeats of a summer rainstorm pound the roof above our heads.

Sliding back into the passenger seat. I reach out with one finger and draw a happy face in the condensation on my window. I turn back to Micah, running a hand down the side of his face like I'm still not sure that he's real. His eyes shine a mix of green and gold, like the forest. "Your eyes are so pretty," I say.

"I know, right?" he says. "They're my second-best feature."

"What's your best?" I ask without thinking.

He glances quickly down at his lap and then arches his

eyebrows suggestively at me.

I laugh out loud. Typical guy. Just when I was thinking this might be the most romantic day of my entire life. Oh, well. Might as well play along. "Prove it," I say. With a grin, I fake like I'm reaching toward the waistband of his jeans.

Micah slaps my hand away playfully. "I might show you. Someday." He laughs, and it is the most beautiful sound in the whole world.

For a moment, we just stare at each other, both grinning like idiots. Both imagining a future filled with so many scary and exciting possibilities.

But first things first.

"So what now?" I ask.

"What do you mean?"

"I mean, what do we tell people? *How* do we tell people?"

"Ah." He nods. "No ancient Chinese guidance for this sort of thing?"

"I'm done with all that. War is totally overrated." I reach over and twine my fingers in his. "So is fighting with the people I care about."

"I agree." Micah squeezes my hand. "You know, we could always let Ebony discover us fooling around in the walk-in cooler. Let her tell people for us."

I frown. "Come on. I'm being serious."

"Me too." He brushes my hair back from my face. "How about this? We've been pretending to date for most of the summer. So I say we just keep doing our thing and let people think what they think. If they ask specific questions, then you can say whatever you want."

"But what *are* we doing?" I ask. "What do you want me to say?"

Micah laughs under his breath. "Oh, so you want me to be that guy, huh?"

"What guy?"

He takes both of my hands in his and turns to face me. "Lainey Mitchell," he starts, in an extra-serious voice. "Will you be my girlfriend?"

I make a noise vaguely approximating a dolphin. Taking a deep breath, I try again. "Yeah."

"Yeah, you'll be my girlfriend or, yeah, you want me to be that guy?" Micah teases.

I pull my right hand free of his and curl it into a fist. "Don't make me hurt you."

He grins. "I think I would like to propose a rule regarding physical violence."

"No such luck. It's too late for rules." Reaching out with one finger, I trace the trinity tattoo on his neck.

Micah inhales deeply and his eyelids flutter closed for a second. Then he reaches over and pulls me toward him again. "I can't even believe everything that's happened," he murmurs as his lips fall gently onto mine.

"I know, right?" I say between kisses. "Most epic summer ever."

And the best part is, it's not over yet.

Acknowledgments

This story would not be what it is without four writing partners that I have been waiting YEARS to lavish gratitude upon: Cathy Castelli, you never lost faith, you believed in me even when I didn't believe in myself. Thank you for your thoughtful comments and unfailing optimism. Jasmine Warga, thank you for years of timely feedback, the MFA perspective, and for railing against the coconuts. You deserve everything wonderful that is headed your way. Jessica Fonseca, thank you for the torture breakfast food and for being a model of patience and determination. You have figured out how to write without losing yourself, and that will serve you well on your journey. Marcy Beller Paul, thank you for being a teacher, cheerleader, confidante, therapist, cab-hailer, and wonderful friend. You, chica, have kept me sane. I look forward to returning the favor, as needed.

More thanks:

To my agent, Jennifer Laughran at Andrea Brown Lit. Signing with you is one of the smartest things I've ever done. I would have written a third book to win you over.

To my editor, Karen Chaplin, for seeing the passion behind Lainey's (and my own) prickly exterior, and for pushing me to make this story come alive on the pages. To everyone else at HarperTeen, from the corner offices to the cubicles, who was involved in this book. You have played a part in making my dreams come true and I will always be grateful.

To my friends and family as always. Especially to Connie for being my Bianca, and to Publicist Mom—the best in the business. Seriously, I could not survive without your love, patience, and random edible gifts. To Team Lainey, for being endlessly awesome. To all the other amazing industry people who are my traveling partners on this journey, including the YA Valentines, the Literaticult, the Apocalypsies, the kidlit Twittersphere, Antony John, Heather Anastasiu, Elizabeth Richards, Jessica Spotswood, Tara Kelly, Rachel Harris, Victoria Scott, Julie Heidbreder, Ailynn Collins, Ken Howe, Christina Ahn Hickey, and Jamie Krakover. To Shelly and Craig Clemons from Darker Violet Designs, for the website and general tech-support awesomeness. I'm sure I'm forgetting someone so [insert your name here]. To everyone who entered my cover reveal contest. Congrats to Emma Chang, my winner. You can see her "book debut" as Emma in Chapter 35.

To the City of St. Louis who took good care of me growing up, and to all the cool '90s bands whose music coaxed me down from the ledges—I will never stop loving you. To everyone from Wiliker's Restaurant, for the flour fights, charred quiche, and years of hilarious antics that have crept their way into these pages. To all the amazing alterna-boys I have been lucky enough to know, especially the one who introduced me to Henry Rollins's spoken-word stuff and the one who introduced me to the Roky Erickson story. To Adam for being "just a guy" and then some. To Evan and Jay for setting the boy-bar impossibly high. When people say Micah is too good to be true, I'm going to tell them about you two.

And finally, to the readers. Always and forever to the readers. In the end, it all comes back to you.